HIGH PRAISE FOR
Romantic Times Lifetime Achievement Award Winner
VIRGINIA HENLEY
and
A YEAR and a DAY

"*A YEAR AND A DAY* IS UNQUESTIONABLY VIRGINIA'S FINEST WORK TO DATE."
—Marsha Canham, author of *The Pride of Lions*

"STEAMY SEX . . . MEMORABLE CHARACTERS . . . BLOODY BATTLES . . . NICELY PACED NARRATIVE."
—*Publishers Weekly*

"THE BEST BOOK EVER WRITTEN BY ONE OF THE GREAT WRITERS OF HISTORICAL EROTIC ROMANCES, the incredible Virginia Henley. Similar to *Braveheart*, the story brilliantly mixes erotic sex and history."
—Harriet Klausner

"I WAS UP TILL DAWN DEVOURING *A YEAR AND A DAY*!"
—Beatrice Small, author of *Betrayed*

"HENLEY KNOWS HOW TO KEEP A PLOT GALLOPING ALONG. That, and an element of frank eroticism, make this one an enjoyable addition to Henley's shelf of historical romance genre."
—*Kirkus Reviews*

Please turn the page for more extraordinary acclaim. . . .

DREAM LOVER

"*DREAM LOVER* IS THE USUAL GREAT FARE FROM MS. HENLEY . . . an authentic historical piece that serves as a realistic but charming backdrop for a witty, exciting adventure. The tale has two fabulous lead characters who struggle with love lost and love regained."

—*Affaire de Coeur*

"A WONDERFUL STORY OF INTRIGUE AND PASSION . . . the pages practically turn themselves."

—*Old Book Barn Gazette*

"ADVENTUROUS!" —*Booklist*

"The pace is brisk and the passions are huge . . . in Henley's universe, love may conquer all."

—*Publishers Weekly*

"STUNNING . . . a lush, highly romantic, adventurous story that dazzles and captivates her fans eager for another glimpse of her sensual storytelling. With unrequited love's searing passion and pain and revenge and desire's power, this master storyteller spins a delicious tale that readers will quickly devour, yet long remember. *Dream Lover* is a dream of a romance."

—*Romantic Times*

"SENSUOUS!" —*Kirkus Reviews*

ENSLAVED

"Readers get two historical romances—a Regency and an ancient Britain—rolled into one great tale . . . and a sensual romance."

—*Affaire de Coeur*

DESIRED

"Readers will find themselves intrigued by the adventure [and] mesmerized by the pageantry."

—*Publishers Weekly*

"A FAST-PACED HISTORICAL ROMANCE filled with several top-rate characters . . . a refreshingly new look at the Plantagenets."

—*Affaire de Coeur*

ENTICED

"A DYNAMIC READ that showcases all of Ms. Henley's hallmarks . . . very sensual."

—*Romantic Times*

"EXCELLENT . . . The pages fly by, as you are drawn into the characters' lives."

—*Rendezvous*

SEDUCED

"*Seduced* never loses steam . . . It's a must read for those who love steamy historical romances. It's bawdy. It's funny. It's a great adventure."

—*USA Today*

Books by Virginia Henley

A WOMAN OF PASSION

THE BORDER HOSTAGE

THE MARRIAGE PRIZE

A YEAR AND A DAY

DREAM LOVER

ENSLAVED

SEDUCED

DESIRED

ENTICED

TEMPTED

THE DRAGON AND THE JEWEL

THE FALCON AND THE FLOWER

THE HAWK AND THE DOVE

THE PIRATE AND THE PAGAN

THE RAVEN AND THE ROSE

Virginia Henley

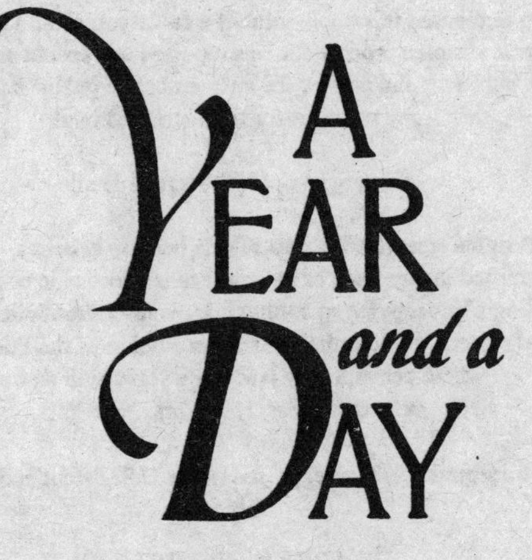

A Dell Book
Published by
Dell Publishing
a division of
Random House, Inc.

This novel is a work of fiction. Names, characters, places, and incidents either are the product of the author's imagination or are used fictitiously. Any resemblance to actual persons, living or dead, events, or locales is entirely coincidental.

ISBN: 0-440-22207-9

Reprinted by arrangement with Delacorte Press

Printed in the United States of America

Published simultaneously in Canada

November 1998

10

OPM

For my new grandson,
Ryan James Henley

1

Submerged up to her breasts in the forest pool, the flame-haired girl shivered deliciously at the feel of the icy water on her skin. She had waited all winter for this first spring dip. Jane Leslie had a wild, untamed streak like the forest creatures with whom she was able to communicate. Because she had this special gift, animals trusted her and came to her hand without fear. Jane had been playing with a river otter that had been swimming beside her, making her dizzy with his somersaults and acrobatics. She had bidden him to cease his antics and now he lay on the bank, slumbering in the spring sunshine.

Suddenly she raised her head, feeling the hair on the nape of her neck rise up the way an animal's hackles do when danger is nigh. Moving only her eyes, she gazed about the leafy bower, trying to identify what had disturbed the perfect tranquility of nature's paradise.

Though she saw nothing, Jane was completely aware of his presence, lurking just beyond the green foliage of the lacy branches. Her ears strained for the least rustle of leaf or murmur of breath, and when she heard nothing, she knew he was a master of stealth. Breathing deeply, she inhaled the smell of the water, the perfume of the first wild iris, the aroma of the forest, and the tang of the sea beyond. Then her nostrils quivered as she caught his male scent. No, she had not been mistaken; he was watching her bathe!

Green eyes gazed through the canopy of leaves, silently observing the bather. He had traveled far and, tired and thirsty, had come to the pool to drink. Now he stared unblinking, as if mesmerized. He licked his lips, his appetite whetted for the tender female flesh that would slake a suddenly aroused hunger. Never taking his eyes from the girl, he moved his weight so that it was more comfortably distributed, as he crouched and waited for her to come out of the water.

The maid lowered her lashes to her cheeks, hiding the excitement she was feeling. Pretending to be unaware of his presence, she dipped her hands into the pool, lifted her arms high, then allowed the water to trickle down her neck and shoulders. Could she tempt him from his hiding place? She had powers that others did not possess. Softly, she began to hum a haunting melody and moved imperceptibly closer to the edge of the pool. Although she appeared calm on the outside, inside her thoughts were in turmoil as her curiosity, excitement, and anticipation soared higher and higher.

Irresistibly drawn by her siren song, he moved forward too on heavily muscled legs. Unblinking, he avidly watched every movement of the small female's body. He marked her for his prey, knowing she could not escape him. She was his for the taking. He raised his proud head, curbing his impatience, as he waited to make his move.

As he emerged through the canopy, Jane's lashes flew up in utter amazement and she found herself staring into the fiercest green eyes she had ever encountered. She had imagined her intruder to be a fox or mayhap a stag; never in her wildest dreams had she imagined encountering a lynx!

Jane was terrified, both for herself and for the sleeping otter. The lynx would devour the sleek creature unless she did something quickly. Bravely, she jumped from the water and tried to scare it away, but the large lynx was not the least bit intimidated. It ignored the otter, focusing its full attention on Jane, and began to pad toward her as if stalking its prey.

Jane gasped in fear and began to run for her life. Her *power* was the only thing that could save her. As she ran, Jane reached for the Celtic touchstone that hung around her neck and she sent up a desperate plea to the goddess Brigantia.

She glanced over her shoulder and realized there would be no divine intervention; in hot pursuit, the lynx was almost upon her. A ragged scream was torn from her throat as her foot caught in a wild bistort vine and she tumbled to the forest floor. The powerful animal loomed over her and with one huge padded paw, rolled her over onto her back.

Jane screamed and closed her eyes to shut out the fearsome vision of the lynx. Her dread was so acute her limbs trembled uncontrollably and her heartbeat thundered in her ears. She sucked in a great shuddering breath as she felt the lynx sniff her hair. Then, incredibly, she felt his tongue come out to lick her cheek. Dear God, like all felines, was he toying with his prey before he devoured her?

Her eyes flew open in alarm and she stared into the

fierce green orbs. His tongue came out again to lick her ear and she sensed for the first time that he was being gentle with her. With tremendous relief, Jane somehow knew he would not harm her.

With her heart still hammering wildly, she gazed up in awe at the sheer magnificence of the creature. His pelt was tawny, the fur about his face and ears was tufted, framing his head with a silvery mane. The wildcat's fur looked soft as thistledown and his huge padded paws hinted at the sheer power he possessed. Jane knew she had no control over him; he was the one in command. He was fearless and fierce, predatory and proud, wild and free.

His tongue moved down her neck to her collarbone and Jane became acutely aware of her nakedness as he began to lick her breasts. As his tongue curled over her nipple, its rough texture sent a frisson of sensation that rippled down inside her belly. Now pleasure mingled with her fear and she experienced a strange excitement unlike any she'd ever felt before that went deep to her core.

The lynx tongued and licked, moving down over her rib cage until she felt wet, warm swirls upon her bare belly. The pleasurable feeling that this aroused in her was so intense that Jane closed her eyes as a low moan escaped her lips.

There was a sudden rustle on the floor of the forest as a hare darted through the trees. The lynx instantly loped after it, disappearing as quickly as he had arrived. Jane took in a ragged breath and lifted her touchstone on its leather thong so she could look into the face of Brigantia. She wondered if the Goddess of Inspiration had sent the hare as an intermediary. Hares were tricksters with powers to effect transformation and control destiny.

As she walked unsteadily back to where her clothes lay, she was completely perplexed by her strange encounter. It occurred to her that it might be an omen, but of what, she had no idea. Her heart still fluttered wildly as she pulled on her woolen gown and stockings. Slowly, the atmosphere around the forest pool reverted to the way it had been before the intruder had arrived. The birds and the dragonflies once again swooped low over the water, and the red squirrels ventured back down the trunks of the oak trees. A turtle stuck his head out of the water and slowly made his way to her feet.

Jane slipped on her leather shoes and headed back to Dumfries Castle where her father, Jock Leslie, was the steward. Dumfries was one of the great border strongholds in the Annandale region of Scotland.

Jane was the youngest of ten children whose mother had died while giving birth to her. She had been raised by her maternal grandmother, Megotta, a fiercely blood-proud Celt. When her daughter had wed Jock Leslie, Megotta had been outraged that she was pledging herself to a man who was not a pure Celt, so she had been doubly determined to instill the Celtic traditions in her grandchildren. Jane, who had seven brothers and two sisters, was Megotta's favorite. She had been born with the gift of healing, which her grandmother believed had been bestowed on her by the ancient Celtic goddesses. Her grandmother hoped she would also develop the gift of second sight, which Jane experienced upon occasion.

When she arrived home, the door of the stone dwelling stood ajar and Jane could clearly hear her two married sisters arguing with her grandmother. Jane's cheeks turned rosy as she realized she was the subject of their disagreement.

She knew her sisters resented her because their father and grandmother treated her as if she were special, allowing her the freedom to explore the forests and care for the animals. But what she did not realize was how jealous they were because she was more beautiful than they were, with her flaming red hair and voluptuous, agile body.

"Ye two can stop yer meddling. Jane is destined for greater things than marriage, and in any case she's far too young," Megotta said firmly.

"Too young?" Mary cried. "I had three bairns by the time I was her age." She placed her hands upon her mounded belly, which held her sixth child in as many years.

"Her wildness is unnatural, she must make an effort to overcome it," Kate asserted. "Folk whisper about her. She's never even been courted, poor wee mite. The men think she's more witch than woman and you're to blame; filling her head with Celtic superstitious nonsense!"

"Ye should take pride in yer Celtic heritage! Nothing is more important than blood!"

"Nothing except bein' handfasted and catching a husband," Mary asserted. "Father will have to pay bride money before any will look at her."

Although Jane got along easily with animals, she was sometimes uncomfortable around people. She knew that because of her strange powers she was different from other people; she was not at all interested in such matters as finding a husband, having babies, and establishing a home, which occupied the thoughts of most other young women. Although Jane seethed with passionate feelings, she tried to keep her emotions to herself because of the whispers and the laughter that were often directed at her. She hid her hurt by pretending not to care that many of the village folk found her odd.

Today, however, she could not control her feelings. As she stepped through the doorway, she confronted her sisters. "I don't want a husband! I prefer to live here with father and Megotta."

Her sisters turned to her, looking shocked. Both were married to cattle herders and had their own stone and wattle homes outside the castle walls. Suddenly, they began to laugh. "She hasna the faintest idea of what she's missing," Kate told Mary.

"I think we'd better enlighten her about what goes on between a man and a lass," Mary told Kate.

"Ye're shameless, the pair of ye!" Megotta cried.

Jane blushed as she stood her ground against her sisters. "It's all right, Megotta. I'm quite aware of what goes on between a man and a woman; I'm simply not interested. I find men extremely—" Jane did not say *terrifying,* because her sisters would likely laugh all the harder. "Coarse," she finished. Jane had never told anyone that she had once been attacked by a man, a fugitive who had been hiding in the forest. The way he had torn her clothes and touched her body had made it plain that he'd intended to have his way with her. She had managed to fight him off with the knife she carried for cutting herbs, but the assault had left her with an indelible fear of strange men.

"And men are no' the only ones who can be coarse," their grandmother asserted. "Take yerselves off home, lest yer fine husbands give ye a good beating fer not getting their dinners on time.''

The sisters shrugged; beatings were an accepted part of marriage.

Jane's dreams were different from those of other young women. Megotta had taught her the things that the ancient Celtic priestesses had practiced, and she wanted to dedicate her life to distilling herbal cures and to healing the people and animals of Dumfries.

Jane's youngest brother, Keith, hurriedly entered the cottage. He was the youngest male Leslie, the only one unmarried and still living at home. A groom at the castle stables, Keith loved horses and was an expert in their care and grooming. ''I have a mare that foaled twins. One is healthy, but I'll lose the other unless ye come, Jane.''

Without a word Jane followed her brother to Dumfries' vast stables. He was her favorite brother, a seventh son who was psychic. The two youngest Leslies had a special bond.

Jane went into the box stall where the mare was nuzzling her newborn, helping it to find her teat. Another foal, extremely small, lay in the straw, seemingly abandoned. A tiny tremor was the only sign of life that Jane saw as she knelt before the newborn. She had learned that touch was equally as important as nourishment where survival was concerned.

Jane placed her hands on the foal's neck and, rubbing with long, smooth strokes, began her magic. Soft, soothing words accompanied her ministrations, coaxing, praising, petting the little animal with voice and hands. She rubbed its back and its belly and its spindly legs, then began again at its muzzle and neck. Gradually, the motion of her hands changed. Her strokes shortened as she dug her fingers into its coat and curried it as its mother's rough tongue would have done if it had shown more signs of life.

"Today at the pool I encountered a lynx."

Keith heard the excitement in her voice. "Were ye not afraid?"

"I was terrified . . . at first. I thought he was going to kill an otter so I tried to scare the lynx away, but I couldn't control its behavior in any way. Then it began to stalk me and I was afraid it was going to attack me." She didn't want to tell Keith about the strange, intimate part of her encounter with the animal. "My touchstone of Brigantia must have saved me."

Keith frowned. "This isn't lynx territory. They range in the craggy mountains beyond the forest. Will you tell Sim and Ben?"

Jane shook her head. Their brothers Sim and Ben were castle shepherds responsible for large flocks of sheep. "I know I should," Jane admitted, "but he was such a magnificent creature, I couldn't bear it if they killed him." She longed to commune with him, to try to join her spirit with his, but the lynx had been the one who had been in control, and she was troubled and perplexed by the encounter. Her fingers moved lovingly over the foai as she talked. "Do you think it was an omen?"

"I do." Keith's usually impish freckled face was solemn; his red hair stood on end as he ran his fingers through it. All the Leslies save this seventh son and Jane were raven-haired. "Great changes are coming—without and within, I fear. Powerful men from afar will come. Scotland will be torn apart."

Jane saw that the lynx was symbolic. He had come down from the far mountains. He tore his prey apart with his great power. Jane shuddered. "Have you told Father of your premonition?"

Keith nodded. "Father has Norman blood and divided loyalties. He says that because Dumfries belongs to the crown, it has changed hands a score of times over the centuries. All of Carrick and Annandale were governed by the Bruces until Baliol became king. Then these lands were confiscated by Comyn, the Constable of Scotland. Father says we are castle keepers, not soldiers, and the changes will no' affect us. But change always has its consequences, Jane."

Although her sisters and the wives of her brothers spent much time at the castle, serving in the dining hall and plenishing the chambers, Jane spent more time in the stables and the stillroom. She seldom ventured into the stronghold where Comyn's men-at-arms were garrisoned. Even though they had been there for three years, Jane still felt threatened by the men's presence. Now, the thought of strange men overrunning Dumfries deeply disturbed her!

The little foal began to struggle and Jane helped it gain its legs. With Keith's help, she guided it to its mother and watched with tender eyes as the mare accepted it. Jane wet her finger with mare's milk, then put it to the baby's mouth. After repeating her action half a dozen times, the little colt began to suckle. As Jane thought over her strange encounter, along with Keith's prophecy, she knew she would rather face the lynx a thousand times over than any man breathing.

2

"Wigton? That's on the border of *Scotland*!" Alice Bolton cried in horror, as she shuddered dramatically.

"I'm not suggesting you be buried alive, I'm suggesting you stay at my castle of Wigton while I go further north," Lynx de Warenne said dryly to his long-standing mistress.

" 'Tis one and the same! I thought when we arrived here on the coast we would soon be sailing to France; I've been looking forward to Bordeaux for months."

"You speak of going to France as if it were a holiday; we go to fight a war," Lynx reminded her.

"War is your life," she said impatiently. She had been about to remove a stocking from her long, slim leg, but now threw down her skirts petulantly. "When I think of all the time I spent in the wilds of Wales for your sake, I could scream, yet now you are asking me to endure further hardship in an even more godforsaken place!"

"Chester Castle was hardly the wilds of Wales," Lynx corrected. "Compared to the barren piles of rock that actually *are* in the wilds of Wales, Chester is palatial, as is this fortress of Newcastle."

"But this isn't Windsor!" she threw back at him. Alicia had been lady-in-waiting to the late Queen Eleanor and had been thoroughly spoiled by living at the lavish royal Plantagenet court.

Lynx shrugged. "Suit yourself, Alice, the choice is yours."

"My name is Alicia; you call me Alice to purposely annoy me! You don't care if I come or stay. I'm just a convenience to you—a habit!"

He fixed her with a glacial stare. "A habit that can easily be broken."

"Oh! You *enjoy* being cruel to me, and after all I've sacrificed for you."

Lynx surged to his full height of six feet, his patience exhausted. "I'll tell you what I don't enjoy—female theatrics. I'll see you anon, madam."

"Don't go, Lynx, please don't leave," Alicia begged frantically. There were at least thirty women in the castle who would willingly take Lynx de Warenne to their beds and she was insatiably jealous of every last one of them. She stared at the closed chamber door with narrowed eyes. He hadn't even slammed it. That proved his indifference to her!

Alicia flew to her polished silver mirror to examine her image. She was as slim as a reed and she was beautiful. What more could a man possibly want? Of course I shall stay in the north, she told herself. How else can I keep some other from sinking her claws into him? He has no idea how predatory some bitches can be!

Alicia moved across her chamber to the wardrobe and took a small flagon from its hiding place. She poured out a measure and sipped it avidly. Alicia had been drinking vinegar for so long, she quite liked its pungent taste. It helped to keep her slim; she would have drunk the horse urine she used to bleach her hair if she thought it would keep off the fat. Queen Eleanor had borne the selfish Edward Plantagenet fifteen children, and nothing quite horrified Alicia as much as the stretched belly and other ravages that childbearing had on a woman's figure.

Lynx dismissed all thoughts of Alicia the moment he left her presence. He thought most women rather selfish and often shallow to boot, though he usually couldn't help but view their shortcomings with some amusement. Lynx found the great hall overflowing with men, drinking, dicing, laughing, shouting—the din was raucous, the smoke from the fires and tallow torches was thick and acrid. His glance swept the vast chamber in search of John de Warenne. When he didn't see his uncle there, Lynx knew he'd find him in the map room.

John de Warenne, Earl of Surrey, glanced up quickly when his broad-shouldered nephew entered the chamber, then his eyes returned to the map he had been poring over.

"Newcastle is bursting at the seams and more are arriving each day. My Welsh archers are camped outside the castle walls, and when the Earl of Ulster's men arrive from Ireland, they'll have to do likewise," Lynx said.

"They won't be here for a few days; their ships haven't yet reached Carlisle. I've ordered Percy to accompany the king north to Berwick. That will give us a bit more room when Clifford and his men arrive." John de Warenne was head general of all of King Edward's armies. He had learned his fighting skills under Simon de Montfort, the greatest warrior England had ever known. "It is sheer folly to underestimate Edward Plantagenet, as the Scots will learn to their sorrow."

"A show of force will likely bring King Baliol with his tail between his legs to swear fealty once more for Scotland and provide Edward with troops to help fight the French. Baliol would have to be blind, deaf, and dumb not to realize Edward set him up as a puppet king," Lynx remarked.

"What he doesn't seem to realize is that Edward Plantagenet can pluck him off his throne as quickly as he set him upon it. If Baliol's henchman John Comyn, Earl of Buchan, is urging rebellion because we are occupied with our plans for France, his brains must be up his arse! Edward could use the army he's gathered to invade Scotland before we sail to France, effectively killing two birds with one stone."

"The irony is that if the Scots nobility united against us they'd be almost impossible to defeat."

De Warenne gave a short, mirthless laugh. "There will be two moons in the sky before they join forces under one banner. The insufferable pride of the clan chiefs prevents them from taking orders from one commander. They would rather fight each other than fight the English."

"Robert Bruce should have been named king, not Baliol, even though he can claim Celtic blood only through his mother. There are few Scots nobles with pure Celtic blood. Most, like the Bruces, are Norman by descent and hold land in both England and Scotland. Scots nobles change sides as often as they remarry." Lynx poured his uncle a horn of ale and handed it to him; only then did the flinty general turn his back on the maps and seem to dismiss all thought of the army for a while.

He sat down before the fire, his glance roaming over Lynx's powerful frame. "Speaking of remarriage, when are you going to take another wife? You grow no younger. I don't want you to end up like me, without a son."

Lynx knew it was his duty to remarry. He held a barony, owned lands in Wales, Essex, and Northumberland, and was heir to John de Warenne's earldom of Surrey with its vast acres and numerous castles. He needed strong sons to hold fast all that belonged to him. If he died without issue, Edward Plantagenet would swallow all the de Warenne holdings.

More than anything on earth, Lynx wanted a son. If he could not be blessed by a son, he would gladly settle for a daughter. He was close to thirty and as far as he knew, his seed had never taken root. Such a deficiency was an embarrassment in a country where large families were both encouraged and expected. King Edward had set the fashion and sired fifteen children on Queen Eleanor, and now that he was widowed, it was rumored that he was looking for another queen so he could begin to sow a second crop.

Lynx had been wed for five years before his wife had died, but the union had produced no children, and deep down he feared that the deficiency was his. None of the de Warennes were prolific breeders; Lynx was his uncle's heir because John had no *legitimate* children of his own.

"You have Fitz-Waren, which proves you are capable of siring sons," Lynx reminded him.

John quaffed his ale, remaining silent for a few minutes, then shook his head in denial. "Fitz isn't my bastard. His drooping eyelid told me before he was two years old that he belonged to my best friend, who was killed in battle. We often shared our wenches . . . When the young lass came to me in tears and confessed she was in trouble, I acknowledged the child."

Lynx now understood why John had never legitimized Fitz-Waren, and in truth his cousin bore no physical resemblance to the de Warennes.

For the hundredth time Lynx thought about taking another wife. Though his first marriage had been arranged, Lady Sylvia Bigod had been everything a man could want in a wife. As well as bringing him wealth, she had been highborn, beautiful, and cultured, and though she was slightly spoiled from living at the lavish Plantegenet court, they had never exchanged an angry word. When Sylvia died from an inflammation of the lungs, Lynx had been steeped in guilt, thinking he had spent too little time with her. Since then, he had been too busy fighting wars and accumulating land holdings to remarry. His thoughts turned to Alicia. Strange that in the two years she had been his mistress, she had never ripened with child. Lynx wanted a family so desperately, he suspected that he would capitulate and wed Alicia if she ever proved fertile. He glanced over at John and promised, "I will look about me for a suitable lady."

Standing gate duty at the castle, Fitz-Waren watched keenly as a hundred horses clattered into the bailey. It was almost dark and Clifford's men were not expected until the morrow. Then Fitz-Waren recognized the de Bohun device on a shield and knew the Earl of Hereford, Constable of England, had arrived.

Suddenly his blood began to surge as he saw a crimson hood thrown back to reveal silvery-gilt tresses, the color of moonlight. *Marjory de Warenne!* Her very name quickened his pulses. Fitz-Waren jumped down from his watch-tower and forced his way through the throng of sweating horses until he had a firm grip on the young widow's bridle.

Jory looked down and gave him a dazzling smile. "Fitz! I'm on the brink of exhaustion, keeping up with these rough louts." Her lashes swept her cheeks. "Be a darling and stable my horse?"

Looking up into the beautiful, fragile face, Fitz knew men would jump to do her bidding even if she had said, "Fall on your sword" or "Drink this cup of hemlock." He cursed himself for a besotted fool and helped her from the saddle, all the while telling himself she was naught but a vain bitch.

Marjory's father-in-law, the Earl of Hereford, elbowed Fitz-Waren aside. Though she was the widow of his eldest son, Humphrey, John de Bohun now wanted her for his second son, Henry.

"It's all right, my lord, Fitz-Waren is my dear cousin. I know you will both excuse me; I want to surprise Lynx." Jory ran toward the castle as lightly as she would traverse the dance floor, despite having spent twelve hours in the saddle with only two short rest stops.

Lynx de Warenne stared in disbelief as his sister swept into the great hall. "Splendor of God, did you just ride in? Who is your escort?" he demanded.

Jory wrinkled her nose. "Unfortunately, it was Hereford. He watches me like a dog with a bone." She reached up on tiptoe to kiss her brother. "Are you growing or am I shrinking?" she teased.

"Don't think to divert me. What the hell are you doing here, Jory?"

She sighed solemnly. "I am in utter disgrace. I will tell you all the grisly details when we are private."

"Come up to my chamber." Lynx signaled his two squires. "Taffy, ask the steward to plenish a chamber for my sister; tell him I don't care who he has to turf out on his ear. Thomas, fetch some ale."

"Ale?" the Irish squire asked doubtfully. No respectable lady drank aught but wine.

Lynx said dryly, "My sister has the appetite of three men-at-arms. It provides the energy for her mayhem."

Jory gave the Irish squire a wink that did peculiar things to his insides. He jumped to do Lynx's bidding, but not before he returned the lady's wink.

When they were alone, Jory threw herself into one of the carved chairs before the fire and lifted her foot in the air. "Help me off with these damned boots."

Lynx turned his back to her, drew her foot through his legs and tugged. The first boot popped off easily, but the second was more difficult to dislodge. Jory placed her stockinged foot against his backside and pushed hard. "You make a lovely maid."

Lynx flung the boots onto the hearth to dry. "You don't need a maid, you need a bloody squire."

"Mmm, what a novel idea. May I have your Irishman?"

"Can you not behave yourself?" he asked repressively.

"No," she replied cheerfully, lifting her skirts to warm her legs. "Have you found a special lady yet worthy of your affection?"

"No, I have not."

"Ugh, that probably means you are still keeping that

awful mistress of yours. When your heart's desire is to have a child, why do you waste your time with Alicia?''

''We are not discussing my shortcomings, we are discussing yours.'' When silence stretched between them, Lynx said sharply, ''I'm waiting.''

''And you do it with such charm,'' she teased. Then, knowing she must confess all, she started at the beginning, picking and choosing her words in order to put herself in the best light.

''When Humphrey was killed in Wales, I grieved so deeply I thought I would go mad, as did others.'' She paused as the inevitable lump of sorrow rose up in her throat. She swallowed hard before she could continue. ''Finally my dearest friend, Princess Joanna, took pity on me and invited me to stay with her in Gloucester. Hereford and Gloucester are only twenty-five miles apart and we had visited often.'' Marjory paused for breath.

''I am aware of the traveling distance between the two cities; get to the heart of the matter.''

Jory sighed. ''My father-in-law objected. When it dawned on me that de Bohun wanted me for his son Henry, I was appalled. I suspect he's already sent for the dispensation. Lynx, I could never marry my husband's brother!''

Lynx frowned. ''You are in disgrace because you refused him? I'll have a word with Hereford.''

''No, no, I haven't got to that part yet. I'm perfectly capable of handling Hereford, for God's sake.''

Lynx made a visible effort to control his impatience. ''Jory, cut to the bloody chase.''

''Well, I suppose you could call it Providence that I

went to Joanna, for within weeks her aging husband took to his bed and died."

The king had married his daughter Joanna to the greatest noble in the realm. Gilbert de Clare had been Earl of Gloucester and Hertford, as well as having owned part of Ireland and Wales, but he had been a good deal older than the Plantagenet princess.

"I'm glad you could be with her. The king and all of England mourned the passing of Gilbert de Clare."

"Oh, it wasn't a love match; de Clare was ancient. Joanna was madly in love with Gilbert's squire, Ralph de Monthermer."

Lynx was shocked. Surely Princess Joanna had not been unfaithful to the powerful Earl of Gloucester? "You aided and abetted the princess to commit adultery!" Lynx accused.

"You are as bad as the rest! All are blaming me as if I pushed them into bed and undressed them."

"The truth, Marjory," Lynx thundered.

"Wellll, perhaps I undid the buttons on her night rail," she admitted, winking saucily. "You know I am cursed with impulsiveness."

"And encouraged Princess Joanna to act impulsively too. No wonder the de Clares are outraged, with the earl not yet cold in his grave. You are usually such a clever little she-devil, how did they find out?"

"We tried our utmost to keep the marriage secret, but the priest must have blabbed."

Lynx de Warenne stared at his sister in horror. "Bones of Christ, lying with him and *marrying* him are worlds apart! What could you have been thinking? Monthermer is a bloody *squire,* for God's sake!"

"Squire no longer; he is nothing less than the Earl of Gloucester and Hertford," she whispered through dry lips.

"Splendor of God, you are absolutely right!" Lynx gasped, quickly realizing the repercussions of Joanna's hasty marriage.

"The de Clares sent a messenger hotfoot to the king and packed me off, back to my ogre of a father-in-law. I promised Joanna I'd ride to the king here at Newcastle and explain everything to him."

"Explain to Edward Plantagenet that his most powerful earldom of Gloucester has been bestowed upon a squire? You must be queer in the head!"

"It runs in the family." Jory's attempt at humor fell on unappreciative ears. She thought Lynx's face looked more grim than she had ever seen it. "You think of Edward Plantagenet as a king; I think of him as a man. There isn't a male breathing who cannot be manip—" Jory saw the warning look on her brother's face and did not dare finish her sentence.

"You and Princess Joanna are like two bloody peas in a pod! The pair of you are far too willful with a high conceit of yourselves."

"That's why we are such good friends."

"The king would be incensed with you. I forbid you to seek him out tonight. Edward has enough on his mind at the moment; this Scottish situation has put him in a towering rage."

The look of defeat on Marjory's face suddenly touched Lynx with compassion. She had undertaken a hundred-and-fifty-mile journey for friendship's sake. He saw the mauve shadows beneath her beautiful eyes, saw the droop of her slim shoulders. "Take my chamber; try to rest. I'll come back and escort you to dinner." Then he went in search of his Welsh squire, Taffy, who had been given an impossible task. There would be no empty chambers in Newcastle this night.

When Marjory entered the hall on the arm of her brother, she had a physical impact on every male lucky enough to catch a glimpse of her. Her pale green gown matched her eyes; her jewels were chosen to draw attention to her feminine curves. From a heavy gold chain dangled a cabochon emerald that swung in the valley between her upthrust breasts, separating, emphasizing, and irresistibly drawing the eye. Its only competition was another gold chain that went round her waist and held a second emerald that rested upon her high mons.

The murmur of men's voices as she passed sounded like growls. To Alicia, on Lynx's other arm, she whispered, "Ooh, they're like a pack of hungry dogs. Shall we draw lots to see who shall be the bone—and who the bitch?" Jory saw the look of revulsion on Alicia's face at the thought of the hall overflowing with knights and uncouth men-at-arms and hid a smile. Personally, she could think of nothing more stimulating than being surrounded by men.

As she swept down the long head table of earls and barons, Jory had a smile for each of them. John de Bohun made a place for her beside him. She went down in a graceful curtsy before him. "Thank you for my safe escort, my dear lord. I shall dine with my uncle John tonight. I haven't had the pleasure of his company in months. But I'm sure Alicia would be most honored to sit at table with England's constable." She knew John de Bohun could not help his proprietory feelings toward her and that he mourned her loss as his daughter-in-law.

Alicia gave her a look that would curdle milk, and as Jory took her place between John de Warenne and Lynx, she murmured, "That should give you breathing space."

John looked down at her with doting eyes. "Hello, Minx, you grow lovelier every day." Lynx and Minx, it was a jest she and Lynx had shared with their uncle since they were children.

"She's in serious trouble," Lynx informed him.

"Not again?" her uncle asked indulgently.

"I simply brought a message to the king from his daughter Joanna."

"You shouldn't really be here," John admonished gently. "Trouble threatens with Scotland; we are taking the army there."

Marjory's face lit up. "You can give me safe escort. I promise to leave as soon as I've had an opportunity to speak with the king. I can go to Carlisle to visit my godmother, Marjory de Bruce. She will welcome me with open arms."

"She will *not,*" Lynx thundered. "Carlisle Castle has been chosen as the mustering point for the armies' supplies and any day now it will be overrun by de Burgh's Irishmen. Carlisle is certainly no fit place for a lady."

Jory's thoughts flashed about like mercury trying to keep one step ahead of her brother, which was no easy task. Suddenly she smiled. "Then I shall go to Wigton. Even you, Brother, cannot deny me access to our own castle." Wigton was only eight or nine miles from Carlisle Castle where the Bruces were governors.

Lynx smiled back at her. "Wigton it is. You will be good company for Alicia."

"Peste!" Marjory swore. "There is always a damn fly in the ointment."

"Why are you in trouble?" John asked. "Because you refuse to remarry? What is it you two have against marriage?"

"I have nothing against marriage—for others. No, I am being facetious. I loved Humphrey very much and would not have chosen to be widowed for all the crown jewels, but now that I have experienced widowhood I realize its advantages far outweigh those of being an unwed maid, or even a wife. I need bend the knee to no man. For the first time in my life I am free to make my own decisions."

"Decisions which are invariably rash," Lynx reminded her.

Jory placed her hand over his. "Lynx, Joanna couldn't help herself. Surely you remember what it's like to fall in love?"

"Love?" Lynx was incredulous. "There is no such thing as *falling in love.* It is a myth created by women, for women. Men may pretend in order to get what they want from women, but I doubt there's a man breathing who truly believes in such nonsense."

Jory lifted her lashes in surprise. "What about Sylvia?"

"Our marriage was arranged, the way all good marriages are. We didn't do anything so ridiculous as *fall in love*!"

Jory studied her brother's face. Lynx de Warenne was one of the handsomest warriors in all of England. His muscular physique and mane of tawny hair caused women to sigh and offer their hearts to him. It was incomprehensible that he had never experienced being in love with a woman. At that moment she felt a great pity for him and quickly lowered her lashes lest he see it.

Lynx changed the subject. "It looks like the king won't be dining with us tonight."

"No, he just received a dispatch that incensed him." John lowered his voice so none but Lynx could hear his words. "Baliol of Scotland has dismissed all officeholders appointed by Edward and confiscated all lands held by the English. The king is presently writing out an order that all Scots fortresses along the border be placed in his hands until the war with France is over."

"Then tomorrow we had better prepare the men to march," Lynx said decisively.

3

King Edward I, the finest lawmaker England had ever known, was in a full-blown Plantagenet rage.

"Whoreson! Dung-eater! Scab-arsed baboon!"

Three men cowered before him, knowing their fate would be sealed once Edward Plantagenet ceased his raving. They had been caught by his spies in the Port of Berwick, smuggling a message to King Philip of France.

"If that dog turd, Baliol, and his prick-licking henchman, Comyn, think I will allow them to form an alliance with France, they have let the maggots devour their gray matter. Splendor of Christ, do they not know I will crush them beneath my boot? Baliol has sat on Scotland's throne for three years, *at my bidding,* and clearly it has been three years too long!

"For months he has been yapping about my ankles, flouting my orders, and for months I have kicked him aside, thinking he would eventually learn obedience and come to heel. Does he not understand that I am the Lord Superior of Scotland?"

The king brandished a parchment in each fist. One was the damning letter to Philip of France that his spies had confiscated, the other was Baliol's Oath of Fealty. Edward's fierce blue eyes stared at the three men before him. "Insurrection! Treason! Betrayal! God will avail him naught now, it is too late."

The leader swallowed hard. "Majesty, permit me to carry your words to Baliol."

Incredulous that the messenger had the temerity to barter for his life, Edward imperiously raised a finger, summoning a guard. "I have my own royal messengers. I have no need of Scots offal! Hang them."

King Edward returned to his privy chambers, high in Newcastle, and summoned the men who had brought in the prisoners. They were in the pay of the palatinate Bishop of Durham, who was in charge of raising an army from Edward's northern levies. In his firm decisive hand the king wrote out a missive, praising the bishop's diligence and ordering him to take his army to Norham Castle on the southern shore of the river Tweed on the very border of Scotland.

A show of force such as you have gathered will put fear in their hearts. I shall join you with mine own army in less than a week.

The king sanded the wet ink, rolled the parchment, melted the sealing wax, and stamped his leopard ring into the soft red wax. As he handed it to the Bishop of Durham's man, he said, "If these Scots forget I am descended from conquerors, they forget at their peril!" As he finished reading the dispatches from the Bishop of Durham, his face began to turn purple. "Call my army commanders to a council meeting!" he ordered John de Warenne.

* * *

Edward Plantagenet entered the large vaulted chamber at Newcastle where his commanders had gathered. The previous day he had been well pleased with the numbers as the armies began to arrive. When Richard de Burgh with his horde of Ulstermen arrived from Ireland the army would total five thousand horse and forty thousand foot soldiers. He had been convinced such a show of strength would bring the Scots to heel.

Today, however, King Edward was enraged. "The Bishop of Durham reports that the English fleet has been attacked in the river Tweed while bringing supplies to the army!" The invaders had sailed out from the great seaport of Berwick, which lay on the northern shore of the Tweed in Scottish territory, and Edward proceeded to vent his temper, reviling Berwick's citizens. Curses and foul oaths echoed around the vaulted chamber.

"The wealth of these merchants has swollen them with arrogance! The fat swines think themselves safe perched behind their fortifications on the north bank! They are about to learn otherwise!"

John de Warenne exchanged a look of understanding with the earls and barons about him. They would have to teach Berwick a lesson before they undertook the French invasion.

There was a commotion at the chamber door as Robert de Bruce pushed past the herald before he could be announced. All present knew the swarthy, handsome Bruce who thought himself the rightful King of Scotland. He made his obeisance to Edward and succinctly delivered his news without preamble.

"Sire, the Scots sent an army down into Cumberland.

It ravaged the northern shires until it reached Carlisle. We rode out to fight the Scots. They suffered a sharp reversal and retreated back to their own territory.''

"The whoresons dared invade England?" Edward Plantagenet's fury bordered on madness.

The earls and barons all spoke at once, disbelief, anger, and outrage swelling their voices to a cacophony. Finally the king lifted his arms. "Silence! The Scots have conspired to form an alliance with France against us, they have sunk our ships and now they have dared to invade England. De Warenne, we would hear what you propose."

The Earl of Surrey got to his feet. He was a decisive general, which was why Edward had put him in command of all his armies. "Your Majesty, I propose we postpone action against the French until we have dealt with this Scottish insurrection."

"We think alike, John." The king brought his fist down upon the table before him with a crash. "We invade Scotland!"

Some cheers went up, mingled with some curses, but all present knew that the die was cast. Once Edward Plantagenet made a decision, he did not go back on it.

Edward's brilliant blue eyes fastened on Robert Bruce. "It is war. Are you with us or with the Scots?" he asked bluntly. Edward knew the Bruces were powerful and he knew they had a secret bond with seven other Scottish earls to support the Bruce claim to the throne. Edward also knew he could not effectively control Scotland without them. But when he had chosen Baliol king over Robert Bruce, the new Scots ruler had confiscated all of the Bruces' holdings in the western marches and handed them over to the Bruces' bitterest enemies, the Comyns. There was no love lost between the Bruces and the Scots King Baliol.

Robert clasped Edward's arm and looked directly into the king's eyes. "We are with you in this." Implied in the pledge was the expectation that in return for their support of the English the Bruces would regain all they had lost. As the two powerful men stared at each other, Edward knew Bruce would eventually demand reversion of the crown of Scotland.

Edward issued John de Warenne an order. "Our first point of attack will be Berwick!"

Lynx de Warenne crossed himself and murmured, "God help the citizens of Berwick. Let us hope when that city falls, Baliol will obey King Edward's summons."

Percy, Stanley, and Bohun joined John de Warenne to discuss strategy, while Robert Bruce gave his Oath of Fealty to the king. "I want the Bruces to remain governors of Carlisle Castle. It must remain impregnable as the headquarters for supplies from Wales and Ireland. Once Scotland capitulates and they hand over Baliol, all the western marches will be reinstated to you," Edward promised.

Lynx de Warenne joined his friend, and the king watched with approval as the two men embraced. The de Warenne and Bruce landholdings in Essex ran together, and the two young men had been companions in their boyhood.

"De Burgh was ordered to land his Ulstermen at Carlisle. Is there any sign of them yet?" Lynx asked.

"Aye. The minute we sent the invaders fleeing back across the border, the Irish sails were spotted in Solway

Firth,'' Robert said with irony. ''But better late than never. They should start arriving here tomorrow.''

''They had better,'' the king stated flatly. ''The army moves north tomorrow.''

Marjory de Warenne felt great frustration. King Edward had been closeted the entire day with his generals, making plans for a march on Scotland, and she had seen neither hide nor hair of him. She reminded herself that this was Edward Plantagenet, the greatest king in Christendom. It was undoubtedly presumptuous of her to expect him to spare time for her when he was making preparations for war, but Jory knew today would be her only chance to plead Joanna's case. At dawn the king would leave and she would be sent to Wigton.

As the afternoon shadows lengthened into evening and still the nobles had not emerged from their war conference, Marjory realized how insignificant women were in men's scheme of things. Women played no part in making decisions. Men ruled the world, fought the wars, made the laws, garnered the wealth, owned the property, and for the most part controlled the lives of their women. The only role available to the female was that of nurturer to the male.

And yet, few women seemed to resent their lot in life. Was she the only female alive who chafed at the restrictions placed upon her? Perhaps if she had had a child, she would be too busy being a mother to be bothered by the inequities between the sexes. Jory felt a pang of regret, then wondered for the thousandth time if she was barren.

Determined to shake off her gloomy mood she lit the candles and poured water to bathe her hands and face.

She might have a chance to speak to the king in the dining hall and beg him for a private word. Jory decided to leave off her head veil. Her silver-gilt hair was by far her prettiest feature and had an amazing effect on the male of the species. Tonight she must look her most attractive if she hoped to gain King Edward's attention.

When Jory arrived in the vast dining hall, flanked by Thomas and Taffy, her eyes first went to the dais and the high, carved chair where the king would sit. Finding the chair empty, her gaze traversed the length of the packed hall, seeking the tall, imposing figure of Edward Plantagenet. Disappointed, she sought a seat just below the dais and thanked the barons who eagerly made room on the bench for her.

The first platters of meat were already on the tables before she caught a glimpse of her brother, Lynx, accompanied by another man. When they climbed up on the dais, Thomas went to attend Lynx. The squire immediately returned for Marjory and led her to the dais.

"There is room with us, Jory; John dines with the king tonight."

"Damn, I've been waiting all day to see Edward . . ." Her voice faltered to a stop as her eyes fell on the man at her brother's side. Splendor of God, here is a man worth looking at, she thought. He was not quite as tall as Lynx, few men were, but the spectacular breadth of his shoulders more than made up for it. Suddenly, Jory's eyes widened as she recognized the darkly handsome Bruce.

"Robert! Is it truly you? Why, I haven't seen you in years. The last time was at the ceremony where your father passed over the earldom of Carrick to you."

Robert Bruce grinned down at her. "You were a child of seventeen and even then beauteous enough to play hell with the hearts of all the Bruce brothers."

"All except you. As I recall you were a wild devil who teased me unmercifully."

"I was no exception, Jory." His dark eyes smoldered as they feasted on her delicate beauty.

She laughed up at him. "You are still teasing me unmercifully and I warrant you are still a wild devil."

Jory was amused when Lynx chose to sit between them and knew her brother had noticed the sparks igniting between her and Robert Bruce.

"I'm sorry you've had no opportunity to speak with the king, Jory. Your journey was a waste of time," Lynx declared.

She glanced at Robert, making a moue with her mouth. "Not completely." Then she added, "There is always tomorrow."

Lynx shook his head. "The king and the entire army leave for Scotland on the morrow."

The teasing light left her eyes. "Is it war?" she asked solemnly. When Lynx nodded, her eyes sought Robert's. "For whom do you fight, my lord?"

"I fight for Robert Bruce," he said quite frankly.

"He stands with us," Lynx confirmed.

"At least for now," Bruce qualified. "I have every intention of smashing my enemy Comyn and taking back my lands in Annandale and Carrick. I welcome Edward's aid," he said with natural arrogance.

"You are Governor of Carlisle Castle; the king expects you to keep it secure," Lynx reminded him.

"I'll return there for the present, but when the real

fighting starts, I'll be in the thick of it. I have enough brothers to keep Carlisle secure."

Jory's face lit up. "I am being banished to my family's castle at Wigton, my lord, which you know lies not far from Carlisle. Will you give me safe escort?" Though she knew perfectly well both her uncle and her brother would provide her with de Warenne knights for her security, she fancied the protection of this powerful Scots earl.

Bruce's mouth curved sensually. "It will be my pleasure."

"Don't be too sure, Robert," Lynx warned. "She is a willful little jade with a penchant for creating havoc."

"I'll keep her in hand," Robert Bruce promised.

Marjory went weak at the thought.

Later that night, Jory paced her chamber trying to find a solution to her problem. She was as tenacious as a terrier and refused to be thwarted when she was this close to her goal. She needed to have a private conversation with the king tonight, and could think of only one place where this might be possible: in his bedchamber. Jory brushed her hair until it fell about her shoulders like a cloak of silk, then she put on lip salve and rubbed a drop of perfumed oil in the cleft between her breasts. Then she draped a veil over her head, concealing her face as well as her telltale hair, and picked up a tray of sweetmeats.

She made her way through the castle to the king's privy chambers. Due to the advanced hour, Newcastle had settled down for the night and the only people she encountered were servants. Jory climbed the steps of the tower that Edward occupied, knowing she would be challenged by a guard at the king's door. When she saw the king's gentleman stationed outside his chamber, she heaved a small sigh, relieved that she did not know him personally.

"His Majesty has retired, he requires nothing more."

"The king sent for me, my lord," she said breathlessly, surprised at her own daring.

He shook his head. "His Majesty ordered no wench tonight."

"Did he not?" she challenged silkily. "King Edward likes something sweet when he retires."

"Don't we all, sweetheart?" he asked, laughing, then reached for her veil.

"Nay!" Jory took a step backward, then lowered her voice confidentially. "My lord, I am not a wench, I am a lady. The king would be angered if my identity became known." She had him half convinced and pressed her advantage. "He told me you would be on the door tonight and that you were the most discreet of all his gentlemen of the bedchamber." While he digested the compliment, Jory scratched on the oaken door and slipped inside.

Edward Plantagenet, wearing a crimson velvet bedrobe, lifted his golden head, sensing, rather than hearing, the intrusion. "Yes, what is it?" he demanded.

She advanced into the chamber and lifted her veil to reveal her face. "Your Majesty, it is Marjory de Warenne."

His brows drew together. "What the devil are you doing here?"

"Sire, I come from Princess Joanna."

The expression on the king's face turned cold. "I've had this Monthermer upstart thrown into irons! The ambitious swine has taken advantage of my daughter. Yet she will not be held blameless in this, nor will those about her who urged this disastrous step.'' His voice and his eyes were like ice. ''They have dishonored the memory of Gilbert de Clare, and his family is greatly insulted. The marriage will be set aside.''

Jory let the veil fall from her hair, then she went down on her knees before him in supplication. ''Your Majesty, Joanna sent me to you to beg your forgiveness and your understanding. She wanted you to hear the truth from my lips before the others poisoned your thoughts with their false tales.''

Jory watched Edward's icy gaze fall upon her lips and hoped he would thaw a little. She saw his gaze lift to her hair and she knew he had noticed her fragrance. As he reached down, taking her hands to raise her, she could see the battle he fought within.

''Say your piece,'' he ordered, but not harshly.

Jory took a deep breath and saw his eyes flicker over her rising breasts. ''Your Majesty, Joanna knows you honored her by wedding her to your greatest noble, the Earl of Gloucester. She did it for love, but not love for Gilbert de Clare . . . Joanna did it for love of *you.*'' Jory wondered if he remembered the terrible tantrums the imperious Joanna had thrown before she'd capitulated and married the aging earl. ''This time she followed her heart; she wed Ralph de Monthermer because she is deeply in love with him.''

''Monthermer is a lowly squire!''

''Never *lowly,* Sire. He was Gilbert de Clare's most valiant warrior. Ralph de Monthermer was de Clare's right hand. He was the one who won glory in battle for de Clare in his declining years. The Earl of Gloucester trusted him with his life and I believe he made Ralph swear an oath to look after Joanna always.''

Jory, caught up in her own tale, began to embroider it a little more. ''It will break Joanna's heart to see her beloved in chains, Sire. Her deepest wish is for you to know Monthermer and learn his worth. The men of Gloucester and Hertford whom he commands hold him in highest respect. Send for him, Sire. Give him a chance to show you his mettle and his loyalty.''

''You plead his case well. What is it about this Monthermer that has blinded both you and Joanna to your duty?''

Jory was suddenly inspired. ''He reminds Joanna of *you,* Sire. That is the great attraction, I swear it.''

As Edward's shrewd eyes roamed over her delicate beauty, his face softened a little. ''I hope Joanna appreciates your friendship. What is it about the de Warennes that makes their loyalty absolute?''

''You honor us with your trust, Sire. To a de Warenne, that trust is sacred.'' Jory hoped God would not strike her dead; 'twas only a slight exaggeration.

Edward took a seat before the fire and indicated that she too might be seated.

''Your Majesty, tomorrow you go to war. For the love you bear Joanna, I beg you not to go into battle without forgiving her. She could not bear it if there was a breach between you. A father's love is so precious.''

Edward smiled at Marjory de Warenne with compassion. ''Do you remember your own father?''

Jory shook her head sadly. ''Lynx remembers him well, but I was too young when he died.''

"He was my dearest friend. 'Twas he who plotted my escape when Simon de Montfort held me captive."

"I know, Sire. I've heard the tale recounted many times."

"His loyalty to me was absolute, as yours appears to be toward my wayward daughter."

Now that the conversation had returned to Princess Joanna, Marjory opened her mouth to entreat the king again. When Edward put up his hand, Jory held her tongue.

"I shall send for this Ralph de Monthermer and judge for myself."

"Thank you, Sire." Jory dipped her knee, knowing she had done all she could and hoped she had tipped the scales in the princess's favor. She picked up her veil. "Godspeed, Your Majesty."

As she hurried from the tower, Jory was confident that all within Newcastle would be asleep at this hour. She almost made it back to her own chamber when suddenly a powerful arm reached out and pulled her into a shadowed recess. Jory was about to scream when she realized it was her cousin, Fitz-Waren, who lifted her veil aside.

"How about a kiss?"

"Damn you for a knave, Fitz, you frightened the wits from me." When he pushed her against the wall and pinned her there, Marjory did not experience any fear, only anger. "Let me go at once."

Fitz-Waren took hold of her chin and brought his mouth down on hers. She pulled away, disgusted. "You've been drinking!"

"Think yourself too good for me after playing whore

to the king? I wager it's something you wouldn't want my father or your brother to learn.'' His hand cupped her breast suggestively.

''Lynx will kill you if he learns of this.''

''Lynx is busy with his own whore.''

Jory knew she must get away from him, but realized if she screamed, she would rouse the castle. She contemplated shouting for Thomas, but could see the passageway was empty and he was no longer outside her door. In a heartbeat Marjory knew she must rely upon herself to escape her cousin's lust. She gripped his leather jack in her fists and brought her knee up sharply into Fitz-Waren's groin.

He doubled over in agony and sank to the stone floor. ''You'll pay for that, you vain bitch!'' he swore between gritted teeth.

4

Jane Leslie climbed the hills behind Dumfries on her way to the forest to gather herbs. She bent to pick a wild yellow pansy and tucked it behind her ear. Once she entered the shaded forest, Jane began to search for speedwell with its pale green, hairy leaves that trailed upon the ground. Speedwell was good for coughs and consumptions. When she came to a boggy place, she identified an alder bush, just coming into bud. Jane gathered handfuls of leaves, knowing there was nothing better for ridding a chamber of fleas that gathered over the long winter. She folded the leaves into the large cloth bag she carried and walked deeper into the woods.

When she saw a patch of dragon-wort, Jane pulled it up by its black-knobbed root and popped it into the bag. It cured many ailments such as vomiting, bruises, bites or stings, and also stopped the bleeding when a woman began to miscarry.

As she neared the forest pool, she grew tense with anticipation, wondering if she would again encounter the lynx. She felt both fear and fascination for the magnificent predator and slowed her pace so that she moved noiselessly.

Jane became aware of his powerful presence almost before she saw him. Completely hidden behind a canopy of leaves, she watched the lynx dip his magnificent head toward the water to drink. He was the most beautiful creature she had ever seen in her life. She watched mesmerized as he entered the water and began to swim.

Jane longed to form a bond with him as she did with other animals. What a rare privilege it would be if some day she could swim alongside him. Then she remembered her brother Keith's words about the lynx being an omen of fateful things to come. Cautiously, she moved back through the trees, then when she was a safe distance away, hurried back to the protective walls of Dumfries.

It was lambing season, and Ben and Sim Leslie were the master shepherds of flocks that numbered over a thousand sheep. That afternoon Jane helped her brothers with the ewes that were in labor. "Sim, have you lost any of your flock to wolves lately?"

"Not many, the dogs are well trained tae warn us when a marauder is nigh."

"That's good." Jane hesitated, then asked tentatively, "Have you ever seen a lynx in these parts?"

"Nay." Sim shook his head. "This is out of their territory. Later, when we take the flocks to graze in the Uplands, we'll encounter big cats. There's lots up in the Pentlands and the Lammermuirs."

Jane lapsed into silence, glad that her lynx was not decimating Dumfries' flocks.

By the time night fell there were three tiny, motherless lambs who would not survive without Jane's tender care. Sim carried them to the stone cottage, where Jane laid them before the hearth to keep them warm.

Megotta had water boiling so that Jane could wash away the blood and mucus that covered her from neck to knees. When Jane was clean she moved toward the hearth.

"Nay, ye will eat before ye tend them. Ye must keep up yer strength or yer power will be diminished."

Jane knew the truth of her grandmother's words. She would have to work over the black-faced lambs for hours if she hoped to save them. She obediently joined Megotta in a bowl of hearty stew flavored with herbs.

"Kate and Mary didn't say anything to Father about finding me a husband, did they?"

Though Megotta knew full well the subject had been thoroughly discussed and solutions suggested, she felt she could overrule Jock regarding his youngest daughter. "Jane, I give ye my word that ye won't be forced tae marry. Put the disturbin' thought out of yer head. There's none good enough in these parts tae be husband tae ye. I'll not see ye sacrificed tae a swineherd or some such lout."

Reassured, Jane filled a small stone bottle from a pan of ewe's milk that stood warming by the fire, then she pushed a clean linen wad into the narrow neck and tipped it up until the linen became saturated. Gently, she lifted the smallest lamb and gave it the linen teat. It seemed too small and lifeless to suckle at first, but Jane's voice and hands began to work their magic.

At the end of half an hour she had managed to get some milk inside the frail creature, and its fleece, now dry and fluffy from Jane's insistent fingers, made it look as if she held a fuzzy ball of wool. She laid it back on the hearth and picked up the second frail creature. With gentle forbearance, Jane ministered to the tiny trio until the hour was late.

Megotta brought a blanket to the hearth. "Get some rest, child." Jane smiled her thanks, as she tucked the lambs about her and lay down before the fire. With their little bellies full, she knew they would doze for the next few hours. Her last thought before she slept was of her magnificent lynx.

Jane drifted into a dream where she found herself back in the forest. *She was in a state of agitation because she knew that eyes watched her. The urge to flee came upon her, but she could not move. When she looked down at her ankles, they were entwined in long vines of bistort that held her fast. Jane could feel the eyes upon her, silently watching every move. Then she knew he was moving closer through the canopy of leaves.*

As she opened her mouth to scream, a lynx glided through the trees. She was so relieved that the creature who watched her was not a man, she sank to the forest floor to catch her breath and still her pulses. Then a terrifying thing happened. Just when she thought she was safe, the lynx began to stalk her!

Slowly, it placed one great padded foot before the other, its green eyes fixed upon her intently. Then it crouched back on its haunches, ready to spring. Again, she opened her mouth to scream as the lynx launched itself at her. When he fell upon her she expected to be torn limb from limb, but what happened was just as horrific to Jane: The lynx transformed himself into a man! Her fear was mingled with awe; never had she seen a man of such size and beauty. Atop powerful shoulders was a mane of tawny hair and brilliant green eyes that could see into her very soul.

He held her fast in powerful hands. She sensed for the first time that he would be gentle with her. With tremendous relief, Jane somehow knew he would not harm her. He inhaled the fragrance of her hair, then incredibly his lips touched her cheek. She watched mesmerized as his tongue came out to lick up and down her throat and over her collarbone.

Jane became acutely aware of her nakedness as he began to slowly lick her breasts. As his tongue curled about a nipple, its rough texture sent delicious sensations running through her body. Fear melted as it was replaced by intense pleasure and a strange excitement began to build deep inside her.

The man's beautiful mouth moved down over her rib cage until she felt wet, warm swirls upon her bare belly. The pleasurable feeling this aroused was so intense, it made Jane close her eyes and low moans escaped her lips. He was in total command of her and that was the way she wanted it!

Jane awoke with a start and blushed at the wanton behavior she had enjoyed in her dream. She pushed all thoughts of the man out of her mind, but the image of the lynx was so powerful it remained with her. She felt compelled to paint herself a new touchstone talisman to protect her and keep her safe.

Her imagination conjured the different goddesses and symbols she might use such as fish, serpents, dragons, and stags, but she rejected all of them, settling instead on the image of the lynx. It was certainly the most powerful creature she had ever encountered. It was also majestic, its beauty proud and awesome. The lynx would be a source of power and energy for her as well as a sacred guardian.

Lynx de Warenne and the other commanders rode north and joined the army the Bishop of Durham had gathered at Norham. From their camp Lynx rode out with the king, John de Warenne, and the other leaders to view the fortified city of Berwick. It was well protected by the sea and also by a deep channel cut by the river Tweed. Berwick Castle was perched on the north bank behind a stockade that was surrounded by a ditch.

"Who commands the garrison?" Edward Plantagenet demanded.

"William Douglas, Your Majesty, reputed to be a stout fighting man," John de Warenne supplied.

"Demand the surrender of the castle," Edward ordered.

John de Warenne chose Lynx to parley with the garrison's commander, while the king and the other leaders retired back to camp. Lynx de Warenne was a fierce warrior who had cut his teeth on subduing Wales. Nevertheless, he abhorred unnecessary bloodshed.

With his squires flanking him, carrying white flags of truce, Lynx de Warenne rode into Berwick Castle and spent a full twenty hours at the negotiating table with William Douglas. Finally, in the small hours of the morning, he saw defeat writ on William Douglas's face. Then and only then did de Warenne allow him a sop to his pride. "I will permit you to ride out with all honor and your men may march out flying your banner and the flag of Scotland."

* * *

Edward Plantagenet, along with all of his commanders, rode up to Berwick's gates to accept the surrender. Hundreds of men lined the top of the stockade to witness the proceedings. When Douglas rode out from the castle, the citizens of Berwick began to jeer at the English, brandishing weapons and chanting taunts and insults. Above the din, one invective could be heard clearly and Edward Plantagenet knew the ridicule was for him alone.

"Longshanks! Longshanks! Longshanks!" they taunted.

The infamous Plantagenet temper exploded like a volcanic eruption. King Edward unsheathed his sword and raised it in the air. "Attack! Attack!"

John de Warenne ordered the light cavalry to the king's side, then quickly organized a battalion of foot soldiers to follow them. Edward, on his great stallion Bayard, leaped over the ditch and galloped to the stockade, flanked by his nephew, Richard of Cornwall, and Fitz-Waren. Their horses sailed over the low stockade, then Fitz-Waren ordered that its timbers be set aflame. The defenders atop it scattered in panic and the English foot soldiers flooded into Berwick like a tidal wave.

Suddenly, one arrow found its mark and entered the eye-slit of Richard of Cornwall's helmet. Edward watched in horror as his nephew fell dead from his horse. His ice-blue eyes sought John de Warenne's as he issued the dreaded order, "No quarter! Put every man of Berwick to the sword!"

Lynx de Warenne knew nothing of the disastrous events taking place outside the castle. Flanked by his squires, he waited at the rear of the long column of surrendering troops. When he finally emerged from Berwick

Castle into the sunlight, a bloody battle was being waged in the streets of the city.

"Why are we not taking prisoners?" Lynx demanded grimly when he finally found his uncle.

"Richard of Cornwall was killed; Edward ordered no quarter!" John told him bluntly.

Lynx jammed his helmet back on his head and turned his destrier around. He and his squires rode through the streets back toward the castle with weapons drawn, but few approached the three great warhorses whose murderous hooves could trample them dead. Without hesitation Lynx de Warenne strode into the great hall of Berwick Castle, which Edward Plantagenet now occupied. "Berwick Castle is ours and the city of Berwick is ours also," he announced. "Further slaughter is unnecessary, Your Majesty."

The blue Plantagenet eyes glittered dangerously. "I ordered every man of Berwick put to the sword!"

"Sire, some of these men are not soldiers, they are citizens, burghers, craftsmen."

"These *burghers* sank our ships and killed Richard of Cornwall! Do you presume to question my orders, de Warenne?"

"I do, Sire. There is no honor in this carnage. When the pages of history are writ, do you wish to be immortalized as England's greatest king and lawmaker or as the butcher of Berwick?"

The king's eyes narrowed. "You argue as passionately as your sister. All the de Warennes are damned presumptuous!"

"I dare speak my mind only because my loyalty is absolute. If you do not call a halt, the hatred between

Scots and English will deepen so that it will be impossible to ever unite the two countries. What I witnessed outside covers me with shame, but worse, it covers *you* with shame, Sire. There are women and children being slaughtered out there."

"Nay, my order was to kill only the men. Call a halt!"

Lynx de Warenne did not linger. He had what he had come for. Now he must get the word out to an army drunk with bloodlust.

Jory de Warenne could not remember a journey she had enjoyed more than the one from Newcastle to Wigton. Both she and Robert Bruce had indulged in an outrageous flirtation that lasted the entire ride. They were exceedingly formal within earshot of others, but the moment they knew they could not be overheard, they teased and toyed with each other in a shockingly intimate fashion. It was a game they enjoyed, made doubly delicious because it was a secret they alone shared.

Jory stood atop Wigton Castle gazing off in the direction of Carlisle, only eight miles away. The Bruce had brought her up to the ramparts knowing it was a place where they could be alone together. Robert stood so close to her, their bodies almost touched. Jory had to lean her head back to look up at him. His dark eyes licked over her like a candle flame. "I know Wigton intimately. It was one of the castles we seized when Baliol came to the throne and we were at odds with the English."

Jory gazed up at him. "I can see you now, breaching her defenses, forcing her to your will, making her yield."

He lifted a tress of silver-gilt hair that was being ruffled by the breeze. "Conquest is in my blood."

As Jory looked up at him she pictured a conqueror, his claymore and battle-ax dripping blood. He wore a breastplate over his massive chest, but his arms and shoulders were naked, travel-stained with dirt and sweat.

Marjory felt her legs grow weak and her body begin to tremble uncontrollably as she watched his fierce gaze sweep over her. Her breath stopped in her throat. "Robert!" She felt herself sway.

He lifted her effortlessly, carrying her toward the stairs. How did he know her own legs were too weak to carry her to her chamber? Jory could not tear her eyes from him. He glistened with sweat and dirt, and the hard metal that covered his chest was hurting her breast that was pressed tightly against him. She welcomed the hurt! With each step he took the world and everyone in it receded farther away.

An ache began deep in her belly, then spread up through her heart and into her throat. Her very skin became sensitized as the wool of her gown touching her body made her want to scream. His arms were so powerful and made her feel so secure, she wanted them about her forever.

Jory was lost, utterly lost. She was limp no longer, and neither was he. He filled her with energy, he filled her with hunger, he filled her with lust! She had no previous experience of the pure animal need. Her swift arousal staggered her. She knew he was experiencing an arousal of his own. No! It wasn't a separate thing at all. They shared the *same* arousal. Equally. It bound them together inextricably with its chains.

Jory flung an arm in the direction of her chamber and he understood the gesture without need of words. He carried her inside, kicked the door closed, then set her feet to the rug while he unbuckled his breastplate. She clung to him to keep from falling, wondering at the madness that gripped her to possess him, and to be possessed.

He had the broadest chest she had ever seen in her life. She couldn't tear her gaze from it. He looked as if he'd been sculpted from bronze; he felt as hard as metal too. Her hands came up to glide over the superb musculature. "Robert!"

His mouth came down to taste his name on her lips. There was nothing tentative about the kiss. It was hard and savage and selfish. Jory realized at this moment that he was uncivilized, and heaven be praised, so was she. Together they tore off her gown and stripped the Bruce naked. Before the last garment fell away, Jory was climbing him as if he were an oak tree. Always before, when she had been intimate with her husband, she had been bathed and scented in the bedchamber. Now she smelled like nothing but a woman. He smelled like a man ripe with lust.

Robert grasped her buttocks, anchoring her as he impaled her on his upthrust shaft. Both cried out with the glory of it. Jory was panting with need, moaning and clawing and crying like a feline in heat. Fused together, they fell to the bed, his weight crushing her. He infused her with so much sexual energy she arched beneath him, lifting his magnificent body for the pure sensual bliss of feeling him plunge ever deeper.

It was as if he were storming her defenses with a battering ram. Jory threw back her head and laughed wildly. Her defenses had come down before he'd ever touched her. Robert's own laughter rolled over her as he pounded his body into hers. It was rough and elemental and like nothing she'd ever experienced in her marriage.

Jory became so frenzied she began to bite him. It turned the tide instantly for both of them. One minute she was drowning in need, the next she was soaring on the crest of a wave of pleasure, her body dissolving in liquid tremors, sheathing his scalding, marble-hard manroot as it burst, spurting his male essence up inside her like molten sparks of fire.

When they were both fully spent, he rolled on his back and took her with him. Jory's eyes gazed down into his, devouring him. The cataclysmic mating had shaken her, changed her. She had always known she was sensual and feminine. Now she realized sensuality paled beside what she experienced with this man. He could do anything to her and she would welcome it, crave it. Her heart soared with her newfound knowledge. He was the magnificent Robert Bruce and she was a perfect match for him!

His eyes traveled up her body as if he owned it, then came to rest on her heart-shaped face. His nostrils flared at the mingled scent of their bodies. She was so fragile, ethereal almost, he marveled that he had not shattered her. He had wanted her beneath him since he'd seen her at Newcastle. Nay, he'd wanted her sheathing his cock five years ago when she was seventeen. "I'm sorry, lass."

Jory's eyes clouded momentarily, then a smile lit up her face. "You lying bastard!"

He laughed then. "Nay, I'm not sorry, I am triumphant."

She touched her lips to his heart, licking the sweat glistening there.

He lifted her off his body and laid her on her back

beside him. Then he came up on his knees, straddling her, his eyes smoldering as his fingers began to explore the prize he had taken.

"Robert, not again!" she gasped.

"Jory, we only fucked. Now I'm going to make love to you."

She felt as if her very bones would melt.

The lovers looked like complete opposites, one so strong, the other fragile; one so big, the other petite; one dark and swarthy, the other so unearthly fair. But under the skin they were perfectly matched, not only sexually, but temperamentally.

The Bruce's lovemaking was slow, unhurried, and completely thorough, but the moment their appetites were slaked and they were both satisfied, he was off the bed and dressing.

"Carry me off to Carlisle," she whispered.

"Don't tempt me."

"Temptation is in my blood." For the space of a heartbeat, she thought he would take her, then the truth of the situation dawned on her. "You won't be staying at Carlisle, will you, Robert?" she asked wistfully.

He scooped her from the bed and enfolded her against him with massive arms. "Soon I go to topple a king from his throne and to take back my castles, then Annandale."

Robert Bruce's resolve and ambition were so powerful Jory almost felt awed by them. "And then take Scotland?" she asked breathlessly.

He searched her face with his dark brilliant eyes. "You've seen inside my heart and read its secrets." He kissed her swiftly, then spun her about and slapped her bottom. "I'm a bloody fool to let a woman come that close. Hurry and dress."

A week later, Jory knew she could stay indoors no longer. The hills and dales were dotted with lambs, an early spring had brought everything into bloom, and the game was plentiful. She decided to go riding, mayhap even organize a hunt. She picked up her skirts and went to seek Alicia, thinking she must be just as ready for diversion as Jory herself was.

Alicia had chosen beautiful rooms in the front wing overlooking the Cumbrian Mountains. The magnificent Skiddaw, whose peak disappeared into the clouds, seemed close enough to touch from her chamber windows. Marjory tapped lightly on her door and waited. When no one answered her knock, she assumed Alicia must be downstairs. Then she heard a low moan.

Jory moved closer to the door and called Alicia's name softly. Again, she heard a moan of distress and immediately turned the knob. There were times when Jory found Alicia Bolton extremely tiresome, but she was filled with concern the moment she saw Alicia doubled over with pain.

"Oh my dear, whatever is it?" Jory asked, rushing to her side.

"It's nothing. Leave me alone!"

"Nothing? But you are in agony—have you been poisoned?" Jory picked up a goblet with dark liquid in the bottom and sniffed it.

"Stop spying on me!" Alicia screamed, holding her belly as if she were in the throes of labor.

Then Jory saw the girl's skirts were soaked with blood. "My God, you're hemorrhaging—let me help you!"

Alicia burst into tears. "Don't tell Lynx, promise me you won't tell him?"

Marjory de Warenne's eyes widened as comprehension dawned. Alicia Bolton was aborting a child! The brownish liquid in the goblet was pennyroyal, a strong abortifacient whose aromatic smell was quite distinctive.

Jory ran to the bed, pulled off a sheet, and tore it into squares of linen. "We have to get this bleeding stopped!" Her heartbeat was drumming inside her ears. God's tears, didn't the woman realize she could die?

"It will stop," Alicia assured her through gritted teeth. "The pain is terrible, but with pennyroyal there is no vomiting or purging of the bowel."

"You've done this before?" Jory asked, horrified. She was shocked at what Alicia had been doing. It was a revelation to discover that her brother was perfectly capable of siring children. How selfish Alicia had been to deny Lynx his heart's desire; he so desperately wanted a child.

"Come, let me help you to bed," Jory said to Alicia, thinking the woman was her own worst enemy. Didn't she realize that Lynx would marry her in a minute if she bore him a child? Jory was on the verge of telling her this, when she reconsidered. *She's not good enough for him!*

"Jory, please, swear you won't betray me?" Alicia begged frantically. "This is punishment enough!"

Though Jory was repulsed by what Alice Bolton had done, she felt compassion for the suffering woman. "I won't betray you, Alicia, but I strongly advise you to confess all to my brother."

5

At Dumfries, all the Comyn men-at-arms along with their commander had been recalled north to the Scottish city of Scone. John Comyn, Constable of Scotland, was gathering an army as fast as he could. He was the power behind his kinsman King Baliol only because he wanted the crown of Scotland for himself one day. Now at the head of the Scots army he had gathered, Comyn swept down through Annandale on his way to England.

Jock Leslie, Dumfries' steward, was angered when Comyn's men rode through Dumfries and stripped it of its livestock and fodder to feed the army. Jock and his sons, along with the other castle retainers, were gathered in Dumfries' bailey to assess matters.

"Dumfries is owned by the crown, and when King Alexander ruled Scotland and the Bruces were wardens in Annandale, we were paid wages for our services. Since the Comyn clansmen have occupied Dumfries we've seen little coin, but at least until now we had the largest herds of cattle and flocks of sheep to fill our bellies," Jock said with disgust. "Goddamn the bloody Comyns!"

"Ye should be ashamed, the lot of ye," Megotta

scolded. "They've gone to fight the English and they can no' do that on empty bellies."

"Christ, woman, only a week ago the Comyns were on the same side as the English. Now they've turned their coats again. I hope to God the Bruces defeat the Comyns and regain Annandale and all their castles. We got paid our wages when the Bruce controlled the western marches!"

"The Bruces are the greatest turncoats in Scotland," Megotta accused. "It's their Norman blood."

Jock's lips twitched. He knew she was trying to goad him; in Megotta's eyes, a Celt could do no wrong, and a Norman could do no right.

Alex Leslie spoke up. "In the forge, when they were gettin' their mounts reshod, the soldiers were complainin' that the Earls of Angus and Dunbar refused the call to arms."

"They're not the only ones, I'll warrant. Every clan this side o' the Forth prefers a Bruce to a Comyn."

"Earl Patrick of Dunbar always was thick as thieves with Bruce. The blood of all the Lowland clans is watered down with filthy English blood. It's too bad our family didna stay in the Highlands. I spit on the Bruce and the English!" Megotta cursed.

"Better get used to them." Keith looked at his grandmother with tender concern. "The English are comin', an' sooner than ye think."

"Ha! If they come to Dumfries to crush us beneath their heel, we'll poison the bastards. Jane and I know our herbs and potions, healing and otherwise!"

"No!" Jane cried. "I would never use my gift for evil."

Jock looked at his daughter's eyes, wide with distress and fear. "Come here, child. Ye have naught to fear. The Leslies are castle keepers. We serve whoever garrisons Dumfries Castle. I am half Anglo-Norman and I know the English are no more monsters than the Scots." He spread his hands. "They are simply men." Jock realized he should have weaned his youngest daughter away from the old woman long ago. Jane should have a husband and bairns to fill her life.

Jane swallowed hard. *Simply men!* That was precisely what she was afraid of. She reached for her talisman and remembered that she'd had a dozen requests for protective touchstones in the past two days alone. Men as well as women wanted them. If there was naught to fear, why were the people of Dumfries suddenly seeking the power of magic to protect themselves?

In Berwick the madness stopped, the dead were buried, and Edward Plantagenet immediately issued orders that whatever had been destroyed in the city must now be rebuilt. The walls of the fortifications were raised higher and the ditch was deepened. To set an example, the king wheeled out the first barrow piled high with mortar and stones.

Within a week, Edward Plantagenet improved the laws and appointed capable men to administer them. He also abolished the hated tax on wool, called the *maltote.* Some of this was done in an effort to atone for the slaughter he had ordered, but word of what the English had done at Berwick spread over Scotland like smoke from a wildfire, choking the Scots and filling them with hatred for the English conquerors.

When King Edward received King Baliol's missive renouncing his fealty, the royal Plantagenet anger was roused again. "The false fool! De Warenne, you will see that he is plucked from his bloody throne, and brought to me on his knees begging for my mercy! Within the month I want Baliol lodged in the Tower of London!"

John de Warenne had so many men-at-arms to deploy, he chose some of Lynx's foot soldiers, along with battalions belonging to Percy and Bohun, to stay behind in Berwick to rebuild and to keep the seaport securely under English control. He directed Anthony Bek, the warrior Bishop of Durham who commanded his own levy of soldiers, to capture King Baliol, then de Warenne took the main body of the army up the coast toward Dunbar where he knew Earl Patrick would remain steadfast to the English. At Dunbar, Edward Plantagenet planned to rejoin his army as it crossed the Lammermuir Hills and cleared the way to the capital city of Edinburgh.

Robert Bruce began to gather up men-at-arms from throughout Northumberland. More Irish and Welsh troops, along with supplies, poured into Carlisle each day, and by the end of the week, Bruce was ready to march into Scotland to take back what had been his.

When word reached him of the massacre at Berwick he knew Comyn, who commanded the Scottish army, would retaliate. Robert Bruce assumed Comyn would march his main army to confront the English. He was astounded when he learned his bitterest enemy was avoiding the English in the east and was instead destroying towns in the west. Comyn's forces were meting out the same mindless destruction that Edward had used at Berwick. He encouraged his army of Scots to ravage the English countryside as soon as they crossed the border, first destroying the monastery of Hexham, then sweeping through Redesdale and the other dales, drawing ever closer to his goal of Carlisle. Every English town and village in the Scots' path was looted then burned, their men, women, and children put to the sword, their livestock driven off, and their churches razed.

Inside the walled city of Carlisle, Robert Bruce waited, ready, willing, and more than able to take on his enemy Comyn, the hated Earl of Buchan.

Comyn selected three thousand of his finest. The Scots relished the idea of a surprise attack, but until over a thousand were inside the city's walls, they had no idea they were the ones who would be surprised!

Leaving one of his brothers to defend the castle itself in the unlikely event it would come under attack, Robert Bruce and his other brothers descended upon the Scots from the north, south, east, and west. The enemy tried to flee, but the encompassing walls held most of them captive, like fish in a barrel. The slaughter was both easy and terrible in its scope. Before the afternoon light began to leave the sky, almost one thousand Scots lay dead in the streets of Carlisle.

Comyn and a handful of his commanders fled through the gates to join the two thousand still outside the walls. He ordered them to stand and fight, but the clan chiefs were reluctant in light of the slaughter. And when the Bruce army poured out of the city, drunk with victory and ready to annihilate anything in its path, the lairds took their men and fled in the direction of the Scottish border.

By the time dusk fell, Robert Bruce and his army had

vanquished the foe. They rode back inside the walls of Carlisle to help the citizens put out the fires that had been set by the enemy. It was only after Robert downed a tankard of ale to ease his parched throat that a picture of Marjory de Warenne flashed into his mind. Wigton was unsafe. He knew he must go immediately and bring her to Carlisle.

Once Robert Bruce deposited Jory de Warenne and Alice Bolton at Carlisle Castle, he set out immediately to rout the Scottish invaders scattered across the English dales and chase them back over the border. So many flocked to the Bruce banners that Robert soon had control over his old territories.

He dispatched his brother Nigel to scout the location of the main body of the English army and deliver the arrogant message that the Bruces would hold Annandale, Dumfries, Galway, and Carrick secure for Edward Plantagenet.

Lynx de Warenne, on night patrol, riding the perimeters of the vast English camp, prided himself on the vigilance of his Welsh archers. Their night vision and hearing were superior to that of English men-at-arms and Lynx believed it did not simply come from training. He believed his Welshmen had a sixth sense that warned them of impending danger. When Lynx heard the signal cry of the night owl he was immediately alerted and caught Nigel Bruce as he slipped into camp.

With a blade at his throat and his heart pumping out of control, Nigel cried out, "A Bruce, a Bruce!"

Lynx lowered his knife, but still kept the intruder in a hammerlock until he got a good look at him. The two men recognized each other at the same moment and the stranglehold turned into a swift embrace of brotherhood.

In John de Warenne's campaign tent Nigel Bruce told what had happened at Carlisle. He assured them that Marjory and Alicia were safe and that the Bruce army had won a complete victory over half the Scots force and had been hard on the heels of the other half, as Comyn retreated to Scotland.

De Warenne's spies had informed him that another force of Scots had seized Earl Patrick's castle of Dunbar, and as he listened to Nigel Bruce, he knew exactly where Comyn was headed. Once the Scots armies were joined, they would make a formidable force, and it was apparent that force would await them at Dunbar.

He asked Nigel Bruce to draw him a detailed map of Scottish territory from the border up to the Firth of Forth and pored over it for the next few hours. By dawn John de Warenne had a plan, but he knew its success depended upon the full cooperation of Robert Bruce and the army he now commanded.

Nigel shook his head. "My brother puts Bruce interests first. I left him ensconced at our stronghold of Lochmaben at the head of the Annandale Valley. When men saw the Bruce banners, they flocked to us; we encountered no opposition. Robert is back where he belongs, holding the western marches. It would take wild horses to drag him from his own turf."

Lynx felt the full impact of John de Warenne's long, speculative look. There was little point in arguing with his uncle when he was in the right. It was rumored that the Bruces had signed pacts with many of the earls of southern Scotland, so without the help of Robert Bruce, victory was uncertain. The fighting could drag on for years, taking and losing the same territory over and over. A decisive battle was necessary to tip the scales and send a message to all of Scotland that Baliol was deposed forever.

"All right," Lynx agreed. "I'll go back with Nigel and persuade the Bruce on one condition." His green eyes were deadly serious as he gave John de Warenne a level look. "I want *your* word, not Edward Plantagenet's, that Robert will be *reconfirmed* in his lands and castles, and that everything that went to Comyn will revert to the Bruces, immediately and without question."

The day after Lynx arrived at Lochmaben, he rode out with his friend Robert Bruce across Annandale visiting each of the Bruce castles from Caerlaverock to Lockryan. As they rode higher up the valley the views became spectacular. "What was the original grant?" Lynx asked.

"My ancestor Adam de Brus, who came over with the Conqueror, was granted lordship of Annandale and two hundred thousand acres straddling the important western route between England and Scotland."

"The Norman lust for land still runs hot in our blood," Lynx admitted. "We are all of us conquerors."

Robert laughed. "As well as Norman, I have Celtic blood from my mother. Is it any wonder I have a compulsion to rule it all?"

As they rode into the prosperous town of Dumfries with its Franciscan monastery and its magnificent stone bridge whose nine arches spanned the river Nith, Lynx could not help feeling covetous.

"I cannot fault you for never wanting to leave here. Annandale is the loveliest country I've ever seen. Don't get me wrong, Essex and Surrey are beautiful and well cultivated, as well as being the most profitable land to own, but the vistas here are so majestic they touch the heart and soul. Can we take a look at the castle?''

Robert grinned at him. ''Dumfries isn't one of mine, it's a royal castle, but it happens to be in my territory. I have an idea! When we defeat Comyn, ask the king to make you Governor of Dumfries, then we can be neighbors.''

Lynx's eyes locked with Robert's. ''Then you'll join the fight?'' Lynx had almost given up hope. He'd talked himself hoarse without Robert's showing the least inclination to lend his support. Lynx had pointed out that Robert should have waited for King Edward to reconfirm his lands and castles before having reclaimed them. The English monarch did not take kindly to arrogance in anyone, other than himself. But Lynx got the distinct impression that Robert Bruce was indifferent to Plantagenet rages.

Now, suddenly, Robert capitulated. Lynx doubted it was for friendship's sake alone. More likely it was the challenge he had thrown out, Lynx decided. He hadn't the faintest idea how much his green eyes reminded Robert of his sister Jory's, as he rode beside him in the April sunshine.

''It's the Bruce!'' Word spread like wildfire through the town of Dumfries and before Robert and Lynx arrived at the castle, all who dwelled within and without were aware of the fact that the Earl of Carrick, Lord of Annandale was riding in. Dumfries had served the Comyns for the last three years, and all save the steward were nervous about the Bruce's frame of mind.

Jock Leslie was at the massive castle doors to welcome the powerful earl, and to provide him with refreshment and to offer whatever services he could render.

"I remember you," Robert said, pleased with what he saw at Dumfries. "How long have you been steward here?"

"Over twenty years, my lord."

Robert introduced Lynx de Warenne, who plied Jock with many pertinent questions about Dumfries.

"I understand that sheep mean wealth in the dales. How large is your flock?"

"Aye, my lord. Dumfries had a thousand sheep. The price of their wool would have kept us all year. Unfortunately, Comyn's army took the sheep before the shearing started."

Lynx saw the look of anger on the Bruce's face. "Does Dumfries have its own forge?"

"Aye, my lord, we also have a gristmill and a brewhouse. We are usually self-sufficient here." Jock Leslie was both honored and proud to answer the questions and give them a tour of the castle. He was deeply gratified when they praised his stewardship. These intelligent men fully understood the concept that castellans were castle keepers and must serve whoever garrisoned Dumfries. "We would be honored if you would stay for dinner, my lords."

Robert Bruce cocked an eyebrow at Lynx, who nodded eagerly. "Thank you, it will be our pleasure to dine at Dumfries."

Jane's sisters arrived at the cottage, more excited than she had ever seen them before.

"Come, come quick! It's the Bruce himself! He's reputed to be the handsomest man in Scotland," Mary cried.

"And the strongest," Kate added. "Women faint at the sight of him!"

Jane saw that Megotta was scandalized by the avid hero worship her granddaughters were displaying and listened silently as Megotta rebuked them soundly. But Jane noticed it had little effect on her sisters and she too was curious. "Let's go and see what the wicked devil looks like," Jane urged Megotta.

They joined the crowd in the bailey to see for themselves the two powerful lords who were visiting Dumfries Castle. As their gazes swept over the two men, one fair, the other dark, it was easy to identify which one was Robert Bruce.

"Who is that with him? He looks like a Norman to me," Megotta said suspiciously.

"Rumor has it he's English, a personal friend of the Bruce," a woman in the crowd answered.

Jane Leslie felt outrage. How dare the Bruce bring an evil Anglo-Norman to Dumfries? Only one person in the crowd did not look at Robert Bruce. Jane's gaze came to rest upon the magnificent man with the tawny mane of hair and brilliant green eyes who stood beside the Bruce. She gasped in disbelief. He was the living embodiment of her lynx!

As her fingers clasped the touchstone about her neck, she became aware of the pulse beating in her throat. Jane blinked rapidly, knowing the image could not be real, but she could not dispel it. The excited voices of her sisters and the noisy crowd fell away until all she could hear was her own wild heartbeat. Jane was aware of nothing and no one save the powerful male whose tawny-gold mane gave him the leonine look of a lynx.

For one heart-stopping moment, it seemed to Jane that the green eyes looked directly into hers and were able to look into her very soul. In a flash she realized that she knew this man; she had seen him before. In a heartbeat, Jane remembered her dream. It came flooding back to her in explicit, shameful detail.

The memories stopped the breath in her throat. In her mind's eye she watched the lynx transform himself into a human male and that man was here before her today in living flesh and blood. Jane's cheeks grew warm as she remembered how he moved with the lithe stealth of a lynx and before she could either cry out or run, he had held her in his powerful hands. This was the enemy! He was a Norman with evil powers to control her—to control them all.

"Megotta, we don't want him here," Jane whispered urgently. "We must get rid of him!"

Then Jock Leslie took the visitors into the castle and Jane and Megotta knew he would extend Dumfries' hospitality by inviting them to dine.

"We'll go to the kitchens," Megotta decided. "We'll get rid of them one way or another."

When Jane and her grandmother entered the kitchens through the rear door, the cooks were rushing about, stirring a cauldron of soup, testing the tenderness of a haunch of venison turning on a huge spit, putting round loaves into a massive baking oven, and throwing vegetables into boiling water.

"I shall make the gravy," Megotta declared, just as Jock Leslie arrived in the vast kitchens.

He took one look at Megotta and strode to her side. "Out of this kitchen now, woman! I'll have none of your malicious tricks today. Would you bring shame down upon our heads?" he demanded. Megotta's protestations of innocence fell on deaf ears. Jock knew the depth of his mother-in-law's hatred for outsiders. "Andrew," he admonished his son, who was steward-in-training, "I'm putting you in charge. Don't allow Megotta back in here under any circumstances!"

After her grandmother left, Jane took herself off to a corner where she waited patiently until the food was ready to be served. Her emotions of fear and hatred were all tangled together, but of one thing she felt certain: the Norman was the more dangerous of the two visitors.

Jane stepped forward as one of the cooks poured soup into a large tureen and laced it with cream and wine. "Andrew, may I serve the soup?" she asked sweetly.

Her brother smiled at her. "Very well, Jane, but don't dawdle; it cools down quickly."

As Jane entered the dining hall, her heart was in her mouth as each step took her closer to Dumfries' honored guests. She was amazed at her own temerity. Would she really have enough courage to carry out her plan? She felt all ashiver as she lifted the ladle to serve Robert Bruce. Her nerve failed her, as she bit her lip and poured his soup without spilling a drop. She glanced furtively at the tawny-haired man sitting beside him and her eyes focused on his lips. She shuddered, remembering the things his wicked mouth had done to her in the dream. She drew in a swift breath as she saw his gaze rise from her breasts to her hair and she saw the swift appraisal and the fierce look of desire that hardened his face. When his sensual mouth curved in a smile of invitation, her resolve hardened. Jane quickly tipped the tureen so that the rich soup cascaded into the man's lap.

Lynx de Warenne jumped up immediately, thankful his leather tunic and chausses had prevented his being scalded. Like lightning his hand shot out to imprison the girl's wrist before she could escape. His angry green gaze swept over the girl with the brilliant hair. "Who the devil are you?"

"A Celt!" she said defiantly.

"A little hellcat who needs taming, I think."

"I am a sworn enemy to the evil English!"

Jock Leslie, who had been bringing his guests the best wine Dumfries had to offer, rushed forward to try to undo the damage his daughter had done.

"Who is this girl?" de Warenne demanded.

"A clumsy serving wench, my lord." Jock was too embarrassed to acknowledge Jane as his daughter.

"She's not clumsy in the least. That was no accident, it was done deliberately." De Warenne's eyes narrowed as he freed her wrist. He knew she'd like nothing better than to fly at him and scratch his face, but she did not dare. "I'd like to teach you manners," he said in a low, rough voice that told her clearly he'd like to do other things to her as well.

"Leave the hall at once!" Jock ordered. "She will be punished, my lord."

As the red-haired maid fled the hall, Robert Bruce spoke up quickly. "Allow me to apologize on behalf of all Celts. Our passionate natures get in the way of rational behavior sometimes."

Lynx de Warenne couldn't help but laugh. He wouldn't mind pitting his own passionate nature against the red-haired maiden's. "Don't punish the girl, Jock Leslie," he said. "I know hatred runs deep for the English, here in Scotland, and the serving wench is no more than an impetuous girl."

Jock summoned raven-haired Kate with an imperious finger. "My own daughter will serve ye the rest of yer meal, my lords. I give ye my pledge that nothing more will mar yer visit."

Jane ran to the stables as if the devil himself were after her. She saw that her brother Keith had put the lords' horses in the best stalls and had found oats for them. As Jane approached the beautiful stallions, she began to talk softly. Though she intensely disliked their owners, the horses were the finest she had ever seen. She threaded her fingers through the silken mane of the powerful gray and was delighted when he whickered.

After talking to them for a while, she became tempted to open and search their saddlebags. Perhaps she could learn the identity of the disturbing man who accompanied Robert Bruce to Dumfries. Perhaps she would unearth a clue that would tell her why he had come and what he was doing here.

As she looked at the contents of the gray's saddlebags, she decided this horse belonged to the Bruce. All they held was water, oat cakes, and a rolled-up plaid. Jane put the things back the way she had found them and moved over to the next stall. She rubbed the sleek black neck of the stallion, murmuring endearments for long minutes before she unfastened the saddlebags to look inside.

Here again the contents were disappointing. All she found were apples, a pair of black leather riding gauntlets, and a parchment of what looked like a map of Annandale to her untrained eye. Since she could not read, Jane refolded it and put everything back the way she had found it; all except for one of the apples.

With one hand she held the apple out to the black stallion, while stroking his neck with the other. Jane almost jumped out of her skin when an angry voice demanded, "What the hell are you doing to my horse?"

She tried to run, but his long strides devoured the distance between them and a calloused hand took her arm in a viselike grip. "Have a care, Norman, I am a witch with strong powers over an enemy of Scotland!"

"Your superstitious claims do not interest me. What I want to know is what did you feed my horse?"

Jane forgot her fear and became indignant. "I would never harm an animal. I gave him an apple. Let me go, you are hurting me!"

"I ought to hurt you, I ought to put you across my knee, you willful little jade."

"Oh-ho, what do we have here? Am I interrupting the prelude to a roll in the hay?" Robert asked with a grin.

"Very amusing," Lynx said dryly, relaxing his grip on the girl. "How the hell can one female cause such havoc in so short a time?"

Robert winked. "You know what they say about redheads: avoid them like the plague!"

Jane stood shaking as she watched them ride from the stables. Relief overwhelmed her that the Anglo-Norman was leaving. But just as she felt this wasn't their first encounter, Jane sensed it would not be their last. The lynx would return. It was inevitable.

6

John de Warenne's plan worked like a charm. As the Scottish army arrived at the first slopes of the Lammermuir Hills, tired from its invasion of Cumberland, the English forces swept down upon it. When the Scots tried to retreat, they ran into Bruce's army, who had come up behind them, and they were trapped between the two enemy forces.

In the fierce battle that ensued at Spottsmuir, near Dunbar, the Scots suffered a crushing defeat. Edward's commanders were battle-hardened veterans, their men-at-arms far better disciplined and equipped than the Scots. By the end of the day, not only was Comyn captured, but one hundred and thirty important Scottish knights, along with the Earls of Menteith, Atholl, and Ross. The following day, Dunbar Castle surrendered.

The evening after a victory in battle was always given over to celebration and feasting. The halls of Dunbar Castle rang with revelry as barrels of ale and casks of malt whisky were rolled up from its cellars that now overflowed with prisoners. In his campaign tent, Lynx de Warenne felt weary and jaded, not filled with the glory that usually accompanied victory.

What the hell is the matter with me? he wondered. Alicia's words came back to him: "War is your life," she had said matter-of-factly, and Lynx could not deny it. He tried to envision his future and what lay before him. After Scotland was subdued, France would become the next military challenge.

Suddenly, it wasn't enough. Lynx wanted more. He hungered for something. He did not quite know what it was, but he knew he would not find it fighting battles in France. Lynx closed his eyes to banish the thought of war, but pictures of the atrocities he had witnessed in the streets of Berwick rose up to haunt him. Children had been squandered, their lives snuffed out like wax candles. Nothing in this world was more precious than a child; he would sell his soul for one of his own.

Edward Plantagenet rode hotfoot from Berwick, regretful that he had missed the decisive battle that would eventually place Scotland firmly in his hands. In Dunbar's great hall, he had the prisoners brought before him, one by one, from the dungeons so he could have a look at them. But more importantly so he could receive their submission as they bent the knee to him and swore their fealty.

As was his practice, Edward sent the prisoners to England to be held at Hertford. Until recently the wealthy and powerful de Clares had kept his prisoners secure. Now he would charge his new son-in-law, Monthermer, with their security and test the man's mettle.

Earl Patrick, restored to his castle of Dunbar, arranged a great feast to celebrate the victory. Edward Plantagenet drank a toast to his supreme commander, John de

Warenne. "You have done well, John. I knew when I chose you to head the army, I picked the best man for the job. You and I were taught by the master himself, Simon de Montfort. A *cautious* general is slow in the pursuit of a retreating enemy; a *great* general strikes as hard when his foe is beaten as when the battle is still undecided."

"Sire, we could not have trapped the Scottish army without the quick and decisive action of Robert Bruce." John de Warenne lifted his goblet to Robert, who stood at his shoulder. "I recommend that you reconfirm his lordship of Annandale immediately."

"If I remember correctly, I said I would consider that once Baliol was captured and deposed," Edward said coldly.

Robert Bruce looked the King of England straight in the eye. "Once Baliol is deposed I shall put in my claim for the throne of Scotland, not just Annandale."

Silence hung in the air as Celtic black eyes stared into Plantagenet blue. "Do you think we have naught to do but win kingdoms for you?" the king demanded.

Sensing hostilities, Lynx stepped to the side of his friend Robert, while John de Warenne summoned all of his diplomatic skills and addressed the king.

"Majesty, your next strategic goal is the city of Edinburgh. We must force the surrender of every castle that lies before us, namely, Roxburgh, Jedburgh, Dumbarton, then Edinburgh. From there it is but a short distance to Stirling. I predict your triumphant progress through Aberdeen and Banff all the way to Elgin will be cluttered with Scots nobles hastening to offer their allegiance. The only danger is that the scattered army will regroup *behind* us and take back the southern and western marches as we move north."

Edward Plantagenet saw clearly that he could not afford to offend Robert Bruce. He needed the powerful earl to protect his back. "You are a great strategist, John, so I leave the matter entirely in your capable hands. And, as you suggest, we shall reconfirm the Bruce castles immediately. The western route between England and Scotland must be kept open to supply our armies."

As the king moved away, taking John de Warenne with him, Robert Bruce looked at Lynx and the two men had a hell of a time concealing their amusement.

"Christ, there's nothing like coming right out and asking for what you want!"

Robert gave Lynx a shove with his massive shoulder. Nodding in the direction of John de Warenne, Robert suggested, "Why don't you try it?"

Suddenly, Lynx knew exactly what he wanted. He raised his head, scanning the crowd for John. When he located him, Lynx strode down the hall without hesitation. As he opened his mouth to speak, John de Warenne said, "I'm sorry, Lynx, but I'm afraid you'll have to forgo bringing the rest of Scotland to heel. The king does not entirely trust Robert Bruce and wants a watchdog put on him. You are the only one who won't arouse the Bruce's suspicion. There is a royal castle at Dumfries that will need a permanent garrison. Will you undertake the unrewarding task?"

His nephew answered with a great smile.

The next morning Lynx de Warenne rode south with twenty of his youngest knights and seventy men-at-arms.

The rest of his men had been placed under the command of his cousin, Fitz-Waren. Lynx had put the matter to his men directly, asking for volunteers, knowing full well that most would prefer to be in the vanguard of the march to subdue Scotland.

When he suggested putting those who wished to remain under the command of his cousin, Fitz-Waren, there had been some dissension in the ranks, and Lynx realized with a shock that his Welshmen neither liked nor respected Roger Fitz-Waren. When Lynx discussed the situation with the two-dozen veteran knights who had chosen to stay and fight for the king, they assured him that John de Warenne kept a tight rein on his bastard son Fitz-Waren and that all would be well. The younger knights Lynx took with him could be used as couriers between Dumfries and the commander of the armies to keep him apprised of their progress.

The night before they arrived at Dumfries, Lynx de Warenne summoned all of his men together after they had made camp. He wanted no trouble once they arrived, and to that end laid down the rules making crystal clear what he expected of them.

"The people of Dumfries are not soldiers, they are castle keepers. We do not go to Dumfries as conquerors, crushing them beneath our heel, we go in peace. You will not make camp outside the walls; you will be housed in Dumfries Castle. We will all dine in the great hall, and at night, those who are not on guard duty either at the castle or in the town will sleep there. The knights will have chambers, two per room.

"We are a garrison, a peacekeeping force who will help the Bruces patrol the western marches and keep open the main supply route from England to Scotland or, more specifically, between Carlisle and Edinburgh.

"Try to keep in mind that though the people of Dumfries are Scots, they are not to be considered the enemy. We want their cooperation, not their hostility." Lynx deepened his voice for emphasis. "All trouble will be reported to me. If you encounter treachery, as I am sure you will, no lives will be taken in retaliation. Once a week I will hold a court of law where punishments will be decided. At all times keep in mind that you are de Warenne men. I will tolerate no uncivilized behavior. You are free to fraternize and conjugate with the females of Dumfries, but no woman will be forced against her will."

When Lynx de Warenne arrived at Dumfries Castle, he ordered his men and the baggage train to wait in the bailey until he had spoken privately with Dumfries' steward. Not one horse was to be stabled nor one wagon unloaded until the correct protocol had been observed.

De Warenne was gratified when the steward recognized him and addressed him by name. Lynx removed his leather gauntlet and extended his hand. "Jock Leslie, you have been steward here twenty years and I ask that you remain in that post." Lynx's shrewd eyes watched the steward's face closely. When he detected no hint of hostility, he warmed to the man. "As you can see for yourself, I and my men have been sent to garrison Dumfries. I would like the integration to be as smooth as possible and I know for the most part that will depend on how you and I deal together." By getting Jock Leslie firmly on his side from the outset, Lynx hoped to reduce resentment against himself and his men.

"I am at yer service, Lord de Warenne."

"From what I have seen here, I find little fault. You obviously do an excellent job with the people you command. I pride myself on doing the same. Nevertheless, there will have to be compromise. If there is something I don't like and want changed, I shall come directly to you, Jock. By the same token, if there is something you do not like, I expect you to come directly to me." The corner of Lynx's mouth lifted. "I won't guarantee that I'll change it; I'm reputed to be rather rigid. But I want you to feel free to discuss anything and everything with me."

Lynx moved on quickly. "I have twenty knights, all arrogant young devils, but they will have no authority over the running of this castle. You are in charge, Jock Leslie, and have no authority to answer to, save me." Again the corner of Lynx's mouth lifted. "You might as well get on with your rat killing."

When Jock didn't quite take his meaning, Lynx waved his hand toward the bailey. "Start issuing your orders immediately. Tell my men where you want their horses and the supplies from the wagons. Tomorrow will be soon enough for you to show me the working of Dumfries."

During the next couple of days the men, women, and children of Dumfries satisfied their curiosity by getting a good look at the men who had been sent to garrison the castle. At first they were filled with trepidation. After all, these men were English and tales of the cruelties the English had committed at Berwick had spread to Dumfries. But when they saw that the commander was the man who had accompanied Robert Bruce, some of their fears were laid to rest.

Word spread quickly that Jock Leslie was to remain as steward with full authority to run the castle as he always had, and the people of Dumfries heaved a collective sigh of relief and realized their good fortune.

Jane Leslie was one of the few exceptions. She did not set foot in either the castle or the bailey. She had spent the last two days with her brother Ben's wife while she gave birth to her fourth bairn. Judith always had long, difficult labors, but Jane's voice and hands soothed her, allaying her fears and easing a great deal of her pain. Jane's gentle touch was like magic and the soft songs she crooned lulled Judith to sleep between her bouts of labored contractions.

Ben had been careful to keep the news that Dumfries had a new overlord and garrison from his wife, thinking she had enough fears to overcome. And as a result, Jane too was blissfully unaware that the castle was now garrisoned by the English.

The baby made his appearance into the world just as the sun began its early morning climb up the sky. Jane bathed the child and put him to suckle at his mother's breast. Judith closed her eyes in well-deserved rest just as Megotta arrived to inspect her new great-grandson.

Jane slipped from the stone house and lifted her face to the warm April sun. Although she'd taken scant rest in the last two days, the miracle of birth was such a stimulating experience that the last thing Jane wanted to do was sleep. She took the path across the meadow and into the trees. Her forest pool was a good two miles from Ben's house, but Jane's step was light, her thoughts all happy as she listened to the birdsong and kept a watchful eye out for the creatures who dwelled among the deep green shadows. The hour was so early, there was a chance she might see her magnificent lynx.

As Jane stepped from beneath the trees' dark canopy into the clearing, a tiny owl landed on her shoulder and rearranged his feathers so that the edge of his wing touched her cheek. His soundless arrival always brought Jane untold pleasure.

Then she spotted her favorite little green heron, the shyest of all waterbirds. He flew to a low branch close-by and stretched his neck down to the water beneath in search of a minnow. "I see you, Crabby Bill," Jane called, watching his head cock to one side when he heard his name. She'd first seen him on the mudflats where the river Nith opened into the sea. The small green heron had been picking up crustaceans and she had immediately named him Crabby Bill. Jane sat down beside the pool and closed her eyes in contentment.

Taking advantage of the early hour, Lynx de Warenne selected a small falcon from the mews and saddled his horse so that he could ride over the demesne alone. He knew that later in the morning Jock Leslie, the steward, would give him the grand tour, but first he wanted to familiarize himself with every acre of land that belonged to Dumfries.

As Lynx rode out across the meadows, hills, and dales, he noticed the paucity of sheep and lambs, noted the lack of milk and beef cattle herds, and saw that no horses grazed in the fields. He silently cursed Comyn for taking Dumfries' livestock. Lynx was well aware that an army must be fed, but it was shortsighted lunacy to kill off an entire herd.

He wondered if pigs were kept in Dumfries' forests as they were in England and urged his mount into the dense woods. Lynx saw no evidence of swine, but the forest teemed with game, both large and small, and he felt a measure of deep satisfaction that Dumfries was not hunted out. When he came to a clearing he dismounted and cast the small falcon, watching it climb high, preparatory to its swift descent.

A piercing scream rent the air, and de Warenne was knocked to the ground as a body hurled itself against him in an unexpected attack. In a flash, Lynx had his assailant by the throat and had rolled over so that his attacker was pinned to the ground. The soft body beneath him immediately told Lynx that his captive was a female and the long, flaming hair identified her as the girl who had annoyed him so much on his first visit to Dumfries.

Jane's brows lifted in shock and surprise as she recognized the man looming above her. She stared into the fierce green eyes and shuddered involuntarily, sensing his savage masculine fire, imagining that at any moment he would start to lick her. She realized almost immediately he was not going to do anything as gentle as lick her. He was angry, prompting fear to rise up in her. "I . . . I pushed you so that the falcon would not kill the birds."

"Pushed me?" he repeated incredulously. "You flew at me like a wild animal!"

"The creatures who come to this pond are my friends. It's a sanctuary; I don't allow hunting here."

"*You* don't allow? Who the devil do you think you are?"

She was reluctant to give him her name and struggled to free herself. But she was pinned between his muscular thighs. As her hands pushed against his chest, her fingers splayed across sleek, rippling muscles. She knew he was the largest man she had ever encountered, and as she lay beneath him the thought of his size and his power overwhelmed her. He could snap her neck with his bare hands. Her breasts rose and fell as she tried to hide her fear. "What are you doing here?" she gasped.

Her luscious breasts were so tempting, Lynx's palms itched to cup and fondle them. His anger melted away and was replaced by hot desire. He grinned down at her. "Anything I wish. I am the new overlord of Dumfries." The erotic possibilities of what he could do to her were endless. At the thought of her soft body imprisoned beneath him, his shaft hardened and lengthened in rampant need.

"That is impossible—you are *English*!" She said the word as if it were an abomination.

"And you are a Celt, I seem to recall from the last time we met. What is your name?"

"Sironi," she said defiantly, using the Celtic name of a goddess that Megotta sometimes called her. Then she remembered she had told him she was a witch with strong powers over Scotland's enemies. Summoning all of her courage she warned him, "You are not wanted at this castle. Great harm will befall you and all who dwell here if you do not leave."

"Your Celtic prophesies make me tremble with fear," he said mockingly. "I am not given to superstitions. You forget I am a Norman." He bent his head to inhale the fragrance of her hair and his hard shaft pressed into her soft belly.

Suddenly she realized she had aroused him and her

fear doubled. She hated him for the lust he felt and she hated herself for the way he made her feel. "Nay, I don't forget you are a Norman!" she spat.

Lynx saw fear darken her eyes and it gave him pause. If he did not stop teasing her, his body would lose control and he would take her here in the grass. He had never forced a maid in his life.

"Silly wench, I should warm your bottom." He climbed off of her and watched her scramble to her feet. "I warrant your talents are more mischief than magic power."

Though Jane felt threatened by him, his disparaging words challenged her. She knew a need to demonstrate her power. She looked up into the tree where his falcon had flown and held her arms up in a commanding stance. "Come to me, Talon!"

The small raptor glided from the treetop and landed on Jane's wrist. She stroked his blue-gray plumage with a finger and spoke to him as if he were a beloved pet, rather than a fierce predator. "You see, I am able to control him."

Lynx de Warenne took hold of the bird's jesses and lifted him from her hand. "You had better learn to control yourself, mistress, now that I am master here," he advised her as he looked deeply into her eyes. Then he remounted and rode off without a backward glance.

7

"Lord de Warenne, this is my son Andrew, who is Dumfries' steward-in-training."

Lynx noticed the resemblance between father and son and invited Andrew to join them.

"I'm sure ye dinna need me tagging along. Actually the kitchens are in turmoil. There are not enough castle cooks or servers. I must go and solve their problems."

"Put my Welshmen to work. There are some excellent cooks among them," Lynx advised.

Next, Jock Leslie took Lynx to the castle forge and introduced the blacksmiths. "These are my sons James and Alex."

Lynx quirked a brow at Jock, but made no comment. He was pleased that the forge was a large one. "I am going to keep you men busy. Many of our horses need reshoeing and our weapons and armor need repairs. I have armorers of course, so you will have to work together. If there are problems, speak up."

From the forge, Jock took Lynx to inspect the castle stores. As they walked, hens and chicks scattered before them. "Do we have geese?" Lynx inquired.

"Very few, my lord."

"Make a note to buy a large flock. My bowmen prefer the feathers of the gray English goose." As they walked, Lynx noticed the children. He always noticed the children. They were happy and healthy with sturdy legs and red cheeks. Jock spoke to all of them, tussling a wee lass's hair or cuffing a lad across the ear. Lynx was surprised when the children addressed Jock as Granddad, for he was no graybeard.

When they arrived at the castle stores, David Leslie voiced his problems without hesitation. "Comyn's men wiped me out. The thoughtless swines fed my store of grain to their horses when the hay ran low."

Lynx nodded as he walked through the storage sheds, noting they were very low on all food supplies. "Buy more. Buy oats for the horses. Stock up on dried staples, beans, peas, lentils, barley—whatever you need."

"I need siller," David said bluntly.

"Then buy some . . . oh, siller means money, of course!" Lynx laughed and looked at Jock ruefully. "You didn't tell me the coffers were low."

"The coffers are empty, my lord," Jock replied quietly.

"Don't look so glum, man, that's easily remedied. We will buy what we need for present use, but we must also replenish the livestock for Dumfries' future needs."

Both Leslies looked relieved.

"We'll buy new flocks . . . I know that sheep mean wealth in the dales. I'll need to talk with the head shepherds and the cattle herders," Lynx decided.

"I'll tell them tonight. My sons Ben and Sim are the head shepherds and the cattle herders are wed to my daughters."

Lynx looked at Jock in amazement. "Christ, man, how many sons and daughters do you have?"

"Only ten, my lord."

"Only?" Lynx almost choked. "To a man who has none, ten offspring is prolific indeed." Lynx's brows went up as another thought occurred to him. "The children call you Granddad because you *are* their granddad!"

Jock nodded happily. "I have thirty grandchildren. No, I lie, I have thirty-one. My son Ben's wife had another bairn in the night."

Lynx stared at him in awe; such a feat seemed almost beyond belief. "I envy you, Jock Leslie."

As they walked to the brewhouse, Lynx's steward said, "May I be so bold as to suggest a handfastin' if ye wish to become a father?"

"Explain this handfasting custom to me," Lynx invited.

Jock thought for a minute, searching for an analogy the Norman lord would understand. "Handfastin' sets decent women apart from the whores. It puts the stamp of approval on a woman lying with a man. In the dales it's usually a preliminary to wedlock. The usual length of a handfastin' is a year and a day. At the end of that time the couple either decides to wed or to part. But if the union produces a child it is legitimate, even if no marriage ever takes place."

"The custom is a safeguard for women and children," Lynx said pensively.

"Aye, my lord; bastardy is frowned upon."

Lynx de Warenne wondered if Jock Leslie was giving him a warning. "My men have their orders; there will be no forcing of women at Dumfries."

* * *

In the late afternoon his steward showed Lynx de Warenne over every room in the castle. The two men hadn't stopped talking and planning since early morning. Inside the fortification, Lynx was hard-pressed to make suggestions for improvement. The drains had been cleaned, the floors scrubbed, the fireplaces did not smoke, and even the dogs were penned up and not allowed to run underfoot.

The furnishings of Dumfries were almost luxurious. In most of the chambers, tapestries covered the stone walls to keep out the cold, many of the upper bedchambers had thick carpets on the floors, and the wide beds all had heavy bed-curtains, woven woolen blankets, and spotless linen. Every bedchamber had a spacious wardrobe and some even had hearths.

The castle, built in true Norman style, was flanked on each corner by a square tower. "This is the Master Tower." Jock led the way up the stone steps to the first level, which consisted of two rooms connected by an arch. "These have always been the living quarters of whoever governed Dumfries."

Lynx noted that every chair was cushioned, every bench padded. The furniture was black oak, polished with beeswax. A games table boasted a set of chessmen, musical instruments hung from the walls, and there was no shortage of polished silver mirrors. When Lynx heard his squires' voices above him, accompanied by a woman's laughter, he climbed to the upper level, where again two chambers were connected by an arch.

He saw immediately that his squires had set up his own bed, carried up his trunks, including his weapons chest, and were busy hanging his clothes in the wardrobe. But it was the woman who caught and held Lynx's attention, as she spread fresh sheets across the bed. She was a comely wench, dark with a generous mouth and well-rounded hips. The curve of her belly told him that she was ripe with child.

"Should you be doing this?" Lynx asked, concerned for her advanced condition.

Jock chuckled. "This is my daughter Mary. You needn't worry, my lord, this is her sixth bairn."

She bobbed him a curtsy and threw him a saucy look. "Welcome to Dumfries, Lord de Warenne."

"Thank you, Mary," Lynx replied, crushing the covetous feeling that gripped him for the child, if not the woman.

"Ye'll want a fire to counter the dampness. Mary, show the squires where the wood is stored," Jock bade.

Lynx stared after the fecund young woman, shaking his head in wonder. "Do you have any unwed daughters, Jock Leslie?"

Jock laughed and joined in the jest. "I have one lass who isna handfasted yet. Ye'd best hurry if ye're interested, my lord!"

Jane had known the lynx would return to Dumfries as surely as she had known spring would return. She thought of him as *the lynx* because he was the embodiment of the magnificent animal with whom she had had the extraordinary encounter. Now she remembered the name of the man who had accompanied Robert Bruce.

"Lord de Warenne," Jane whispered the name aloud and felt her heart flutter with trepidation. The incident at the forest pool had been unfortunate and disturbing, yet somehow it had had an air of inevitability about it, as if it had been preordained. Her emotions had been in such turmoil, but luckily she had managed to mask the fear and the awe she felt for him.

Jane lifted the touchstone she wore about her neck and gazed down at the painted lynx. The tawny mane, the green eyes, the massive shoulders bore an uncanny resemblance to de Warenne, and she could not help but feel the man posed a threat to her.

Jane did not return home but instead sought out her brother Keith at the stables. He was the only one who seemed to understand the things she felt and did, without finding her strange or, worse still, laughing at her. Jane liked the smell of the stables. The mingled scent of horse, hay, and leather played counterpoint to the acrid smell of horse manure. But when she saw a group of unfamiliar men-at-arms she was filled with trepidation. Jane turned on her heel and was hurrying from the stable when Keith caught sight of her.

He dropped his currying brush and rushed after her. "Jane, don't run off. Come and look at the horses—they're the finest I've ever seen, especially Lord de Warenne's black stallion." Keith took hold of her arm to stay her flight.

"I cannot . . . those men—" The words stuck in her throat.

"Come up to the mews while I return Talon to his perch." Keith took the falcon on his wrist and led the way up to the loft where the hawks were kept. "The men are knights who belong to the new lord."

The hooded birds of prey recognized the voices and

screeched for attention. Jane gently stroked the breast of a female merlin, quieting her immediately. ''I've seen him,'' she whispered ominously.

''Lord de Warenne?''

Jane nodded. ''I saw him before.''

''Aye, he came with Robert Bruce, Earl of Carrick.''

Jane shook her head. ''I saw him before that.''

Keith, realizing she was trying to tell him something, gave her his full attention.

''Do you remember when I saw the lynx at the forest pool? Well, I saw him there again.'' She lifted the Celtic touchstone on its leather thong. ''I took the lynx for my magic symbol. I thought if I could merge my spirit with his, it would give me power and strength. Anyway, the lynx came to me in a dream and he turned into a man . . . It was Lord de Warenne.''

Keith nodded slowly. ''That is second sight . . . seeing things before they happen. Have you had any visions?''

''I saw him at the forest pool this morning, but I don't think he was a vision. I think he was real.''

''The lord's name is Lynx.''

''What?''

''His name is Lynx de Warenne.''

Jane's lips parted in surprise and dismay, for that is what she had called him, *the lynx.* ''Keith, what does it mean?''

''I know not. Yet his destiny and that of Dumfries are somehow bound together. There *is* a purpose; perhaps a divine one, perhaps not. But whether for good or evil, only time will tell.''

"I believe that my new touchstone will protect me against him!"

Keith's eyes examined her face. "He has frightened you. Jane, I don't believe he is a threat to you."

"I'm not afraid of him," she assured her brother, lifting her head proudly, but deep inside she was afraid of him and of the things he made her feel.

That evening when the Leslie women gathered at Judith and Ben's house to welcome the new bairn into the family, an air of excitement prevailed. The breathless talk was all of Lord de Warenne, his handsome young knights, and the swarthy Welsh bowmen. The young women downplayed any anxiety they felt toward the newcomers. Yet the edge of apprehension they felt added to the thrilling knowledge that the men were dangerous and undefeated in recent battles.

"Judith, ye're missing all the excitement. His knights are so tall, ye'll never believe yer eyes," Kate informed her. "The Welsh bowmen are no' so tall, but they make up for it with brawn!"

Mary, bursting with self-importance, announced, "*I* made his bed today!"

The others turned to her eagerly. "The lord's bed?"

"Aye. He was greatly concerned for me, working in my condition."

The girls laughed. "Making a bed isna work!"

Mary continued, holding up her hands. "He was this close to me. He could have reached out an' touched me."

"An' did he?" Kate asked suggestively.

"No, Father was there with him," Mary said with a wink. The young matrons hooted with laughter.

As Jane put Judith's children to bed, she listened to the Leslie women. Whenever they got together, their favorite subject was the male of the species, and Jane had always been puzzled that they did not share her fear of men. She kept it to herself that this morning his powerful hands had touched her body intimately as he'd held her pinned beneath him. Jane shivered, remembering his savage masculinity; while the other women were greatly attracted to him, Jane felt wary of him.

Jane kissed the children and sang them to sleep, with a soft, soothing melody. But on the inside she was seething with passionate emotions. She was apprehensive that when she fell asleep tonight, the lynx would come to her in her dreams.

Lynx de Warenne lay abed in the Master Tower, going over the day's events in his mind. All had gone exceedingly well, far better than he had anticipated, and he knew most of it was due to the competence of Dumfries' steward, Jock Leslie.

All that was needed to make the demesne flourish was money for new flocks and herds, and the de Warenne coffers were healthy. He did not consider it a waste to spend personal monies, even though Dumfries belonged to the crown. In the back of his mind, Lynx had the notion that his sojourn in Scotland might just be long-term.

Though the subjugation of Wales had taken place a decade and a half ago, Edward Plantagenet and his armies had still found it necessary to spend most of the last ten years building great castles along her borders to hold the wild tribesmen under control. Lynx doubted the Scots would be any easier to control.

His mind moved on quickly to Dumfries' immediate needs. A few hunts would supply them with venison, boar, and game, and the river Nith and the open sea of Solway Firth would provide an abundance of fish and shellfish. If he established a market in the town of Dumfries, Lynx knew it would attract produce and supplies from miles away, perhaps even from across the border in England. And he would encourage ships to bring in goods from Wales and Ireland.

He reminded himself to visit the Franciscan monastery on the morrow to learn if they produced aught more useful than prayer, and for the umpteenth time, he pushed away a thought that refused to leave his mind entirely.

When Lynx had finished reviewing the day's events and had gone over his plans for tomorrow, he allowed himself to examine the thought carefully. Jock Leslie had a daughter who wasn't spoken for. Was this Providence? Was this his chance to beget an heir? Breeding seemed no problem whatsoever for the Leslies.

A moment of self-doubt assailed him. Did the fault lie within himself? The de Warennes were not prolific breeders; neither he nor Jory had produced a child. Still, he argued with himself, his father had produced not one but two children. If he mated with a Leslie woman, mayhap the odds would be in his favor!

Lynx imagined how shocked the nobility would be if he wed a commoner. John de Warenne would disapprove of such a union, but Lynx cared naught for that. He was a man who made his own decisions regarding his personal life. The king would not be best pleased either, yet hadn't Princess Joanna just married her husband's squire?

His thoughts turned to the young Leslie woman. Her appearance, age, and temperament were of little importance to Lynx de Warenne. If she could give him a child, the rest was immaterial. All that mattered was that she be willing. The accepted custom of handfasting somehow made the idea more plausible. If the union produced no child after a year and a day, the union could be dissolved. On the other hand, if the young woman became pregnant, he would marry her immediately.

Lynx's thoughts became clouded as he recalled the feelings of loss he had suffered when his wife Sylvia had died. He hadn't spent enough time with her and had been ridden with guilt. He assured himself that would not happen if he wed a girl of lower station. There would be no romantic involvement whatsoever, for either of them. The relationship would be a simple one. She would be the mother of his child. In return she would receive the respect and honor due her as his wife.

Try as he might, Lynx could think of few disadvantages to the idea. Alicia would throw her usual tantrum, but when he pointed out to her that their relationship would remain unchanged, what possible objection could she have? In any case, Alicia had no say in the matter and would be miles away in Carlisle for the next few months.

Lynx's thoughts returned to Jock Leslie. His steward was the key to any such plan. He would speak to Jock in the morning. If he and his steward could come to terms on an agreement regarding this matter, that would be all that was necessary.

Now that he had made up his mind to pursue the hand-fasting, Lynx felt more at peace with himself than he had in a long while. He fell asleep visualizing himself holding his baby son. When his dream began, he was surrounded by children who looked like him.

8

The following morning Lynx de Warenne decided to ride to Lochmaben to buy livestock. The Bruces derived a great deal of their wealth from the herds of cattle and flocks of sheep that covered most of Annandale. Lynx asked Ben and Sim Leslie to accompany him since they knew far more about sheep than he would ever know. Lynx also invited their father, Jock Leslie, to accompany him. The six- or seven-mile ride up the valley to Lochmaben Castle would give Lynx the opportunity to lay the proposal for the handfasting before his steward.

Lynx left his squires at Dumfries, relying on their innate common sense to handle whatever might arise in his absence. Though lower in rank than the young de Warenne knights, Thomas and Taffy had their lord's full authority to take charge should it become necessary.

At midmorning, Jane was startled when her brother James came bursting through the doorway of the stone house, his arms and face streaked black with soot and sweat. Jane stepped back when she saw that a tall, fair-haired stranger accompanied him.

James addressed Megotta. "There's bin an accident at

the forge! One of the lord's knights has bin burned. Fetch some ointment!''

Megotta's face and attitude became stony. ''My healing salve is for Scotsmen, not filthy Englishmen!''

James's mouth fell open. ''Are ye daft, woman? We need yer help!''

Megotta folded her arms across her scrawny chest, pressed her lips together, and replied firmly, ''Ye'll not get it!''

Taffy stepped forward. ''Ma'am, I'm Welsh, not English. Some of our Welsh are healers as you are, but they are unfamiliar with the plants and herbs that grow in these parts. Could you tell the medicine men the properties of some of the local plants?''

''I could, but I won't.''

When James spotted Jane, he turned from Megotta in frustrated fury. ''Jane, will ye come?''

With an apprehensive glance in Taffy's direction, Jane nodded her head and ran to get her medicinal box.

On the way to the forge Taffy said, ''Lord de Warenne will be most grateful to you, lady.''

Jane saw relief and gratitude writ plain on the squire's face and saw something else there too. The well-muscled youth had a blush upon his cheek when he spoke to her, and Jane was discomfitted to realize that the young man found her attractive.

When they reached the forge, a circle of men were gathered about a young knight sitting upon a stool. Another knight, obviously a concerned friend, knelt before him. As well as Jane's brother Alex, Lord de Warenne's squire Thomas stood by looking helpless, while two dark Welsh archers conversed in Celtic.

At the sight of the men Jane hesitated, but felt James's hand at the small of her back urging her forward. She was met by the heat of the braziers and immediately realized the hot air would add to the knight's misery.

"Please," Jane appealed to her brother Alex, "bring him outside where it's cool and sit him on the grass."

The young knight's tunic had been removed and Jane saw that his burn extended from his left elbow all the way up his arm and across his shoulder. She also saw that he was in agony. As she knelt before him to examine the injury, seven men crowded about her, all talking at once.

A furious Thomas told her the two brainless young knights had been wrestling and that there would be hell to pay when Lord de Warenne returned. The injured man's friend, Sir Harry, the knight with whom he'd been wrestling, proclaimed it had all been his fault and Sir Giles must not be blamed. The two dark Welshmen began to question Jane about the contents of her medicinal box, pressing her to tell them what herbs she used to heal burns.

Filled with dismay at the men crowding about her, Jane turned beseeching eyes upon her brother. "James, please, make them step back."

When he realized Jane was agitated simply by being among strange men, he urged the men to give her some space. "Ma sister is very shy of men. If ye want her to help, ye'll have to stand back an' keep yer tongues from clatterin'."

"Alex, I need a bucket of cold water," Jane directed, and watched three men run to do her bidding. Jane took a clean linen cloth from her box and looked into her patient's eyes. "Sir Giles?" When he nodded in response, she said softly, "This will take the fire from the burn."

Jane noticed how bloodless his face was and that his eyes welled with tears that he stubbornly refused to shed. She dipped the linen into the cold water and wrung it out over the man's shoulder and arm, over and over again. Her repeated action fell into a deliberate rhythm and seemed to have a hypnotic effect on the wounded knight. She never actually touched the cloth to the burn, but squeezed cold water over it like a waterfall.

When two buckets had been emptied, she knelt before Sir Giles, patiently waiting for the breeze to dry the arm and shoulder. From her box Jane took a pot of aromatic green unguent and spread it thickly, coating the entire area, which had already begun to blister.

When the air no longer touched his skin, Giles closed his eyes, a tear running down his cheek. "You have the gentlest touch I've ever known, demoiselle," he whispered hoarsely.

His friend, Sir Harry Eltham, drew close. "Do you need bandages, demoiselle?"

Jane looked up into his face with alarm, but when she saw how young he was and how concerned he was for his friend, some of her apprehension melted away. "No, it is better not to bind it. The unguent must be applied every few hours."

Impulsively, Sir Harry grabbed her hand and lifted her fingers to his lips. "Thank you, demoiselle."

Embarrassed, Jane snatched her hand back and gave her full attention to her patient. She knew the terrible shock his system had received; a burn caused a greater degree of agony than the pain of other injuries. Jane knew she had the power to alleviate and diminish that pain, perhaps even eliminate it altogether.

"Please lie prone," she asked shyly.

Sir Giles obeyed immediately. She was the only one who had been able to help him.

"I want you to distance yourself from the pain. *You* must do it, but I will assist you." Jane's fingers brushed the long hair from the nape of Giles's neck then pressed down firmly at the base of his skull. After about two minutes, she ran her fingertips down the length of his back on either side of his spine and repeated the strokes a dozen times.

"It has gone!" Giles said with a dazed look of disbelief on his face.

As Sir Harry and Taffy came forward to help Sir Giles to his feet, Jane held up her hand to stop them. "He should rest," she said firmly. She handed the jar of unguent to Sir Harry and told him to put on more in about four hours.

"Thank you, demoiselle, we are forever in your debt."

"You are an angel of mercy, lady," Taffy said. The looks on the young men's faces were akin to worship.

Thomas came forward with the two dark Welshmen at his heels. "Lady, this is Rhys and Gowan, our Welsh healers. Will you show them where to gather the herbs for that green salve? The plants are strange and it is imperative that our Welsh healers learn the properties of the herbs that grow here."

Jane hesitated. "My grandmother has taught me to guard our knowledge of healing plants."

Thomas said shrewdly, "If you will not pass on your

knowledge to our Welsh, Lord de Warenne will order you to nurse all his men who fall sick."

The threat thoroughly intimidated her as it was meant to. "I'll teach them what I know about our plants," Jane reluctantly agreed, "but I will not go into the forest with strange men unless my brother James comes with us."

By late afternoon they had gathered a dozen different plants, filling big cloth bags with Scotch thistle, alkanet, bryony, and hemlock. As Jane listened to them converse with James, she realized the two Welshmen were not so very different from her brother. Their English was sprinkled with Celtic words and their appearance was also similar, with their dark hair and muscular, stocky builds.

As Rhys and Gowan began exchanging their knowledge of the medicinal properties of plants with her, Jane lost her fear of the Welshmen. As they picked and examined the plants Jane pointed out, they realized there were great similarities between what grew here in Scotland and what grew in Wales.

Jane pointed to a plant that seemed to grow everywhere. "That is balm, one of the two herbs that go into the green unguent for burns."

"What is the other, lady?" Rhys asked.

"Scotch thistle, which also grows in abundance here."

"Thistles are prickly-headed instruments of the devil. How do you pick them?"

"Ah, there is a secret to it. If you pluck them gingerly, they will cause sharp pain to your fingers, but if you do it boldly, grasping the whole head firmly, the thistles collapse and feel like thistledown. Here, let me show you."

When Rhys attempted to pick one, it stabbed his fingers cruelly and Gowan laughed at him, but he didn't give up, and his second attempt brought success.

When they sat down in a clearing to share bread and cheese, the exchange became lively. They were amazed at the things Jane knew about herbs, things they had never dreamed of. She pulled betony from her cloth bag. "This is good for belching."

"To start it or to stop it?"

Jane laughed. "To stop it of course, who on earth would want to start belching?" She pulled a leaf-covered branch from her bag. "This is black alder, it gets rid of lice."

They hung on her every word and by the time they returned to Dumfries and followed her into the castle still-room, their admiration for the young woman was plain for all to see.

Inside Dumfries Castle word had spread like wildfire that Jane Leslie had tended the burned knight and Jane's sisters were pea-green with envy.

When Lynx arrived at Lochmaben, he was surprised to learn that Robert Bruce had returned to Carlisle for a couple of days. Nigel Bruce took de Warenne to one of their tenant sheep farms where Lynx paid for a flock of two hundred black-faced sheep, which he allowed his shepherds to select.

He watched with interest as Ben and Sim culled the animals they wanted from the huge flock, then turned them over to their shaggy-coated black-and-white dogs to herd into a pen.

"Best brand the lambs when ye get them to Dumfries,

there's a good deal of raiding that goes on in these parts," Nigel advised.

"By the English?" Lynx asked.

"English my arse! 'Tis the bloody Scots who do the reiving," Nigel informed him.

Lynx de Warenne fixed his shepherds with an icy green stare. "I will hang any man caught lifting Dumfries' sheep, and by the same token a harsh punishment awaits any man of Dumfries who goes out raiding others."

Lynx was disappointed that Robert was away. He had held off approaching Jock Leslie until he saw what his friend's reaction would be to the proposed handfasting of his steward's daughter. But when he thought it over, Lynx realized that he had already made his decision, so Robert Bruce's reaction was immaterial.

As Lynx de Warenne and Jock Leslie rode back down the Annandale Valley, followed at a fair distance by the two shepherds and the newly acquired flock, he decided to broach the matter that dominated his thoughts.

"Jock, your daughter who is not yet spoken for—would you consider handfasting her to me?"

"Are ye serious, my lord?"

"I've never been more serious in my life. If she conceives, I'll marry her immediately."

"Ye would truly make my daughter Lady de Warenne?" Jock asked doubtfully.

"I would consider it a small price to pay for a son."

"What if her first child is a lass?"

"A son or a daughter—it would make no difference. I'll wed her when she conceives, not when she is delivered."

"That's uncommonly generous, my lord. Are ye not heir to a great earldom?" Jock asked with suspicion.

"The earldom of Surrey," Lynx confirmed.

"How could ma daughter possibly become the Countess of Surrey?" Jock asked, seemingly overwhelmed at the idea.

"By giving me a child," Lynx said simply.

"How soon do ye want the handfastin'?"

"Immediately. The king could send for me at any time. Do we have an agreement?"

"We do, Lord de Warenne."

"Good." A short laugh escaped from between his lips. "All that remains is for your daughter to agree."

"Nay, my lord. I spoke for her when I agreed, as is my right. My daughter Jane will be honored beyond belief. But of course ye will wish to meet her, question her, see if she meets with yer approval."

"Jane?" Lynx tested the name upon his tongue. "She mustn't be forced."

"Forced?" Jock almost choked. "Forced to wed into the nobility and become a countess someday? Her answer will be *yes* and she'll have naught else to say in the matter."

Lynx grimaced. If he knew aught about women, she would have a hell of a lot to say in the matter!

"No! No! No! How could Father ever think I would agree to such a thing?" The Leslie women had once again congregated at Judith's house.

"Don't be a silly fool, Jane. I definitely heard the word *handfasting*. Any of Lord de Warenne's men could take ye without a legal handfasting," Kate pointed out.

"I bet it's one of the Welsh bowmen who wants ye, or do ye think it could be one of the lord's squires?" Mary pressed her. Both sisters were breathless with excitement over what they'd overheard their father tell their grandmother, Megotta.

A picture of Taffy flew into Jane's mind and she recalled how he had flushed when he'd spoken with her. "Oh Lord, I hope and pray not. Megotta promised me I would never have to wed," Jane said wretchedly.

"It has naught to do with Megotta. It's what Father says that counts," Mary assured her. "They were having a terrible row and Megotta lost the argument. Father was furious with her over refusing to tend the knight who was burned. He told her in no uncertain terms that de Warenne was master of Dumfries now and that his word was law."

Jane wrung her hands in distress. "Oh, may the goddess Brigantia protect me! What if it's Sir Giles? I tended his burn and took away his pain, and out of some sort of gratitude, mayhap he thinks he must repay me by offering for me."

"But Sir Giles is a knight," Kate pointed out. "Surely he wouldn't reach so far beneath himself."

Jane bit her lip. "Of course not, how silly of me."

"Still, he might have fallen under her spell. Jane has strange powers," Mary insisted, unable to keep the jealousy from her voice.

Judith's new babe had fallen asleep at her breast. She put him in his cradle and joined the other women. "This is the opportunity of a lifetime, Jane. We've all been worried that no man ever offered for ye."

"I don't want a man!" Jane said desperately.

"But it's not what ye want, it's what Lord de Warenne

wants. If he handfasts ye to one of his knights, ye'll be called Lady Jane," Judith pointed out.

Kate and Mary exchanged a look of alarm. "Mayhap when the lord sees her, he'll change his mind," Mary said hopefully, wishing she'd never urged her father to find Jane a husband.

"When he sends for ye, make sure yer hair is plaited neatly away from yer face," Kate advised.

"And wear yer brown woolen dress," Mary insisted.

"Oh no, that will make her look too plain," Judith protested.

Kate and Mary soon overruled Judith. Better by far that their little sister be *plain* Jane, rather than *Lady* Jane!

When Jane arrived home, her father was waiting for her. Megotta's face looked like a thundercloud and obviously she was talking to no one. She took herself off to her room and slammed the door in protest.

Jock totally ignored his mother-in-law and bade Jane sit with him before the fire. "Ye did a good thing today, Jane, tending the knight's burns. Lord de Warenne wants to speak with ye."

"Tonight?" she asked in great alarm.

"Nay," Jock said laughing. "Tonight he is busy tearing a strip off his young knights fer their irresponsible behavior in his absence. I've never seen a man so grim-faced."

Jane felt relieved. If the lord was angry with his knights, it was unlikely he would listen to a request for a handfasting. "I heard a rumor Lord de Warenne wanted to see me about a handfasting," Jane said cautiously.

"Christ! Rumors are thicker than ticks on a sheep

hereabouts. Yer sisters overheard me telling Megotta, no doubt.'' He wasn't really angry, he was too excited. He ruffled Jane's hair. ''This will mean such good fortune for our family. 'Tis an unlooked for opportunity of a lifetime.'' He didn't want to spoil the surprise for her. ''Go up to the castle in the morning. Lord de Warenne wants to tell ye himself what he and I have agreed to.''

Jane's heart sank. ''You've already made an agreement? Father, I don't want to get handfasted! I want to use my healing powers as the ancient Celtic priestesses did.''

''You sound just like Megotta! I'm sick an' tired of her putting ridiculous ideas in yer head. It is yer duty to obey me, not yer grandmother. Get off to bed!''

Jane did not dare to argue further with him. Megotta must have protested the handfasting and what good had it done? She knew she would have to summon the courage to face Lord de Warenne and make him understand her refusal.

After she undressed, Jane looked down at the lynx touchstone that lay between her naked breasts. Her pulses raced at the thought of seeing Lord de Warenne in the morning. There was a strange thread that linked their destinies, which excited and troubled her beyond belief. He was easily the most powerful man she had ever encountered. He stirred passionate emotions inside her, the most predominant of which was fear.

Jane knew that tomorrow she would somehow find the courage to defy him. She was going to refuse the handfasting and tell him plainly she wanted no man breathing, not now, not ever! The thought of pitting her will against his made her feel weak all over. But she was going to say no to Lynx de Warenne and enjoy doing so!

Early the next morning, however, some of Jane's bravado had fled. She couldn't dispel a feeling of dread at seeing Lord de Warenne because at all of their previous encounters he had become angry with her. Then an idea came to her. As well as making herself unappealing as a candidate for a handfasting with one of the de Warenne men, she would disguise herself in the hope that he wouldn't recognize her.

With Megotta's help, she bound her breasts tightly so that her chest looked as if it were almost flat. "Make it tighter, I want to look thin and scrawny."

"Are ye sure ye can breathe, child?"

"Yes, I'll be fine. Oh, whatever will I do with my hair?"

"We'll pull it back and cover it with a linen head cloth."

In the brown woolen dress Jane entered Dumfries Castle and was met by Thomas, the lord's squire. He looked at her curiously, but made no comment about her appearance. He led her to a small chamber off the great hall where Lord de Warenne conducted the castle's business. He bade her wait, disappeared inside for a moment, then came out and motioned for her to enter. Jane lifted her chin, walked into the chamber and heard the door close behind her.

His back to the mantelpiece, Lynx de Warenne stood watching the door. When the young woman entered, disappointment washed over him. "You are Jane Leslie?" he asked.

"Yes, my lord," she said softly, almost overwhelmed by his commanding presence.

Splendor of God, Lynx thought, she was nothing like Jock's other buxom daughters. "How old are you?" he asked brusquely.

"Eighteen, my lord." Jane lowered her eyes.

"I'm almost thirty," he stated baldly. He watched her lashes flutter up in surprise. She's too young, too innocent, and too unwordly, he thought. Then he chided himself. Were these not the qualities a man wanted in the mother of his child? Surely these qualities were preferable to guile, deceit, and wantonness? Still, he had more or less expected a brood mare, not the unbroken filly standing before him who had perhaps never been ridden.

In Lynx de Warenne's experience women were calculating and manipulative. Was it possible that this girl had led such a sheltered life she was as yet untainted? She seemed to be in awe of him and he assumed it was because he was of noble birth and she was not. Such an advantage would give him the upper hand. She would defer to him in all matters. He would be able to control her with a look or a word.

Lynx looked her over from head to toe. She was certainly a plain little thing. Still, he wasn't looking for a mistress or a roll in the hay; he was in the market for a mate. He plunged forward. "Your father and I have agreed to a handfasting."

Jane gathered all of her courage. "My lord, do I have your permission to speak plainly?"

"Of course."

"I do not know who has asked for me. Perhaps one of your Welsh bowmen because I have healing powers, or perhaps your squire Taffy, who has confused me with an angel of mercy, or even Sir Giles because I took his pain away and he thinks to repay me. But whoever it is, my answer is no. I do not wish to be handfasted to any of them." Jane took a deep breath to stop her knees from shaking. "My lord, you will not force me, will you?"

"Jane, your father has agreed to handfast you to *me.*"

Jane's brows rose in disbelief. "You?"

She gazed up into his green eyes, then allowed her glance to slide over him from his mane of tawny hair, across his impossibly wide shoulders, to his powerfully muscled chest, down to his strong, long legs. Then her gaze traveled back up his body, rested for a full minute on his firm, unsmiling mouth, and came to rest on his lynx-green eyes.

Jane's fingers closed over her touchstone. Had the goddess Brigantia deserted her? She was so shocked and stunned that suddenly all the pent-up fear she felt for this man began to surge up inside her. It rushed through her veins, pierced her heart, then flowed upward into her throat, making it impossible for her to breathe. Jane put a hand to her head as outrage overwhelmed her, dizzying her senses. The dominant figure of Lynx de Warenne blurred, then she swayed toward him as if her will had been snatched away by the invisible hand of Fate.

9

Lynx caught her as she swooned. He looked down at her, appalled, adding "delicate" to the list of Jane's shortcomings. Then he looked more closely. There was something familiar about her face. He pulled off the linen head cloth and the bright color of her long hair identified her immediately. Splendor of God, it was the willful young woman who had given him nothing but trouble! But what the devil has she done to her breasts? he wondered, looking at her chest. Lynx ran his hands over her body and instead of soft flesh beneath her dress, he felt something stiff and unyielding. With consternation he guessed that she had bound her beautiful breasts in a deliberate attempt to disguise her lovely figure.

He reached inside the loose woolen dress to rid her of her tight binding. As he pulled the linen strips away, one luscious breast sprang from its confinement and Lynx could not resist cupping it in his palm and running his thumb across its tip until it peaked. Then his hand sought the other full breast, massaging it until its tip also peaked into a tiny jewel.

The moment Jane was able to breathe, she opened her eyes and stared at him in outrage. Lynx withdrew his hands from beneath the loose woolen dress, feeling a reluctance that surprised him.

"Why the devil did you try to disguise yourself?" he demanded.

"You have a terrible temper, my lord, which becomes aroused every time you see me. I covered my hair and bound myself hoping you would not recognize me." Her breasts rose and fell with her apprehension.

His eyes lingered on them appreciatively; they were lush and lovely. "You will make yourself ill, doing such a stupid thing!"

"I am never ill, my lord," Jane said proudly. Then she realized her mistake. If she had claimed delicate health, he would not want her.

"Why didn't you tell me from the outset that you were my steward's daughter? Why did you deliberately lie to me, telling me your name was Sironi?" He surprised himself by recalling her name.

"I didn't lie, Lord de Warenne. Sironi is my Celtic name."

He set his back to the fire and stared down at her. What the hell was he getting himself into? "It is my turn to speak plainly." Lynx de Warenne's deep voice cut into her thoughts. "I was married before, but the union produced no children. I have vast land holdings and will inherit an earldom. I need an heir; that is the reason I offer this handfasting. If you conceive, a marriage will take place immediately. If you do not conceive, the handfasting will be dissolved in a year and a day and your father will be paid compensation."

Now anger began to mingle with her fear. "Why did

you choose *me,* Lord de Warenne?'' She brushed away the feeling that somehow their destinies were entwined.

''Your father has bred ten children, most of whom have proven prolific breeders themselves. The odds are in favor of your producing children.'' He looked at her gravely. ''What do you say, Jane? Will you try to give me a child?'' He made it plain that this would be nothing more than a business arrangement.

Though her knees were trembling, she lifted her chin and dared to refuse him. ''I am sorry, Lord de Warenne. Most women would consider your offer to be a great honor, but I am unlike other women. I do not wish to be handfasted or married. I have no desire to become a wife. I have been given the power of healing and want nothing more than to pursue that calling as the ancient Celtic priestesses did.''

Lynx was shocked that she was actually turning him down. She was a rustic commoner, how dare she? ''Your father does not approve of this Celtic hocus-pocus.''

''That is because he has Norman blood. My grandmother, Megotta, has taught me the ancient rituals of the Celts and shown me the magic healing properties of herbs. She promised me I would not be handfasted.''

As he watched her, he realized this young female was the complete opposite of his highborn late wife, and yet there was something about her that attracted him. She challenged him, and Lynx de Warenne decided to take up that challenge! He went to the door and beckoned Thomas. ''Fetch the old woman,'' he directed.

When he returned he said, ''I take it you dislike children.''

''What a dreadful thing to say—I love children. My

brothers and sisters have dozens of wee ones and I love and adore all of them!"

He looked relieved, but he did not smile at her. In fact his face remained grave. When a knock came on the door he said, "Please excuse me, I'll be back in a few moments."

De Warenne was not so polite to the crone who stood glaring at his squire Thomas. "Jock Leslie has agreed to handfast his daughter to me, but you, madam, are an impediment."

"My granddaughter is a Celt. I don't want her mating with the enemy!" she said angrily.

His green eyes were glacial. "I am lord here, and I will be obeyed. If you object to this union I will send you back to the Highlands, where you will have no further contact with your family."

Megotta's anger flared at his ruthless male attitude and still she defied him. "I would rather go back to the Highlands than live under the heel of the English!"

His gaze flicked over her. If she was rash enough to pit her will against his, she would lose the battle. "And never see your granddaughter Jane again?" he inquired.

He saw the pain and the sadness in her eyes. Regretting the need to be harsh with this old woman, he quickly added, "On the other hand, if you convince Jane to accept this handfasting, I will not be ungenerous to you, or your family. I already have her father's permission and I don't need yours, but I would prefer it if you gave Jane your blessing." He opened the chamber door and ushered her inside.

"Jane, your grandmother has something she wishes to say to you in private. I'll wait outside."

When the door closed, Jane cried, "Megotta, it is Lord de Warenne who wants to handfast me. I have refused him, but I know Father will be furious with me. Thank heaven you have come to support me."

"Jane, I have changed my mind. I want you to get this Lynx de Warenne in your power. If you give him a child, he will make you a countess and you and the child will have greater wealth than you have ever imagined."

Jane was distraught. "Has he threatened you?"

"No, no, child, but your father has already agreed to it and I have no authority over you, so you must take advantage of this opportunity that is being offered to you."

Jane's hope dissolved like snow in summer as the chamber door opened and de Warenne came back into the room. Jane felt as if a hand reached inside her breast and crushed her heart. One by one she gathered her feelings and emotions together, getting them under control, then tucking them away deep inside. With not even her grandmother to support her, she had little choice. Through bloodless lips she murmured, "If my father and you have an agreement, I will honor it, my lord."

Lynx de Warenne felt a deep measure of satisfaction, but he was careful not to gloat over his victory. He bowed formally. "I'll draw up the legal paper for us to sign. You might as well go and get your things."

"Today?" she asked, shocked.

"Yes, today. I see no reason to wait until the morrow."

Lynx prided himself on being a man who faced the unpleasantries of life and put them behind him immediately. But as he watched Jane Leslie depart, he realized bleakly that it would be a damned awkward bedding.

* * *

"Well?" Jane's sisters demanded the moment she opened the door. "We've been waiting here ages!"

"I said *yes.*" Jane spoke as if she were in a trance.

"We know ye said *yes,* ye feckless creature," Kate said impatiently. "What we want to know is *who*?"

"I am to be handfasted to Lord de Warenne."

"Ha, and I'm to be crowned Queen of Scotland!" Kate cried.

"Ye are a little liar!" Mary accused.

Megotta came into the room. "She speaks the truth. Yer father has sold her to the powerful heir to the de Warenne earldom!"

Jane's eyes flooded with tears and she ran to her own tiny chamber so they would not see her cry.

"What would he want with Jane?" Kate asked Megotta blankly.

"She's a Celt and a virgin. Don't ye see it is to humble us all? The English own us and will grind us beneath their heel, dragging our pride through the dirt. Jane has special powers and de Warenne wants to put his brand on her."

"The rumors are true, she is a witch!" Mary concluded, totally ignoring Megotta's words.

"She must have cast a spell on him. Why else would he take her to his bed?" Kate cried enviously.

Her sisters followed her to the tiny chamber where her pallet lay. As Jane lifted two woolen dresses and a cloak from their hooks on the wall and folded them neatly, Mary said, "Now? Ye're moving into the castle? The handfasting is today?"

"Yes, I must hurry."

Mary looked at Kate and without a word they departed

and headed to the castle where the handfasting would take place.

As Jane added her stockings and aprons to the pile, a desperate idea came to her. She bundled up her things and sought out Megotta. "I'm going to run away!"

Her grandmother looked alarmed. "Where will ye go, child?"

Jane didn't have a good answer. Anywhere seemed better than Dumfries Castle at the moment. "I'll hide in Selkirk Forest. There are isolated parts that are said to be a refuge for people who have lost their homes through a dispute with an overlord."

"Jane, you cannot run away. I would be blamed! De Warenne is a hard man. He would punish me severely."

Jane decided to take her grandmother with her, then reluctantly she changed her mind. How could she ask the aging Megotta to give up her home to live in the wild? Just then a knock came on the door, and when Megotta opened it, Taffy loomed on the threshold. "I've come to get my lady's baggage."

"Ye'll no' set foot in my home!" Megotta cried, blocking the squire's entrance.

Jane's heart plummeted. It was too late for her to steal away now, and in any case she had nowhere to go. She knew she would have to obey her father's wishes for the handfasting, but her resolve hardened. When the year and a day were up, she would be free to leave. She would not stay with de Warenne one moment longer. Jane went to the door, her cheeks rosy because of her grandmother's rudeness. "I'll bring you my medicinal box, Taffy. I can manage the rest."

Jane gathered together her small pots of paint and

brushes. She had no touchstones left. She would have to gather more from the seashore where there was an abundance of the smooth, curiously shaped stones. She returned to the door and handed Taffy the medicinal box, which he swung to his shoulder.

"I can carry more, my lady."

Jane glanced down at the things in her arms. "There is no more."

Taffy recalled the times he had staggered beneath Lady Alicia's baggage and in the process lost a little more of his heart to Lady Jane.

Inside the castle, Taffy led the way to the Master Tower and climbed the stone steps to the first two rooms. "These are to be your rooms, Lady Jane; Lord de Warenne's are up above." He swung the wooden box from his shoulder. "I'll be back shortly, my lady."

As Jane stared about the chamber, its luxury intimidated her. Her feet felt rooted to the carpeted floor as her eyes looked their fill. She had been in the great hall many times and earlier today had spoken to the lord in the small room off the hall, but this was the first time she had ever been inside one of the castle's towers where the private chambers were located.

Jane stared at the rich tapestries, the cushioned furnishings, the musical instruments, and the games table with its carved figures set out upon a board. Finally, it was the hearth with its dancing fire that drew her. She stepped close and felt comforted by the heat of the flames. The chamber was so spacious she would never get used to it. Her eyes lifted to the archway with dismay as she realized there was yet another chamber beyond. Jane gathered her courage and went through the arch.

The bed stopped her in her tracks. She had never seen anything like it before. Her own bed had always been a small pallet close to the floor. The bed her brother Ben and Judith slept in was wide enough for two people, but it rested on a wooden frame close to the floor. This bed was vast; and so high off the floor there were wooden steps beside it. Velvet curtains hung from high corner posts and the luxurious material had rings attached so that the curtains could be drawn about the bed to keep out the drafts and envelop those inside in privacy. A forbidden image of herself and Lord de Warenne enclosed inside the intimacy of the bed-curtains made Jane's knees turn to water.

She banished the wicked picture immediately and opened the massive wardrobe. Now she understood why there were no hooks on the wall for clothes; the hooks were inside the wardrobe. Jane hung up her cloak and her two woolen dresses, one black and one gray. She placed her shifts and stockings in a wardrobe drawer and set her painting supplies in another. She turned from the wardrobe and caught her image in a mirror.

She jumped back in alarm, thinking someone was in the room with her. When she realized there was no one there, that it was simply an oval of highly polished silver set in a wooden frame, she stepped closer to examine it. She stared at the female reflected before her and knew she was looking at herself. Jane had never before looked into a mirror, and she found it an unsettling experience. She had seen herself in the forest pool, but that had only shown her a blurred image of herself. The mirror showed her clearly and precisely what she looked like.

Jane caught her breath and touched her fingertips to the polished surface, tracing her brows and her slanting cheekbones. She saw with chagrin that her eyes were almond-shaped and deep brown, exactly like a doe she had seen with her fawn. Her lips were too full, her hair too bright! Why did her hair have to be red; why couldn't she have raven tresses like her sisters? Jane turned from the mirror with a sinking heart.

She heard a knock on the outer door and ran through the arch to open it. Taffy directed a bevy of castle servants. One brought soap and towels, another carried fresh white linen sheets, a young boy carried in a scuttle of coal for the fire, and two men servants carried in a ladies' slipper-shaped bathing tub. Still another servant brought a matching basin and jug, filled with water, and Taffy himself brought her a tray holding watered wine, goblets, and sweetmeats. She watched as fresh torches were placed in the wall brackets, ready for lighting, and a huge square candle in its own brass stand was carried in.

When the servants withdrew, Taffy said, "If there is anything you desire, lady, please tell me. It is my responsibility to plenish your chamber."

Before she could thank him, another knock came at the door. Taffy opened it to find Thomas. "Lord de Warenne has the papers ready—" He stopped in mid-sentence. "She cannot go down looking like that," he said in a low voice.

Taffy bent toward him and murmured, "She has no gowns, no jewels—nothing pretty at all."

Thomas's eyes swept over Jane from head to foot. "Wait here," he ordered Taffy.

Thomas sought Lord de Warenne in the small room off the great hall. Jock Leslie and his eldest son, Andrew,

Dumfries' steward-in-training, were already present as Jane's witnesses to the legal handfasting.

When Lynx looked up from the papers on the table, Thomas said, "The lady has no decent clothes, my lord."

Jock Leslie looked offended. "Until now she has led a simple life."

Lynx bade his squire, "Fetch the lady as she is. Her clothes matter not; her signature is all that counts."

Jane entered the small chamber wearing her brown woolen dress and sturdy leather shoes. She was flanked by the lord's squires, who would act as his witnesses.

Lynx had one moment of misgiving. Thomas was right, she looked exactly like a peasant girl. He executed a formal bow to her. "You have not changed your mind?"

Her lashes flew to her cheeks, trying to mask the fear and outrage she felt. How could she change her mind when he had threatened her grandmother? How could she refuse the handfasting with her father's stern eyes upon her? Being in a small room with five men who would hear her give her pledge was most intimidating. She shot de Warenne a look of pure hatred and shook her head.

Her father gave her the words. They were simple enough. Lynx de Warenne came to her side, took her hand in his, and waited for her pledge.

"I, Jane Leslie, pledge thee my troth in handfast for a year and a day." Her words were clear, without hesitation, surprising even herself, but silently she added: *And not one moment longer!*

"I, Lynx de Warenne, pledge thee my troth in handfast for a year and a day." His deep solemn voice rolled over her, filling the room, dominating the very air they breathed.

In fact, the verbal pledge was enough to make the agreement binding, but Lynx wanted everything to be legal for both their sakes. He was in a position of power, while Jane Leslie had no power at all. If she conceived and aught happened to him before they could wed, Lynx wanted his child to be his legal, ironclad heir, so was leaving nothing to chance.

When Lord de Warenne handed her a quill, Jane was thankful she knew how to sign her name. When she was finished, he took the quill from her hand and signed "Lynx de Warenne" with a bold flourish. Though Jane could not read, she studied his signature intently, so that she would recognize it in the future. She had no idea how she had kept her hand from trembling. So, it is done! she thought wildly. The lynx owns me body and soul for the next year.

When the witnesses added their signatures to the paper, Lynx sanded it and rolled it up. He said to Jock, "We'll have a small celebration in the hall tonight. Thank you all for attending us." Lynx held out his arm in a polite, formal gesture and Jane felt panic rise within her. Where was he taking her? What would he do? It was only afternoon; surely he would wait until nighttime to consummate their union?

Her pulses raced and her heart began to pound as she tried to recall what had happened at her sisters' handfastings. She swallowed with difficulty as she remembered that their husbands hadn't waited five minutes before they had taken them to bed! With great trepidation Jane placed her hand upon Lord de Warenne's arm. As he led her through the hall toward the Master Tower, their thoughts mirrored each other's: *It is done . . . there is no turning back.*

Thomas and Taffy trailed after them, quietly talking in earnest. "The hall will be crowded tonight. Every man jack of them will want a good look at her," Taffy said tight-lipped.

"He pretends indifference to the way she looks, but I know better," Thomas asserted. "Lord de Warenne's pride rivals that of King Edward Plantagenet. We have to do something; dinner is less than two hours away."

"I'll search every wardrobe in Dumfries. Perhaps there is a gown some female discarded," Taffy offered.

"I'll look through my lord's wardrobe and my own," Thomas said. "We'll have to find something for her."

Lynx opened the door to Jane's chambers and swept her inside. It suddenly dawned on him that she had no maid to fetch and carry for her, no female to bathe and dress her. "Would you like your sisters to be with you to serve you?" he asked politely.

Jane's face showed relief at his suggestion, even though it was ridiculous. Kate and Mary would never serve her. She was the youngest and had always served *them.* "Thank you, I would like their company, though I am used to doing for myself."

He frowned. Did she not realize her status had been elevated above that of all other women who had ever lived in Dumfries Castle? "I hope you will be comfortable here. This tower should serve us well. My rooms are above, up these steps, but I needn't disturb you every time I come and go. My chambers open onto the parapet walk and there is another staircase that leads down from there. You will have relative privacy." And so would he, Lynx thought silently. There was no way he would allow this young woman to disrupt his life.

When Lynx saw Thomas hovering at the open door, he welcomed the interruption. "I'll take my bath now, Thomas."

"The servants are bringing Lady Jane's bathwater, my lord."

"Good, I'll take my bath at the same time."

Jane went stiff as she pictured herself naked as they bathed together. She sagged with relief as she saw the two men disappear up the stairs and she realized she had misinterpreted her lord's meaning.

Lynx sat submerged to the hips, his long legs bent at the knee so the tub could accommodate his length. He scrubbed first at the hard calluses on his hands, then at his nails with the luffa.

"Will you wear the green, my lord?" Thomas took the dark velvet tunic from the wardrobe.

Lynx frowned. "It's on the plain side for a festive occasion, don't you think?"

"Even so, it will make you look a peacock beside Lady Jane."

"Ah," Lynx murmured, lathering the soap into his hair. "Has she not even one suitable gown?"

Thomas laid the green tunic on the bed and picked up the bucket of water beside the tub. He dumped it over Lynx unceremoniously. "She has nothing, no bedgowns, no jewels, no ribbons; she doesn't even have a hairbrush.

She uses a currycomb that looks like it came from the stables."

"Then take her some of my brushes and combs for God's sake, until we can remedy the situation. Get cloth from the stores and have some gowns made for her. There must be seamstresses and needlewomen here in the castle or in Dumfries' town, and there must be women who card and weave wool. Ask Jock, he'll know."

"Aye, my lord, but that doesn't solve tonight's dilemma, does it?"

Tonight's dilemma. Thomas didn't know the half of it!

As the squire opened and closed drawers and chests, his eye fell on the cloth jupons that Lord de Warenne wore over his chain mail. The fancy silk ones were reserved for tournaments. Thomas realized that one of these would make a pretty night rail, though it would be open at both sides. He felt his groin harden and grinned, knowing the jupon would more than serve the purpose. His hand hesitated over a black silk one emblazoned with a silver lynx, then moved on to choose a far more suitable plain white silk jupon.

Meanwhile, Taffy didn't have much luck finding discarded gowns. Women were too avaricious to leave their garments behind when they departed. He consulted Sir Giles Bernard, who was the most fashionably dressed knight in his lord's mesne. Sir Giles opened his wardrobe along with his heart when he heard of Lady Jane's plight. Giles selected a deep purple calf-length tunic. On Jane it would fall to her ankles. He generously added a heavy silver chain for her to use as a belt.

Because there was not one yard of ribbon to be found in all of Dumfries, Taffy went out into the castle garden to get flowers for Jane's hair. He cut a hawthorn branch covered with blossoms, dethorned it with his knife, and fashioned it into a small crown. As he headed toward the Master Tower, he was relieved to see that Jane's sisters had come to help her dress for the celebration.

10

Jane was thankful that her favorite sister-in-law, Judith Leslie, accompanied Mary and Kate when they came to her new chambers. Her sisters kept telling her how lucky she was to have Lord de Warenne choose her for a mate, but as Judith helped her into the huge tub, she looked into Jane's eyes with gentle concern. "Are you afraid?"

Jane sank down in the warm water. She was about to deny her fear vigorously, but Judith's soft words brought a truthful response from her lips. "Yes, I'm afraid . . . I don't know what to expect from him."

Kate laughed suggestively. "Expect the worst."

"That way, you won't be disappointed," Mary added.

Judith chided them both. "Jane has no experience with men. She needs our advice, not dire warnings!"

"Just keep your mouth shut and your legs open," Kate advised. "Men don't want conversation, they want action."

"The bigger the man, the bigger the appetite, if you know what I mean," Mary informed her, holding her hands apart to show her the size of his parts. "They don't call it a *yard* for nothing!"

Kate laughed at Mary's rude gesture.

"They are just teasing you, Jane, take no notice of them," Judith urged.

"Oh, I know they are enjoying themselves at my expense."

Kate stopped laughing. "All right, then, here's some real advice. Don't cry, no matter how much he hurts you. Men hate tears."

"It's time to get dressed, Jane. Step out of the water." Judith held up a big towel.

"No, I'm going to drown myself," Jane said, only half jesting.

"Stop feeling sorry for yerself; every other woman in Dumfries would sell her soul to be handfasted to Lord de Warenne," Mary informed her.

"She's right," Judith admitted. "It's a blessing, not a curse. Try to please him and obey him in all things and everything will go well for you, Jane."

When she was dressed, Judith brushed Jane's hair until it fell brilliantly to her hips. Against the purple velvet of the plain-cut tunic, her hair was a lovely red-gold.

When Lynx de Warenne came to escort her to the hall he stared in surprise at the transformation that had taken place. Instead of a peasant girl he found a beautiful young woman in her place. He was impressed by his squires' efforts on behalf of his lady. The simple wreath of flowers crowning her glorious red hair was more exquisite than costly jewels. She looked more desirable to him than any woman he had seen in a long time.

As they entered the noisy hall filled with his men and all the people of Dumfries Castle, including the entire family of Leslies, Jane gripped his arm so tightly, he knew immediately she was terrified. Unlike most women she seemed to dread being the center of attention.

"I'm sorry, Jane. Everyone is curious about us. Once they've had a good look at you, I'm sure the novelty will wear off." He put his hand over hers and squeezed his encouragement. Up on the dais Lynx held up his hands for silence. His speech was short and sweet in deference to her shyness. "I present the Lady Jane. Please join me in a toast to welcome and honor her." Lynx raised his goblet and everyone in the hall toasted Jane.

A thunderous cheer followed by applause rolled around the hall. Jane lowered her eyes. She did not dare look up at the sea of men before her, nor raise her eyes to acknowledge her family. Neither did she dare steal a glance at Lord de Warenne. But she was acutely aware of him. When they were seated, his chair was elevated higher than hers as befitted his station, and his two squires stood behind their chairs to serve them.

"It is customary for you to acknowledge the toast."

Her lashes flew up, she stared at him for a moment, then picked up her goblet of wine and drained it.

Lynx quirked an eyebrow in amusement. "A simple 'thank you' would have been a more appropriate response for a lady."

The wine brought instant heat to her cheeks. It felt as if a bright red rose unfurled in her breast and brought her a small measure of recklessness. "If you had wanted a lady, my lord, you should not have chosen *me.*"

"Are you deliberately trying to goad me, *chérie*?"

Thomas refilled her goblet and Jane eyed the wine uncertainly. Seeing her speculative glance, Lynx recalled the time she had deliberately spilled hot soup on him. Before she could reach for the goblet, he took her hand and gave her a warning glance.

Jane read his thoughts and the corners of her mouth lifted in amusement. "Have no fear, the wine is too good to waste on you." She pulled her hand from his as if his touch offended her.

"Insolence will soon make me tire of you," he said silkily.

"I am relieved it won't take a year and a day."

Lynx masked his own amusement. Her wit was unexpected and it secretly delighted him. He enjoyed sparring with her. It was infinitely preferable to the fear she had displayed at first.

Jane usually had a good appetite and the food placed before her looked and smelled delicious, but her throat felt tight and she knew she would not be able to swallow one bite with everyone's eyes upon her.

Lynx watched her toy with her food. It annoyed him. Why did women eat like birds, starving themselves for vanity's sake? His sister, Jory, was the only woman he knew who relished her food and there were few men breathing who didn't find her attractive.

Welsh harpers strolled about the hall, providing music while everyone dined. When the meal was almost done, a balladeer stepped to the center of the hall and sang an epic love tale, set to music. Jane had never felt so uncomfortable in her life. Her cheeks flamed with fire, while her hands turned to ice. Her feet were extremely cold as well, for she had come down in her stocking feet. Her sturdy leather shoes had seemed inappropriate with the elegant tunic, and she posessed no slippers. From the tail of her eye she saw Lord de Warenne beckon Thomas, though she could not hear what he said.

"Christ, no more soulful love songs. Summon a piper and let's have something Scottish and lively."

Everyone in the castle seemed to be enjoying themselves except Jane. She felt as if every eye watched her with speculation as the hour grew later. She looked over at the long table where her family sat. Megotta was not there, but her brothers and sisters were having the time of their lives. Jane wished she was sitting with her brothers instead of here on the dais beside the sharp-eyed de Warenne.

Lynx followed her glance. "Your brothers seem to be enjoying themselves."

Does he disapprove of their behavior also? she wondered with pique. She lifted her chin. "They love to laugh; they are very witty. You don't seem to have much humor . . . or wit. Perhaps you are witless?" Jane was aghast at her own daring.

His eyes narrowed. "You enjoy pricking me with your words. Soon it will be my turn to do the pricking."

Jane stiffened with fear and rose to flee. His hand shot out to grasp her wrist and he forced her to sit. "You will not rush from my side before my men. You haven't the faintest idea how a lady should act. You will be gracious. Smile at me. At least have the courtesy to pretend you are happy to be handfasted to me."

"Pretense is exactly what it is." As the pressure on her wrist increased, Jane smiled. But through her teeth she said, "I hate you, I hope I am barren!"

Lynx de Warenne was on his feet instantly. He swung her up into his arms and raised his voice. "Stay where you are and enjoy yourselves. Our steward will keep the wine flowing.'' A great cheer went up when they saw the lord would carry his woman from the hall.

Taffy stepped close to Lynx de Warenne and murmured, ''Your lady is very young, my lord.''

Lynx was startled. Surely the young devil didn't fear for her? He ignored the remark and strode from the hall. His two squires followed him while the rest of his men took out their dice or challenged each other to wrestling matches. He felt Jane clutching his shoulder and glanced down at her. Her face was whiter than the hawthorn blossoms in her hair.

Lynx carried her up the steps to the first level of the Master Tower and opened her chamber door. Incredulously, he heard Thomas's voice in his ear. ''She is extremely innocent, my lord.''

He slipped inside and set her feet to the carpet, then Lynx turned to confront his squires. ''Christ, do the pair of you think to tutor me?'' Then he firmly closed the door in their faces.

Now that Jane was alone with him, all her bravado fled. ''My lord, I'm sorry, I didn't mean what I said. It was just a game to see who could make the cruelest remark.''

Lynx saw the fear in her eyes. Eyes that were the lovely soft brown of a doe. The last thing he wanted her to feel was trapped. His face softened as he looked down at her. ''Do you think we can begin again? It was an ordeal for you tonight with every eye upon you. Let's both forget the things we said to each other.''

''Yes, that would be best,'' she murmured.

Lynx stood awkwardly, wondering exactly how to go about the business of impregnating her. It was a unique situation, one that he had certainly never encountered before. If the female he was with had been a whore, she would know exactly how to go about the task, with encouragement from him. If the female he was bent on seducing had been a lady, she would expect and welcome his advances the moment the chamber door closed.

His mind went back to his wedding night, seeking clues. That deflowering had gone easily enough, Lynx recalled. Lady Sylvia Bigod had clung to him avidly and the clinging had gone on for five years. He reminded himself that this situation was completely different and banished all thoughts of his late wife. Lynx decided that at all costs he must remain polite; he could not allow things to degenerate into another battle of words. "Did you enjoy the music, my lady?" he inquired courteously.

Knowing how easily her tongue got carried away when she was nervous, Jane decided to speak as little as possible. She stood hesitantly, gazing across the chamber at the fire. "Yes, my lord."

Silence descended.

Lynx advanced into the chamber, spied a stringed lute on the wall, and again asked politely, "Do you play?"

Jane's lashes flew up. Was he asking her to play some sort of mating game? When she saw he was looking at a musical instrument she replied, "No, my lord."

Again there was silence.

Lynx took a few more steps into the room, noting that Jane remained just inside the door, exactly where he had deposited her. His glance fell on the games table with its carved pieces. "Do you play chess, my lady?" Was that a desperate note he detected in his own voice?

"No, my lord." She could have bitten off her tongue

the moment she said it. If they played a board game, it would postpone the consummation.

He watched her gaze return longingly to the fire. "Are you cold?"

"No . . . yes . . . no, my lord."

Lynx laughed and immediately felt better. "Well, which is it?"

"My feet are cold," Jane blurted out.

Lynx laughed again. Cold feet was something they had in common! He held out a hand. "Come and be warm." He watched her come forward slowly and pulled a cushioned chair closer to the fire. She sat down primly with folded hands and lowered lashes. Lynx sank to his knees, folded back the hem of the velvet tunic, and saw that she wore no shoes.

He bit back a surprised comment as he realized she had no slippers. Instead, he took Jane's foot in his big hands and began to massage it. It was indeed icy to the touch, yet her cheeks flamed. He massaged the other foot, watching her breathing become agitated.

His hands were unbelievably strong and warm. As he rubbed her stockinged foot, she felt his heat begin to seep into her. It felt wonderful, but his closeness took away her breath. As her breasts rose and fell, she saw his eyes upon them. Her nipples peaked of their own volition and she feared he would soon have her naked.

"Are you afraid of me, my lady?" he inquired, still using the formal, polite tone.

"No . . . yes . . . no, my lord."

This time he forced himself not to laugh. "Well, which is it?"

"I don't know, my lord," she murmured, fingering the soft velvet of the tunic she wore.

Lynx knew he would have to breach the barrier of formality that existed between them. "Jane," he deliberately used her name, "let's try to be comfortable with each other. All of this formality is getting us nowhere." He rose to his feet and moved across the chamber to pour them wine. He saw immediately from its pale color that it was only watered wine, too diluted to warm the blood. Lynx headed for the stairs that led up to his own chambers. "I'll get us some wine."

While Lynx was upstairs he took the opportunity to divest himself of his clothes. He shrugged into his black velvet bedrobe to cover his nakedness and took up a flagon of wine. He hoped one would be enough. Lynx also hoped Jane would take the opportunity to undress and put on her own bedrobe, but when he came down the stairs, he found her exactly as he had left her.

As he poured them each a goblet of the red wine, he realized she wasn't going to make it easy for him. The onus rested squarely on him. Perhaps she wasn't simply innocent, perhaps she was woefully ignorant on top of everything else. He took the wine to the fire and handed her the goblet. He watched her covertly as she tentatively took a sip. It was obvious she had as little experience with wine as she had with men. It appeared he would have to teach her everything.

"Like this. Take a mouthful and roll it about your tongue to savor the taste." He swallowed and watched as she imitated him. She repeated the action, then quaffed deeply, half draining the cup. Her eyes became bright as an idea suddenly occurred to her. She must ask him to teach her how to play chess. She would keep filling his goblet until he passed out, as she had seen her brothers do upon festive occasions.

"Now I'm hot," she announced.

Lynx nodded. "The wine warms your blood from the inside, just as the fire warms you from the outside."

She rose and moved away from the fire. "Would you teach me how to play chess, my lord?"

He realized that she was avoiding the intimacy that must inevitably happen between them, and reluctantly decided to give her a little more time. "You cannot learn an intricate game like chess in one night, but we can begin the first lesson." Lynx de Warenne curbed the impatience that had started to build inside him. He wanted to give her a lesson all right, but it had nothing to do with chess.

They sat down facing each other with the small games table between them. The chess pieces were tall and beautifully carved from ivory. He picked one up and handed it to her. Their fingers touched and she drew away as if he had burned her. "That is the king, the most important piece on the board. He outranks everyone."

As she gazed down at the tall figure in her hand, she realized he could be speaking of his own position here at Dumfries.

"Each player has sixteen pieces to move; eight principal pieces consisting of a king, queen, two bishops, two knights, and two—"

"Castles," Jane said, reaching out a finger to trace the carved turrets.

"The castles are called rooks. The other eight pieces are pawns."

That is what I am, a pawn! Nervously, she rolled the king between her palms.

As Lynx watched her hands manipulate the king, he felt himself growing hard. He cleared his throat. "You win by, er, *checkmating* your opponent's king." He picked up his goblet and drained its contents.

"Let me get you more wine, my lord," Jane said breathlessly.

"Thank you." Lynx reached over and removed the tall king her fingers were playing with before he became further aroused. As he gazed across at her, the chess lesson forgotten, he knew he needed some answers before he proceeded, and the questions could not be formal and polite; they could only be blunt.

"Jane, do you know what happens between a male and a female?"

"Yes. I have seen the animals."

"Animals?" he echoed.

"I have seen the animals mate."

Splendor of God, was she talking about a rutting ram or a rampant stallion? There were times, he admitted, when the sex act *was* like that between a man and a woman, if you were lucky, but it certainly wasn't what he had in mind for tonight. He passed a hand over his eyes, needing a moment to collect his thoughts. "Go and put on your bedgown, then we'll talk."

Jane looked at his goblet and wished he would drain it again. How much wine would it take to make him fall asleep? He was less formal and stiffly polite than he had been. Perhaps she had made a mistake. Perhaps the wine would induce him to carry out the consummation sooner rather than later. Already his attitude was far less proper.

Needing to put some distance between them, Jane went into the bedchamber.

She looked at the white silk jupon lying across her pillow. This must be what he'd meant by bedgown, but she didn't know how she was ever going to let him see her in such a scandalous garment. Jane tried to swallow her dismay. She had made her pledge to give herself to the lynx and if the silk garment was what she was expected to wear as his lady, then she had little choice. She ignored a tiny voice from within that told her she had never worn anything as fine as silk. Would it feel as beautiful as it looked?

She removed the wreath of flowers from her head, unfastened the heavy silver chain, and lifted off the purple velvet tunic. She quickly slipped the white silk jupon over her head to cover her naked breasts and pulled it down over her bare bottom. Timidly, she glanced into the mirror. The dark woolen stockings could be seen through the side slits in the jupon and they looked hideous!

Jane's hopes plummeted. She did not want to look hideous in the eyes of this arrogant, powerful lord; Jane desperately wanted to look attractive for some strange reason she could not fathom. She peeled the woolen stockings from her legs, folded them on top of the velvet tunic, and picked up the wreath. The hawthorn blossoms looked wilted, but Jane dutifully fitted it back onto the crown of her hair. She stood for a moment, loathe to leave the privacy of the bedchamber, until her eyes fell on the high, wide bed. It represented such a threat to her, she knew she must put as much distance as she could between the bed and herself.

Lynx stared in disbelief as the small figure appeared in

the archway. What in the name of God was the girl wearing? If he wasn't mistaken, it was one of his silk jupons. It was then that it dawned on him she had no bedgown and this must be the handiwork of Thomas, trying to improvise.

His mouth went dry as she walked across the room toward him. As she passed in front of the fire, her body was outlined through the fine silk, displaying her long legs and her lush breasts. Lynx picked up his wine and drained it, then he handed Jane her half-empty goblet and watched her do the same. Lord have mercy upon him; how would he curb the rampant desire he was feeling?

Lynx de Warenne rose to his feet, looming above her, dwarfing her. "Jane, do you know what a man looks like; how he is fashioned?"

"Not a naked man, my lord." Suddenly, inexplicably she was wildly curious.

He took a deep breath. "Then it is high time that you learned." He sat down in the chair and lifted her onto his lap.

Jane sat perched on his knees, which were covered by his black velvet bedrobe. She looked at him expectantly, both dreading and desiring him to make the first move. He removed the wreath from her head and combed his fingers through her long, red hair. When he brought a handful to his face to inhale its scent, she gasped, expecting his tongue to come out and lick her cheek as the lynx had done in the forest. When it did not happen, she gazed into his green eyes, then dropped her gaze to his beautiful mouth. Surely that was relief she felt, not longing.

As Jane sat unmoving, Lynx prompted, "Are you not curious?"

"Yes, my lord," she admitted innocently.

"Then I suggest you explore me."

She looked into his eyes to see if he meant it. He did. Slowly, her hand came up to his chest to peel back the black velvet. His chest was covered by a thick pelt as tawny as his long mane of hair. Jane wondered if he realized the startling contrast the black velvet made against his bronzed skin and tawny hair, and suddenly, she knew that he did. That was why he had deliberately chosen it.

Delicately, she raised her bottom and pulled the bedrobe from beneath her. He was now divided in half down the center of his body. One half was soft black velvet, the other smooth bronze skin. One half was soberly clothed, the other blatantly bared. Yet even more startling was the feel of his thigh beneath her bottom, with only the thin layer of silk separating their naked flesh.

She tried to fight the feeling of excitement that rose up inside her, but it was so strong she felt as if she were being carried along on a tidal wave. As her fingers unerringly reached to lift the other half of his robe, Lynx once more began to harden. She looked down with wide-eyed curiosity as his shaft became fully erect.

Jane knew enough about male animals to know this happened before they mated, but his size surprised her. "Do all men grow this big?" she asked in wonder.

Lynx felt his balls tighten. He had never considered the question. "More or less, I suppose."

A ghost of a dimple appeared beside her mouth, then it vanished. "I think *more,* rather than *less,* my lord."

Lynx shrugged out of the bedrobe. "Are you warm enough now?"

"Oh yes; actually I'm overheated," she admitted breathlessly.

His shaft pulsed and he cautioned himself to go slow. Lynx took her hand and brought it to his groin. After a moment he placed her fingers around his cock and moved them slowly up and down. "Rapid movement creates friction," he explained swallowing hard. "And both of our bodies produce a natural lubrication to ease entrance into your—" he caught back the word he was going to use and substituted, "body."

As she listened solemnly, it pleased him greatly that he detected neither repulsion nor dread for the physical act he was leading up to. He wondered briefly if she really was virgin. He swallowed the question; there was a surer way of discovering if she was untouched than asking. Some women were consummate liars.

Lynx slipped his hand into the open side of the silk jupon to touch her hip, then moved it down between her legs. When he came into contact with the soft curls covering her mons he said, "Open for me, Jane."

No! *Never*! her mind cried, but slowly, sensually, her thighs yielded to his questing hand.

He saw her blush as she opened for him and heard her gasp as he slid a finger up inside her. She was unbelievably small and tight, unquestionably virgin, and for her sake Lynx almost wished it were otherwise. With his other hand he stroked her beautiful hair. "Jane, you do realize there will be pain the first time?"

"When you mount me, yes."

Lynx felt his phallus jerk, then he felt Jane contract on his finger and his cock reacted shamelessly. "I'll try not to hurt you," he said hoarsely. "I'll try to be gentle."

Jane could not recall ever having seen a gentle mating. The male ravaged; the female submitted.

"Do you feel my finger?"

"Oh yes," she murmured breathlessly.

"Does it hurt?"

"No, my lord."

"Your sheath is very tight—it will have to stretch to accommodate me. It will be infinitely easier on you if you do not resist me," he cautioned. "Will you cooperate, Jane?"

She licked dry lips and whispered, "I'll try, my lord."

He withdrew his finger from her tight sheath and brushed aside the front panel of silk so that she was exposed from the waist down. The sight of her red-gold curls made his cock jut straight up. With his hands on her waist, Lynx lifted her. "Straddle me," he whispered.

As Jane opened her thighs and slid her knees on either side of his hips, Lynx forgot all about the handfasting being a business arrangement. He was hell-bent on seduction as desire and longing rose up savagely to claim her virginity.

Lynx positioned the tip of his phallus on her pink cleft, held her eyes with his, then slowly surged up inside her. He stopped when he gauged he was a little less than halfway inside her, to allow her to get used to the new sensation. His hands stroked her back, coaxing her lovely young body to yield to him fully.

Jane was surprised that she felt no pain. She felt full of him, full to bursting, but it did not really hurt. She wanted to scream, but it was from excitement at what the lynx was doing to her.

"Take a deep breath; try to relax," he murmured.

She thought she might drown in the depths of his green eyes.

His hands slid down from her waist to grasp her hips. Then he drew her down swiftly and firmly while at the same time he thrust upward ruthlessly, piercing the impediment that guarded her innocence.

A cry tore from Jane's throat before she could swallow it.

Lynx pulled her against him. "Hush, it's done," he soothed. He could not bear the thought of hurting her further and reluctantly decided to withdraw for a moment. Stroking her hair with his big hand, he gently lifted her off his lethal weapon. The white silk garment she wore was now stained with bright drops of blood.

He gave her a minute to recover. "You were very brave. How do you feel?"

"Tender . . . I ache a little. Do you hurt, my lord?"

"Nay." He was touched at her concern for him. "Well, perhaps I ache a little too."

She slipped her small hand down to rub his shaft and Lynx almost came out of his skin.

"I thought it would take much longer," she confided, wishing it had not ended so soon.

It dawned on him that she was still in ignorance. "We haven't completed coitus yet." By the look she gave him he knew that she did not understand his meaning, so he added, "I think we'll be far more comfortable in bed."

Lynx set her feet to the floor and took her hand to lead the way. At the archway, in full view of the bed, he felt Jane's slight hesitation. Overruling her reluctance, he picked her up and carried her the rest of the way.

Jane was secretly pleased that he gave her no choice. The high, wide bed was an experience she longed to sample, but the contemplation of such a thing overwhelmed her. Now it was about to happen, the knowledge that the lynx would share the intimacy of the bed, lying beside her naked, sent a thrill running through her that she could hardly contain. When he pulled down the cover and slipped her onto the snowy sheet, Jane almost screamed with excitement. Her eyes swept over his naked splendor as he stood poised, then she watched him climb onto the bed and stretch his length beside her.

Lynx made no effort to cover them, but rolled toward Jane, resting on one elbow. "Do you still ache?" he asked with concern.

Jane nodded, unable to speak because of his closeness. He had not yet touched her, but she knew he was going to and all her senses were heightened. She held her breath as he reached out his hand and slipped it beneath the silk jupon. When he touched her mons a great shudder ran through her body. Then his big hand covered her pubic bone, cupping her and pressing down firmly. The heat from his touch seeped into her body.

"Breathe, Jane," he murmured, and with a great gasp she took in air then let it out along with all her body's stiff resistance. She had never been aware of her mons before tonight, now it felt sensitive, warm, alive. The heat and pressure of his powerful hand was so delicious she felt as if her core were melting. Jane didn't think anything could feel more exquisite. She was wrong. When he began to rub the heel of his hand slowly across her pubic bone, she closed her eyes and moaned softly with pure pleasure. When she opened her eyes she saw that Lynx had grown fully erect in a heartbeat.

For her sake, Lynx didn't wish to draw it out this first time. There was no need to tamp down his desire to make it last. His knowing hands had worked their magic so that Jane was not in great discomfort, but she could be by the time he was done. It would be unkind to spend an hour arousing her body, then leave her unsatisfied. He doubted it was possible for a virgin to be orgasmic her first time.

Purposely leaving her breasts covered by the silk, he played with them through the sleek, slippery material. He rose up on his knees, straddling her thighs, then reached down to position his jutting erection against her cleft. To tear her hymen, Lynx had used a brutal thrust, this time, however, he entered her with care. He pushed inside her gently, an inch at a time, until he was seated to the hilt, then he forced himself to remain still so that she might get used to the fullness. Lynx had never experienced a woman so tight and scalding hot in his life. When he began to move, he knew it would not take many thrusts before he spent.

When Lynx covered her, Jane put her hands up against his chest in a defensive gesture, but she realized immediately she might as well push against the stone walls of the castle. As he slid slowly into her, she held her breath, afraid he would stretch her beyond her endurance. When at last he stopped and held himself motionless, she was shocked at how much she enjoyed the feel of him inside her. Jane took a deep breath and yielded herself to him, welcoming his great power.

Knowing she held Lord de Warenne inside her filled

her with awe. His massive chest brushed against her cheek and she could hear the thud of his heart. Then he began to move against her and she was enveloped in his male scent. Jane felt empowered. Lynx de Warenne was the most magnificent man she had ever encountered and he had chosen her for his mate. It gave her a new feeling of confidence. Suddenly, she felt him stiffen, heard him gasp, then his body arched as his white-hot seed poured into her.

It was the most cataclysmic thing that had ever happened to her, and yet she yearned for more. She gazed hungrily at his mouth, longing for him to lick her from neck to knees. She wanted to put her mouth on his body and learn the taste of it. Her breasts and belly and lips ached and quivered for his touch. It took a long time for the fire in her blood to cool. Because of the strangeness of the bed and because she was unused to lying with another, it was a long time before Jane slept. But she did drift off to the edge of sleep, where thoughts became entangled with wishes and dreams. How strange that he had not kissed her. The corners of her mouth lifted. It was just as well. If his lips had touched hers, she would have devoured him.

Lynx lay on his back, his arms crossed above his head. Jane Leslie was unbelievably desirable. He was well content with the choice he had made, though he chided himself for letting passion rule the night. He had thought it would be so easy to keep a formal distance between them and not allow his emotions to become involved. He had promised her the handfasting would be a simple business arrangement, but already he had stepped over the bounds.

From now on he vowed to have better control over himself.

When he was certain she slept, he dropped a kiss on the top of her head, swung his long legs to the floor, then climbed to his own chambers to sleep in his own bed.

11

In Carlisle, Jory and Robert Bruce did not have the luxury of a bed. The lovers wished to keep their liaison a secret and as a result had to ride out from Carlisle Castle for their tryst. Long hours of keeping their eyes and hands from each other made their desire mount to such a peak, they could think of nothing but making love.

Jory kept her late afternoon appointment with a Carlisle dressmaker, but afterward she did not return to the castle. Instead, she rode out through the gates of the town to a prearranged meeting place with Robert. It was the mystical time of twilight when he spotted her, but he did not draw rein. Instead he galloped by with a wild whoop, challenging her to catch him.

Jory loved a dare, and soon she was neck and neck with him. "Where are we going, you devil?"

His grin flashed. "There's something I want you to see."

The long grass covered their horses up to their hocks, while a lone kestrel flew overhead toward his roost for the night. Suddenly they rode over a ridge and there before them stood a stone turret, twenty feet high. Robert reined in, dismounted and came to lift Jory from her saddle.

"What is it?"

"A lookout post built by the Romans one thousand years ago."

As she came down into his arms, her lovely gilt hair brushed his face, causing him to shudder with longing. He kissed her deeply, tasting her, inhaling her unique scent, groaning as she pressed her breasts close and kissed him back with sensual abandon.

Robert slipped a possessive arm about her and drew her close against his side. His other hand swept out dramatically. "This is Hadrian's Wall. It was the first thing ever to separate England and Scotland."

"It was built to separate the civilized *English* from the barbarian *Scots,*" Jory teased. "And rightly so, you are still wildmen!"

"Only some of us," he said, bending low to nip her ear with his teeth. "But you are right, Jory. They built it to guard the boundary between the Civilized World and the Outer Darkness beyond."

Her eyes swept from the sandstone masonry of the tower to where his finger pointed, and saw the long wall with its dragon back snaking across the landscape.

"Come," he urged. "Come into my country. I want to make love to you in the land I intend to rule!" Robert Bruce helped Jory climb to the top of the once turreted and castellated wall and dropped to the other side. Then he held up his arms, and without hesitation, Jory sprang down to him. "Look at these things," he urged.

She peered closely in the twilight and saw the symbols of phalluses carved into the stone. "They come in a glorious variety," she marveled.

Robert laughed. "Superstition—to fend off the evil

eye. You can have your pick of small or large, curved or straight; some are even bewinged, or have bells tied to them."

"You know which I pick," Jory mumured, moving against him playfully.

"Did you say prick?" he teased, pressing his hardness into her soft belly.

"Oh, yes please," she whispered breathlessly.

They slipped up inside the turret where Robert spread his cloak over the ancient stones, then stripped off his clothes. Jory resisted removing her own garments so that they could both indulge in the pleasure of his undressing her. As he uncovered her, inch by delicious inch, his lips worshiped her. Then his tongue licked her from neck to knees until her cries were carried on the wind across the rugged terrain of the wild border country.

It was two full hours before they allowed each other to dress. Both knew they must take what they wanted while they were together. They only had tonight. As they wrapped their cloaks about themselves and untethered their horses, Jory knew a moment of apprehension for him.

"Would you betray King Edward?"

He lifted her chin. "Would he betray me?"

"Without a moment's hesitation," she said softly. "I fear for you, Robert."

• "You think me reckless, but in this I am a canny Scot. My grandfather, Robert Bruce, did all in his power to become rightful King of Scotland. When he died, unsuccessful, it was my father's turn. He spent his life trying to accomplish the same goal, and he too was unsuccessful. Now it is my turn. Our motto has become: 'If at first you don't succeed, try, try again.' Jory, I shall become King of Scotland, one way or another. Perhaps it will be as simple as outliving Edward Plantagenet. He grows old. His son is a weakling who will never be able to hold this land, even if his father wins it for him."

Her moment of apprehension passed. If any man could do it, Robert Bruce could. Before they arrived back at the castle, he kissed her good-bye. She clung for one brief second, then bade him Godspeed until they could meet again.

The ladies of Carlisle Castle were gathered in Lady Bruce's solar when Jory joined them.

"You've never been at the dressmakers until this hour," Alice Bolton accused.

"Nay, afterward I paid a visit to an astrologer to have my future foretold."

"And what are you going to be when you grow up?" Alicia asked acidly.

"Fair of face, irresistible to men, sweet and kind of nature."

"You are already that!" Fourteen-year-old Elizabeth de Burgh giggled. She had come from Ireland with her father, the Earl of Ulster, and had been left in the care of Lady Marjory Bruce at Carlisle, with her two Irish serving women, Maggie and Molly, who shadowed her every waking moment. Elizabeth, who found the older and sophisticated Jory absolutely fascinating, had already lost her heart to Robert Bruce and was inordinately homesick for Ireland. Jory had immediately befriended the young girl and they had become allies against Alicia, who had little patience with a child of fourteen.

Lady Bruce poured a goblet of wine for Jory, her goddaughter. "You look frozen. Come and be warm by the fire. Alicia has been entertaining us with the tale of how she met your brother, Lynx."

"It's very romantic." Elizabeth de Burgh sighed.

Jory blinked. Her brother was the least romantic man she knew. "If you like romance, you should hear Lady Marjory's story."

"Oh, you don't want to hear that old tale again," Lady Marjory demurred.

"Yes we do; let me tell the legend," Jory insisted. "She was the very beautiful and very young, widowed Countess of Carrick when she encountered the handsome Robert Bruce hunting on her estates. She fell in love with him at a glance and instructed her men to abduct him. They weren't seen again in public until they were man and wife!"

"Now for the truth," said Lady Marjory, blushing prettily in spite of her years. "We did fall in love, violently I might add, but I was a ward of King Alexander of Scotland. Robert knew the king wouldn't allow us to marry, for that would make Robert the Earl of Carrick. So he kidnapped me and forced me to wed him. To save his neck I put the tale about that it was *I* who abducted *him.*" Lady Bruce looked at Jory. "The Bruce men have always been wild devils; 'tis folly to underestimate them."

Jory realized that she and Robert might be fooling the others, but her godmother was far too shrewd to have the wool pulled over her eyes for long. It tore at her heart that Robert was leaving, but it was probably best for the present.

Though Jory was an irresistible lure, she was not the

main reason why Robert Bruce had come to Carlisle. He needed to learn where his enemies lay and had decided to set a trap, using as bait a baggage train of supplies that he dispatched from Carlisle along the main route of the western marches to Ayr and Glasgow. Galloway was ever a hotbed of unrest, always in need of arms and provisions, and Bruce needed to know just where, along the route, the wagons and packhorses would be raided.

When Jane Leslie awoke she found herself alone and wondered just when Lord de Warenne had quit the bed. She slipped her hand into the neck of the silk jupon and lifted the talisman from where it lay in the valley of her breasts. As she gazed down into the green eyes, much to her surprise she realized that she had enjoyed making love with Lynx and she felt disappointed that he was gone this morning.

Impatiently, she swept back her disheveled hair, feeling angry with herself for getting emotionally involved with him. The only reason he wanted her was for the heir she might produce for him. On top of everything else, he was an Englishman, not a Celt. Images of last night, when their bodies had been one, came flooding back to her. In the cold light of morning she was ashamed at how wantonly she had responded to him. She reminded herself that she did not want to belong to any man, least of all an Englishman!

When a low tap came upon the outer door, Jane felt panic rise up. She scrambled from the bed, saw the crimson spots of blood on her night rail, and grabbed Lynx's black velvet bedrobe from the chair where he'd left it.

When she wrapped it about herself, his scent enveloped her, angering yet exciting her at the same time.

It was Taffy with her breakfast, and behind him were servants carrying her bathwater. She was too shy to ask him where Lynx was, but the squire answered her question without knowing it.

"My lord has arranged for the sewing women to make you some new garments. They await your pleasure in the solar, my lady. Lord de Warenne is with the messenger from the king who rode in early and will not be able to take breakfast with you this morning."

"Thank you, Taffy," she murmured, then looked up with dismay as her sisters, Mary and Kate, entered her chamber without knocking. When the squire withdrew, her sisters exchanged sly glances. "We came to see if you survived last night," Mary announced.

"I survived very well, thank you," Jane asserted.

"I'm surprised ye can even walk this morning," Kate said avidly.

"Is his appetite as big as his yard?" Mary probed.

When Jane didn't answer them, Kate scoffed, "There's no way Plain Jane could satisfy the lord's appetite. I'll wager he left her bed in disgust when all he got was tears."

Mary took a handful of the black velvet Jane held about her. "Is this his robe?" She rubbed the luxurious material between her fingers with envy. When Kate also reached over to feel it, the robe fell away to reveal the white silk marked with the blood of Jane's virginity.

"Well, well, it looks like he took her cherry good and proper," Mary said, unable to disguise the envy she felt.

"She'll be too fine to associate with the likes of us, now," Kate accused.

"That's not true!" Jane protested.

"Good, then we'll join ye for breakfast," Mary decided, helping herself to the food Taffy had had especially prepared for his lord's new lady. Kate joined her, pointing out the disadvantages of belonging to de Warenne. "You do realize your life will be completely different from now on? You'll have no more freedom to run wild about the forest playing with animals. And a Norman will never allow you to dabble in Celtic mysticism. He'll put a stop to that nonsense immediately!"

Mary added spitefully, "If you do produce an heir for him and he marries you, think of all the wifely obligations you will be burdened with. The rigid formality of being the wife of such an important lord will curb your freedom day and night. I pity you, Jane."

Jane looked at her breakfast tray and saw that every last tasty morsel had been devoured. "Would you like my bath, too?" she challenged.

"No thanks, it's gone cold!" Kate said with glee as she and her sister decided they'd lingered long enough where they had no right to be.

As Jane sank down into the tepid water, her sisters' comments made her wish that Lynx de Warenne would leave Dumfries and never return. Then Taffy's words took on significance. If a messenger had come from the king, Lynx might be leaving her. She lifted her touchstone. Perhaps if she wished hard enough, he would leave and never come back. As she held the talisman in her hand, his powerful image crystallized and became clear. Suddenly she felt comforted. Lord de Warenne *was* going to leave

Dumfries; she would be free of him soon. But will he return? she wondered wildly.

Lynx de Warenne reread the message incredulously. How was it possible that such chaos had broken out among his Welsh archers when he had scarcely been gone a fortnight? The king's order was writ plain. He was to return immediately and bring his men under control. His Welsh were actually threatening to join the Scots, and King Edward was in a fine rage.

When Lynx read the missive from his uncle, John de Warenne, he cursed foully and realized he should never have placed his men under the command of his cousin, Fitz-Waren. They had sustained so many losses that they were refusing to obey Fitz-Waren's orders and had threatened to join the enemy!

Lynx summoned the steward of Dumfries. "I am recalled to the front lines, Jock, and only God or the devil knows how long the fighting will last. I can leave only a token force here to defend Dumfries, but you are close to Lochmaben and must send to the Bruce if danger threatens."

"Will you return here, Lord de Warenne?"

"Unless I am killed in battle, I pledge to you that I shall return. Likely it will not be until we have captured Baliol and the Scots acknowledge Edward Plantagenet as king."

"Well, let's hope ye get the job done before winter sets in," Jock said optimistically. "The season is so fierce and cruel, fighting would be nigh impossible."

"I will leave you money to buy more herds. I have total trust in you to run Dumfries in my absence."

* * *

At the noon meal in the hall, Lynx informed his men that they were rejoining the army at Jedburgh, a distance of only fifty miles away. "Four knights will remain here at Dumfries, along with a dozen Welsh archers." His eyes sought Sir Giles, whose burns were still healing. "Bernard and Eltham, you will remain here along with Royce and Caverley; the rest of you pack up your gear and be prepared to depart before nightfall." Lynx was aware that Sir Giles and Sir Harry would think they were now paying the price for their juvenile behavior, but the truth was they were his youngest knights and he felt a grave responsibility to preserve their lives.

When the meal was done, Lynx was surprised by the arrival of Robert Bruce at the head of a large baggage train.

"I'm testing the route through the western marches. It's the surest and fastest way I know of to locate where trouble lies in wait." Robert grinned.

"I'm rejoining the army," Lynx said shortly.

"Trouble?" Robert inquired.

"Nothing I can't handle," Lynx replied grimly. "Will you keep an eye on Dumfries while I'm gone? I'd like to find the castle still standing when I return."

The Bruce grinned. "I told you Annandale would seep into your blood."

Lynx's green eyes held those of his longtime friend. "I've handfasted my steward's daughter."

The Bruce's grin widened. "You lusty dog! That was quick, or was the fruit so ripe it fell into your hand?"

Lynx grinned back. "Believe me, lust had nothing to do with it. She comes from a prolific family of ten. The simple truth is I want a child, but now that too will have to wait."

Robert winked. "There's always tonight."

Lynx laughed. The Bruce's arrival would postpone his departure until the morrow.

Robert Bruce was consumed by curiosity to see the woman who had taken the fancy of Lynx de Warenne. Since she was not noble, he reasoned that she must truly be a temptress. He did not get a chance to meet her until the evening meal, when he was taken completely aback. It was the beauty with the glorious red hair who had deliberately spilled the soup on his friend. No doubt that had been her provocative way of gaining Lynx de Warenne's attention.

She had announced she was a Celt, and as Robert appraised her, he knew it was true. Her almond-shaped eyes and slanting cheekbones proclaimed her heritage. She seemed as delicate as a fawn, and Robert, who had been ready to tease her unmercifully, quickly changed his mind. Jane Leslie was as ethereal as Jory, perhaps not quite as naughty as his own beloved, at least not yet. But if he was not mistaken, Jane had something else. She had a mystical quality that set her apart from other women.

Robert glanced at Lynx. On the surface they seemed a mismatched couple; a lynx and a lamb waiting to be devoured, yet no one really knew the secret, intimate currents that enswathed a pair who mated. The Bruce noticed the thong about her neck. "You wear a Celtic touchstone?"

Jane's gold-tipped lashes lifted as Robert produced his own. "Mine is the Celtic horse."

"The emblem of power and sovereignty," Jane said softly.

"May I see yours?"

The beauty of the lynx took his breath away. "Who painted this?"

"I did, my lord."

"You have a rare gift." He'd warrant she had others. Robert was aware of Lynx's scrutiny, though he remained silent. The Bruce raised his eyes to meet his friend's and smiled his approval.

When Lynx saw how much Robert seemed to like Jane, he suddenly felt possessive of her. They shared a Celtic heritage and would have much in common. The ease with which they spoke together made him feel like an outsider.

"I understand you have many brothers and sisters?" Robert asked with interest.

"Yes, we are a big family." Jane knew how enamored her sisters and her brothers' wives were of Robert Bruce. She knew just how delighted the young women would be to meet him. "Come, my lord, I will introduce my family to you. It will be such an honor for them."

Robert followed Jane to the table where the Leslies sat. He spoke to the men and smiled at the women, who were all dark like himself. "Do you carry on the old Celtic traditions?" he asked with interest.

"We know the music and the dances," Sim Leslie's young wife offered.

"Do you have Celtic costumes?"

"No, my lord, but we have amulets and Jane has a purple head veil with mystic symbols. Would you like to see them?" she offered eagerly.

''Yes, and I would like to see you perform an authentic Celtic dance for me.''

The young women looked to Jock Leslie, who sat at the head of their table. ''In honor of the Earl of Carrick's visit, I think a dance would be in order.''

Jane was both surprised and delighted. Her father usually discouraged the ancient rituals of their culture. The young women left to get their amulets, and Jane, without consulting Lord de Warenne, went to her chamber for her head veil. She unfolded one of her linen aprons that she used to protect the fine-spun veil and took out the circlet of copper that fit about her head to hold it in place. It was fashioned like a serpent, which was the ancient symbol of the earth healer, Sironi.

When Jane returned to the hall, wearing the sacred veil, the other young women awaited her. Each wore arm amulets of copper bearing ancient symbols. Some bore the Celtic cross, others the sacred Tree of Life; still others displayed entwined fish or birds. ''All these different sacred symbols represent the union of celestial and earthly forces, as does the dance we will perform.''

As Lynx sat watching Jane, he thought she looked especially beautiful tonight. He was intrigued by her, as his eyes followed the wavelike movements of her arms and the spirals she created with her fingers. He could not deny the attraction he felt.

''The ancient Celts celebrated the earthly forces,'' Robert explained to Lynx. ''Spirals are a natural pattern found in wind and water currents, even fern fronds and shells are spiraled. They represent a continuity of life with no beginning and no end and the pathway that leads to the divine source.''

The dance ended to much applause. Lynx de Warenne came down from the dais and took Jane aside. "My lady . . ." He paused, realizing he sounded too stiff and formal, and began again. "Jane, I have been ordered by the king to rejoin the army. I leave at dawn."

Relief washed over her. She had been silently scheming how to postpone going up to bed with Lynx by continuing to dance. She assumed he would go straight to bed without her so he could get a good night's rest. Jane curtsied to him. "I bid you good night, my lord."

Lynx stared down at her, not believing what he was hearing. "I am taking you to bed with me. I could be away for months. This will be our last chance for you to conceive."

Jane's relief melted away as he took her firmly by the hand and led her back to the dais.

Robert stood as they approached. "Your dance was exquisite, my lady. I thank you with all my heart."

"Jane wishes to bid you good night, Robert."

"Good night, Jane. My friend is the luckiest of men." Robert winked at Lynx, then said, "I think I'll propose a wrestling match for the men's entertainment." The Bruce was a champion at wrestling who had never known defeat. He and Lynx had been matched many times over the years, but it usually ended in a draw. Robert was broader, but Lynx had the advantage of longer limbs.

"I would be the first to challenge you," Lynx said with a grin, "but I have other sport to occupy me this night, my friend."

12

As she climbed the steps to her chamber, Jane could feel the heat from Lynx's arm seeping into her fingertips where they rested on his sleeve. Behind them she could hear his squires following, and felt her cheeks burn while at the same time she was all ashiver. Lynx opened the door for her, ushered her into the chamber, then paused on the threshold to speak with his squires.

Lynx's glance went over both men and settled on the younger. "Taffy, I've decided you must stay at Dumfries with my lady. I want you to take special care of her and guard her in all ways." Lynx seldom gave a reason for his decisions, but this time he added, "I have no one else I can trust completely." His glance moved to Thomas. "Be ready at dawn."

Taffy looked at the closed door with dismay. How could Lord de Warenne leave him behind. And yet a part of him was happy he had been given the task of protecting his lady.

Thomas gave him a warning. "When the lord said ye were to protect her in *all* ways, I hope ye took his meaning."

Taffy frowned. "I will care for her as if she were my own."

"Ye'd better not, ye great oaf. I know ye fancy her, but ye'd better plant no seeds in the lord's furrow."

"I don't think of her that way!" Taffy protested.

"Ye're a man, there is no other way to think of a woman."

Jane walked slowly to the fire, gazing down into the flames. One of them was blue, and superstition said that was the devil dancing. Her thoughts were in turmoil. She was determined not to respond to him as she had last night, yet she was aware that he had a strange power over her that was difficult to control. Her palms nervously caressed the soft velvet of the new green gown the needlewomen had fashioned for her. It was the most costly garment she had ever worn. She turned to face him when he came into the chamber and closed the door. Her spirits flagged a little when he did not seem to even notice what she wore.

Why do I care? she rebuked herself. Tears suddenly stung the back of her eyes and she quickly veiled them with her lashes to conceal all emotion. She hoped he would not sit before the fire and take her onto his knees again, and when he made no move toward the big chair, a wave of relief washed over her. She wished he would go upstairs and leave her in peace. If he was departing at dawn, he should go straight to bed, but she knew it was her bed he would go to, not his own. She bobbed a small curtsy. "Excuse me, my lord," then she went into the adjoining bedroom.

Jane put away her Celtic veil and with a pang of reluctance removed the green velvet dress and hung it carefully in her wardrobe. How could he not have noticed such a lovely gown? Jane donned the crisp white night rail the needlewomen had sewn for her, thankful it was not as revealing as last night's garment.

Lynx moved through the archway carrying two goblets of wine. The disappointment he experienced when he saw what Jane was wearing caused him to pause. The silk jupon with its slitted sides that revealed her legs had been far more conducive to mating than the pristine garment enveloping her at the moment.

As he moved to his own side of the bed, Jane held out his black bedrobe. He reached for it politely though he had no intention of donning the damned thing, then quaffed deeply of the wine. He watched Jane slip beneath the covers and lie stiffly as if sharing a bed with him were a duty she wished to avoid. He said gruffly, "Your wine."

She sat up, took the goblet eagerly, and rolled a mouthful about her tongue as he had instructed her last night. Would she remember her other lessons as well? Lynx felt himself harden as he remembered last night's unexpected pleasure. He removed his restrictive clothes and climbed into bed naked, then he drained his goblet and enjoyed the feeling of his blood as it heated. He watched her with approval as she too drained her cup.

When she lay back down he moved closer, then reached a hand to unfasten the tiny buttons below her chin. His fingers came into contact with her touchstone and he lifted it to see it better. "Did you really paint this, Jane?"

"Yes, my lord."

"Its detail is amazing. Where did you encounter such a beast?"

"At the forest pool," she answered truthfully.

"Do you realize how dangerous a lynx can be?"

She looked up into his wide green eyes and saw the humor in his question. The corners of her mouth went up. "You mean he could devour me anytime he wished?"

Lynx felt his cock pulse as he realized she might be referring to him. He watched her glance flicker over his tawny hair, then glide across his wide chest.

"He is the most magnificent beast I have ever seen."

She seemed timid, yet perhaps danger excited her. He understood how a person could feel that way for he often courted danger himself. He slipped his hand up beneath the voluminous nightdress and felt her body shiver as his fingers unerringly found her cleft. She was dew-moist and it gave him hope that she would not find their mating painful tonight. To that end Lynx teased her with his touch, then stroked her woman's center with calloused fingers.

In spite of her earlier determination not to respond to him, his touch aroused such pleasure for her, Jane wanted to scream with excitement. She longed to touch him and return some of the intense pleasure he gave her, but she did not dare explore him tonight since he did not invite her. A gasp escaped her lips when she could no longer hold it back, and she arched her mons into his hand when a powerful finger pushed inside her.

The moment her tight sheath gripped his finger, Lynx's shaft began to buck in anticipation. Christ, how he would love to draw out the mating, thrusting hard and slow for an hour of sleek pounding until his sexual energy was fucked out, but he knew he could not. With an iron will he forced himself to be gentle, nestling inside her until she became used to his fullness. "Wrap your legs high about my back," he murmured.

Jane opened her thighs as wide as she could and felt him slide deeper. She loved the weight of him, the scent of him, and when he began to thrust gently, she suddenly felt something inside her building and tightening as if he were drawing her to the edge of a great precipice. She hovered on the brink, but did not have the courage to fling herself over the cliff. Then she heard Lynx cry out and forgot her own body's sensations, as he erupted inside her. She certainly felt that. He collapsed on top of her and she tightened her legs to hold him at her center. When he rolled away, she told herself she was glad it was over. She was happy that he was leaving, because she was afraid of the things he made her feel when they were together.

What if this separation were permanent? she wondered. Jane had made a wish that he would leave and never return. What if he should die as a result of her wish? She wanted to be free of him, but she certainly did not want harm to befall him. She should have painted him a Celtic touchstone to keep him safe in battle, but now there was no time. She looked at him with alarm.

"Did I hurt you?" he asked, misinterpreting her expression.

"Nay, my lord, there was no pain."

But no pleasure, either, he thought, feeling quite selfish. Her look of alarm must be connected to the fact that he had not reassured her that he would return. How could he have been so thoughtless to one so lovely, aye, and generous too, he admitted. He leaned toward her on his elbow. "Jane, I'm sorry our time has been so short . . . I will likely be gone for months, but I shall return to Dumfries when the fighting is done."

If you do not fall in battle, she thought wildly. She lowered her eyes. He must never suspect her thoughts, for that would make him think she had no confidence in his fighting skills. He was the powerful Lynx; he would triumph.

When she saw that he was asleep, Jane took the leather thong from about her neck and carefully slipped it over his tawny head. The spirit of the lynx would protect him.

Lynx de Warenne reported to King Edward before speaking with his Welsh archers, although at least a dozen of his knights had approached him with what sounded like valid complaints against Fitz-Waren.

"I had hoped to keep you in Annandale to watch the Bruce's activities, but the fighting men you left behind are so undisciplined, they are a threat to our campaign." Edward's blue eyes blazed fiercely. "Get them under control, de Warenne, or heads will roll!"

"Aye, Your Majesty," Lynx said grimly, then rode immediately to where his men were camped.

His bowmen eyed him warily and he knew he should never have left. The Welsh were a reticent, closemouthed people, to outsiders at least, and he did not expect them to rush forward with complaints. He spoke with the Welsh lieutenants, knowing they would take his words to the men-at-arms.

"You have sustained heavy losses and I shoulder my share of the blame for it. I should never have put you under another's command and pledge I will not do so again. I am returned to stay. My squire is setting up my campaign tent now. I will hear any man who wishes to speak.''

Not many Welsh entered his tent, but every English knight came forward and said his piece. Fitz-Waren had ordered whole villages burned and pillaged, the peasants slaughtered wholesale, including children. Women had been used unmercifully for sport to quench the bloodlust that ran rampant among Fitz-Waren's own men. The Scots had retaliated in night raids, setting ablaze the tents of his bowmen. Lynx de Warenne's anger grew hotter by the minute, until he became so saturated by the tales of horror that his rage turned to ice in his veins.

The light was fading from the sky when Fitz-Waren rode into camp, accompanied by his light cavalry officers. ''Well, well, Cousin, I heard you were back. Apparently you could not bear to forgo the glory of battle, nor share in its rewards.''

Lynx walked toward him, slowly unfastening his breastplate and sword. When he'd removed them, he handed them to Thomas and waited calmly until Fitz-Waren dismounted. The moment Fitz's feet touched the ground, Lynx's powerful fist shot out and smashed into his jaw, knocking him from his feet.

Fitz was up in a flash, fighting back with black fury. Lynx knocked him to the ground again, then coldly, calmly, waited for him to get back up. Fitz drew his knife and lunged wildly at his attacker. The pain shot up through his shoulder as Lynx deliberately broke his knife arm.

Fitz looked about for aid from his officers, but they dared not help him with the malevolent faces of the Welsh bowmen glaring as they gathered in a wide circle. Maddened with pain, Fitz-Waren attacked like a raging bull. Lynx de Warenne's implacable fists pounded his face to a pulp. Only when he lay in a heap, unable to rise, did Lynx walk away.

Thomas looked down at the bloodied man with contempt, then he reached into his chausses and deliberately pissed on the ground where Fitz-Waren lay, making sure his humiliation was complete.

Early in May both Jedburgh Castle and Roxburgh Castle surrendered to the English. On the opposite coast, John de Warenne's forces took Dumbarton, a few miles from Glasgow, then the two armies converged on Edinburgh from opposite directions. The great city was able to hold out for only a few days before yielding to the onslaught of Edward Plantagenet.

All during May, Lynx de Warenne and Fitz-Waren avoided each other as much as possible; neither wanted to stir the ire of the king. When Lynx met his uncle John again, he made no mention of the bad blood that had been stirred up between himself and Fitz-Waren; the commander of the armies had quite enough on his plate at the moment.

From Edinburgh, the army moved north to the city of Stirling, but found the castle had been abandoned by its Scots garrison when they arrived. Every last one of Baliol's advisers distanced themselves from him now that all hope was gone that he could hold on to the throne. Then, early in July, at Brechin, Baliol renounced his kingdom to Edward Plantagenet's representative, Anthony Bek, the Bishop of Durham. He appeared before Bek wearing the plain white robe of a penitent. He placed his staff of office in Bek's hands and formally renounced all claim to the kingdom of Scotland.

Well satisfied, Edward Plantagenet acted leniently, sending Baliol to Hertford, only technically a prisoner. He was restricted to a twenty-mile area near London where he was even allowed to hunt in the king's forests south of the Trent.

Now King Edward Plantagenet planned a triumphant progress through Aberdeen and Banff, as far as Elgin. Lynx de Warenne curbed his impatience to return to Dumfries. The fighting seemed to be over, but King Edward wanted a show of force as he rode north receiving the oath of allegiance from the Scottish nobles.

Jane Leslie suspected that she was carrying Lynx de Warenne's child within a sennight of his departure, because her courses stopped immediately. She told no one in her family, but kept the knowledge to herself. It was a secret she would have to share with one other when the time came, but it was bound to make Lord de Warenne happy, for that was the sole reason he had handfasted her.

Her first reaction was one of sadness. Discovering that she was carrying Lynx de Warenne's child meant she would be forever bound to a man who did not love her. He had vowed to wed her and make her his countess if she conceived, but that was the last thing she wanted. She would never be able to live her life freely again. Jane eventually resigned herself to her pregnancy because she would never hurt anything, especially not her own child. Then gradually, Jane became secretly happy about the new life she carried. Though she had no wish to be a wife or a countess, she was now looking forward to becoming a mother.

After the lord had departed, Jane returned to healing the animals for her brothers, while her sisters treated her much as they always had. When they ordered her about, however, and tried to take advantage of her because she was the youngest, she soon put them in their place. Jane was still generous with them though, occasionally letting them borrow a new gown the needlewomen had sewn for her, and allowed them to come and go in her tower rooms.

Jane greatly enjoyed the riding lessons that Taffy gave her. She had ridden ponies since she was a child, but she had never had the luxury of her own horse before. Lord de Warenne had left instructions with his squire to provide Jane with a well-bred mare suitable for a lady. Jane fell in love with the beautiful white horse immediately and took Taffy's suggestion of the name Blanchette, which was Norman for white.

Keith looked after the lovely white horse for her and also accompanied her on long rides, but he was the first one to suspect she was carrying Lynx de Warenne's child and advised Jane to curtail her riding. "The lord would run mad if you lost his child through negligence."

"You are right, Keith, but please don't tell the others about my baby. They would be at me night and day with their superior advice."

"I won't say anything, Jane, but when the dough begins to rise, they'll know ye have a loaf in the oven. Perhaps Lord de Warenne will return soon. Baliol has been deposed and every noble across Scotland is scurrying to Edward Plantagenet to swear allegiance."

"I am so relieved the fighting is finished. I prayed to the great goddesses every night to keep the Lynx safe."

"Jane, the fighting is *not* finished. There will be a lull until the Scots regroup. There is a young leader who has already lifted his head and will rouse the Scots people to fight again."

"No!" Jane cried. "I don't want our people to be enemies."

Keith laid a comforting hand on her shoulder, realizing he should not worry her in her delicate condition. "Jane, do not fear. Lord de Warenne will return and all will be well for a good while."

When Edward Plantagenet arrived at Scone, he removed the Stone of Destiny on which every Celtic king had been crowned and sent it to Westminster Abbey in London. Back in Edinburgh he did likewise with the Holy Rood along with the Scottish regalia and official documentation. Edward Plantagenet wanted to drive home the fact that Scotland was now subordinate to England. He called a parliament at Berwick for the twenty-eighth day of August 1296 and ordered every landholder in Scotland to appear there to reaffirm his allegiance to England.

Robert Bruce planned to attend. He wanted signed and sealed documents that stated officially the Annandale lands were taken back from Comyn and returned to the Bruces.

At Carlisle, Robert Bruce's mother decided not to go to Berwick. Her beloved husband, Robert Bruce the elder, was ailing and she made the decision to take him back to their English estates in Essex before winter set in.

She gathered the ladies in her solar and explained her decision to them. "Will you return to England with us, Jory, Alicia?"

Jory spoke up immediately. "Oh no, Lady Bruce. Everyone who is anyone, either in England or Scotland, will be at Berwick at the end of the month. I wouldn't miss it for the crown jewels! It took King Edward only five months to accomplish what he set out to do and there will be celebrations like we have seldom seen before."

"*Only* five months?" Alicia Bolton said with asperity. "It felt like a lifetime!"

Young Elizabeth de Burgh entreated, "Oh, Lady Bruce, may I go with Lady Marjory to Berwick?"

"But, my dear, your father entrusted you to my care. The Earl of Ulster is a man I shouldn't care to vex."

"Oh, please, Lady Bruce? The fighting is over and I long to see my father again." She dared not add that seeing Robert Bruce was an even greater longing in her breast.

Jory added her persuasion. "I shall take Elizabeth under my wing, Godmother, aye and appease Edward de Burgh if he cavils."

"And what about Lynx de Warenne?" asked Lady Marjory Bruce with raised eyebrows. "He's the one most likely to send you all packing."

"Ah, that is where dearest Alicia comes in. She shall be our secret weapon," Jory declared, carefully keeping sarcasm from her voice. "How could Lynx possibly resist her?"

Though Alicia liked to be flattered, it in no way lessened her anger toward Lynx. He had tricked her into accompanying him north then blithely ridden away without looking back over his shoulder. The faithless cur was off taking his pleasure wherever he found it, month after endless month, while she dried up at Carlisle. To pay him back she would have been unfaithful to him, but the problem was that the Bruce brothers had ignored her, refusing to poach on Lynx de Warenne's property, then even they had gone north to their Scottish castles. Alicia damned Scotland and everyone in it!

In the months they had been separated, she didn't believe for a moment that Lynx de Warenne had been faithful to her. Women everywhere followed him with their eyes, casting blatant invitations his way. She would tolerate his making an occasional visit to a whore, but if any other had dared to set her sights on him, Alicia decided she would take a terrible revenge. Any such female would wish she were dead, rather than tangle with her!

13

Berwick Castle began to bulge at the seams from the horde of Scottish nobles pouring in with claims for their land. After the castle filled, the city of Berwick itself became clogged with wealthy men and women vying for elbowroom with the thieves, beggars, and whores.

Edward Plantagenet arrived at Berwick with days to spare, leaving his armies behind him to march south with all speed. John de Warenne accompanied the king, knowing that Percy, Clifford, Ulster, and the rest of his generals would see to their own men.

Lynx de Warenne set an easy pace for his bowmen; a two-hundred-mile trek on foot was no small undertaking. Fitz-Waren, on the other hand, spurred on his light cavalry, arriving in good time to secure rooms in Berwick Castle. Fitz hoped against hope that Jory de Warenne would show up, and if she did, he had a chamber next to his own to offer her.

The lust he felt toward Jory had grown since his fight with her brother, and if she came, he had made up his mind to fuck her. His beautiful cousin was a cock-teasing little bitch who begged for it, so this time he would give it to her. He stretched out on the bed in his chamber, imagining her beneath him. The corner of his mouth lifted; Jory would come, all right. She loved being on the front row of any important gathering.

When Jory arrived at Berwick Castle, her first order of business was locating Edward de Burgh, Earl of Ulster. Although Elizabeth adored her powerful father, she was still young enough to be terrified of his disapproval.

"Elizabeth, darling, do stop trembling; I'll make sure his wrath does not descend upon you."

"You don't know him," Elizabeth said faintly.

"He's a man, that's all I need to know," Jory assured her with a wink.

Alice Bolton followed them into the bowels of the castle, hoping they would soon be rid of the fourteen-year-old.

Jory's quick eyes soon picked out a man wearing Ulster's badge on his sleeve who gave them directions to de Burgh's chambers.

"What the devil are ye doing here?" he thundered, when his eyes fell upon the dark head of his daughter.

"She came with me, my lord earl," Jory said, letting her hood fall back as she swept down into a curtsy deep enough to reveal the valley of her breasts to the man who ruled half of Ireland. Jory held out her hand and de Burgh gallantly raised her, kissing her fingers in the process. "Lady Marjory, is Lady Bruce here?"

"Alas, my lord, her husband's health was such that she took him to England where the clime is kinder. She insisted that Elizabeth accompany her, but I could see the poor lady was already overburdened and so promised to take your lovely daughter under my own wing."

De Burgh recalled Jory's state of widowhood. "Thank ye, madam, that was most kind."

"Not at all, my lord. Elizabeth is delightful company." When she saw he was at a loss over what to do with his child, Jory offered, "I shall be happy to chaperon her here in Berwick, and her serving women never let her out of their sight."

"Again, I thank ye. Fortunately, I have sufficient chambers for both of ye."

Jory knew the earl's squires and servants would be turfed out immediately, but took it as her due. She glanced questioningly at Alicia, who replied smugly, "Don't worry about me, I'll be sharing with Lynx."

"Of course. Let us go and greet my worthy brother."

After a long, futile search, Alice Bolton came to the furious conclusion that Lynx de Warenne was not in Berwick. She wanted to slap Jory in the face for dragging her all this way. She had been jostled and gaped at by men whose thick Scottish burr assaulted her ears and now wished heartily that she had accompanied Lady Bruce back to London. One uncouth lout who leered at her was actually wearing a bearskin whose odor made her gag. The sparkling amusement in Jory's eyes made everything twice as bad. "He'll pay for this," Alicia said between clenched teeth.

"Hello, Coz, I never expected to see you here," FitzWaren drawled as his gaze lingered on Jory's breasts.

Her eyes narrowed. "Unfortunately, I cannot say the same for you, Fitz."

"Hello, Roger, have you any idea where Lynx might be?" Alicia asked hopefully.

"I'm not his keeper. Were you counting on him to

secure rooms for you? You surely must know by now his men come first." His eyes were drawn back to Jory. "For the small price of a smile you may have this chamber next to mine."

"The price is too high," Jory said sweetly. "The Earl of Ulster has offered me his hospitality, but my friend here is in sore need. Smile at the man, Alicia."

As the pair watched Marjory de Warenne depart, Alicia said, "I don't know what ails her; one minute she is all smiles, the next, her tongue could clip tin."

"I know what ails her; she needs a good bedding!" He stared after her, hating her, lusting for her, then hating himself for it.

Alicia giggled. "I never thought of that. Widowhood must be very trying."

Suddenly, Fitz-Waren's eyes filled with speculation as an unexpected opportunity presented itself to him. De Warenne's mistress must also be suffering from nighttime starvation and Fitz-Waren decided that tupping his cousin's strumpet would bring him a great deal of satisfaction.

Alicia's sharp eyes saw the look and it gave her ideas of her own. The fact that he was Lynx's cousin would make her revenge all the sweeter!

When Jory returned to the chambers where Ulster was housed, she found him conversing with Robert Bruce as young Elizabeth sat listening, entranced.

"Lady Marjory, do ye know the Bruce?" Ulster asked.

In the biblical sense, Jory thought wickedly, but with an impersonal smile, said, "Aye, my lord, he is a friend of my brother."

"Is Lynx here?" Bruce inquired.

"I'm afraid he hasn't yet arrived."

"When he does, he can find me in the east tower," Bruce said smoothly.

"I shall remember, my lord," Jory promised. "Please excuse me, gentlemen, I must find our baggage before some knave makes off with it."

Elizabeth reluctantly followed her from the room. "I wish you had asked Robert Bruce to dine with us," she said dreamily. "Men can't resist you, Jory. You even have my father eating out of your hand."

"Then I hope you are taking notes," Jory teased.

"Oh, I am," young Elizabeth de Burgh replied earnestly.

It was after midnight before Jory unobtrusively slipped up to the east tower disguised as a page. Robert's eyes brimmed with amusement as he twirled her about, viewing her from every angle. "Cock's bones, you make a comely lad, but even a blind man wouldn't be deceived."

"And why not, pray tell?"

He pulled her toward him, caressing her breasts. "Because boys don't have lovely titties, like these." His hands moved lower. "Nor a round bum like this one."

Jory lifted her mouth to his. "I missed you fiercely, you rogue, though I shouldn't admit it."

"And I, you, my love." He pulled off her cap and lifted a handful of her pretty hair to his lips.

"Robert, I've been thinking about how we can be together for a while. Why don't you invite Lynx to visit your great castle at Lochmaben?"

"You underestimate your brother's intelligence."

"Nay, I'm well aware I cannot manipulate him," Jory sighed.

"You won't need to," Robert said with a grin. "He will be asking for lordship of Dumfries Castle, only eight miles from Lochmaben."

Jory's eyes widened. "I see your fine hand in this." Then her eyes widened farther. "And feel your fine hand, too, you devil!"

"Feel this," he invited wickedly.

Jory complied. She had a few demands of her own she couldn't wait to issue.

"Cock's bones, I never undressed a lad before. It has a hint of the forbidden about it," he teased, stripping off the tight hose of a page boy.

She lifted her mouth to his. "I didn't know what forbidden was until you took me in hand." She teased him with her tongue. "Turnabout is fair play, Robert. Now I want to take you in hand . . . and mouth."

"Do whatever you fancy, sweetheart," he murmured huskily, lifting her and carrying her to the bed.

Jory came over him in the dominant position. "Tonight *I* intend to make love to *you* . . . at least the first time." She took the greatest delight in removing the clothes from his powerful body, then her mouth began its hot, wet trail down his naked torso toward the goal she desired.

In Fitz-Waren's chamber, Alice Bolton sipped the third cup of dry red wine he had poured for them. She rather liked the taste; it reminded her of vinegar. Her inhibitions were at low ebb as she allowed Fitz-Waren to make free with her slim body. She experienced a moment of power;

Lynx wasn't the only member of the de Warenne family she could attract.

She soon discovered that Roger was not the lover Lynx was. In fact, some of the things he demanded of her were demeaning, but her pleasure was not derived from the sex acts she performed; her pleasure came from the satisfaction of knowing she deceived Lynx with his own cousin. When Lynx arrived, Alicia knew she would forgive him for bringing her north and even for his neglect; what she could never forgive was his indifference.

The next morning Edward Plantagenet sat in the great hall of Berwick, receiving every landholder from Galloway to Caithness. William Ormsby, an English High Court justiciary, sat on the king's right, while a dozen clerks recorded the names of those who had come forward to get their landholdings reconfirmed and pledge their allegiance to Edward. During the next month he would receive the submissions of over two thousand men, including all of the Scottish clergy. The list of names filled thirty-five skins of parchment, and the arrogant English nobles looking on dubbed it the "Ragman Roll."

As Edward performed his kingly duties with great satisfaction, Lynx de Warenne and his squire Thomas shouldered their way up to the castle. Lynx couldn't believe the crush of humanity that had squeezed into the Port of Berwick. Even the graveyards were packed, with tombstones serving as beds. He had no choice but to order his men to set up their tents in hayfields outside the city.

John de Warenne spotted Lynx's tawny head above the crowd in the great hall and the two men embraced warmly, relieved to find each other unscathed from the recent fighting. Lynx could see that John was bursting with news.

"I have reason to believe Edward is going to appoint me Governor of Scotland!"

"Congratulations, John. You won the country for him, so it's only right you govern it. I want lordship of Dumfries; I'm delighted you'll be in a position to give it to me."

"Don't you want to go to France with Edward?"

"I do not. I've handfasted the daughter of Dumfries' steward. If she quickens with child during the year of the handfasting, I'll wed her."

"Then I should congratulate you; but, Lynx, surely you know you could look to the highest ladies in the land?"

"It is the child that matters to me, John, not the wife; and Jane Leslie comes from a family of prolific breeders."

"Ah," John said, as understanding dawned, "so that's the attraction."

"By the look of this horde, we'll be here a month of bloody Sundays. By the time I get back to Dumfries, I may have been gone six months; half my year will be gone."

John laughed and thumped Lynx on the back. "Then you'll have to double your efforts to make up for lost time."

Thomas approached the de Warennes with a frown furrowing his forehead. "There's not a cubbyhole left, my lord; even the bedbugs have been displaced."

"Pitch my tent with the men."

"Oh, I haven't given up yet, my lord." Thomas took a

pair of dice from his doublet. "Never underestimate the luck of the Irish."

"It might be politic for us to head toward the dining hall, or we won't be fed either," Lynx suggested.

When they arrived in the crowded room, Lynx de Warenne came face-to-face with Alice Bolton. He stared at her in disbelief. "How dare you come to Berwick without my permission, madam?"

"My lord . . . Lynx . . . Lady Bruce returned to England. Would you rather I had gone with her?" she asked archly.

Lynx suddenly realized that wouldn't have displeased him in the least, then cursed himself for a coward. He knew he was tiring of her, but she had given him two years of her life and deserved better of him.

Fitz-Waren strolled up to John de Warenne. "What a crush; everyone and his whore are here."

Alicia flushed furiously, and Lynx gave Fitz-Waren such a malevolent look, he stepped back.

"Excuse us," Lynx said curtly, steering Alicia away from the others. "You should not be here. This parliament has been called to conduct important business of the realm. You should have stayed put until I sent for you."

"It was Jory's idea that we come! She insisted; I had little choice in the matter."

Lynx's grim expression softened somewhat. "Speak of the devil," he murmured as Jory and Elizabeth de Burgh emerged through the crowd of men.

Jory stood on tiptoe to kiss her brother. "Don't be fierce with me for coming, Lynx, history is being made here in Berwick."

His laugh rang out. "As if you give a tinker's damn for

history. 'Twas the victory celebrations you couldn't resist, flaunting your beauty before the Scots nobles and dancing until dawn every night.'' When it became known her uncle was to be Governor of Scotland, Lynx realized she would be coveted by every last one.

''Speaking of Scots nobles, Robert Bruce was asking for you. He's in the east tower.''

Lynx saw Elizabeth de Burgh blush prettily at the mere mention of the Bruce's name. She was no more than a child, yet her head was filled with romantic notions. Females were all alike, he decided cynically.

Since his dice were loaded, Thomas had no difficulty securing a decent chamber for Lord de Warenne, and Lynx soon came to appreciate the comfort of a room over his campaign tent, when the parliament dragged on for a fourth then a fifth week. It seemed that Alicia had learned her lesson and waited for Lynx to send for her. He was in no hurry to see her, however.

Finally, when he was private with his sister, Lynx told her about the handfasting.

Jory exclaimed with delight, ''At last, you are in love!''

''Splendor of God, of course I'm not in love. Jane Leslie and I hardly know each other. Two days after the ceremony, the king recalled me to the army, and by the time I return to Dumfries I'll have been away six months.''

''You must be highly attracted to her; why else would you take a steward's daughter to your bed?''

''To get her with child, of course. If she conceives, I intend to wed her.''

"There is something in de Warenne blood that makes us enjoy flaunting convention," Jory said lightly.

"What the devil have you done now?" he demanded.

"Me? 'Tis you who will raise eyebrows, wedding beneath your station!"

"When I told Robert Bruce and John, their eyebrows stayed in place; as for the rest, I don't give a damn. It's my life."

"And when you told Alicia?"

The muscles in his jaw clenched. "It has nothing whatsoever to do with her; she's my mistress, for God's sake."

Marjory momentarily closed her eyes in prayer. *I ask only one thing: please let me be there when Alice Bolton finds out!*

The month of September and half of October passed before the last name was recorded on the Ragman Roll and it was time for Edward Plantagenet to announce those who had been chosen to rule Scotland in his name. A hush fell over the crowded hall as the king named the three key officials he had appointed. John de Warenne, Earl of Surrey, was named governor, and William Ormsby, the English High Court official, was named chief justiciar.

The murmurs of approval abruptly died when the third name was announced. The king appointed Hugh de Cressingham as treasurer. Both English and Scots despised this self-serving political upstart. Rumors were already flying that he had appropriated the money for rebuilding Berwick to his own use.

That evening, John de Warenne's chambers were thronged with well-wishers as well as those who wished to curry favor with him. Fitz-Waren suddenly found himself being fawned upon now that his father was the Governor of Scotland, and his natural cupidity sprang to the fore. Fitz quickly realized that he could make himself a fortune. The idea of becoming filthy rich appealed to his greed, but not quite as much as did the power he would wield. He stroked the brow over his drooping eyelid and contemplated just what post he would request from his all-powerful father.

Lynx de Warenne drank a toast to his uncle's appointment as governor and to Robert Bruce's lordship of Annandale.

"Christ, you could have heard a cockroach fart in the hush that fell when Cressingham's name was announced," Bruce said.

"Making him treasurer was a grave mistake. Edward should have appointed at least one Scottish noble as viceroy. Mark my words, his choice will come back to haunt him," Lynx predicted.

"He thinks Scotland crushed, but by ramming home his power, he arouses a determination to rise and fight." Robert winked to temper his words. "Well, at least in me he does."

"God's teeth, cease this talk of fighting. Let us enjoy our castles in peace, at least through the winter."

"Let's see, it's mid-October—five months to the end of winter. I'll lay ye odds the Scots can't keep the peace that long!"

"I'll take that wager, but only because most Scots nobles will be out of the country. Edward has offered freedom to some of the men captured at Dunbar if they take up arms for England in the invasion of France."

"Just so long as he keeps my enemy Comyn locked up, I'll be happy."

When the chambers emptied and the Bruce sought his east-tower room, John de Warenne had a nightcap with his nephew. "As governor, I willingly grant you lordship of Dumfries, Lynx, but there is a small string attached. It goes without saying you will keep an eye on our friend Robert's activities."

14

As Lynx de Warenne and his men neared Dumfries, his spirits lifted. The Scottish border country was even more beautiful in the autumn than it had been in the spring when he had left. He had given his knights and Welsh bowmen their free choice. Some had decided to go to France with the king, a few had chosen to return home to Wales, but the vast majority of his knights and bowmen remained at his side.

It was a good thing Dumfries Castle was large and his steward, Jock Leslie, efficient. Housing such a horde should present no problem, though feeding them through the winter might present difficulties. Lynx's thoughts progressed from Jock Leslie to the man's daughter. His hand closed over the touchstone Jane had painted. When he left Dumfries he recalled that he had been riding a full hour before he'd discovered the Celtic talisman.

His first instinct had been to remove it. He was not superstitious, that was for the ignorant masses. A stone dangling about a man's neck would not keep him safe; only superior fighting skills could do that. Jane Leslie must have slipped her touchstone over his head while he slept, thinking it would protect him. He glanced down at it now and knew he had not kept it about his neck because the young girl had put it there. He wore it because the lynx had taken his fancy.

He grimaced. He must stop thinking of her as "the young girl." She was *Jane,* the lady he hoped would give him a child; the lady who just might become his wife and the future Countess of Surrey. Lynx shook his head; try as he might, he could not picture Jane Leslie as a countess. She had been allowed to be wild and free and was unlike most other women. De Warenne was a man who seldom doubted himself. He did not regret the handfasting, yet in hindsight, he was not convinced of the wisdom of it.

A female cry of distress brought Lynx back from his reverie. He wheeled his destrier and rode back down the line. His friend Robert Bruce, also riding to Annandale, did likewise. Both had immediately recognized Jory's voice.

"My palfrey has gone lame . . . she must have picked up a stone!"

Lynx dismounted and aided Jory from her saddle. He lifted the mare's hooves and examined them carefully. "If she did, it's gone now. We are only about two miles from Dumfries, I think she'll hold out."

"Oh no, Sheba is most dear to me, I shan't ride her while she is lame."

"Marjory, for pity's sake, don't delay us now we are almost there," Alicia urged irritably.

"Lady Marjory may ride with me," the Bruce offered politely.

Lynx gave his friend a quelling glance and lifted his sister onto his own saddle, then mounted behind her.

When Lynx's squire Thomas took Sheba's reins, Jory rewarded him with a grateful smile.

Robert Bruce winked at his friend. "Delays are inevitable if you are foolish enough to travel with women."

"*Some* women would try the patience of a saint," Lynx responded with a grin.

"And some *men* are so full of themselves, they need to be taken down from their high horses," Jory said sweetly.

"She must mean you," Robert quipped. "Englishmen are noted for their arrogance."

"They are second only to the Scots, which never ceases to amaze me, since *they* have so little about which to be arrogant!"

Lynx laughed at his sister's wit, then glanced at Alice Bolton. In the beginning she had been as amusing as she had been beautiful. Lately, however, she seemed devoid of humor. He felt it would be heartless to dismiss her and hoped that sooner or later she would tire of their arrangement.

As Dumfries came into view, Lynx again galloped down the line. Jory put her fingers in her ears as her brother bellowed out orders. "Assemble in the bailey. The steward will need a head count and a horse count. Take the supply wagons to the far end and begin unloading immediately. Use the river Nith to bathe."

"Must I bathe with your men?" Jory's eyes were alight with mischief.

"Not you, Minx, though I wouldn't put it past you."

Robert Bruce reined in beside the pair mounted on the black destrier. "We are for Lochmaben, so I'll bid you adieu. I'll ride over in a couple of days when you're settled in."

"Bring your brothers," Lynx invited. "My castle is your home."

"It will be one day, my friend," the Bruce said, laughing, though Lynx knew he was deadly serious. "Lady Alicia, Lady Marjory." Robert Bruce saluted them with equal gallantry, then his men rode off toward the valley.

As they clattered into Dumfries' bailey, Lynx dismounted and lifted down Jory. "Take your palfrey to the stables. A lad named Keith will tend her for you. You can't miss him, his hair is the color of a torch."

Jane Leslie was in the loft above the stables trying to soothe the falcons and other hunting birds that had inexplicably set up a racket since before dawn. At the thunder of hooves, she ran to the narrow aperture and saw the horde of cavalry and foot soldiers. Lynx had returned! This was the reason the raptors were restive. They had known before any human that a multitude of men approached.

Jane's hands flew to her belly. She stood transfixed, her feet rooted to the plank floor, her pulse beating so rapidly from a mixture of excitement and fear that she thought she would faint. Sometimes she wondered how she had had the temerity to go to his bed!

Now, after half a year, he was here and she knew that after such a lengthy time apart, he would be like a stranger and she would have to summon her courage to face it all again! One small part of her wanted to run to him and give him the news of his child, but her shyness made that impossible in front of four hundred men.

Suddenly, the babe she carried quickened, and a cry escaped her surprised lips. Jane wrapped her arms about her belly and sank onto a wooden bench to catch her breath. She sat very still, half expecting her precious burden to turn a somersault, but all movement ceased, and after about five minutes, Jane stood up on shaky legs and descended from the mews into the stables.

Her brother Keith was deep in conversation with the most beautiful female Jane had ever seen. Her hair was the color of moonlight and her clothes were exquisite. She wore an underdress and tunic for riding in a deep shade of amber embroidered with golden thread.

Keith's head shot up as Jane appoached. "My sister will be able to help, lady. She has the healing touch."

Jane felt the impact of imploring green eyes, exactly the shade of Lord de Warenne's. "She went lame about two miles back, but she doesn't seem to have picked up a stone."

Jane ran her hand down the palfrey's flank and the little black horse whickered as if in greeting.

"Sheba likes you," Jory declared.

"All animals respond to ma sister, lady. She has a special gift."

Jane saw the lady's eyes roam over her with curiosity, resting on her rounded belly for a brief second. Then she looked into her eyes. The two young women smiled at each other. Then Jane crouched down and began with featherlike strokes to massage the mare's leg, gradually increasing the pressure of her fingers until she was kneading it. When she straightened up, Keith walked Sheba across the stable floor and Jory saw that the limp had vanished.

"You healed her!" Jory cried.

"No, my lady, I only took away her pain. She has traveled too far . . . she needs rest."

Jory took hold of the girl's hands. "I thank you with all my heart."

Keith said, "I'll put her in a box stall, away from the other horses, lady."

"Thank you both. I'll be back later to check on her."

Jane stared after the ethereal-looking female as she ran lightly from the stables. "She is the lord's sister. Did you see her green eyes?"

Keith nodded. "I could even see her aura; she exudes vitality. Father will need me to find a place for all the horses." He paused on his way outside. "I told ye he'd come back, Jane. Have ye seen him yet?"

Jane shook her head and slowly followed him to the stable doors. Her eyes found Lynx de Warenne immediately among the hundreds of men. Mounted on the huge coal-black destrier, clad from head to booted foot in dominant black, shouting orders, he was easily the most overpowering figure of authority she had ever seen.

Panic rose up within her. With his having been away for months, she couldn't help but feel he was a total stranger; a frightening stranger! Her hand crept up to her tightly braided hair, then she glanced down at her clothes. She had put on the plainest gown she owned to tend the hawks in the mews. Suddenly she remembered that she had sent her bed-curtains to the castle laundry to be washed. Wasn't it just like a man to return when she was least prepared for him? She decided to slip around to a rear entrance of the castle and get her bed-curtains from the laundry before she was noticed.

* * *

Jory and Alicia were greeted by a strapping dark Scot who welcomed them to Dumfries. Jory gave him a quizzical glance from beneath her lashes and offered him her hand. He did not take it to his lips, but shook it heartily. "Ladies, it is my pleasant duty tae accommodate you."

Jory bit back a spicy retort and said, "You are far too young to be Jock Leslie."

"I'm his son Andrew, the second steward."

"Ah, I've been told by my brother the Leslies are worth their weight in gold."

"And your brother is . . . ?" Andrew flushed with pleasure.

"Her brother is Lynx de Warenne, lord of this castle," Alicia interjected. "We would like the best chambers that Dumfries has to offer."

Jory bit her lip. Alice Bolton hadn't the faintest notion that she was addressing the brother of the lady whom Lynx had handfasted . . . in fact she hadn't the least notion that Lynx even *was* handfasted. She is in for a very nasty shock, Jory thought with glee. "If you can possibly manage it, I'd like my chamber to be as private as possible." When Robert visited her, they would need seclusion.

"And *I* will need chambers close to my lord," Alicia declared, managing to sound both arch and coy at the same time. The implication was unmistakable.

Jory saw Andrew Leslie's dark brows draw into a frown as it dawned on him that Lord de Warenne had brought his whore to Dumfries. Lord in heaven, would he run straight to his sister with the news? She and Alicia had scarcely set foot in the castle, yet trouble was already brewing! Jory knew she must distance herself from Alice Bolton.

"I notice Dumfries has lovely towers, Andrew. Would it be possible for me to have a tower room?" She spoke to him as if he were the most important man on earth and was relieved to see that she had diverted him, at least temporarily. He escorted her to the Lady Tower, for which Jory thanked him most sincerely. Then watched with worried eyes as he stiffly led Alicia away to "accommodate" her.

Lynx de Warenne ran a hand through his mane of hair and stretched his shoulder muscles. He was well pleased with his steward's efficiency. In less than three hours, the supply wagons had been unloaded, the fodder stored, their armor and weapons hung in the armory, the horses put out to pasture, and every last man in his mesne given suitable lodging.

"Well done, Jock. The only question that remains is will you be able to feed us all?"

"The kitchens are hives of activity, my lord, but we will need a few more cooks," Jock replied with understatement.

"Feel free to recruit my Welshmen. They're not used to being idle and they have healthy appetites. Every man will earn his keep one way or another." Lynx started toward the river.

"We may not have enough hot water for all yer men to bathe, but we certainly have enough fer you, Lord de Warenne."

Lynx waved his hand dismissively. "A quick swim in

the Nith will suffice, Jock. My sister has likely already used every last drop of hot bathwater in all of Dumfries."

When Lynx finally entered the castle, Alicia met him with a catalogue of complaints.

"Some dour-faced idiot has given me the wrong rooms. Then your stupid squire has compounded the error by carrying my trunks up there instead of to the chamber that adjoins yours, as I instructed him to do! In fact, every order I've issued at Dumfries has been ignored!"

"Then I suggest you stop issuing them," Lynx said bluntly.

"Oh! You delight in abusing me!"

Calmly, Lynx put his hands to her waist and lifted her from his path. "Alicia, use the chamber assigned to you tonight."

"I want you to tell the castle servants who I am!" she insisted.

"Did it ever occur to you to be just a tad discreet?"

Alicia was speechless at the suggestion. His uncle was the Governor of all Scotland. Surely Lynx de Warenne must realize how important he was and, as his chosen lady, how important *she* was?

Lynx spotted his squire Taffy. "Excuse me, madam, I have more pressing matters to attend to." Putting distance between himself and Alicia, he muttered, "Bloody women! What problems has your charge created during my absence?" Lynx demanded of Taffy.

"None whatsoever, my lord. Lady Jane is no trouble at all. She is the least demanding lady I ever served. She already knew how to ride a pony, but I found her a well-bred mare as you instructed and I am sure you will be pleased with the way she handles the animal . . . she outrides me, now."

"An undemanding woman?" His mouth curved in amusement. "There's a unique concept. Sorry to put an end to your tranquil existence, but Jory and Alicia are here."

"Yes, my lord, I carried up their baggage."

"You poor sod, you must have the stamina of an ox."

Taffy grinned. "It's good to have you back, my lord. I even missed Thomas."

Lynx couldn't help but laugh. "For God's sake don't tell him, he's insufferable enough."

"I've unpacked for you, my lord, and laid out fresh clothes."

"Thanks; I bathed in the river with the men. I'll see you in the hall." Lynx climbed the stairs to the Master Tower. He entered one of the chambers beneath his that belonged to Jane. It was empty, so without pause, he went up to his own rooms. He looked about him with satisfaction as he removed his soiled clothes. It felt good to be back at Dumfries. He knew he had made the right choice, picking Scotland over France.

The responsibility of keeping the peace between Scots and English rested lightly on his shoulders. In Lynx's experience, men were men. When dealt with fairly, they would respond in kind whether they were Scot or Hottentot.

He donned the dark tunic and hose, then pulled on black boots whose leather was soft as butter. He slicked back his wet hair and fastened it with a thong at his nape, then selected a heavy gold chain, a cabochon emerald ring, and his favorite dagger. Lynx suddenly realized he was ravenous. He picked up a russet apple from a bowl of fruit and bit into it with relish, then descended the stairs that led to Jane's chambers. Again, he found the room empty. He wondered idly where she was and stepped to the archway to glance into the other chamber.

Jane was standing on a high stool with her back toward him, putting up clean bed-curtains. Feeling decidedly playful at the sight of her, Lynx came up behind her silently, hoping to surprise her. As she stood on her tiptoes to thread the heavy material through the curtain ring, he growled low in his throat and pounced. "I've got you now!" he exulted, as he snatched her into his arms.

Jane shrieked and stared up into devilish green eyes as her heart pounded and her pulses raced madly.

Lynx stared at the small mound of her belly. "Splendor of God, are you with child?" He dropped the apple and his eyes widened. "You *are* with child!"

"Yes, my lord." Jane held her breath, uncertain of his reaction.

"But that's marvelous! What a clever girl you are." Lynx began to laugh with joy and Jane let out her breath and laughed with him. Suddenly he sobered. "Are you mad?" He felt anger and joy simultaneously. "What the devil are you doing up on a stool endangering the baby! You must not engage in these kinds of activities while you are in such a delicate condition. There are servants to do this sort of thing. In fact, you must not engage in any work at all until after the child is born."

Jane felt resentment rise up in her as she envisioned every freedom being taken away from her. He was far too dominant, issuing orders the moment he returned. "We are only handfasted, not wed," she reminded him. "You have no authority over me."

The expression on his face was incredulous. "I have every authority over you. Shall I prove it by ordering you to bed until my child is born?"

Jane's resentment melted into panic and she knew she must placate him, rather than challenge him. "Don't be fierce with me, my lord. I am perfectly well and so is the baby. It won't be here for three more months."

Lynx's momentary flare of anger changed to concern. Gently, he set her down in the big chair and carried over a cushioned stool. "Put your feet up," he suggested. "The baby you're carrying doesn't appear to be very big, are you sure it's all right?" Without waiting for a reply he ordered, "You must eat more." A terrible thought struck him. "Christ almighty, that young fool Taffy has let you ride! The irresponsible young devil has no notion of the danger to which he has subjected the child."

Lynx began to pace. "No more riding. I'll have a litter made for you. You must be more careful . . . nothing must happen to this child."

"Lord de Warenne, I swear to you that the baby will be all right."

Lynx stopped pacing and looked down at her earnest face. "You must think me the world's greatest fool."

"Nay, my lord, I think you the world's most concerned father."

He laughed then. "I'm going to be a father! If I don't tell someone, I'll burst. I'll announce it in the hall!"

Jane tried to rise, but he stayed her with his hand. "Don't exert yourself, lady, I'll have a tray sent up. There must be no more running up and down stairs!"

Jane hadn't known what Lord de Warenne would say or do when he first saw her. She had both dreaded and anticipated his greeting. Would he be pleased about the child? Would he embrace her? She certainly hadn't expected his grave anxieties over such a natural condition. Jane felt frustrated. He had demanded that she eat more, stop riding, and stay in her chamber with her feet up!

She told herself that when he became accustomed to the pregnancy, he would see how irrational his orders were. Lynx de Warenne had embraced her after all, but that had been before he realized she was carrying his child. He had been in a teasing mood, growling like a lynx and playfully pouncing on her. Jane sighed; was she relieved or disappointed that his game of seduction had ended so abruptly? She pushed the question away and decided to go down to the stables to take another look at the palfrey's leg.

Jane murmured the mare's name as her hands slid down over Sheba's fetlocks. She was so deep in thought she did not see the lady approach and was unaware of her presence until she spoke.

"I didn't introduce myself before, or even ask your name, and you have been so kind to my mare. I'm Marjory de Warenne."

Jane straightened and saw Lynx's sister extend her hand. She had changed into a gown the shade of amethysts and Jane thought she looked even more beautiful than the first time she had seen her. "My name is Jane Leslie, my lady."

"Jane Leslie?" Jory's green eyes swept over the plainly clad girl before her in amazement. For once she was rendered almost speechless. Her glance paused on the girl's midsection, then Jory lifted her eyes to the young woman's face and smiled tenderly. "Jane, I'm so very happy to meet you. Does my brother know he's going to be a father?"

"Yes, and I know he is overjoyed at the thought of a child, but he wants to totally control me. The child is everything to him while I am nothing more than a broodmare."

"Oh, my dear, I'm sure Lynx doesn't think of you that way. You are a very beautiful young woman. I'll help you to get him to view you as desirable in your own right," Jory promised. "But, Jane, you shouldn't be tending my horse, you are the Lady of Dumfries!"

"Nay, I'm not a lady because I am not of noble birth. I am not married to your brother, I am handfasted for a year and a day. 'Tis a Scottish custom whereby a man and woman live together. At the end of the allotted time they either decide to marry or to part." She decided to be forthright with Jory. "I never wished to marry. This is what I like to do. I have a gift for healing animals. Your Sheba has a weakness in her legs, but with the right exercise, I can make her legs strong."

Again, Jory was momentarily speechless. "How kind and thoughtful you are. Jane," she said impulsively, "let's be friends?"

Jane nodded. "I would like that very much."

Jory's eyes sparkled. "Oh, my dear, I'm going to turn you into Lady Jane. Nay, more than that; when I'm done with you, you'll be *Lady Jane Tut*!"

15

Jory entered the dining hall accompanied by Alicia and Elizabeth de Burgh. "Let's sit here, let's not go up on the dais tonight," Jory suggested as she was eagerly greeted by Lynx's knights.

Alicia agreed instantly. After the indifferent way Lynx had treated her, she decided to respond with cool disdain. A rebuff might be just what he needed to make him eager for her company.

When de Warenne arrived, accompanied by a dozen knights and their squires, all were laughing in great good humor. They filled the dais, never seeming to notice that the ladies sat elsewhere.

As the fish course was followed by haunches of roast mutton, Lynx was relieved to see that as usual his steward had coped, and an influx of over four hundred hungry men had not daunted him. Tonight, Lynx felt there was no finer place on earth than Dumfries. He no longer doubted the wisdom of the handfasting he had entered into with Jane Leslie; she had proven amazingly fertile.

A great feeling of well-being enveloped him and spread to include everyone in the vast hall. Finally, he would have an heir and the child would be born here at

Dumfries. He took a deep breath of satisfaction and in that moment felt omnipotent. Lynx surged to his feet and held up his hands to quiet the din.

As Jory gazed up at him with affection, she wondered why on earth Jane was not at his side.

Alicia caught her breath as she watched Lynx. He was the most compelling man she'd ever known and now that his uncle was Governor of Scotland, he was a rare prize indeed. She instantly changed her mind about treating him with disdain.

"Raise your cups with me and drink a toast to Dumfries." Hundreds of hands were raised. "I am about to become a father!"

Pandemonium broke loose. Men hooted, whistled, and banged their dagger handles on the tables.

Jory looked at her dinner companion's stunned face and murmured, "Alicia, you're leaving teeth marks on your goblet."

Alicia banged her goblet down so hard, her wine sloshed over the rim. "Where is the slut? I'll soon put an end to her little schemes!"

Lynx came down from the dais and joined the Leslie family, who were all sitting together tonight. All his men joined him in toasting them, then Jock Leslie proposed a toast to Lynx de Warenne.

Alicia hissed, "Who are these people?" as her eyes narrowed on the females at the Leslie table.

"Jock Leslie is Dumfries' steward. Jane is his daughter," Jory explained.

"He's been dallying with his steward's daughter? Then she's just a servant," Alicia said with contempt.

"It's not *dallying;* Lynx and Jane are handfasted."

"Handfasted? What the devil is that?"

" 'Tis an honorable Scottish custom, whereby a man and woman are pledged for a year and a day. If they suit each other, they marry."

"Honorable custom my eye. 'Tis just another scheme concocted by men to get between a woman's legs! As if Lord de Warenne would wed a slut!"

"But, Alicia, you expected Lynx to wed with you," Jory pointed out sweetly.

"You bitch! You think this amusing. You knew about this and didn't have the decency to tell me. Which one is she?"

"Oh, Jane isn't here. A tray was carried up to her. She and Lynx share the Master Tower."

The knights at their table were listening avidly to Alicia's outburst of temper. When she realized the display she was making, she stopped speaking immediately and began to plot in silence.

It seemed that each and every one of his men came to congratulate Lord de Warenne and drink to his health and that of his unborn heir. When the atmosphere in the hall proceeded from boisterous to uproarious, Elizabeth de Burgh's women ushered her up to bed. Jory took herself upstairs shortly thereafter, but Alicia lingered, biding her time.

She decided to take a page from Jory de Warenne's book and make herself sweet and amenable. It was said that you could catch more flies with honey than vinegar, and Alicia was ready to try it. Actually, she was ready to try anything. Alicia waited until Lynx finished a game of dice, watched him rise, half expecting him to stagger from all the drink he had consumed, and approached him. He seemed to stiffen at her approach, but she smiled up into his green eyes and said softly, "Congratulations, Lynx, I am so happy for you."

She watched his eyes narrow. "You are *happy,* Alicia?"

She placed her hand on his arm. "I know how long you have wished for a child. You must be so happy tonight . . . and if you are happy, then I am too."

"Thank you, Alicia, that's most understanding of you."

"Well, we do have an understanding, don't we?"

She saw that his eyes were no longer narrowed against her, they had taken on an owlish quality. "I thought you'd be—"

"Jealous?" She laughed softly. "Your relationship with the mother of your child has absolutely nothing to do with me . . . with us."

"That is true."

Alicia wanted to draw his dagger and plunge it into his cold heart, instead she deepened her smile. Her fingers caressed his muscled arm. "I'm here for you, Lynx." She laughed up at him and teased, "Why else would I brave this barbarous land?" She bade him go back and enjoy himself, and as she left, she glanced back at him over her shoulder, making sure the invitation was crystal clear.

Up in her chamber, Jane tried to finish all the food Taffy had brought up to her, but it was impossible. She pushed the tray aside and brought out her touchstones and paints in an effort to calm her excitement. When she heard the tap on her chamber door, her heart slammed against her ribs and Jane walked to the door on weak legs, wishing he had not come so early.

When Jane opened the door to find Marjory, she was vastly relieved. "Oh, do come in, my lady."

"Jane, if we are going to be friends, you must call me Jory."

"You have green eyes, like Lynx."

"Cat eyes. Yours are far prettier, you have doe eyes."

Jane received so few compliments, she was unconvinced.

"Lynx announced your wonderful news in the hall tonight. Why on earth weren't you at his side?"

"All those men . . . anyway, I don't think my lord wanted me there."

"Nonsense, he would have displayed you like a trophy, you know what men are like!" Jory looked at Jane's face. "No, you don't know what men are like. What fun I'm going to have teaching you!"

"My lord told me I mustn't exert myself and sent food up for me. He said the baby doesn't look big enough and told me I must eat more, but I couldn't finish it all."

Jory looked at the food that remained. "Good God, if you ate all that, you'd be big as a pig full of figs! Take no notice of what Lynx says; what does he know?"

"But I must obey him," Jane said resentfully.

Jory began to laugh and couldn't stop. "Oh, how droll you are. Oh, I'm going to *pee*! Jane, what on earth makes you think you must obey him?" Jory asked, wiping away tears of mirth.

"He is the lord here—he is all-powerful."

"That is true, but you are the *lady* here; his power is your power. You must wind him about your finger. Men don't admire meek and submissive women, not real men anyway. They admire women who are willful and a little bit wanton."

"I feel no power, Jory."

"That is because you don't exercise it. Let's see, could you gentle a stallion and make it eat out of your hand?"

"Easily."

"Then think of Lynx as a stallion."

Jane laughed. "That would be easy enough."

"Great fun, too. Think of it as a game," Jory suggested.

"I don't know how to play games."

"Then I'll teach you! Men love games, they play them all the time, both literally and figuratively. They dice, they play chess. Take the king . . . he plays war games, his chess pieces are countries. My uncle John de Warenne's chess pieces are his generals."

"I thought games were for gambling."

"They are, Jane. Men are addicted to gambling. It's a love-hate thing. They love to win, hate to lose. It's the *risk* that tempts them."

Jane could clearly see that Jory herself would be tempting to a man. "You have such beautiful clothes."

"Don't you?"

Impulsively, Jane took her hand. "Let me show you." They went through to the bedchamber where Jane opened her wardrobe. She showed Jory two woolen dresses. "These are what I used to wear. Before Lynx went away he left orders the needlewomen make me some new garments."

Jory looked at Jane's gown. The material was fine enough, but its color and style left much to be desired. "I design my own clothes, choose my own colors, and you must do the same."

"I couldn't."

Jory put her finger to Jane's lips. "Repeat after me: *I will and I shall!*"

"I will and I shall," Jane whispered tentatively.

"Now put your hands on your hips and say it as if you mean it."

"I will and I shall!" Jane repeated, then dissolved into laughter.

"Splendid! Now, what colors do you like?"

"I like what you are wearing."

"Amethyst? Yes, this color would look lovely with your red-gold hair. Jane, you can wear colors that I can't, such as yellow. I look best in pastel shades, but you would be vivid in bright jewel tones. Just imagine yourself in sapphire blue."

"I couldn't."

Jory's eyes flashed their warning.

"I will and I shall," Jane declared with a smile that revealed her dimples. "Oh, I wish my hair was as pretty as yours."

"Perhaps it is, but we'll never know if you wear it tortured into tight plaits. You should wear it down. Is it as long as mine?"

"Longer, but I c— I will and I shall," Jane amended. "Jory, it's easy to say it, but doing it will be so much harder."

"Of course it won't. We'll transform you overnight. You will be Jane when you go to bed, but when you open your eyes in the morning, you will be Lady Jane Tut!"

Jane stopped laughing. "Bed," she murmured. "What time is it?"

Marjory knew that the thought of Lynx had wiped all others from Jane's mind. "When Lynx comes tonight," Jory warned, "he'll be more than a little intoxicated. You know what men are like when they've had far too much to drink." She looked at Jane's face. "No, you don't know." Jory explained, "They are extremely amorous, but completely incapable."

When Jane looked uncertain, Jory elaborated, "The only thing that swells gloriously forth is loud snoring!"

It was a point of honor that Lynx remain on his feet longer than his knights or men-at-arms. And of course the English tried to outdrink the Scots, a virtual impossibility. It was long past midnight when Lynx made his way to the Master Tower. In mid-step he realized that he was about to disturb Jane. Rest was extremely important for a mother-to-be. What a thoughtless devil he was.

Lynx did an immediate about-face, albeit very carefully. Then he tried to recall where Alicia's room was. "Of course, it's in the west wing," he muttered, striking his forehead with the heel of his palm. "How could I forget when she complained so much?"

"Lynx," Alicia said softly. She had almost given up hope, but now felt a surge of smug satisfaction.

"Alicia."

"Come in, darling. I've missed you so much." He seemed rooted to the spot, so she pulled him across the threshold and closed the door. Lynx leaned back against it to steady himself as she came into his arms. Lust surged up in him as he pushed her gown from her shoulders and set his mouth to her throat.

"It's warm in here."

"Well, you know how to remedy that." Alicia unfastened his dagger, then took his hand, urging him toward a chair. "Let me take off your boots."

"You are very generous, Alisha." He slurred her name, reaching out to touch her breasts.

"More generous than the little mother?" she asked archly, playfully pushing him into the chair.

"We won't speak of Jane," he said stiffly.

Alicia wanted to scratch his eyes out. She spun away and stared into the fire, trying to control her anger and her sharp tongue. She took a deep breath and slipped her gown off, letting it slide down her body until the soft garment formed a pool at her feet. She knew the firelight would turn her skin to gold.

A sudden noise behind her made her turn from the fire. She stared at Lynx in horror. His head had fallen back and a loud snore resonated about the chamber.

Though Lynx was gone before first cock's crow, every servant at Dumfries knew Lord de Warenne had spent the night with his mistress. It was Alicia herself who made sure that Marjory knew in whose chamber her brother had slept.

"I'm surprised at you, Alicia. After all he had consumed, you actually let him into your room?"

"He was most insistent and most amorous."

"I can imagine," Jory said sweetly without a trace of sarcasm. Jory knew she must get to Jane before the malicious tongues did their damage. She had been going down for breakfast, but now excused herself from Alicia and returned to her tower room. Jory opened her wardrobe, selected half a dozen garments, and carried them to the Master Tower.

Taffy was just entering with a breakfast tray. Jory gave an exaggerated sigh. "I have been replaced in your affections."

"Yes, my lady." Taffy blushed. "I mean no, my lady."

"You are forgiven; she has my heart too."

Jory knocked before she entered. "Good morning, Lady Jane, I've brought you some of my clothes until you get new gowns made."

Jane caught her breath at the lovely garments. There was a pale lavender underdress with a vivid magenta tunic, there was a peach-colored gown and another in a shade of turquoise. "I can't take your clothes," Jane demurred, with a look of pure longing.

"Yes, you can. I shall put them in your wardrobe," Jory said firmly, disappearing through the archway.

Jane's sisters walked in without knocking. Mary helped herself to the food on the breakfast tray, while Kate asked slyly, "How was the homecoming? Did he keep you up all night?"

"My lord didn't come," Jane said low.

"That's because he spent the night with his *mistress*!" Kate informed her.

Jory swept through the archway, anger turning her eyes to glittering green ice.

"My lady!" Kate swept down into a curtsy. Mary hastily swallowed a mouthful of food, trying not to choke, and followed her sister's lead. "Good morning, my lady."

"These are my sisters, Kate and Mary."

"Good morning," Jory said coolly. "Why do you bend the knee to me?"

Mary glanced at Kate. "Out of respect, my lady."

"And why do you respect me?" Jory asked sweetly.

Again a glance was exchanged. "Because you are Lord de Warenne's sister."

"Let me explain something to you. *This* is Lord de Warenne's *lady*. Jane is the future Countess of Surrey. You should be on your knees to her. Have you any idea how influential she can be to you and your families? Think of your children's futures. She will be able to secure appointments at court for your sons, good marriages for your daughters. Show Lady Jane some respect. Kate, you may start by knocking and waiting for her permission before you enter her chamber. Mary, you may go to the kitchen for your breakfast, or to the hall, but you may not touch Jane's food again." Marjory smiled. "Thank you, that will be all. Oh, by the way, Lady Jane refused my brother this chamber last night because he was legless with drink. He slept elsewhere because he had no choice."

Kate and Mary filed out quietly.

"Oh, Jory, does he have a mistress in the castle?"

"Jane, all men have mistresses . . . Alicia is nothing more than a habit, an old habit."

"Alicia . . ." Jane said softly.

"That isn't even her real name . . . it's Alice Bolton. She means nothing to him. Lynx chose *you* to be the mother of his child, not a slut like Alicia."

Jane sank into a chair as her memory went back over Lynx de Warenne's own words. *I need an heir; that is the reason I offer this handfasting.* He had been plain enough and she had known from the outset that it was a sort of business arrangement. Even when they had shared a bed, shared their bodies, he had not spoken of love, nor even affection. The subject of faithfulness and fidelity had not even been broached.

"I'm being silly," Jane admitted. "That part of his life is separate and has naught to do with me."

She sounded so forlorn, Marjory's heart turned over. "You care for him, don't you?"

"Yes, I do." Jane closed her eyes, seeing his image on her closed eyelids.

"Oh, darling, you must never let him know your heart's secret. You must appear to be blithely indifferent to him. No man breathing can accept a woman's disinterest. You'll soon have that stallion eating out of your hand."

16

In a small paddock behind the stables, Jane had set up a plank of wood four inches from the ground. With Sheba on a lead attached to her bridle, Jane urged the palfrey to jump over the low barrier.

"This exercise will strengthen the weak muscles in her legs," Jane explained.

"Now that you've shown me what will help her, I'll be able to do it myself," Jory decided.

"I really shouldn't be wearing your exquisite gown when I work with the animals. I'll ruin it."

"Nonsense, you can just have another one made. Nothing is more important for a woman than looking beautiful at all times."

For the first time in her life, Jane did feel beautiful. She had brushed out her red-gold hair, then tied back her curls with a peach ribbon that matched the color of her dress. "But it's so woefully impractical."

"You will need a maid to look after your clothes. Young Elizabeth de Burgh has two women. I'll need a maid also, now that I intend to stay in one place longer than five minutes."

A tall figure emerged from the stables and strode purposefully in their direction. "What the devil are you doing?" Lord de Warenne demanded, towering menacingly above Jane.

"G-good day, my lord. I am working Jory's palfrey to strengthen the weak muscles in her legs."

He looked at her incredulously. "Have you gone mad? You are carrying a child—you cannot work with animals in your delicate condition."

Jory's first impulse was to jump in and defend Jane, but with difficulty she held her tongue.

"I am in no danger, my lord."

"I am speaking of my child."

His words hurt her. "Your child is in no danger. I have worked with animals all my life."

"Well, my lady, you will work with them no longer," he said implacably.

With a fleeting glance at Jory, Jane lifted her chin and said, "I will and I shall."

Jory gasped.

Without a word, Lynx's powerful arms swooped out and lifted Jane from her feet. Grim-faced, he bent a look upon his sister. "She is defiant enough without your aiding and abetting her!" He strode from the paddock, through the stables, and didn't halt until they were in the Master Tower.

The feel of his arms about her sent a thrill up Jane's spine. Though his face was dark with anger, she knew that as long as she carried her precious burden, she was in no danger. She accused him anyway. "Why are you being fierce with me? I am in more danger from your anger than Jory's little palfrey."

"You don't seriously think I would harm my child?"

Jane put her head on one side and her hands on her hips. "You don't seriously think I would harm *my* child?"

Lynx looked at her in exasperation. She was being even more defiant than usual. A sudden thought occurred to him. "You are angry because you have been listening to gossip!"

"Lord de Warenne, I am not angry with you . . . you stir no emotion in me whatsoever."

Lynx stared at her. His eyes were drawn to the rounded mound of her belly beneath the peach silk. Could that be true? he wondered. "You've heard no gossip?"

Jane's mouth curved. "Oh, I've heard the gossip, my dear lord, but I have little interest in what you do with your mistress." Her laughter infuriated him.

His eyes narrowed dangerously. "One of the things I shall demand from a wife is obedience!"

"We are not wed yet, my lord."

Lynx fought to control his temper. Every woman in the world wanted the last bloody word. He was determined not to let her have it. His green eyes turned to ice. "And are never likely to be, Mistress Leslie."

He set her down inside her chamber and then slammed the door.

A moment later, Jory appeared. "You handled yourself splendidly, Jane."

"I feel wretched. He was so cold with me, Jory."

"He may have sounded cold, but he was as mad as fire or he wouldn't have slammed the door."

"He said he would never marry me."

"Of course he will marry you. Handfasting might be an honorable custom to a Scot, but not to an Englishman. Lynx wants his child to be legitimate more than anything in the world. Of course, when he asks, you must refuse him."

Jane brushed away a tear. "Why?"

"Men want what they cannot have. Do you want Lynx to wed you because of the child, or wed you for yourself?"

"Jory, you know the answer."

"Then you must become a challenge to him. Refuse him, and he will turn over heaven and earth to win you."

"Do you think I should pack my things and go back home?"

"Oh no. Save that trump card to play later in the game, and speaking of games, I must teach you how to play backgammon and chess. You must become an expert at board games so that you can *let* him win."

Jane's dimples appeared. "That doesn't make sense."

"It makes perfect sense, because there are times when it will be imperative that he lose. It all depends on what stakes you are playing for." Jory reached up and took down the stringed lute from the wall. "I'll teach you music, too. You must learn how to entertain a man on a long winter's eve."

Jane recalled that the first time Lynx brought her to these lovely chambers, he had asked if she played chess or played a musical instrument. "Oh, thank you, Jory. Lynx already taught me the names of the chess pieces, but if you would take the time to teach me how to play, I would be so grateful!"

Lynx inspected the new flocks of sheep and cattle, thinking there should be more, but when he learned that Ben and Sim Leslie had taken the majority to the Uplands to graze, he was well satisfied with the numbers. He spent two hours with David Leslie in the storehouse, taking inventory of what supplies Dumfries had and what they would need. He appointed Keith Leslie to cull the horses that needed new shoes and get them to the blacksmiths.

Thomas was already at the forge, getting de Warenne's armor and weapons cleaned and repaired. Every piece of equipment in the armory must be checked; no small undertaking for an army of almost five hundred. Lynx designated a stone building as a slaughterhouse and put his Welshmen in charge. They knew that the hide of every animal killed for food must be cured and the leather used for boots, harnesses, and a dozen other necessities.

As Lynx bathed and changed his clothes before he went down to dinner, his spirits were high. His anger with Jane had soon melted away. How could he be at odds with the young woman who had given him his heart's desire? He had decided she must be in the dining hall beside him tonight to stem the flood of gossip. Lynx opened the door to summon her, then thought better of her climbing stairs and descended to her chamber.

His eyes went immediately to his child, before they lifted to her face. "Are you well?"

"Yes, my lord."

"I had heard that a woman suffers from nausea when she is carrying a child."

Jane was glad that he had not seen her the first couple of months when the mere smell of food set her off retching. He would have ordered her confined to bed. "No nausea," she said, smiling.

"Good, then you will dine with me in the hall."

The smallest look of apprehension came into her face.

It did not escape Lynx. "Jane, we are a castle of men—you simply must get used to us."

"So says your sister, Marjory."

"I carp at Jory sometimes, because of her impulsiveness, but she is a good role model for you. She is accomplished in all the feminine arts and is invariably sweet-tempered."

Jane lowered her lashes to hide her amusement. If he knew only half the things Jory had advised her to do, he would banish his sister from Dumfries!

Lynx seated her on his left and shared his trencher with her. He cut the meat with his knife and selected all the most succulent pieces for her.

Jane was flattered until she realized he wasn't doing it to try to please her; it was his way of making sure his child got the best. She smiled at her misapprehension of his motives and ate the meat. She too wanted the best for her baby.

Lynx urged her to try everything and she did her best. He seemed to search his mind for conversational topics, but Jane soon discovered that every utterance came back to the baby, the only thing they had in common.

As Lynx looked out from the dais at the crowded hall, he knew most eyes were on him and Jane. By giving her the place of honor and showing his respect for her, every man here would do the same. For appearance's sake, Lynx could not linger in the hall tonight. He had no choice but to accompany Jane back to her chambers.

Her pulses quickened as he closed the door behind them and followed her into the room. Jane took a deep breath and tried to remember all of Jory's advice. She spied the games table and invited, "Would you care to play a board game, my lord?"

"Chess?" Lynx asked hopefully.

"Good heavens, I'm not up to chess yet, but I'll try a game of Fox and Geese if you will help me." Jory said men loved to be asked for their help. She also said men preferred to be the Fox with only one game piece, pitting their wits against an opponent's many Geese.

Jane placed the Fox upon her palm and held it out to him. "I choose the Geese."

Lynx had two of them in his possession before she sought his advice. He pointed out the danger that threatened two more of her pieces and she prevented him from seizing them. Gradually, however, the sly Fox outwitted the silly Geese and he had far more of her pieces than she did. As Jory had advised, it was time to drop one of her pieces to the carpet.

As Jane bent over to retrieve her game piece, Lynx's eyes strayed to her breasts. She bent lower, affording him a better view. Within a minute she watched him surreptitiously shove another piece over the board's edge. "I'll get it, my lord," she offered graciously, bending low to give him exactly what he wanted.

Though he had never seen Jane's breasts naked, he could tell that they were much larger now. In fact they were luscious. As he pictured what they must look like, his hands itched to touch them.

Jane deftly moved her Goose and scooped up his Fox. "You were being kind to me, Lord de Warenne, letting me win." She laid her fingers on his arm. "You shouldn't make it easy, you should make it *hard* for me."

His cock began to swell. Lynx shifted uncomfortably.

She has no idea she has said something sexually provocative.

Jane, of course, knew exactly what she had said, though she had no idea of the effect of her words. They played again and Lynx soon gained control over both the game and his body. A moment of lust was not going to make him risk harming his child. His body's needs would be slaked elsewhere.

Marjory had shown Jane how to jostle the games table so that the pieces would scatter if she was losing badly, but Jane didn't mind losing to him. She drew in a swift involuntary breath as her baby suddenly jerked.

"What is it? Are you in pain?" Lynx demanded.

"No . . . no, pray don't be alarmed. The baby moved and took me by surprise."

"Is that normal?" His eyes were filled with concern.

"Perfectly normal, so my grandmother tells me. The more it moves, the healthier it is."

Lynx lifted the games table that sat between them and set it aside. He held out his hand. "Come."

Jane's eyebrows rose in a question.

"Come to me." He opened his thighs and she stepped hesitantly between them. He placed a proprietary hand upon her abdomen and waited. Nothing happened.

He looked at her expectantly and she flushed deeply. Did he think she could make it happen? Then she felt a flutter and could see by his expression that he too had felt it. Suddenly, the baby jerked again and Lynx's face showed his delight. "He kicked me!" The wonder of actually being able to feel his child filled him with awe. He searched her face. "Do you think it a boy or a girl?"

"I have no idea, my lord, though there are dozens of theories for predicting, none of which are infallible."

"Such as?" he prompted, seemingly fascinated.

"Well, some women claim if you are constantly sick and the child kicks continually, it's a male; if it gives no trouble, it is a female."

"Women say such things because they are biased against males."

"Another way is to suspend a small touchstone over the child. If the pendulum swings back and forth, it is a male; if it moves in a circle, it is a female."

"Superstitious hocus-pocus," he scoffed.

"Do you still have the lynx I gave you?"

He nodded and reached inside his tunic with his free hand.

"It kept you safe."

He opened his mouth to refute its power, and Jane, anticipating his denial, put her fingers to his lips. "The lynx is very special to me."

Swallowing his words, he took the touchstone from about his neck and put it over her head. "Now it will keep you safe," he said firmly. The lynx talisman nestled between her lush breasts and once again lust rose up in him. Lynx removed his hand from her as if he had been burned. He stood and bowed politely, his manner as stiff as his body.

"You need your rest. Thank you for a most pleasant evening. Good night, my lady."

"Good night, my lord."

Long after he disappeared upstairs, Jane could still feel the heat from his hand. She lifted the lynx touchstone and looked down into its green eyes. "Thank you," she whispered. She imagined the stone still held his body heat as she touched it to her cheek. With a sigh of longing she went to her wardrobe and took out his black velvet bedrobe; if she couldn't have him in the bed with her, this was the next best thing.

The moment Jane fell asleep, her dream began. She was running through the forest; the lynx loping along at her side. The pair didn't stop until they reached the edge of the pool. They paused together, Jane's hand resting lightly on the tawny tufted mane. They plunged together, swimming side by side, joined by an invisible, mystical power. Then came the magical transformation. Her lynx turned into a man who lifted her into his arms and carried her from the water. The man was Lord de Warenne. His kiss was deep, his ravishing deeper still.

Upstairs, in the wide bed, Lynx lay motionless, thoughts of his child filling his imagination. He tried to picture a boy and then a girl, but knew it was impossible to visualize a true image. All that really mattered was that the child be healthy. Lynx was thrilled that he had felt it move. He suddenly wished that he had undressed Jane so that he could have touched her naked belly. Then he wished that he had shared her bed so that he could lie beside the child all night.

Lynx threw back the covers and his feet hit the floor. He would go down now. Then he hesitated. It would be selfish to disturb her sleep. Lynx lay back down. What the devil was the matter with him? The best thing he could do for the child's welfare was marry its mother. He would make the arrangements tomorrow. Once he had made the decision, he turned over and fell asleep.

* * *

At breakfast time, Jane went down to the hall with Jory's prompting. "I shouldn't sit up on the dais without Lord de Warenne taking me there."

"You are wrong, Jane. That is your place," Jory said, leading the way onto the dais.

"Sit beside me," Jane implored. She sat down and watched Lynx enter the hall with her father. A woman caught up with him and possessively touched his arm.

Jane clutched Marjory's hand. "Oh no," she murmured wretchedly. "Is that Alicia with my lord?"

"Aye, she doesn't usually arise this early," Jory said dryly.

"I had no idea she would be so tall and slim and beautiful."

"She's not slim, she's bony, with no breasts to speak of; and she's far from beautiful."

"Her hair is blond," Jane said hopelessly, realizing Lynx must be attracted to fair women.

"She's not naturally blond, she's mousy brown," Jory insisted.

"She's lovely," Jane contradicted.

Alice Bolton watched Lynx go up onto the dais. The first thing he did was take Jane Leslie's hands and raise her up for a polite kiss of greeting.

Alicia's eyes narrowed as she assessed the girl. She was small and red-haired, neither of which were desirable in a woman. However, she was vexingly young. Alicia's eyes focused on her belly and she shuddered. The girl wasn't very swollen yet, but within the next couple of months she would become disgustingly distended. Nothing repelled Alicia as much as childbearing. Better her than me, she thought with malice. Alicia decided then and there that she would not allow this girl to be a threat to her. She would watch and listen, and sooner or later would find a way to destroy her. She had done it before, and with accomplished courtesans. This little serf would be no match for her.

"I trust you had a good night, Jane."

"Yes, thank you." She could feel her cheeks growing warm. Her night dreams had been wondrous, but now that she had seen Alicia, she doubted her nocturnal fantasy would ever become reality.

Lynx piled her platter high with food. "Eat as much as you can. We want the child to grow strong and healthy."

When he looks at me, all he sees is the child.

"I spoke to your father about the wedding. I plan a two-day hunt to ensure the marriage feast doesn't empty the larders, then we can proceed."

Jane's heart lurched against her ribs. "Yes, my lord." She felt Jory kick her under cover of the table. "No, my lord." She stopped eating and folded her hands in her lap.

Lynx smiled politely down at her. "What is it, lady?"

"I need to speak with you in private, Lord de Warenne."

Again, the polite smile. "You will have to learn to call me Lynx."

"Yes, my lord," she murmured.

"Do you have a problem, Jane?"

"No, my lord, I don't have a problem," she said softly, a smile playing at the corners of her lips, "but you might."

17

"What did you say?" Lynx spoke low, almost silkily, his voice carrying a much greater threat than if he had shouted at her.

Jane stood before him in her chamber in the Master Tower, wishing herself a thousand miles away. "I will not marry you . . ." the terrible silence dragged out until she felt intimidated enough to add, "just yet."

De Warenne's face was set in such a hard expression that it looked as if it had been carved from rock. He walked around her, examining her from all angles. "Is that or is it not my child you are carrying?" he asked bluntly.

"It is, my lord."

"Did I not handfast you with the understanding that if you quickened with child, I would wed you?"

"You did, my lord."

"I am convinced you will be an excellent mother."

"Thank you, my lord."

"I am also satisfied you will be an adequate wife."

The word "adequate" stung Jane.

"Am I missing something here?" he asked politely.

"Yes, my lord." She had to bend her neck to look up

at him. "A handfasting is for a year and a day. A marriage may take place before the year is up, but only if *both* parties agree to it."

"You don't believe I will make you an adequate husband?" he demanded with disbelief.

"Oh yes, yes I do, my lord."

"Then, splendor of God, what is your objection?"

Jane swallowed hard. He was not a patient man and clearly his was running out. "*Adequate* may be good enough for you, Lord de Warenne, but it is not good enough for me."

He stared at her as if she had used an obscenity. For a moment he was so stunned by her reply that he was speechless.

Her insides felt like jelly. At least he's looking at you for once and not the child, she told herself.

"I am of noble birth, have wealth and lands, am heir to an earldom, and have offered to wed you and someday make you a countess, yet you consider me only *adequate*?" His brows drew together showing that her words had insulted his pride. "What more do you want from a husband?"

Jane lifted her chin so that her eyes met his. "I want a caring, loving, respectful husband who will share his life with me."

Lynx de Warenne stared at her in amazement. She had more pride than any noble lady born, and she knew exactly what she wanted.

Jane lowered her gaze and said softly, "I cannot marry you yet. I would like more time, my lord."

"By all means, Lady Jane, take all the time you need." He swept her a mocking bow.

Lynx made his way to the room off the great hall. Jock had reported some minor disputes that had arisen between his English knights and the Scots at Dumfries during his long absence and he had decided to hold a court to hear the complaints. Jane had irritated him beyond measure. He was stung by her refusal to marry him immediately. Most women would be overjoyed by an offer of marriage from him. But apparently Jane was so unworldly that wealth and titles meant nothing to her. She seemed to place no importance on the fact that marriage to him would elevate her from the servant class to the ranks of nobility. No doubt that intimidated her and was the reason why she had asked for more time, he told himself.

But deep down Lynx knew that wasn't true. She wasn't intimidated at all; rather, she had sounded extremely haughty when she'd declared that *adequate* wasn't good enough for her. Reluctantly, Lynx admitted to himself that he knew exactly what she wanted. She wanted him to be a real husband who would share his life with her; she wanted to be loved.

When he arrived, the chamber off the great hall was filled with complainants, most of whom were Scots. For the most part, the charges were petty. A shepherd claimed de Warenne knights continually rode through his flocks of sheep, scattering them. A groom complained that his knights arrogantly ordered the stable hands about as if they were slaves. At least half a dozen men charged that his knights had slept with their wives. When de Warenne asked if the women had been forced or willing, the Scots became sullen and didn't seem to think that should matter. "Bloody women!" he muttered under his breath.

Lord de Warenne stood. "Thank you for speaking plainly. Rest assured I will address your grievances immediately. I will do my part to control my knights, and I suggest you do your part to control your wives. Good day."

He told Thomas to summon every de Warenne knight to the hall. When they were assembled, he gave them a scathing set-down. His method for ruling men was simple: he set extremely high standards and expected his men to reach them.

"Some of the complaints I have received are petty and therefore beneath de Warenne knights. You will refrain from scattering the flocks when you ride out."

"But there are sheep everywhere, my lord," Montgomery complained.

"There will soon be a hell of a lot more when the main flocks are brought back from the Uplands. Sheep mean wealth in these borderlands and you'll be damn glad of mutton on the table in the dead of winter." He changed the subject. "I've had complaints from the stable hands." He looked grimly into the face of each knight present. "If any man here doesn't take care of his own horse, he will no longer be a de Warenne knight." He paused to emphasize his edict.

"And now to the matter that seems to irk the Scots the most. They complain that you are fucking their wives." One side of Lynx's mouth twitched. "I won't ask for a show of hands."

The knights laughed at his acerbic humor.

"I know you think you are irresistible devils and I know the women throw themselves at you, but try to limit yourselves to unmarried females and widows—or learn discretion.''

Lynx beckoned Thomas. ''I'd better lay the law down to the men-at-arms. Have them assemble in the bailey.''

Once he was satisfied his rules were understood, Lynx told them to prepare for a hunt. Though there was to be no wedding feast, a two-day hunt was necessary. Moreover, the stags and boars would be at their fattest after the summer months and the game at its most plentiful.

When Marjory learned of the hunt and asked to be included, Lynx gave her a flat ''no.'' ''Jory, I'd appreciate it if you'd occupy your time teaching Jane the ways of a lady. Perhaps it will give her the confidence she needs. I think the idea of becoming Lady de Warenne overwhelms her.''

''I shall endeavor to teach her the things she will need to know,'' Jory promised innocently. ''How flattering that you want her to be like me.''

''God's bones, I wouldn't go that far,'' Lynx said dryly.

Jane was in the middle of having some of her new gowns fitted. Her chamber was awash with vivid colors from garments piled on chairs and the settle. When Marjory arrived, Jane had on an emerald tunic over a pale green underdress. ''This is so wasteful. The tunic will be too tight in another month.''

''Why don't you put two rows of buttons down the sides to allow for expansion?'' Jory suggested to the sewing woman. ''Jane, buttons are marvelous. They make my gowns fit my body much tighter, but in your case they will make them fit looser.''

"Buttons are expensive," the Scotswoman said with tight lips.

"If they weren't, we wouldn't want them," Jory said lightly. "Lady Jane must have the very best; Lord de Warenne insists upon it."

Jane removed the emerald tunic and handed it to the sewing woman who gathered up the garments to carry away with her.

"Lady Jane would like these to be ready tomorrow," Marjory said firmly as she held open the door for the woman.

"Jory, you are so bold."

"The bloody woman would dress you in sackcloth if she had her way. You must learn to be assertive with servants, Jane. My brother wants me to teach you to be a lady and the first lesson is to be high-handed with everyone, starting with Lynx."

"He is infuriated with me."

"Then you are doing everything right. Provoking your lord isn't just a pleasure, it's a duty!"

"Jory, you are so bad."

"I know. When they go off hunting tomorrow, why don't we go hawking?"

"I'd love to, but hawking is a man's sport," Jane said with surprise.

"Not anymore. In England, the ladies have taken such a fancy to falconry, the men complain we are turning the sport frivolous and effeminate. Our smaller hands can manage the jesses and tyrrits easier than theirs."

"Your brother has forbidden me to ride."

"Oooh, and you are just shaking in your boots."

"Jory, he can be extremely intimidating."

"Darling, he can't use corporal punishment on you; he won't maul you."

"He'll maul my pride."

"Yes, he's very good at that," Jory admitted. "But to tell the truth, when you refused to wed him, you mauled his."

"The birds do need exercise," Jane wavered, "and I'm quite used to handling them, though they can be very cruel and fierce."

"That's because they're females," Jory pointed out.

"The best raptors *are* females; I never thought about it before."

"Lynx always flies a female, and the fiercer his falcon, the more he admires her."

Jane laughed. "You are teaching me to be bad."

Alicia, filled with jealousy and insecurity, laced with a great deal of vindictiveness, recruited Kate Leslie as her maid. Servants never stayed with Alicia for very long because she had the temper of a viper, striking her hapless maids whenever the real target of her rage was unavailable. In selecting Kate, however, she had an ulterior motive, so she treated her fairly well. Since Lynx adamantly refused to discuss the subject of Jane Leslie, Alicia had latched on to her sister, and the girl was proving to be a pipeline of information.

"You have beautiful gowns, Lady Alicia. My sister Jane is having all new clothes made."

"Really? That seems like an unnecessary expense for my lord with her belly expanding every day."

"Well, that's the only reason he handfasted her, so she would breed." Kate couldn't disguise her envy.

"Do you know if plans are being made for a wedding?"

"Nay, none that I know of, but my lord did promise to wed her if she conceived."

That's the only hold the little slut has on him, Alicia thought. Eliminate the child and you eliminate the wedding!

Just after sunup, almost two hundred men left for the two-day hunt. Jane watched from her tower window, wondering if she had done the right thing in refusing to marry Lynx. He had not come to her chambers last night, and though he had sat next to her in the hall, he had been polite but aloof. When the mood took him, Lynx de Warenne could be cold and remote. She'd missed the warmth she knew he was capable of showing.

After breakfast, the sewing woman brought all the dresses she had made for Jane. When she received more praise than she had ever heard in her life, the woman was suddenly mollified over the extravagance of the garments.

"Thank you, I never dreamed I would ever have such lovely clothes."

"An' why shouldn't a Scots lass be dressed as pretty as the English?"

When she was alone, Jane couldn't resist trying on every one of them. Until lately, clothes had meant nothing to her. Now she realized they were one of women's greatest pleasures. When she tried on the white silk, she was enchanted with her appearance. Nothing she had ever worn contrasted so dramatically with her long red-gold hair. White was sinfully impractical, but it made her feel like a goddess.

Jane was so absorbed in her lovely new clothes, she had no idea that Robert Bruce had ridden in. She finally tore herself from the mirror and hung all of her new garments in the wardrobe. Jane couldn't resist showing Jory how she looked in the delicate white silk, so she decided to return the gowns Marjory had lent her.

When Jane arrived at Jory's tower room, she wasn't there. Jane suddenly remembered the plan to go hawking and concluded Jory was probably at the stables. As she was hanging the gowns in the wardrobe, she heard the deep voice of a man and recognized immediately that it was the Bruce. She also heard Jory's provocative laugh.

"I'm going to make love to you until Lynx returns," Robert Bruce declared passionately.

Jane's jaw dropped open. She quickly climbed into the wardrobe and pulled the door half-closed behind her. She could see the couple plainly in the mirror on the other door of the wardrobe. Jane closed her eyes and prayed that they would soon leave. She could not close her ears, however.

"Where is your sense of honor, sir, to take advantage of me in my brother's absence?" Jory purred.

"I have no sense of honor, and that enhances all my other senses," Robert warned intensely.

They stopped talking, but Jane could hear rustling. She opened her eyes and was stunned to see them both naked. She watched, mesmerized as Robert lifted Jory high and let her slide down his body. Then they went wild.

The things the Bruce did to Jory aroused her until she was panting and scratching and biting him. Jory slithered to the floor and Robert mounted her, unleashing all the sexual energy that had been dammed up inside him since they'd last touched.

Jane watched in shocked fascination as he arched and spent himself. But, as if he'd never have enough of the delicate beauty beneath him, he went on his knees, thrust his dark head between her legs, and began making love to her with his mouth. Jane could not believe what she was witnessing. She had a dizzying sense that this couldn't really be happening.

Marjory began to writhe and cry out her pleasure, becoming so splendidly uninhibited that she arched her mons into his demanding mouth, threading her fingers into his hair to hold him close for the ravishing. Dear God in heaven, would they never be finished? Jane wondered frantically. Finally, Jory screamed and clung to him as if she were about to die. They lay still, catching their breath, looking into each other's eyes.

Jane heaved a sigh of relief as she saw Robert get to his feet, but her mouth gaped open as she watched him lift Jory in his arms and carry her to the bed. They whispered and murmured love words and endearments so intimate, Jane knew that they had been lovers for some time. They made love so tenderly, it seemed a sacrilege to watch and listen. Lovemaking such as theirs demanded privacy.

Jane crouched in the wardrobe, her emotions so entangled she began to tremble. Marjory draped herself in a sheet as she watched her lover dress. Before he departed, he gave her a swift kiss and murmured, "I'm staying the night."

Jane had a cramp in her back and could remain still no longer. When she reached behind her to rub it, her elbow hit the wardrobe. Jory flung open the door with a cry of outrage. "My God, what are you doing in there?"

"I wasn't spying, Jory. I brought back the dresses you lent me, I recognized the Bruce's voice when he said he was going to make love to you . . . and I hid." Jane stepped from the wardrobe looking pale and upset.

"Oh, Jane, Janie . . . I've shocked you!"

Marjory led the trembling girl to the bed. Her mind darted about like quicksilver, trying to recall the things she and Robert had done. Jane was so unworldly and innocent, she must be deeply shocked by the things they'd done. "I'm sorry, Jane, please don't be upset. I know the things we did must seem wicked to you, but you must understand this is what lovers do."

"Oh, Jory," Jane whispered huskily, "what you have with Robert . . . that's what I want with Lynx."

Jory's legs turned to water and she sank down on a stool. "Oh, darling, we are mad in love with each other."

"Yes," Jane said dreamily.

"A passion like ours is rare. I didn't have it in my marriage, though I loved my husband," Jory tried to explain.

"I want Lynx to love me," Jane said wistfully.

"He has never been in love; he told me so himself."

"But he was married."

"Marriage doesn't guarantee love, Jane. In fact it is very often the death knell to love. Most married couples merely tolerate each other."

Jane thought of her brothers' and sisters' marriages and knew there was truth in what Marjory said. "I don't show it, but on the inside, I feel just as passionately about everything as you do.'' As she spoke, Jane caressed her baby with loving hands.

''Well, I don't think it's hopeless. Lynx already loves his child and is passionately protective of it.''

''Once I have the baby, he won't notice me anymore.''

Suddenly Jory knew she had to redouble her efforts to make Jane so desirable, Lynx wouldn't be able to resist her. ''You'll have to learn how to attract a man's attention. Let him see some of the passion you feel inside. Refuse to be ignored. Think of yourself as the Chatelaine of Dumfries. Put yourself in charge here. Let Lynx see your fine hand in everything.''

Jane smiled. ''I'll storm the castle.''

''Actually, that's not a bad idea. Think of it in terms of a military campaign. You not only want the castle, you want to capture its lord. Don't settle for anything less than unconditional surrender! You'll need men to practice on and who better than the Bruces?''

''Are they all here?'' Jane blushed to the roots of her hair.

''Robert brought two of his brothers. We'll recruit them.''

''Jory!'' Jane protested.

''Robert will enjoy making Lynx jealous and it will throw the scent off he and I being lovers. It's a secret you alone share, Jane.''

''I won't give you away, I promise.''

''Let me get dressed and we'll meet downstairs. I suggest you save that exquisite white silk for Lynx's return from the hunt tomorrow eve.''

* * *

"Father!" Jane summoned Jock who was on his way to the kitchens.

He looked down at his daughter dressed in brilliant turquoise. "Ye look very grand today, lassie."

"I need your help. I must learn to be the Chatelaine of Dumfries and I want to do it well, not just adequately. How shall I address you? I cannot call you Jock."

"Ye will address me as 'steward' and I will address ye as 'Lady Jane.' "

"Very well. Since we are entertaining the Bruces, what do you plan on serving for dinner?"

With twinkling eyes he listed what was on the menu, though he did it with every formality.

Jane considered, then made a couple of suggestions of her own, purely for the practice.

"That sounds excellent, Lady Jane." He bowed and was about to continue to the kitchens when she said, "And, steward, I was not informed when the Bruces arrived, as I ought to have been."

"An oversight on my part, Lady Jane."

"Please see that it doesn't happen again." She looked at him gravely. "Was that all right?"

"Aye. Always use a high-handed tone with servants."

"That's what Jory told me, but I wasn't sure."

"Lady Marjory has the right of it."

Jane next sought out her brother Andrew. She briefly explained about her position of chatelaine and told him she would need his help. "The Earl of Carrick and his brothers are our guests, but Dumfries lacks entertainment in the hall. Get a piper for us, but also see if you can find jugglers or acrobats. Elizabeth de Burgh has told me her father's castle employs strolling minstrels and actors who put on plays in the hall."

"But the Earl of Ulster owns half of Ireland. He lives like a king in his palatinate."

"Surely we can do something on a small scale. At least let's be civilized."

Andrew stared after his sister in amazement. He'd never realized it before, but there was more to Jane than met the eye!

When Jane encountered the Bruce, her cheeks suffused with color as his eyes swept over her from head to foot.

"Lady Jane, you are absolutely blooming." He lifted her fingers to his lips in a gallant gesture. "It looks like we'll be celebrating a wedding soon."

"Perhaps not as soon as my lord would like," Jane said shyly.

"You refused him?" Robert asked incredulously.

"I told him I needed more time."

Robert threw back his head and laughed. "Lady Jane, I'd like you to meet my brothers Nigel and Alexander."

"I am delighted to meet you. I am so sorry Lord de Warenne is off hunting."

"Must be daft in the head to desert such a beautiful lady," Alexander declared.

"Never fear," Nigel said, tucking her arm into his. "I'll take good care of you in Lynx's absence."

18

Up on the dais, Jane asked Marjory to sit in Lynx's place and she directed Robert Bruce to sit on her other side. The moment the meat was served, Jory leaned forward and said, "Jane knows about us."

Jane closed her eyes in mortification.

Robert leaned forward and looked at the two ladies blankly. "Oh, you mean that we were childhood friends."

"Jane knows all," Marjory murmured.

The Bruce still looked baffled. "Do you mean that my mother is your godmother?" he asked politely.

"Give it up. Jane was in my wardrobe this afternoon."

"Ah," Robert replied, realizing his bluff was pointless. Then he took one of Jane's hands and squeezed it. He smiled into her eyes and said, "Celts don't betray each other."

Alexander, sitting next to him, said, "They do it all the bloody time!"

"Who the hellfire is interested in your opinion?" Robert asked.

Alexander grinned. "Lady Jane is—just ask her."

Nigel Bruce, seated on the far side of Marjory,

leaned forward and said, "If you two uncouth swines don't stop making Lady Jane blush, I'll wipe the floor with you."

With a rapt look on her face, Jory declared, "This is such fun, it takes me back to when I was fourteen."

Robert teased, "The only difference is that back then we were all in love with you. Now it is Jane who has our hearts."

Early in the afternoon of the following day, the hunters began to return. Jane and Jory were in the meadow beyond the stables where the Bruce brothers were giving them pointers on flying hawks.

Lynx hailed Robert Bruce from his saddle as he galloped across the meadow. Jane handed her goshawk to Robert so that she could greet Lynx, but the Bruce put a protective arm about her to hold her back. "Don't touch him, Jane, he's all bloody."

Lynx's gaze flicked over Jane's primrose velvet gown and flushed cheeks, and thought once again how pretty she was. Her hair reminded him of a cloak of fire. No other woman he had ever known had such glorious hair, and her figure was so softly rounded and lush it aroused him.

"We're back early. We bagged more game than we could carry. If I'd known you were coming, Robert, you could have hunted with us."

"Your lady entertained us royally in your absence." Robert grinned. "Congratulations are in order. You are a very lucky man." Both Alexander and Nigel pounded Lynx on the back and shook his hand.

"Shall I prepare a bath for you, my lord?" Jane offered sweetly.

Taffy, whose brows lowered the moment he saw the Bruce put his arm about Lady Jane, said, "I'll do it, my lady, there is no need to trouble yourself."

"I'm learning the duties of a chatelaine," Jane explained.

Lynx, who thought he might have enjoyed Jane's attentions if Taffy hadn't interfered, said shortly, "I'll bathe myself. Robert, you have information for me?"

The Bruce handed the goshawk to Nigel and he and Lynx went off toward the castle.

"Taffy," Marjory said, giving the squire her most seductive smile, "Lady Jane needs your help. She needs to practice her social skills on the opposite sex. Can you pretend to be utterly devoted to her?"

Taffy flushed. "I *am* devoted to her, Lady Marjory."

Jory gave a mock sigh. "She steals all my admirers."

"Shall we take our birds into the forest?" Nigel asked, carefully placing the goshawk on Jane's gloved hand.

"Lady Jane may not ride at the moment," Taffy said repressively.

Nigel looked at Alexander. "Are we going to take orders from a Welshman?"

"Like hell we are," Alex replied cheerfully, and the two men picked up Taffy and deposited him in the horse trough outside the stables.

"Oh, no, 'tis all my fault!" Jane said, stricken.

"Pay no heed. That is how men amuse themselves," Jory said lightly. "Especially big men; it helps use up all their disgusting energy."

* * *

Lynx avoided the communal bathhouse and instead sat in a wooden tub in his chambers where he and Robert Bruce could talk in private.

"Don't let your weapons rust. I expect trouble to break out any day," Bruce said.

"I get regular dispatches from the governor. He doesn't seem aware of a threat."

"The trouble will start in the Highlands. All will remain quiet this side of the Clyde and the Firth of Forth, at least for the time being."

"That's because of *your* presence here," Lynx declared. "It is crucial that Bruce remain loyal to Edward, since Annandale straddles the vital western route between England and Scotland."

"My spies tell me that Andrew de Moray has escaped from Chester where the king imprisoned him. The Morays have the lordship of Bothwell and rule vast stretches of land as far south as Lanarkshire."

"Edward has Bothwell Castle strongly garrisoned," Lynx reminded him.

"Aye, but they have other strongholds in Moray, Banff, Inverness, and Ross."

"Moray couldn't have escaped without help in high places."

Robert picked up a bucket of water and unceremoniously dumped it over Lynx. "Exactly!"

As Lynx dressed he studied Robert's dark features. Robert knew he would dispatch this information to John de Warenne. But Lynx wondered what Robert wasn't telling him. There were de Warenne spies out there, but obviously they were not as informed as the Bruce's.

In the hall at dinner, Lynx noticed the addition of music immediately. As well as bladderpipes, strolling musicians played harps and timbrels. Between courses, pages came around with finger bowls and towels.

"I see my sister Jory's fine hand in the improvements," Lynx said to Jane.

"Nay, my lord, you see *my* fine hand. I also told the steward to order us some silver forks. I understand the late queen introduced them to England, so I've decided to introduce them to Scotland."

Though his eyebrows elevated, Lynx managed to keep the amusement from his eyes. Lady Jane had begun to take her position seriously. Behind them, Thomas and Taffy vied with each other to fulfill her every wish, and she rewarded their efforts with a brilliant smile. Though Lynx made no comment, he was acutely aware of the competition for Jane's approval. It must be because she was his lady, so he decided to do nothing to discourage it.

His eyes were drawn again and again to Jane. In the fine white silk with her lovely red hair whispering about her hips, she was as attractive as any lady he had seen at court. After the meal he watched beneath hooded lids as men surrounded her. Not just the Bruces, but two of his knights, Sir Giles and Sir Harry, were dancing attendance on her as well.

When Jane bid everyone good night, Lynx was torn. He wanted to talk with the Bruces, but he also wanted to go upstairs with Jane. He decided he could do both. Lynx told Robert he would join him shortly, then he put his hand beneath Jane's elbow and murmured, "I'll see you safely upstairs."

As they ascended the steps, he looked down at her. "I had a most pleasant homecoming."

"I'm so glad, my lord."

To Lynx, her voice sounded cool and polite. He could not tell what she was thinking and suddenly wished that he could. Sometimes Jane had an air of mystery about her. He told himself it was due to her Celtic blood.

When they were inside her chambers he said, "When you were flying the hawks today, I appreciated your not riding out, Jane. My orders forbidding you to ride must have sounded arbitrary. I do not mean to constrict you; I am concerned for your safety as much as the baby's."

"Thank you. That means a great deal to me. Now I shan't deliberately flout your orders."

Was she teasing him? he wondered. As her mouth curved into a delicious smile, it suddenly occurred to Lynx that he had never kissed her. He took both her hands and drew her inexorably toward him. Then he dipped his head to kiss her good night. He intended to kiss her lips, but she turned her face slightly and his lips grazed her cheek.

"Good night, my lord."

"Good night, Jane," he said, a bit perplexed. But then he thought, Yes, she was definitely teasing him!

Jane had not been to her forest pool since Lynx had returned from fighting, so after their company had departed the next day, she wrapped up warmly, took her herb knife, and decided to go to her special place. Lynx had told her he didn't mean to restrict her and she felt relieved. She had always enjoyed being solitary and prized her freedom.

As Jane approached the pool, the hair on the nape of her neck seemed to stand on end and she had a premonition that something was wrong. She stopped still in her tracks, looking, listening, scenting. She heard a panting sound, faint but distressful. It led her in the direction of a leafy, low-lying branch. She bent down to pull it aside and stared into the green eyes of the lynx!

Startled, she let the branch fall back into place, but not before she had seen that the magnificent creature had been wounded. With her heart in her mouth, Jane clutched her touchstone and said a quick prayer to the goddess Brigantia. Then slowly, she lifted the branch aside. An arrow was embedded in the top of his foreleg, where the leg joined the lithe torso.

Jane looked deeply into its eyes and talked soothingly. "Hush, I will help you. Be still and I will take your pain." Gently, she stroked its tufted fur with her fingertips, drawing off its pain as she knew she could. When the eyes of the lynx became glassy, she knew she had mesmerized the animal enough to lessen its pain.

Now she left it so she could gather white willow leaves from a tree on the far side of the pool. She knew of nothing better to staunch the bleeding of wounds. Next she picked a couple of huge dock leaves and scooped a handful of mud from the water's edge, then Jane tore a piece of cloth from her underdress, soaked it with water, and carried it all back to the wounded beast.

With gentle fingers she eased the arrowhead from the wound and watched with hammering heart as the blood flowed freely. All the while, murmuring a singsong litany of soothing phrases, Jane cleansed the wound, covered it with white willow, packed on the mud, and securely bandaged it with the cloth ripped from her gown.

Tomorrow she would bring it meat lightly laced with

poppy to make the wounded animal sleep. She would have to feed it for a few days until it had healed enough to be able to hunt again. She allowed the branches ablaze with autumn leaves to fall back into place and washed her hands at the pool. Anger at the hunters swept over her. This was a Welsh bowman's arrow! Yet she knew she could not go back to the castle and complain. The lynx's life depended on her guarding it with a cloak of secrecy.

Before she left, Jane took her herb knife and drew a magic circle about the hiding place. She visualized a silver-blue flame shooting from the tip of her knife as she drew the circle of fire and felt secure that nothing could penetrate it.

Lynx de Warenne sent a sealed dispatch to the governor, whose headquarters were in Edinburgh. His lieutenant, Montgomery, was a swift rider who should reach his uncle sometime tomorrow. From the stables, the forest beyond the meadow was clearly visible and Lynx saw Jane disappear into the trees.

His first impulse was to send Taffy after her, but the squire was nowhere to be seen. When Lynx spotted Jane's brother Keith, he pointed toward the trees and told him Jane had gone into the forest alone.

"She's gone to the pool, my lord; she's been going there since she was a child."

"Yes, our first encounter was at her forest pool, but I'd feel better if you'd keep an eye on her."

Keith, who liked de Warenne, promised that he would.

Within the hour, a courier arrived, giving Lynx cause for concern. He liked neither the message nor the messenger. John de Warenne informed him that Fitz-Waren had been granted lordship of Torthwald Castle, and his uncle had sent the message with one of Fitz's light cavalry officers.

Lynx masked the animosity he felt toward Fitz's officer. Torthwald was not too much farther away than the Bruce stronghold of Lochmaben; far too close for Lynx's peace of mind. He had the distinct impression that a watchdog had been set down in their midst. The appointment had the king's stamp of mistrust all over it. It was a common Plantagenet ploy to set one against another.

Fitz-Waren's man also delivered personal invitations, one for Lynx, the others for Marjory and Alicia, to visit Torthwald Castle. Lynx took all the letters and informed the messenger that he would see that the ladies received them. De Warenne told him there would be no reply, then turned him over to his steward for refreshment. Lynx certainly intended to visit Torthwald, but he would do so covertly, without Fitz-Waren's knowledge.

By the time Keith Leslie decided to check on Jane's whereabouts, she was already on her way back to the castle. Keith did not want her to know he had been asked to keep his eye on her and played his role so well, he did not think Jane was the least bit suspicious. At the same time, Jane was so cautiously evasive about what she had been doing, Keith suspected nothing.

Jane made her way to the castle kitchens and came away with a small haunch of venison. She knew she could not ask for raw meat without prompting questions, but her explanation to the cook about her condition making her ravenously hungry at odd hours was accepted with understanding.

The next morning she set out with the meat, some of which she had laced with poppy, and a pot of ointment made from yellow loosestrife which was good for quickly closing up a wound so it could heal cleanly. This time she made sure that Keith did not see her go into the forest.

With her heartbeat pounding in her eardrums, she parted the brilliant foliage and found the lynx where she had left him. She tossed him the meat and moved away to let him eat in peace. Animals were unpredictable when food was present. As she walked toward the pool she could hear his low growls as he devoured the venison.

Jane picked up a pair of nosy hedgehogs who had come to see what she was doing and carried them to the safety of the far side of the water. She also shooed away a doe and a flock of doves. By the time she returned to the lynx, he was dozing from the opiate she had fed him.

Quickly she cleansed the wound of its caked blood and mud, then covered it with a thick layer of the healing salve. Again, she bound it so the lynx could not lick it off.

Back at the castle, as Jane made her way to the kitchens, she jumped with guilt as Lynx spoke her name and caught up with her.

"I am on my way to Lochmaben. I may not return until tomorrow." Actually he was going to Torthwald, but didn't want even his squires to know. "If there is aught you need—"

"Thomas and Taffy will take good care of me," she finished his sentence for him.

Lynx stood looking at her with a bemused expression

on his face and she suddenly felt compelled to explain where she was going. "I'm on my way to the kitchens. A good chatelaine always knows what the cooks are preparing," she lied.

She looked so pretty, Lynx had a sudden urge to touch her. He put his fingers beneath her chin and raised her face until their eyes met. "You will make somebody a very good wife." His green eyes were filled with a teasing light.

Jane's pulse began to race. For once he was actually smiling at her. She swept her dark lashes down over her eyes and murmured, "My lord, you are flirting with me."

Lynx laughed. "It is permitted," he murmured back, and touched his lips to hers. He found that one taste was not enough. He looked down at her soft lips and hungered for more. His mouth came down on hers with an aching tenderness. Then his powerful arms tightened about her soft body as she pressed herself against him. Lynx parted her lips with the tip of his tongue, then thrust inside with slow, insistent strokes.

His hot, hungry mouth sent tiny tremors through Jane's body. His masculine scent stole her senses as she yielded her mouth for his ravaging. He drew her sensual lower lip into his mouth as if it were a ripe cherry, and held her so tightly her breasts were crushed against the hard muscles of his chest. Before the lingering kiss ended, it had aroused an unquenchable longing deep inside her.

Jane was weak with desire when he departed, and thrilled with the knowledge that he was beginning to respond to her. But she was relieved that he would be away for a couple of days so that she could tend the lynx secretly. Jane knew if Lord de Warenne learned of the risks she was taking, he would be livid. He would never understand, and he would never forgive her. He would lock her up for the remainder of her pregnancy and throw away the key!

Under cover of darkness, Lynx de Warenne tethered his horse and walked the perimeter of Torthwald Castle. Try as he might, he could find no way inside without being discovered. Fitz-Waren had the walls so heavily guarded, there was no chance to even swim the moat without being seen.

The following day, he rode out across the surrounding dales and talked with shepherds and cattle herders. The rumors of atrocities at the castle seemed so exaggerated, Lynx doubted most of what he heard, but he was sure of one thing. Hatred for the English conquerors was spreading like a contagion.

He spent the afternoon in the village of Beattock, but the people were so closemouthed and suspicious of him, he found no one who would answer his questions. Lynx realized he would have fared much better if he'd had Jock Leslie or one of Jock's sons with him. In the evening he went to the village of Torthwald. The people were surly and afraid. When he saw the gibbets with their grisly fruit, he understood why.

As Lynx de Warenne rode back to Dumfries, the grim realities of trying to conquer a people brought his spirits low. He thought of all the castles garrisoned by English across Scotland and wondered how many were being ruled by an iron fist rather than conciliation. Were the English so blind they could not see such brutality would only strengthen the Scots' resistance?

Lynx believed that John de Warenne would be a moderate governor, even though the other viceroys, Ormsby and Cressingham, were incapable of moderation. He knew the first thing he had to do was get Fitz-Waren removed from Torthwald. On the ride home, the heavens opened and cold rain poured down in sheets. The glorious autumn weather had lasted into November, but winter threatened. By the time he stabled his horse at Dumfries, Lynx felt sick at heart. He wanted the heirs of his body to hold this castle in peace and prosperity. He prayed it was the weather that had drowned his optimism and put him in such a dark mood.

Because of the drenching rain, he did not take the outside steps to the parapet of the Master Tower. When he reached Jane's chambers, he hesitated, in the hope that she would hear him and speak. He lingered for long minutes in the silence, feeling strangely empty. Then he made a decision and slowly undressed.

As he moved toward the bed he said, "Jane, are you awake?" He thought he heard a swift intake of breath. "Don't be alarmed, it's Lynx." He slipped into the warm bed and moved across it until he was against her back.

"My lord," she gasped, rising up.

His strong arms went about her to draw her back down. He stroked her hair. "Hush, Jane. Go back to sleep."

Their breathing was the only sound that disturbed the silence. As she lay with her body touching his, she knew it would be impossible to go back to sleep. But she lay still as his long, strong body shared her warmth. In a while she felt his hand slide over her belly where it lay possessive and content. Jane smiled into the darkness, feeling surprisingly contented, too.

19

In the morning Jane awoke alone in her bed. She had not heard Lynx leave. Could she have just dreamed that he'd slept nestled against her? No, his body had left its imprint in the feather bed. Her hand touched the linen sheet, imagining she could still feel his warmth. She wondered why he had come to her. Was he troubled? He hadn't come to talk, and it certainly wasn't desire that had brought him to her bed. There was only one answer: his unborn child had drawn him to her.

Jane wished with all her heart it were otherwise, but she decided she wasn't going to waste her day longing for the impossible. When she was dressed, she made her way to the kitchens, secured a leg of mutton for the lynx, and wrapped it in a linen towel. His wound had almost healed and she hoped that within another week he would be able to hunt for himself.

To avoid being followed by Keith, she did not go near the stables, which was the shortest route to the forest pool, but instead walked across the clearing behind the laundry, toward the trees.

From his chamber window in the Master Tower, Lynx watched Jane as she headed toward the woods. Where the devil was she going and what was she carrying? He had asked her brother Keith to keep an eye on her, but it looked as if she were deliberately avoiding the stables. As Lynx watched her, he knew she was not out for a morning stroll, but had a definite purpose in mind.

He had been mulling over whether to pen a letter to the governor or go to Edinburgh himself, but Jane's actions now filled his thoughts and he knew his mind would not rest until he discovered what she was up to. Lynx made his way to the laundry, then crossed the clearing and entered the forest at the spot where he had seen Jane disappear. He did not resort to stealth, but strode through the trees knowing instinctively which direction to take. It wasn't long before he glimpsed her some distance ahead of him. He saw her pause and turn with alarm, ready for flight.

"Jane, hold!" he commanded her. She stopped in her tracks as if rooted to the spot, as he closed the distance between them. The look on her face clearly betrayed the fact that he had caught her at something she didn't want him to know about and that she wished him a thousand miles away.

"What are you doing?" he asked bluntly.

"What do you mean, my lord?"

"It's a simple enough question. What are you doing?"

"Nothing." Her breasts rose and fell with her agitation.

"Clearly, you have come to the forest for some purpose."

"I have come to gather herbs," she said, indicating her cloth bag, yet gripping it close as if she would keep the contents from him.

Lynx raised a powerful hand and took the bag from her. He did not know what he expected to find, but it was certainly not a leg of mutton and a pot of ointment. He pulled out the meat. "This is in case you fall hungry while you are gathering your herbs." He knew her dainty appetite. The suggestion that she would eat a whole leg of mutton was palpably ridiculous.

She opened her mouth to speak.

"Do not lie to me, Jane." His face and his tone were grim. His first suspicion was that she had come to aid some outlaw or fugitive hiding in the forest. He had her neatly cornered and suddenly he watched her evasiveness turn to anger as she took the offensive.

"It is *your* fault," she flared. "You and your careless hunters! I am simply tending an animal I found wounded by an arrow."

For a moment, Lynx felt badly. He knew how tender-hearted she was with animals and the creatures of the forest. "Jane, in a hunt, it happens. We try for clean kills, but it happens. Where is it?"

"I won't tell you!" she defied.

He gave her a level look. "You don't need to tell me. It is near the forest pool. I will go with you."

"No! No!" she cried with passion. "Go away, leave me alone! You set my brother to spy on me and now you are following me yourself."

Her reaction was so explosive he immediately knew she wanted to keep her secret from him at all costs. What the hell creature would devour a leg of mutton? "What animal are you feeding?"

He watched her press her lips together and lift her chin in defiance, but he also saw her fingers clutch her touchstone protectively. His eyes widened in disbelief. "Splendor of God, it is that lynx you told me of!" His long strides carried him in the direction of Jane's forest pool.

She ran after him, knowing his intent. "No, no, please don't kill him!" But she saw that his hand was already drawing out his dagger. Her concern was all for the lynx and the fury de Warenne directed toward it. She did not even think of the fury he would direct toward her.

At the edge of the pool he stopped and looked intently for a spot where an animal might lie concealed. Infallibly, his keen eyes fell on the low-lying branches with their brilliant foliage, and without hesitation, he strode toward them.

"No!" Jane sobbed, dashing ahead of him and flinging herself down in front of the place where the lynx had taken refuge.

His big hand closed about her wrist and he plucked her from the forest floor as easily as if she were a wildflower and thrust her behind him. He tore back the branches with his knife at the ready, then cursed aloud when he found the lair empty, the wild beast gone. Lynx de Warenne's accusing gaze swung to Jane and she saw the enormity of the risk she had taken through his eyes.

"You care for naught but the child! You are obsessed!" she flung at him, too afraid to retreat into the defensive.

" 'Tis a damn good thing somebody has a care for it." His voice and his eyes were like ice. To stop himself from shaking her until her bones rattled, he ran a frustrated hand through his tawny mane. "You have deliberately put my child in danger's way, risking its very life, without a thought in your empty head. Does your own child mean nothing to you?''

The cruel and false accusation angered Jane. ''I love my child very much, I would never do anything to harm it! Please try to understand that I was in no danger from the lynx. I have the power to communicate with animals and to heal them when they are hurt. I think it is about time you got to know me and recognize my special abilities.''

''Not one more word!'' Lynx ground out. He pointed in the direction of the castle. ''On your way, lady.''

As Jane hurried through the trees ahead of him, his ominous silence blanketed her. He did not speak again until the walls of Dumfries closed about them. ''You are confined to the castle,'' he said shortly.

Alice Bolton had just returned from her daily visit to the stillroom with Kate Leslie, where they had been distilling a new concoction purported to bleach hair. Alicia and her maid saw Jane arrive, almost in tears, with Lynx de Warenne close on her heels. The couple's body language screamed to all witnessing the scene that they had been fighting, even before they heard Lynx tell Jane she was confined to the castle.

A sly smile of satisfaction curved Alicia's lips as she watched Jane rush past her to ascend the stairs. ''Your sister is upset. Take her some more of my special wine and find out what the trouble is,'' she instructed Kate. ''We can wash my hair later.'' Alicia knew she had allowed this young woman to gain a profound advantage over her and hoped to use the quarrel as leverage. While Lynx was angered with the girl, she would try to lure him back to her bed. Tonight in the hall she would leave her hair uncovered and wear one of Lynx's favorite gowns.

Kate arrived shortly, obviously out of temper with her sister Jane. "She would barely speak to me, my lady. She puts on fine airs these days, pretending to be better than the rest of us."

"Did you give her the wine?"

"She set it aside with the other wine I took her. Was there something in it?" Kate whispered suspiciously.

"Of course not," Alicia lied. "Wine loosens the tongue. I thought it would make her confide in you. Didn't you even learn what caused the quarrel?"

Kate, wishing to avoid a tongue-lashing, said quickly, "It must have been the child, Lord de Warenne has no personal feelings for my sister."

Alicia's lips thinned. "Of course. He has forbidden her to ride and now he has confined her to the castle. The care and attention he bestows upon the child must make her seethe with jealousy, and the brat isn't even born yet." *If the little bitch would drink the wine, she would abort!*

Alicia unpinned her head veil. "Let's get my hair washed. I must look particularly beautiful tonight."

Various plans flitted through Alicia's mind as Kate ministered to her faded locks. Her maid obviously could no longer get Jane to confide in her, but she had her uses. She had free access to her sister's chambers in the Master Tower, which was an absolute necessity for the scheme that Alicia's brain had concocted. "I may have a gown that will fit you, Kate. I'm surprised your sister isn't more generous with you." In Alicia's experience, a bribe worked miracles.

Before she went down to the hall to dine, Alicia

brushed out her hair and adorned herself with the sapphires Lynx had given her long ago. He treated her with casual indifference these days, and she must take this opportunity to change all that. Excitement stirred her blood. She had seen Lynx's anger, barely controlled, and it aroused her. Alicia shivered as she pictured the battle scars on his naked body. They were the visible proof of the danger he constantly faced.

When Lynx went to the hall for dinner, he knew Jane would not be there. After a quarrel, it was a woman's way to keep to herself as if she were the injured party. Well, it would be a good long time before he would ask her to sit with him in the place of honor again. She could dine in her chamber and consider her reckless behavior.

He spotted Thomas and saw that Alicia had engaged his squire in conversation. Lynx was annoyed because there was no way to avoid her. As he approached, he noticed cynically that she wore a favorite sapphire-blue gown with the jewels he had once given her.

"Good evening, Lynx." Her voice was soft; he knew she was about to ask for something.

"My lord, would you permit me to join you this evening?"

An outright "no" would be too surly, even in his dark mood. He considered fobbing her off with an excuse, but realized he couldn't be bothered. "Why not?" he said carelessly, taking a seat below the dais and helping Alicia into the chair beside him.

When Thomas poured them wine, Alicia took up her goblet and drank deeply. "Lynx, I want to apologize to you."

"For what?" he asked bluntly, wise to the soft, cajoling ways of women.

"I've been so angry with you. I've been completely ignoring you, punishing you for bringing me north. But the truth is, I was terribly spoiled and feeling utterly sorry for myself."

As he looked at her he thought her so thin, she was almost haggard. Unwittingly, he was comparing her with Jane's soft, lush figure.

"Now I realize I've not been punishing you, Lynx, I've been punishing myself. I sorely miss your company, my dearest lord, and beg you to let us still be friends?"

As Lynx watched and listened to her, he realized his desire for his old mistress was a thing of the past. And suddenly Lynx felt sorry for her. How lonely she must be. It was unfair to Alicia to keep her buried here in the borders. "I'm going to Edinburgh shortly—"

Before he could finish, she began begging him. "Oh, Lynx, please take me with you. I promise you won't regret it!"

His shrewd eyes searched her face. "A woman like you isn't suited to being buried in the country. You probably hate Dumfries. I can see you would be must happier in Edinburgh." He put his hand over hers to soften the suggestion he was going to make. Here was his opportunity to get her out of Dumfries permanently. "In Edinburgh Castle, the spacious governor's residence is very much like court. They are continually entertaining both English and Scots nobles who come to swear fealty. Why don't I secure you chambers there, or buy you a little house of your own nearby?"

"What a wonderful idea! We can be together whenever

you visit the city, which will be often I hope. Thank you so much, darling."

Lynx removed his hand and picked up his knife. "Keeping you here is unfair to you." *It is also unfair to Jane!* It suddenly occurred to him that perhaps Jane Leslie had refused to wed him because he kept a mistress at Dumfries. Alicia was not a permanent part of his life, but Jane did not know that.

When the meal was over, Lynx excused himself. He smiled down at Alicia, grateful that she was not going to cause difficulties. He could afford to be kind now that she realized they could be nothing more than friends. "I'll let you know later when we'll be leaving."

Alicia smiled back. "Yes, later."

Lynx talked over his proposed journey to Edinburgh with his knights, deciding who would accompany him and who would stay behind. Then he consulted with his steward and finally his squire.

Thomas rubbed his nose. "I'm not sure ye should leave Taffy to look after Lady Jane, my lord. He doesn't know how to be firm with a lady and lay down the law, at least not with that particular lady."

"And why is that?" Lynx asked with a frown.

Thomas chuckled. "Because the lad is in love with her."

His frown deepened. Thomas might find that amusing, but Lynx did not. "Then the job is yours," he told Thomas. "She's confined to the castle for her own good." The thought of being left behind soon wiped the amusement from Thomas's face.

De Warenne retired to his chamber to pen a note to Robert Bruce. While he was away in Edinburgh, he would feel better if the Bruce kept a weather eye on Dumfries. Lynx sanded the letter and pressed his ring into the wax seal. As he began to unfasten his doublet, a low knock came on the outer door. Assuming it was Thomas, he bade him enter. "I have a note for . . ." His words trailed away as Alicia appeared in the archway. *God grant me patience!* "Alicia, why are you here?"

"You invited me."

"Invited you?" His voice rose with incredulity, carrying to the chamber below.

"Oh, not in words . . . you invited me with your eyes."

He stared at her in disbelief as she began to remove her bedgown.

Below, Jane heard the sound of a woman's voice, though she could not make out the words she spoke. Extremely curious, she climbed the steps that led up to Lord de Warenne's chambers and listened at the door.

"Tonight, I could see that you wanted me as much as I wanted you. The way you looked at me, undressing me with those passionate green eyes. That's why I wore your favorite gown and the sapphires you gave me."

A wave of guilt swept over Lynx as he realized his desire for this woman was long dead. It was all in her imagination. How could he get rid of her without destroying her vanity? The moment he rejected her, she would start a screaming match. "Alicia," he began, firmly closing her bedgown, "I want you to go back to your own chamber. We've been together long enough for you to know I like to be the aggressor. When I want you, I will come to your bed."

"I understand, darling; walls have ears."

He walked her across the room with a firm hand at her back and opened the door, determined to be rid of her.

Below, Jane sat on the stairs, staring blindly into the darkness. Don't you dare to cry! she told herself. It doesn't matter to me that she wore his favorite gown or that he bought her jewels, she told herself fiercely. Instead of tears, she felt anger rise up inside her until she was ready to explode. He's taking her to Edinburgh! she thought furiously. You care more for your mistress than you care for me. Damn you to hellfire, Lynx de Warenne!

Jane crept down the stairs quietly. With shaking hands she lit a candle, and her eyes fell on the flagons of wine. With trembling fingers she reached for a cup.

Buoyed with confidence, Alicia lit the candles in her chamber and turned down the covers on the bed. She knew that Lynx hated it whenever she sought him out in his own chamber and she hadn't been foolish enough to do it often. But tonight she just hadn't been able to help herself. He had not come to her in so long, she feared that he was tiring of her.

Alicia poured a cup of wine and assured herself that she had done the right thing. Now that she had let him know how she felt, he would come to her bed again. The minutes ticked by and stretched into an hour. Her confidence began to slip.

She poured herself another cup of wine and began to pace the chamber. Why was he not eager for her company? It was because of the little slut he had handfasted. Because he had planted his seed in her belly, she was becoming the most important thing in his life. The pennyroyal Alicia had put in the wine could not work if the stupid girl did not drink the wine!

After another hour dragged by, Alicia realized Lynx de Warenne was not coming. Why would any man turn down a sexual overture? It made no sense to her. She had swallowed her pride and gone to him and this humiliation was her reward! She rushed to the mirror to examine her appearance. She opened her bedgown to reassure herself that she was still as slim and attractive as ever. Her own belly was concave, not swollen and distended like Jane Leslie's. Then it fully dawned on her that it wasn't the girl who was her rival, it was the child!

But everything would be all right. Lynx was taking her to Edinburgh. Alicia clung to that thought like a drowning woman clutching at a straw. Then suddenly, she could deny the truth no longer. He was taking her to Edinburgh in order to get rid of her. That was the reason why the couple had been fighting this morning! Jane Leslie had demanded that Lynx get his mistress out of Dumfries!

Alicia flung the cup at the mirror, denting its polished surface. It was time to change her plan. Planting seeds of suspicion might be just as effective as actually aborting the child. She had held off too long. *She who hesitates is lost!*

20

Jane did not go to bed. She sat in a chair before the embers of the fire, a cup of wine at her elbow, as she struggled with her unhappiness. Should she just swallow her pride and make the best of the humiliating situation? Should she confront Lord de Warenne and tell him how she felt? Should she go to Alicia and scratch out her eyes?

Jory de Warenne said men didn't want a woman to be meek, but preferred one who was willful. So, since he had confined her to the castle, Jane decided to rebel against his authority by going home. She knew her father stayed at the castle most nights, so she would have to face only Megotta. Jane did not pack her belongings, she would take nothing he had given her. And deep inside, she hoped he would come for her and make everything right between them.

It was not yet daylight when Jane slipped from the castle and made her way to her old home. When she arrived, the candles were burning and she was surprised to see Sim and Ben sitting by the hearth, deep in conversation with Megotta. Jane hadn't even known they had returned from the upland grazing. The autumn weather had held so well they had stayed a month later than usual.

When she entered the room, all three abruptly stopped talking as if they had been caught at planning a crime. The air was permeated with guilt and secrecy, and Jane immediately forgot her own problem, sensing there was more far-reaching trouble here. Her grandmother swung about and spoke to someone Jane could not see.

"Did you tell Jane?" Megotta demanded.

Keith stepped from the shadows. "No, I did not."

Jane ran to Keith. "What is it? What's wrong?"

"She has the second sight, just like Keith. 'Tis impossible to keep things from her," Megotta whispered.

"When we were in the Uplands we learned about a new leader who is recruiting Scottish rebels. Men from every station in life are flocking to join him. Second and third sons who have naught to lose are gathering an army to fight the English oppressors. His name is William Wallace; his goal is freedom. Countless numbers are secretly supporting him, unwilling to live in slavery," Ben explained.

"He is a Celt, like us. We've seen him, listened to him. He is restoring Scots pride that the English tried to crush out of us. Half the shepherds in the borders have pledged to Wallace," Sim added.

Jane stared at her brothers, aghast. "My God, you have already committed yourselves. That's what has kept you away until November, you have secretly pledged to this cause!"

"We are Celts," Ben declared.

"You are dead men if de Warenne learns of this," Keith warned.

"No one outside this room must learn of this," Jane

insisted frantically. "At all costs keep it from Father. If you persist in this, you will be signing death warrants for all of us!"

"Are ye so blind, ye don't know why de Warenne is here in Dumfries?" Keith demanded. "He is here to stamp out any spark of rebellion. His uncle is Governor of Scotland, for Christ's sake. Even the Bruce stands with the English. They have spies everywhere."

Sim and Ben exchanged fearful glances. All they had actually done was let the rebels have a few of their sheep, but that was enough to get them hanged.

When their sister Kate arrived, they were all eating breakfast. "I heard you were home," she said, addressing Sim and Ben. "I just came to say hello." Kate's eyes widened when she saw Jane sitting at the table. "What are you doing here?"

Jane tossed her head. Kate was interested only in female gossip and Jane fervently hoped to keep it that way. "You know Lord de Warenne and I had a quarrel. I decided to move back home."

When Kate left, Jane warned them all. "She cannot be trusted. She is thick as thieves with de Warenne's mistress." Jane tried to ignore her brothers' pitying looks.

"Yer father never should have sold ye to him!" Megotta spat.

"You know I had no choice but to agree to the handfasting." Jane wished she had not come home, wished she had not learned of Ben and Sim's reckless behavior. Now her loyalties were hopelessly divided, and she felt as if she were being torn in half.

* * *

"My sister Jane has run home to our grandmother," Kate told Alicia. "She has defied Lord de Warenne's orders!"

"I have little interest in your sister. Lord de Warenne is taking me to Edinburgh. Go and get me a breakfast tray, then you can help me pack." Alicia couldn't believe that Fate was smiling upon her by giving her this timely opportunity.

The moment Kate departed, Alicia took her supply of pennyroyal from the cupboard where she kept it concealed and made her way to the Master Tower. She slipped into Jane's room and laid the herbs down next to the wine. It took less than a minute. Now all she had to do was tell Lynx what the girl was up to. The foolish slut had played right into her hands.

As Lynx was leaving the hall with his sister, Jory, he encountered Alicia. It looked as if she had been waiting for him and he schooled his face to reflect a patience he did not feel.

"My lord, I must have a word with you in private."

"Alicia, what is it?" He saw her glance at Marjory.

"I am certain you want no other ears to hear what I must tell you."

Lynx was just about at the end of his rope with this woman, but knowing he wouldn't have to put up with her for much longer, he took her into the small chamber off the hall.

"Jane Leslie is trying to abort your child."

Lynx grabbed her by the shoulders. "You lying bitch!"

" 'Tis true!" she cried. "Her sister found the stuff in her chamber. She's been dosing herself with pennyroyal, but it hasn't worked, so she's gone to her grandmother to get the job done properly. The old witch, Megotta, performs all the abortions at Dumfries! Ask anyone!"

Lynx flung Alicia aside and strode to the stairs of the Master Tower, then took the steps two at a time. He had confined Jane to the castle; she would not dare leave. But all the while a voice inside himself whispered that Jane would indeed defy him. Defy him, yes, but surely she would never destroy her child!

When Lynx found her chambers empty, he told himself she could be elsewhere in the castle. He threw open her wardrobe and felt better when he saw her clothes were still there. But when his eyes fell on the pennyroyal and Jane's herb knife, he felt immeasurably worse. He picked up the cup of wine and sniffed it. His gut twisted sickeningly and he recognized the sensation as fear. Lynx de Warenne began to run.

Jane jumped to her feet in great alarm as the front door was flung open and Lord de Warenne swept in like the angel of death. Jane almost swooned with fear for her brothers. How had he learned of their dealings with William Wallace so quickly? He knocked a cup of milk from her hand, shouting, "Don't dare drink that filthy stuff!"

Jane sank to a stool on shaky legs as she realized with relief that his anger was not directed at her brothers, but at her. She watched him point an imperious finger at Megotta. "Old woman, if you have done aught to destroy my child, prepare to die!"

"Lord de Warenne, what are you saying? What is it you think we have done?" Jane cried.

"You are aborting the baby!"

"No, no, on my honor, I swear that I am not!"

"Women have no honor," he thundered.

Jane stepped close and took hold of his forearms. The moment she touched him, she felt his fear, experienced his agony, knew the anger that engulfed him. She dug her nails into his flesh to get his attention. "Lynx, I swear to you on my soul, I have not done this thing." She grabbed his hand and drew it to her belly. "Feel, feel! The baby lives . . . the baby thrives."

Some of the madness left his green eyes as he focused on the child that kicked inside her belly. Jane reached up and touched her fingers to his cheek. "My lord, I know how much you love this child. Please understand that I love it too, with all my heart and all my soul."

"Then why did you come here?" he demanded.

"I wanted to defy your orders! I heard your mistress in your chamber last night and I was furious with you! Who accuses me of this deed?"

"Alicia, and your sister Kate. I have seen with my own eyes the abortificiant herbs you gathered."

"I will go with you now and face my accusers."

Jane walked beside him in silence back to the castle. Her face was pale, her hands trembled, but her step was resolute. Jane climbed the stairs of the Master Tower slowly, the child now grown so much, her steps were slightly clumsy.

Her eyes fell on the pennyroyal immediately, then lifted until they looked directly into Lynx's eyes. "I swear to you I did not gather this herb."

"The wine too is laced with the filthy stuff."

"Kate brought me the wine . . . praise God I did not

drink it,'' she murmured. Again she looked into his eyes. ''You will have to decide who you believe.''

Jory came in through the open door. ''You both look so awful, what trouble is Alicia brewing between you?''

The lump in Jane's throat almost choked her. ''She told my lord I was trying to abort his baby.''

''My God, she will stop at nothing to get what she wants. Lynx, I have something to tell you, something I should have told you long ago.''

Marjory led Jane to a chair. ''Sit down before you fall down,'' she said softly, then beckoned her brother into the adjoining chamber.

''When Alicia and I were at Wigton, I found her hemorrhaging from a self-induced abortion. I was frightened to death for her, but she assured me she would be all right, because she'd done it before. She begged me not to betray her secret to you and I foolishly gave her my word.''

''Damn you, Jory, why did you not tell me?''

''Because at the time I pitied Alicia and feared how angry you would become if you knew the truth! But her lies about Jane free me from my promise of silence.''

Lynx de Warenne ground his teeth. ''Breathes there a woman anywhere in this world who can be trusted?''

Jory shuddered as he stalked from the room; her brother looked capable of murder.

Kate had almost finished packing Alicia's fine gowns when de Warenne walked into the bedchamber. ''Leave us.'' His tone was so curt, his eyes so threatening, Kate dropped the garment she was folding and fled.

De Warenne confronted Alicia without preamble. "In the time we have been together, did you conceive?"

Alicia stared, knowing she was damned no matter her answer.

"*Did* you?"

She flinched as if he had struck her and uttered a half-truth. "I did, Lynx, but I lost it. I didn't want to tell you because I knew how much you wanted a child."

"So, it's true." The green fire in his eyes turned to ice.

"Damn Marjory de Warenne to hellfire!" Alicia cursed.

"Madam, it is you who are damned." He looked at her trunks, filled to overflowing with the things he had given her. "I'll see that you have safe escort to Edinburgh, or England or wherever it is you decide to go."

Alicia stared at the closed door, two spots of humiliation burning holes in her cheeks. He was ending it! How dare he think he could do that? She wanted to destroy the arrogance she had once found so attractive. Well, he might think it was finished, but it wouldn't be over until she had extracted her revenge. She'd go to neither Edinburgh nor England. She'd go to Fitz-Waren at Torthwald. "I'll bring you low," Alicia vowed, "and I'll use your own cousin to do it!"

Marjory urged Jane to lie down. "You've had such an upsetting morning, I think you should go to bed."

"But I'm not ill."

"Still, you should rest. You are very pale. I'll stay with you, if you like," Jory offered.

Jane conceded. "I'll put my feet up and perhaps I'll paint a touchstone . . . it's very soothing."

"Oh, will you make me one? Robert wears a talisman. Do you really believe they have magic power?"

"His symbol is the Celtic horse, which represents sovereignty. I believe the touchstone has the power to protect, but Robert's destiny lies within himself."

Jory searched Jane's face. "Do you know his destiny?" She quickly put a finger to Jane's lips. "No, don't tell me—I want things to stay the way they are."

"The wheel of life turns, Jory. Everything changes. How would you like me to paint you a divine couple representing the sacred union of male and female energy? It stresses each partner's need for both independence and cooperation to enrich life's journey."

"That sounds perfect. Since the beginning of time people have believed in the mystic power of symbols. Let me tell you about the Roman phallic symbols on Hadrian's Wall that Robert showed me."

As the pair became absorbed in designing the touchstone they studiously avoided the subject of Lynx de Warenne and the unpleasant confrontation that had taken place earlier. It wasn't until hours later that they heard a low knock on Jane's chamber door. Jory opened the door, then quickly excused herself so that Jane and her brother could talk in privacy.

"Are you feeling poorly?" Lynx asked.

"No . . . Jory thought I should rest. I've been painting her a touchstone."

Lynx took a few restless paces, then came back. He obviously felt awkward about whatever he had come to say. He hooked his thumbs into his belt. "You won't have Alice Bolton to contend with anymore. She's gone."

Jane saw that was all he was going to say about the

woman, there would be no detailed explanation. "Thank you for believing me." Jane knew that he did not completely believe her, but he was giving her the benefit of the doubt. He had made his choice between herself and Alicia, but she knew that in his heart Lynx de Warenne did not trust any woman.

"I acted too harshly this morning." Jane knew it was the closest he would ever come to an apology. He strode to the window, then came back to the settle where she reclined. "I am a military man, responsible for my own army. I am used to issuing orders and having those orders obeyed without question."

Was he explaining himself to her or taking a stand? "I am used to complete freedom," she countered softly.

The gulf between them was wide. If it was not to widen further, clearly they would have to compromise. Jane's glance fell on the divine couple she had been painting, and she was struck by how closely it represented their union. Their need for independence was too great. They must learn to cooperate and start to trust each other before they could find any happiness together on life's journey.

"I prefer that you stay at the castle rather than go back to your old home."

Jane was grateful that he had not issued an order and she saw that it was a great concession on his part. "I'll stay, my lord, and promise to do nothing incautious that could harm the baby." They felt awkward and ill at ease with each other, but at least they were no longer quarreling.

"I am going to Edinburgh to see the governor. The time apart will give us a breathing space from each other. I never meant to make you feel like a prisoner, my lady."

They were back to being formal and polite. When he returned they would have to start all over again.

"Godspeed, Lord de Warenne."

When Lynx de Warenne arrived with his knights at the governor's headquarters in Edinburgh Castle, he was surprised to learn that Robert Bruce was already ensconced with his uncle. When his arrival was announced, Lynx was allowed to join them. One look at the Bruce's lowered brows told him his friend was incensed about something.

Wearily, John de Warenne held up his hands. "I have enough trouble, Lynx. If you are here to report more of it, I might be tempted to slay the messenger."

"The king has freed Comyn," Bruce growled.

John de Warenne explained the circumstances to Lynx. "By the time I got your message that Andrew Moray had escaped, he was already organizing a rebellion in the north. Edward freed Comyn on the condition that he put down the rebellion and keep the peace north of the Forth."

"Moray is a *kinsman* of Comyn for Christ's sake!" Bruce cursed.

"That's precisely why Edward chose Comyn," John pointed out.

The Bruce still protested. "They'll work hand in glove with each other. Comyn has his eye on the throne of Scotland for himself!"

"He's not the only one." John de Warenne looked pointedly at Bruce.

Lynx rubbed his chin. "I think Comyn has persuaded Edward that it is not safe to give the Bruce a free hand in

Scotland. He has likely pointed out that your power will grow unless Comyn acts as counterpoint. It's the king's favorite game to set one noble against another; it leaves Edward conveniently free to sail to Flanders."

"Damn you both. The things you say about the king border on treason," John warned. "I don't know what you expect from me, I cannot and will not countermand the king's orders," he told Bruce flatly.

"I want a formal complaint sent to Edward Plantagenet. Comyn shouldn't have free rein in the north. The Earls of Atholl and Fife should be made wardens."

"Your suggestion has merit; I'll pass it on to the king," John agreed reluctantly.

"Is there trouble elsewhere?" Lynx asked John.

"Has either one of you heard of a man called William Wallace?"

Both men shook their heads.

"I've a report here from Henry Percy that this Wallace and a band of ruffians attacked and killed Percy's steward in the marketplace of Ayr. Percy issued a warrant for his arrest, but they failed to find him." John de Warenne brandished a report from the sheriff of another county. "They couldn't find Wallace because he was attacking a peel tower in Lanark!"

"Who is he?" Lynx asked.

"A nobody! No lands! No title!"

"I hate to point out the obvious," Lynx said, "but a man with nothing to lose makes the most formidable enemy."

John de Warenne seemed confounded. "When the king departed, most of the Scottish leaders had sworn their fealty, the armies had disbanded, and every main stronghold was garrisoned by English. I was convinced their cause was hopeless.''

''Never underestimate a Scot,'' Robert Bruce said lightly.

Lynx de Warenne sensed a warning behind his friend's words.

''I've an anteroom filled with petitioners and I'm drowning in a sea of paperwork. Can we talk later?'' de Warenne asked.

Lynx was concerned about his uncle. He looked as if he had aged ten years in less than two months. Clearly, John de Warenne was far better suited to the battlefield than administration.

They left through a side door and the moment they were alone, Robert Bruce said, ''Let's get something to eat and I'll fill you in on William Wallace.''

Lynx raised an eyebrow. ''You said you'd never heard of him.''

''I lied. I've known of the king's enemy for some time.''

21

Robert Bruce drained his tankard of ale and wiped his mouth. ''I knew trouble would spring from some quarter, so I set a trap. When I took the baggage train from Carlisle along the western route, I expected it to be raided before it reached Glasgow. I wasn't disappointed, though trouble came a hell of a lot closer than Glasgow. The packhorses were snatched at Ayr by a reckless lad called William Wallace.''

''You didn't kill him, you didn't arrest him. What *did* you do?'' Lynx asked bluntly. He had no illusions about Robert, the Bruce would do what was expedient for himself, not the crown.

''I listened to him, I sized him up, I assessed him.''

''And your conclusion?''

''Wallace is formidable. He's a young giant. You are a tall son of a bitch, but Wallace must be six and a half feet. He has shaggy, wheaten-colored brows and beneath them strange, pale eyes, lit with a zealous light. There is a wildness about him, a bloodthirsty ruthlessness that borders on madness. He wields a gigantic double-edged claymore as if it's an extention of his arm.''

Bruce called for more ale. ''On the other hand I don't

believe his cause will succeed. He may be able to lead farmers, shepherds, outlaws, the common people of Scotland, but the nobles and clan chiefs will never accept his authority. They enjoy absolute power over their own clans. They'll fight when and where *they* choose, and accept orders from none."

"You discussed an alliance with this William Wallace!" Lynx guessed.

Robert laughed. "You're a shrewd sod, Lynx. I'll deny it to the death, but we did explore a few . . . possibilities. The upshot is that Wallace supports restoring Baliol to the throne, which goes against my interests, so we formed no alliance."

"No alliance perhaps, but I'll wager you struck some sort of a bargain with the bastard," Lynx accused.

"More of an understanding. He sure as hell won't be raiding any more Bruce baggage trains."

"But he's attacked Percy's steward."

The Bruce shrugged. "*I* used to be the warden of Ayr but the king in his wisdom gave it to Percy." He cocked an eyebrow and leaned in close. "I don't give a shit what Wallace does to Percy, so long as he gives me and mine a wide berth."

"It's been rumored for years you have a secret pact with seven earls to put you on the throne when the time is right."

"That was my grandfather and father before me. The earls change sides more often than they change their underdrawers. I put more faith in you, my friend, than all the earls in Scotland."

* * *

The following day Robert Bruce returned to Annandale, but Lynx remained at Edinburgh Castle at the request of John de Warenne. Though his uncle had a hundred clerks and scribes, it was obvious the governor needed Lynx's aid. Before he did anything, however, he had to clear the air with John. "Did you put Fitz-Waren at Torthwald as a watchdog over the Bruce and myself?"

John looked startled. "Nay, why would you accuse me of such? The last thing I want is bad blood between you two!" In actuality John had dangled Torthwald before Fitz-Waren in order to get rid of him. The young rogue had swaggered about Edinburgh, lining his pockets, causing him nothing but trouble. "Since I gave you Dumfries, I thought it only fair that Fitz get Torthwald."

"It's a pile of stone compared to Dumfries, but that's beside the point." Lynx wanted to tell John about the atrocities in Torthwald village, but knew Fitz could easily justify the hangings since his garrison was there to put down trouble. If he accused Fitz-Waren of anything, John would jump in and defend him. It had happened in the past. Nevertheless, Lynx pressed him with a question. "Why did you use one of his officers to courier a message to me?"

"Fitz said he had letters of his own going to Dumfries."

"I don't want him privy to my business. I prefer to use my own couriers," Lynx said bluntly.

"Damn it all, why does there have to be this petty jealousy between the two of you? It's only natural that Fitz be envious of you because you are the heir to the earldom, but I expect better of you. I know he has faults, but I would ask you to overlook them and settle your differences for my sake."

You have no idea what he is, John, Lynx said to himself. You think him merely weak and envious, but I know evil when I see it. John's shoulders seemed stooped beneath his new responsibilities, so Lynx kept his mouth shut.

John sighed heavily. "I've pouches of dispatches from all over Scotland I haven't even opened yet, most of them reporting trouble no doubt."

"I'll go through them and pinpoint the trouble spots," Lynx volunteered. "I do have some good news for you, John. At long last I'm going to be a father."

"Well, congratulations, Lynx! That makes me as happy as it makes you. Are you married yet?"

"Not quite. Mayhap we'll have a Christmas wedding."

But as Christmas approached, Lynx de Warenne had no hope in hell of being at Dumfries for the holy days. So many complaints came from Scone regarding William Ormsby, the new justiciar, that Lynx went to investigate. The justiciar had set up his courts in Scone and most of the reports accused him of legalized stealing.

Lynx found the complaints justified. Ormsby was extorting money by levying fines on every Scot in a hundred-mile radius. If a man did not pay his fine, he was outlawed. With only a handful of knights, Lynx could do nothing but lay the facts before the governor.

Meanwhile William Wallace was stirring up trouble wherever he could and men were flocking to his cause daily. In Lanark, the sheriff, William Heselrig, who held down all resistance with an iron hand, was killed by Wallace and the English headquarters there were destroyed.

Lynx dispatched his lieutenant Montgomery to Dumfries for more of his men. He also sent letters to his sister, Marjory, to Jane, and to his steward explaining that he could not be home for Christmas, but promising that they would hold the festivities at the New Year, which was in keeping with Scottish custom.

Lynx was almost torn in half, wanting to be at Dumfries, filled with anxiety about the approaching birth of his child, yet knowing his duty took precedence over his personal life. When he reread his letter to Jane, he saw that it was filled with dire warnings, and orders that she must follow. He tore it up and began again, two or three times. Finally he simply wrote that he hoped she was well and begged her not to go into Selkirk Forest because it was crawling with outlaws.

Lynx's search for Wallace was fruitless. The zealous young outlaw was fast becoming a champion of the common people and every household was helping to conceal him. Wallace was especially brutal with English priests and nuns, driving them from their churches with fire and sword, killing any who did not flee. Because of this, Lynx de Warenne began looking at the Church of Scotland with suspicious eyes.

The money to finance this uprising was coming from some source, and none was richer than the church. Moreover, the Church of Scotland had a network of communication with every diocese in the country. Every bishop had sworn allegiance to the king, but Lynx de Warenne was cynical enough to know that beneath their frocks, bishops were men like any other.

Suddenly winter arrived with a vengeance. Snow covered everything and the temperature plummeted to freezing. As a result all attacks and hostilities ceased. Both John de Warenne and Lynx knew it was only a lull; the trouble would start up again as soon as the weather permitted.

Lynx prepared detailed reports for the governor about William Ormsby, the justiciar, and what he had seen in Scone. Then he laid out the many complaints against William Wallace and documented many of his treasonable acts. Lynx also informed John of his suspicions about the involvement of the Church of Scotland. "Will you send these to the king?"

"Certainly the reports on William Wallace," John said firmly.

"What about the justiciar?"

John shook his head, worry lines furrowing his brow. "I know what the king's answer will be. He will tell me I wasn't put here to spy on his English officials, I was put here to govern! Edward Plantagenet only wants to hear that those he appointed are holding this country secure. He won't question the methods."

Lynx informed John that he was going home to Dumfries for the New Year, while there was a lull in the hostilities. He pledged that he would return with enough men-at-arms to put down all resistance and restore peace to the entire Lowlands. "I'm going to ask the Bruce to help us. It might take some persuading, so give me a fortnight or so."

It was the worst Christmas Alice Bolton had ever experienced. The holy days were an excuse for Fitz-Waren and his knights to indulge in a drunken debauch. The torches in the hall burned night and day as the men indulged in fun and games that ranged from downright childish to depraved.

They brought full-grown rams into the hall for a ram race, then made wagers on who could ride them the longest. When this activity palled, they turned their attention to the female servants of the castle and the girls from Torthwald village, who were considered fair game to satisfy the sexual appetites of the merrymakers, whether they were willing or no.

Before long, every man in the castle dangled a naked wench from his knee. When the sex games aroused the men's bloodlust, ewes were herded into the hall for a sheep-sticking, and by dawn the flagstones ran red.

The minute Fitz-Waren showed signs of sobering, Alicia lured him to her bed and kept him there for three days. Alicia added her hatred for Lynx de Warenne to Fitz-Waren's and nurtured it until it was full-blown. While she catered to his sick appetites, she planted seeds of discontent.

"Fitz, your father is the Governor of Scotland. Where is your pride? You shouldn't allow yourself to be buried in the wilds, living in this barren pile of rock, among peasants. Your abilities are being wasted here. A man with your talents would be much more suited to the administration of the country. Think of the fortune you could make!"

"I tried all my life to shine in my father's eyes, but so long as that fucking Lynx de Warenne was around, my father hardly acknowledged my existence!"

"It is not right that Lynx de Warenne is your father's

heir. He is not worthy! Why don't you convince your father that Lynx plots against the crown with Robert Bruce?"

Fitz's hand tightened on Alicia's buttock and he squeezed brutally. "Is it true—does he plot with Bruce?"

"Does it matter whether it is true or not, so long as John de Warenne believes you?"

"The old swine wouldn't believe anything I said against the saintly Lynx." His eyes narrowed dangerously. "But the king might believe it."

Alicia fed his vanity. "What a brilliant idea, Fitz! Obviously there's more to you than an oversized cock," she purred. "Discredit Lynx de Warenne and your father might make you his heir!"

"My father will never make me his heir so long as Lynx de Warenne lives and breathes."

Alicia smiled and cupped his testes. "I'm sure a man with your balls could arrange a tragic accident. Really, Fitz, I can't believe you've let him live this long. Lynx hates you so much, I'm sure he'd eliminate you if he ever got the chance."

Murder was not a new idea to Fitz-Waren, so the seeds Alicia sowed fell on fertile soil. In the meantime he'd join his father in Edinburgh. The governor must send frequent reports to the king. It would be a simple matter to add a few hints about Lynx de Warenne plotting to gain the crown for his great friend Robert Bruce. Such information would not fall on deaf ears, especially if he reminded Edward that when he commanded Lynx's Welsh bowmen they threatened to defect to the Scots.

"Pack your bags, Alicia, we're leaving this stinking midden tomorrow."

* * *

Christmas at Dumfries had been fairly quiet. A light powdery snow transformed the dales' huge mountains from purple to white and added to the children's enjoyment of the holy days. Marjory de Warenne and Elizabeth de Burgh had accepted an invitation to join the Bruce festivities, which went on for days, but Jane stayed snug at Dumfries, not risking the wagon ride to Lochmaben.

A week after they returned, the women all sat with Jane before a warm fire in her chamber. She had plenty of company these days because her time was drawing close. Her brother's wife, Judith, along with two needlewomen, were helping her sew swaddling clothes for the baby. Jory and Elizabeth were also plying their needles, even though the results of their labor caused much merriment and laughter among the women.

Periodically Jane struggled to her feet and put her hand to her back to ease the dull ache that plagued her when she sat too long. As she passed the tall window, she paused and gave a little cry.

Jory jumped up to aid her. "Is it time?"

"No, no." Jane pointed through the window where dark riders were visible against the white landscape. "It's Lynx!"

"How can you tell? They're too far away."

"Perhaps it's the way he sits his horse; I could never mistake him for any other."

"Well, it's about time the callous devil returned. I shall give him a piece of my mind!"

Jane smiled at Jory. "Was it not you who told me a man always needs a warm welcome? Was it not you who told me a man hates a shrew and a nag above all things?"

"You actually pay attention to what I say?" Jory teased.

"I write it down in my journal," young Elizabeth de Burgh said solemnly.

Jane had plenty of time to make her way down to the hall. She knew Lynx de Warenne and his knights would see to their own horses before they sought the warmth of the castle.

The men came into the hall together, stamping their feet and brushing snow from their shoulders. The women were waiting for them. "Welcome home," they chorused and were rewarded by grins of gratitude.

Lynx looked from Jory to Jane. "I'm sorry I missed Christmas and wasn't here to welcome in the New Year."

Jory opened her mouth and the others held their breath. "Don't give it a thought, at least you are in time to celebrate Twelfth Night." The ladies let out their breath and dissolved into laughter.

"I fail to see anything amusing, but it feels damn good to be welcomed with laughter." Lynx took Jane's hands in his as his glance swept her from head to foot. "Are you well?"

"Very well, thank you, my lord."

"Happy New Year, Jane. I've brought a cradle from Edinburgh carved with roses and thistles. Just wait till you see it."

"We saw the packhorses loaded down with gifts," Jory informed him archly, "so we decided to forgive you."

"They're all for Jane . . . sorry about that, Minx," he teased, knowing he couldn't fool his sister for one minute. As he stood there Lynx was filled with an overwhelming sense of anticipation, yet at the same time he couldn't shake off his feeling of apprehension. Now that he had seen Jane and knew the child would be arriving soon, his feelings heightened in intensity.

Once again, he was torn, needing to spend the evening in the hall with his men to prepare them for what lay ahead, but wanting to be with Jane and his child. "Will you join me in the hall, lady?"

Jane blushed and shook her head. "In my advanced condition I would draw every eye. I'll be more comfortable in my chamber."

"Above all things I want you to be comfortable. After I talk with the men, may I join you?" he inquired politely. Lynx wanted to ask her a hundred questions. He clenched his fists at his sides, wanting to put his hands on her belly, knowing a need to hold both her and his child. But he knew that Jane was far too shy and reserved for him to do any of these things while others were present.

"Come whenever you wish, my lord," she murmured sweetly and moved toward the stairs.

Suddenly Lynx didn't give a damn who was present. He swept her up in his arms and carried her up to her chamber in the Master Tower. He sat her before the fire, drew up a stool for her feet, and put cushions to her back. When he was certain she was comfortable, he dropped a kiss on her head and promised, "I'll be up as soon as I can."

Lynx de Warenne stood on the dais in the vast dining hall and spoke to the men as they were eating and while they were a captive audience. He told them he had pledged their support to the governor and warned them to be prepared to go wherever they were needed.

He confirmed that the lull in hostilities was due only to the weather and when trouble broke out again, they would be leaving for Edinburgh. He told them flatly that if the hostilities were not stamped out and their enemies were allowed to unite, another full-scale war threatened just down the road.

Lynx de Warenne wanted his men to be fully prepared for whatever lay ahead of them. He told them to ready their horses, their armor, and their weapons. He informed them they would be responsible for their own supply wagons and listed what they would carry in their baggage train.

Then he reminded them of Scotland's treacherous winter conditions, pointing out that they would need extra warm clothing and bedding. Most of his men-at-arms were veterans, many had fought in Wales and knew that a mountain blizzard could mean death by freezing or starvation.

Once he had prepared them for the worst, he raised a horn of ale and said, "In the meantime, we are going to enjoy a belated Christmas and New Year's celebration. I hear the Bruce's festivities lasted three days. Surely we can do better than that? Does anyone here object to a week's holiday?"

The response from the men was deafening.

22

As Lynx opened her chamber door, Jane gave a great yawn and set aside the tiny nightgown she had been sewing. She struggled to arise and Lynx waved his hand to stop her. "Nay, don't get up on my account."

She smiled softly. "I'm not. I have to move about to relieve the ache in my back."

"Then let me help you." He was beside her instantly.

"Just hold out your hand and I'll pull myself up." He did as she instructed and Jane levered herself from the chair. "Oh, that made it so much easier than doing it myself. Thank you."

They lapsed into an awkward silence, the same gulf separating them as when they parted. Lynx desperately wanted to close the void that had opened between them. For one thing he wanted to touch his child, and for another, he wanted to sleep in the same bed with her in case she needed him. They had fallen into the habit of being scrupulously polite with one another and he searched his mind for a way to toss politeness out the window.

Lynx wondered how she would react if he said exactly what was on his mind. *I want to see you naked.* Suddenly, Jane yawned again and he saw that her eyelids were drooping. Lynx leaped across the chasm. "You can hardly keep your eyes open, let me undress you."

Jane's eyelids lifted quickly enough, then her lashes fanned her cheeks as she guessed what he wanted.

Lynx held out his hand to her and she placed hers in it and allowed him to draw her close. He sat down before the fire and opened his thighs so she could move between them. Then he undid the buttons on each side of her smock and drew it over her head. Her fine lawn chemise clung to her body, outlining her shape. To his discerning eyes she was carrying the child much lower now than the last time he'd seen her.

As he reached to lift off her shift, Jane modestly turned her back to him. She was naked now, standing between his thighs, yet still he had seen only her back. He reached up to undo her thick plait and her hair tumbled over his hands like flaming silk. Lynx said thickly, "Turn for me, Jane."

Very slowly, Jane turned until she faced him. Lynx drew in a swift breath. It was the first time he had ever seen a naked female heavy with child, and he was absolutely enthralled. The curve of her belly was pronounced, yet beautiful in its elliptical shape. Her breasts were full, round, firm, and luscious. The skin of her breasts and belly was so taut and smooth, it looked like cream satin.

The firelight played across her flesh, turning it from cream, to golden, to flame. Her hair whispered about her shoulders, possessively clinging, curling, covering her delicate collarbone. The outward curve of her precious burden shadowed her mons, making it seem an extremely private and secret place.

"You are so beautiful, you stop the breath in my throat," he said reverently.

Tentatively at first, he brushed his fingertips across her skin, then when he found her flesh so firm and warm to the touch, he became bolder and caressed her mounded belly with loving hands. "I want to sleep with you tonight."

She leaned into his hands, loving the feel of them against her skin. "I don't sleep much these nights, it's difficult to be comfortable. I lie on my side and cushion the baby with a bolster."

"Let me be your bolster; lie against me tonight."

She nodded shyly and before he lifted her into bed, Lynx put his lips to her firm, fragrant flesh and covered her with kisses. Then Lynx stripped off his clothes and joined her in the bed, ready to accommodate her any way he could.

"I need your back," Jane whispered.

Obligingly he turned on his side and presented his broad back to her. Jane moved against him, putting her left arm about his chest, then she slipped her left leg between his, so that the baby lay against his back. She felt so secure in the warm nest that soon her eyes closed and her breathing deepened in slumber.

Lynx, knowing the child was safe between the two people who had created it and loved it, felt a deep contentment steal over him. When he knew that Jane finally slept, he relaxed and fell asleep with the baby rhythmically kicking his back.

Lynx awoke with a start, not knowing how long he had been asleep. Beside him, Jane was struggling to sit up, while trying to muffle sounds of distress. The chamber was pitch-black, so Lynx swung his legs from the bed and fumbled about the night table until he had the candles lit.

"Is the baby coming? Stay calm, I'll get help." He sprang up and was halfway to the door before her words penetrated his brain.

"No, please, don't alert the castle, please, Lynx."

He came back to the bed, running a hand through his tawny mane of hair until it stood on end. "I thought your labor had started."

Jane put her hand on his arm to keep him at her side. "It has only just begun, it will go on for hours yet. It's barely midnight, I think; the baby won't be born before daylight."

Lynx looked at her in alarm. "Don't you want the midwife or one of the other women? Tell me who you want."

"I want only you, for now."

Lynx took a deep breath. Whatever Jane wanted at this moment, Jane was going to get. "Sweeting, what do you want me to do?"

"I want you to stay with me, talk to me, help me make it through the darkest hours of the night until dawn breaks."

He picked up her bedgown, spun from soft cream lamb's wool, and wrapped it about her, then helped her from the bed. He rekindled the fire, pulled up the big chair, and took her onto his lap. Tenderly, he brushed a curl from her temple. "Are you afraid?"

Jane looked into his green eyes and knew if she admitted the truth, he might panic. Not only was she afraid for herself, but fear for her baby threatened to overwhelm her. But at all costs, Jane knew she must not transfer her fears to Lynx. In her woman's wisdom, she knew this was a time when they must give each other strength.

The corners of her mouth went up. "How can I be afraid when you are holding me?"

He pulled her head against his shoulder and stroked her hair. He felt her body stiffen as a pain knifed into her. When it passed, she whispered, "Talk to me."

He said the first thing that came into his head. "Did you read the letter I sent you?" Feeling a need for honesty between them, he admitted, "I tore up the first three that I wrote . . . they were filled with orders."

Jane too wanted no more secrets between them. "I cannot read," she whispered, "but Jory has promised to teach me. I put your letter beneath my pillow."

Lynx laughed, recalling the struggle he'd had with the damn thing. "I didn't learn how to read until I was nine. My tutors had to beat it into me. All I cared for was horses and swords and battle strategy. Then John de Warenne told me I couldn't become his squire until I could read. I learned fast enough then."

He talked to her for hours, discussing everything from religion to what it felt like before going into battle. Whenever Jane was gripped with an agonizing labor pain, Lynx talked her through it, masking his own fear so he would not communicate it to her. Every hour he rubbed her back, massaged her feet, and brought her endless drinks of water.

All the while he kept talking. At one point he even found himself wanting to tell her of his first marriage and the difficulties they had encountered, but realized this was neither the time nor the place. Instead, he asked her about names for the baby. If it was a girl, Jane said she wanted to call her Jory, and if it was a boy, they settled on Lincoln, which was his late father's name, as well as his own.

Toward morning her contractions were coming closer together and Lynx was relieved when Taffy arrived with a breakfast tray. His young squire took in the situation with his first glance and ran to tell Lady Marjory. Soon the chamber was filled with women. The castle midwife arrived and Elizabeth de Burgh brought Molly and Maggie, both experienced midwives in their own right. Judith Leslie appeared and Jane's sister Mary soon followed. Both of them had given birth in the last few months.

Lynx became alarmed as Jane's moans increased. Then she began to pant and her lovely hair became drenched with perspiration. "Can't you do something for her?" he demanded grimly.

Molly, a plainspoken Irish woman, did not approve of a man being present at such a time. "Jane is small; your baby enormous. This is what childbirth is like!"

Lynx appealed to Judith. "Can't you give her something for the pain?"

Judith shook her head helplessly. "Only Megotta knows which herbs to use."

He saw Jane murmur a request to Jory, who went to the wardrobe and brought back something made of black velvet. Jane clutched it to her possessively and closed her eyes. "This is my bedrobe," Lynx said, at a loss.

Jane opened her eyes and murmured, "It brings me comfort."

A great lump of guilt rose in his throat as he acknowledged that he was the author of all this misery. He felt Jane grab his hand and knew she needed desperately to communicate something to him. He went on his knees and bent his head close to her bloodless lips.

"Lynx," she whispered, "please leave me now . . . I cannot scream in front of you."

He gathered both her hands in his and kissed them, then he got to his feet and strode from the chamber. He did not stop until he was at Megotta's house.

When she opened the door at his insistent hammering, Megotta demanded, "What do you want?"

Lynx searched his mind for a way to get through to her. "I want some common ground between us so we can communicate."

"We will never have common ground!"

"You and I have much in common. We both have a towering pride that rules our lives, but we both care deeply for Jane . . . Help ease her suffering, Megotta."

"She's giving birth to a Norman; she deserves to suffer!"

The old crone was so blood-proud, Lynx wanted to strike her. Despite her harsh words, he could see from the expression on her face that she was concerned about Jane. He decided to use cunning to manipulate her. He shrugged his shoulders and made to leave. "We have two Irish midwives in charge; Jane can manage without you."

The word "Irish" did the trick. "Irish? They'll botch the job!" Megotta grabbed her medicinal box and scurried past him in her headlong rush to the castle.

Because of the impending birth, Dumfries' steward wisely put the holiday celebrations on hold, and since there would be plenty of time before the castle started rejoicing, he directed the maidservants and young pages to gather holly, ivy, and evergreen boughs to decorate the hall. Then Jock Leslie took pity on Lynx and kept him occupied for the next few hours as best he could.

With the help of David Leslie, who was in charge of the stores, they did an inventory of the food supplies Dumfries had on hand, calculated what Lynx's men would take in their baggage train, then made a list of what would be left. Then they did the same with fodder for the animals. Though the supplies seemed adequate, Lynx knew it was wise to set aside a healthy reserve that they could call on in an emergency. He arranged to send half a dozen men to Carlisle for the extra provisions.

Lynx realized the time would pass more quickly if he focused his attention on the task at hand, but still he had difficulty separating his mind completely from what was happening in the Master Tower. As he walked to the armory, Lynx thought he heard the wail of a baby, but it was a familiar enough sound at Dumfries and he was soon distracted when his chief armorer admitted to a dilemma.

Apparently there were some weapons missing. The armorer had assumed they were at the forge for cleaning and repairing, but when a tally had been taken, the count had come up short. Lynx made a mental note to query his knights and went himself to the blacksmith forge to question James and Alex Leslie. They pleaded ignorance of any knowledge of the weapons' whereabouts, so Lynx decided not to interrogate them further until he had spoken to his men-at-arms. But he wasn't entirely convinced they knew nothing; weapons did not get up and walk of their own volition.

Back in the castle he wandered about aimlessly and was inevitably drawn to the vast kitchens by the savory smells of roasting meat and baking pastries. Oxens and whole stags were spitted and turning over in gigantic, walk-in fireplaces built into the walls. The outer kitchens were filled with his Welshmen, plucking game and skinning hares for tomorrow's feast.

Suddenly, Lynx felt as if the walls of the castle were closing in on him. The heat of the kitchens was suffocating and he knew he needed a dose of fresh air. He went to the stables, saddled a favorite mount, and headed into the wind. He followed the river Nith to its mouth and rode along the pebbled shore of the Solway Firth where it opened into the sea. The weather was too harsh for any ships to be anchored in the small port today.

The wind was bitter cold, but he welcomed it, breathing in the salt air as if it were the elixir of life. The rocks and shells on the beach were coated with ice, so he did not ride recklessly, but cantered slowly, savoring the lashing waves and the endless screams of the seabirds. Lynx did not want to think, only feel. By becoming one with the windswept slate sky and the roiling pewter sea, whose turbulence was infinitely greater than his own, he achieved a measure of calm within.

When he headed back to Dumfries, the afternoon light was fading from the sky. He gave his horse a good rubdown and an extra measure of oats, then headed for the castle. He expected the first man he met to give him the news that he longed for yet dreaded at the same time, but though the men in the hall greeted him, they gave him no news.

Lynx knew he must go to Jane and face whatever awaited him behind the closed door of her chambers. Splendor of God, where would he find the courage? He looked down at his hands in dismay, realizing he stank of horse. As he climbed the outside stairs to his own tower rooms he wondered if his decision to bathe and change was one of cowardice.

When he opened his chamber door, he found both Thomas and Taffy awaiting him. Expecting the worst, Lynx braced himself.

"Where the blazing hell have ye bin?" Thomas demanded.

"They asked for you two hours ago," Taffy added, pouring hot water from the cans into the wooden tub.

"The child?" Lynx questioned.

"Bloody women!" Thomas cursed. "Do ye think they'd let us men know anythin' at all? They're like a coven of witches, performin' their rites, guardin' their secrets. They hold the whip hand when it comes to childbirthin' and well they know it! At a time like this they close ranks, press their lips together, and look down their superior noses at the male of the species."

At Lynx's look of alarm, Taffy tried to reassure him. "We heard a baby cry hours ago."

Lynx stripped off his clothes and stepped into the water, thankful that the child was at least born, but worried mindless over whether all was well. With Thomas's aid he threw on his clothes and stuffed a bag of gold coins into his doublet, then with trepidation he opened the door that led down to Jane's chambers.

The outer room was filled with women and every last one of them had a smug look on her face.

"Congratulations, my lord, you have a fine, great son."

"Biggest lad I've seen in years!"

Lynx's anxious green eyes sought out his sister's for confirmation. Jory looked ready to burst with excitement. "Hurry, she's waiting for you."

Lynx felt numb. Somehow he managed to cross the room and walk through the connecting archway. Jane was sitting up in bed, absolutely glowing. A smile lit up her face and her eyes were soft with love. She looked radiant. Lynx was stunned. As he reached her side, he said hoarsely, "When I left, I thought you at death's door."

"I needed to scream, then I felt a lot better. Thank you for bringing in Megotta, she gave me something that took away a good deal of the pain." Jane pulled aside a corner of the shawl that covered the baby. "You have a son, my lord."

Lynx looked down at the child with disbelief. "They told me he was big; he's the smallest scrap of humanity I've ever seen!"

"He *is* big . . . big and beautiful and perfect. Say hello to Lincoln de Warenne the Third."

He pulled aside the shawl so he could get a better look at his son, then he shook his head in wonder, as a smile tugged at the corners of his mouth. The big eyes already had a hint of green and pointed tufts of tawny down covered the baby's head. "His name may be Lincoln the Third, but he looks like a lynx cub to me."

"Thank you for letting me have him to myself for the first few hours. I felt so possessive of him, I didn't know how I was going to share him. But now that you are here, I don't mind at all. Here, take him." Jane gently scooped up her son and offered him to his father.

He reached out gingerly, fearing his clumsiness would do the child an injury, but once he held him securely in his arms, Lynx's natural instincts took over and he vowed no harm would ever come to his child so long as he drew breath.

"You must be dying to show him off. Take him down to the hall and let the men see him," Jane said proudly.

But suddenly Lynx understood what Jane meant when she had said she was possessive of him and didn't want to share him. He also better understood the women in the outer room wanting to keep and savor their secret. Just for a while, just for tonight, he didn't want to share his son with the castle. Lynx's entire universe encompassed this chamber alone and he wanted to remain here with his child and its mother, where they could be private and undisturbed and shut out the world.

Lynx handed the baby back to Jane. "Tomorrow will be soon enough." He entered the outer room, sincerely thanked all the women for their help, and gave every one of them a piece of gold. "We want to be alone now," he explained firmly, "but I'd like the pleasure of telling the men myself, ladies."

The women filed out, more than happy to keep the secret of the child's gender from the inquisitive men of Dumfries, who normally ruled the roost.

When Lynx returned, he did not take his child from its mother's arms, but slipped down on his knees beside the bed and stroked the backs of his fingers across the tawny tufts. "Jane, I want to thank you from the bottom of my heart for giving me a son."

The corners of her mouth lifted with delight. "Nay, *I* want to thank *you* for giving *me* a son. I couldn't have done it without you," she teased.

Her words made him remember how the child had been

conceived and he felt humbled. Jane had given him this child out of simple duty to her lord, and Lynx knew he would be eternally indebted to her. "Jane, you simply have no idea how grateful I am to you. I want to reward you. Ask anything of me and if it is within my power, I will gift you with it."

Jane wanted only one thing from Lynx de Warenne; she wanted his love. And suddenly she didn't think it was an impossibility. The void that stretched between them had narrowed during the hours of her labor. He had tended her with loving hands and surely that was the first step toward tending her with a loving heart. Out of gratitude she knew he was willing to marry her, but she wanted more than his gratitude.

Jane knew he was so joyous at becoming a father, and so well pleased with the child, that he would want more children. She sensed that his next words would be about marriage, because Lynx felt it was his duty to make her his wife. She spoke up quickly. "There is one thing I would like, if you will indulge me."

Briefly he pictured an expensive jewel. "Just name it."

"I know you are going to speak of marriage again . . . would you let me pick the time?"

He stared at her in disbelief. Tomorrow he'd had every intention of sending for the priest and overruling her objections. But she had anticipated him and cleverly held him in check. His green eyes flashed their annoyance. The little minx was going to pit her will against his!

His son opened his mouth and began to scream. He watched Jane murmur a soothing word of love and lift the child to her breast. Lynx was mesmerized as he saw the little mouth fasten to her nipple and his son's fists clench and unclench on her breast as he took undisputed possession of it.

Lynx's face softened as the intimate picture touched his heart. He smiled at Jane and murmured, "I can refuse you nothing."

23

Not only the castle, but the entire village of Dumfries decided to celebrate the birth of Lynx de Warenne's heir. The moment that the news leaked out the next day, it flowed through the wide, friendly streets of the town until it reached the Franciscan monastery on the north bank of the river Nith. A great peal of bells rang out and didn't stop for a full twenty-four hours.

A courier on a fast horse was dispatched to the Bruce at Lochmaben asking him to stand as godfather to Lincoln de Warenne the Third, and before evening descended, Robert, Nigel, and Alexander, as well as their brother Thomas, who had ridden over from their castle of Caerlaverock, headed down the Annandale Valley toward Dumfries with packhorses piled high with presents.

Jane was up and about, glowing with health and happiness and feeling light as thistledown. She refused to let her baby out of her sight, but the ladies insisted she could not carry him herself until she was stronger, and vied with each other for the privilege of toting him about.

With Jory and Elizabeth, to say nothing of Molly and Maggie, passing his son around possessively, Lynx hardly got a chance to look at him, let alone hold him. So he sought out Jock Leslie to ask him to recommend a competent nursemaid to help Jane and take charge at the same time.

"I prefer a mature woman over a young girl, a no-nonsense, capable nursemaid who will put her foot down when it's necessary."

"I think Grace Murray would be yer best choice, my lord. She's in charge of the castle maids and knows how to knock their heads together when they misbehave."

"Send this Grace Murray to me and I'll have a word with her; she sounds ideal," Lynx decided.

Jock cleared his throat in preparation for what he was about to say. Lord de Warenne had always dealt fairly with him and Jock plucked up his courage to broach what might be a delicate subject. "I expect ye'll be planning brothers an' sisters fer yer son, my lord?"

Lynx grinned. "I'm sure as hell not going to stop, now that I've sired one."

"When ye handfasted Jane, there was a promise of marriage—"

As the words hung in the air, Lynx's piercing glance met his steward's and held. "I have been trying to marry your daughter since the day I returned three months back and saw my child ripening in her belly. On my honor, it is Jane who is dragging her feet over the marriage, not I."

Jock was outraged. "I'll soon settle her nonsense, my lord; make yer arrangements with the priest."

"No, Jock. I don't want her pressured in any way. I've given Jane my word that she can decide when we'll marry."

Jock looked at Lord de Warenne as if he had lost his mind. "Beggin' yer pardon, my lord, but ye've never fallen into the trap of lettin' a woman have her own way?"

"She gives me little choice, she's refused me outright on several occasions."

"Did ye not beat her?" Jock demanded.

A ludicrous picture of a muscular six-foot man beating a delicate girl of less than a hundred pounds flashed across his mind. "Of course I didn't beat her."

"There's yer mistake! A firm hand applied to the bottom on a nightly basis will bring total obedience; I guarantee it, my lord."

"Thank you for your advice, Jock," Lynx said solemnly. He was astounded at the ignorance of most men when it came to women. A nightly beating would not guarantee total obedience; more likely it would guarantee infidelity or a cup of hemlock.

Lynx spoke with Grace Murray, then satisfied with her capable manner, appointed her his son's nursemaid, starting tomorrow when the festivities would begin. Then he went up to Jane's chamber to inform her of his decision, sensing that he would meet with resistance.

Jane was nursing the baby, while Jory fussed over the temperature of the baby's bathwater and Elizabeth de Burgh decorated the carved cradle with blue and white ribbons.

His blunt tongue almost ordered the women to leave, then a more subtle idea occurred to him. "Ladies, I need your help. The Bruces have just arrived en masse and there is no one in the hall to welcome them. Would you be so kind?" Lynx saw the pretty blush that suffused Elizabeth's cheeks and knew he had dangled the perfect bait to lure her downstairs. He did not notice the green flame ignite in Jory's eyes, but was grateful when she followed Elizabeth from the chamber.

Lynx secured the door against all intruders and came back. He could not take his eyes from the enchanting picture of his son suckling his mother's breast. "Are you exhausted?"

"No, no, I'm too filled with happiness, there's no room left for exhaustion."

If only she'd admit to being tired, his next words would be easier. "I've appointed Grace Murray as the baby's nursemaid. She's a capable woman who will give you all the help you need."

Jane's face fell as she clasped her son closer to her breast. "I don't want any help. I want to look after him myself!"

His hand reached out to lift a silken curl from her shoulder. "Sweeting, you may not *want* help, but you *need* help. The young pup kept you up all night. How long can you keep that up? Jane, you'll still be in charge. Grace will take her orders from you. When you've tended him all day, doesn't it make sense that Grace look after him through the night so you can rest? She can share this room with him."

"But he needs feeding in the night," Jane explained.

"Then we'll get a wet nurse. God's teeth, you can't nurse him day and night."

Jane glared at him defiantly. "I will and I shall!"

He looked at her in disbelief, yet he felt admiration for her. "You shout those bloody words at me like a battle cry. Lady, are you not willing to compromise?"

They stared at each other for a full minute, but this time Jane refused to lower her eyes from his. Then the corners of her mouth went up. "You are conceding a great deal, Lord de Warenne, to compromise with a woman. I agree to have Grace as his nursemaid, I even agree to let her share his chamber, but day or night he will be brought to me to be fed at my breast and no other."

Since he had accomplished what he came for, Lynx acceded to her declaration graciously. "It shall be as you wish." A teasing light came into his eyes as he brushed back a red-gold tendril from her temple. "This stubborn streak of willfulness you have developed is damned attractive. I like nothing better than a challenge."

She ran the tip of her tongue over pink lips. "You thought the harmless little kitten you handfasted had no claws."

Watching that tongue, Lynx grew hard. His son's eyes closed in contented sleep and a bright nipple popped from his mouth. Lynx's cock began to pulse.

"I am no harmless kitten, I am the mother of a lynx cub. I not only spit and scratch, I bite too!"

A blazing hot desire spread through his veins until he could feel his need pounding from his throat to the soles of his feet. His groin was so engorged, it felt as if it might burst. It was the very first time Lynx had ever felt lust for this woman. *His* woman, he reminded himself. She was doubly desirable because she was forbidden to him for a few days yet.

With an iron will he tried to banish the lust that raged within, but he found it impossible. The best he could do was bank the fires in his blood so that he did not lose control. If he could keep his rampant sexuality caged for two or three more nights, he would be able to unleash it and let it run wild. He tore his glance from her lush breasts and forced his mind from erotic thoughts.

"I know the hour is advanced, but would you consider having a late supper with the Bruces and letting them have a glimpse of our son before you retire?"

Jane's dimples came out of hiding. "I can't wait to show Robert my beautiful little treasure."

Lynx's shaft bucked again as her words provoked his wicked thoughts. Not until she handed him his sleeping son did his blood begin to cool.

"I'll be down as soon as I've bathed my breasts and changed my gown."

His blood began to heat up again at the thought of watching her do these things. "I'll wait for you and we'll go down together," he said thickly.

Jane was surprised that Lynx had not whisked away his son to display him like a trophy before his friend Robert and the Bruce brothers. She had given him the opportunity to take the baby, but he seemed intent upon lingering in her chamber.

Was he just being polite, offering to wait for her, or had she at last taken his fancy? If such was the case, she had Jory to thank for it. Her advice had been priceless. *Men don't admire meek and submissive women, not real men anyway. They admire women who are willful and a little bit wanton.*

More of Jory's words came back to her. *You must become a challenge to him.* Jane smiled; had Lynx not just admitted that he liked nothing better than a challenge and that he found her willfulness damned attractive? Jane's lashes swept to her cheeks. If she wasn't mistaken, she had heard Lynx's voice roughen with what might be desire. *Men want what they cannot have.* Since willfulness had worked out in her favor, was it not time to try being *a little bit wanton*?

The front of Jane's gown opened and closed to allow her to feed the baby. She deliberately left it undone and reached behind her to unfasten the back. She pretended a great deal of difficulty and smiled a secret smile as Lynx laid his son in his cradle and hastened to her aid. She presented her back to him, knowing full well that his view of her breasts from his great height would be totally unimpeded.

Jane drew in a swift breath as she felt his fingers come into contact with her naked back and she allowed him to hear it. She was amply rewarded when she felt him sweep aside her hair and touch his lips to her nape. Was it gratitude or was it desire? Jane decided to find out.

She leaned back against him and instantly felt his erection against her soft bottom. Pretending to notice nothing she moved away, stepped from her gown, and walked over to the washstand to pour rosewater into the bowl. Lynx followed her as if she were a lodestone. She felt his hands cup her shoulders, then slide her shift down so that she was naked to the waist. When his lips touched her bare flesh, a delicious shiver ran down the entire length of her spine. She turned her head to look up at him over her shoulder and their gazes met and held.

She saw green fire burning in his eyes as he lifted a handful of her hair. He rubbed the silken tresses against his cheek, then inhaled its fragrance. "I want to wrap myself in your hair. The feel of it arouses me to madness," he said huskily.

Slowly, she turned to face him, and watched as his

possessive gaze was drawn to her upthrust breasts. Silently, seductively, she offered him the sponge in blatant, sensual invitation. Lynx took the sponge from her, dipped it into the rosewater, and with gentle, loving hands bathed her beautiful breasts.

Jane gasped at the exquisite sensations he was arousing deep inside her. His touch was a silken torment, teasing and arousing her until she was smoky-eyed with desire. When Lynx dried her breasts with the towel, its rough texture made her cry out with pure pleasure and she felt her nipples harden into erect little buds. With deliberate slowness, Jane took up a tiny pot and lifted off its lid.

"What's that?" he asked in fascination.

"Glycerin . . . I put a drop on each nipple to keep them supple." She watched the dark pupils of his green eyes dilate.

"Let me do that," he said thickly.

"If it would give you pleasure." Jane knew it would certainly give her pleasure. His faintest touch made her weak with longing.

As he touched his fingertips to her nipple, she watched him almost come out of his skin, but she did not count on the effect it would have on her. As he moved to her other breast and rubbed the bright tip with the glycerin, she felt a wetness begin between her legs, then she felt her woman's center convulse and she was taken with a delicious shudder. She watched his eyes lift to her mouth and knew he was about to take her in his arms and cover her with kisses.

Though Jane wanted nothing more in the world, she remembered Jory's infallible advice. *Refuse him, and he will turn over heaven and earth to get you.* She was ravenous for the kiss and decided to allow him just one, to whet his appetite for more. As his mouth came down on hers, her lips parted to welcome the savage ravishing. She realized the moment his lips took possession of hers that he was the one in control, not her.

Lynx did not release her mouth until their kiss built to an intensity that neither of them had ever experienced before. With a little cry, she pulled away quickly and went to her wardrobe for a fresh gown. "We must hurry, my lord, 'tis very rude to keep our guests waiting."

As Lynx descended the staircase with his son clasped in his right arm and Jane holding his left, the cheers and applause of the Bruce brothers standing at the bottom rose up to surround them.

Jane felt herself lifted from her feet by Robert's massive arms as he planted a kiss upon her mouth. "Well done, Jane!" Then he took the child from Lynx, unwrapped the shawl, and inspected him from head to foot. "Looks like a lynx cub to me . . . You do realize he's a Scot?"

Until that moment Lynx hadn't thought of it, but he realized he'd be ragged unmercifully for producing a Scot and might as well concede with good grace.

"I've brought him a magnificent Bruce cradle on condition you'll name him after me," Robert declared.

Lynx took back his son. "He's already got a cradle I hauled all the way from Edinburgh and his name is Lincoln de Warenne the Third."

Jane slipped between the two rivals. "He can use two cradles; one upstairs in his nursery and one down here in the hall. And I've decided his name shall be Lincoln Robert de Warenne."

Robert slapped his friend on the back. "Ho! The lass is ruling the roost now, I see."

Nigel and Alex Bruce hooted. "Better get her under control or she'll put a ring through your nose and lead you about like a prize bull!"

"Let's get our feet under the table so we can start the toasts. Bring on the whisky!" Thomas Bruce demanded.

Marjory said to Jane, "We can toast with hypocras. It's deliciously spicy, you'll love it."

"Malt whisky not good enough for you, Jory?" Thomas teased.

"I've developed a taste for some things Scottish, but whisky isn't one of them."

Lynx laid the baby in the cradle and they enjoyed an intimate supper with only the Bruces for company. The de Warenne heir slept blissfully through the noisy toasts and raucous laughter. When they were all replete with food and drink, Jory signaled Taffy, who brought in an armful of presents that St. Nicholas had left on Twelfth Night.

Each gift bore the name of one person sitting at table. Most of the men found a dagger or dirk when they unwrapped their favors, but Robert Bruce was momentarily puzzled when he opened the wrapping and found a piece of ribbon onto which had been stitched two Christmas bells. He turned the piece of frippery over and over in his hands, trying to recall where he had seen a similar object before. Then it came to him and he quickly stuffed it inside his doublet as tears of laughter rolled down his face. He was well aware that Jory was delighted with his reaction, though he was far too discreet to glance her way.

All eyes focused on Jane as she unwrapped her gift. Marjory had had the castle needlewomen working for days on a gown that would show off Jane's slim figure. It was fuchsia velvet with long trailing sleeves, lined in white satin. The low neck and the hem were bordered with a wide band of pearl and crystal beads.

Jane gasped, then burst into tears. "Oh, Jory, it's the loveliest gown I've ever seen, how can I thank you?"

"By wearing it tomorrow and taking your rightful place as Chatelaine of Dumfries."

The Bruces heartily agreed, telling her she was the most beautiful mother in Scotland.

"Thank you for coming to our celebration," Lynx said warmly. "We planned it for Twelfth Night, but the lynx cub decided to put in an appearance, so tomorrow will be more like Fifteenth Night."

"I'm Lord of Misrule," Nigel Bruce declared, "and I want no arguments from the old men of the family."

Marjory gave Robert a saucy wink. "Since we have so much to celebrate tomorrow, I suggest we have an early night."

Without glancing in Jory's direction, Robert winked at Jane and declared, "Well, I'm certainly ready for bed."

Jane knew Robert and Jory were sending each other messages right under the others' noses, and her laughter trilled out like silver bells. Lynx frowned. Why did Jane find everything Robert said so damned amusing?

When Jane arose and went to the cradle to lift her son, the men watched her avidly. All four Bruces envied Lynx de Warenne his woman and his son this night. As Jane headed toward the stairs, Lynx took his sister aside. "Jane was so thrilled with the gown. I want to give her something like that, but I brought gifts only for the baby."

"It's a good thing I know what a thoughtless swine you are. I had another gown made and hid it in your own wardrobe. Since she's never had anything pretty, she lusts for lovely things. Can you imagine how rewarding it would be to gift her with furs or jewels?"

Lynx felt his erection start and cursed softly under his breath. "You are a paradox of bitch and angel."

"And I've taught Jane everything I know, you lucky lout."

When Lynx closed the door of Jane's chambers, the lynx cub opened his mouth and started to scream. "Splendor of God, is he going to keep us up all night again?" Lynx ran a frustrated hand through his tawny hair. "What the hell are we going to do?"

Jane smiled. "I'll feed him, then you can walk him. The combination will work like a charm."

An hour later as Lynx walked the floor and watched his son fall asleep in his arms, he offered up a prayer of thanks for the priceless gift that had been bestowed upon him. Truth be told, there was nowhere in the entire world he would rather be at this moment than guarding his firstborn son. It was a labor of love and he realized it was his first intimate experience with the emotion. Lynx cradled him beneath his heart for another hour, then very gently, very quietly, laid him beside his sleeping mother and climbed the stairs to his own chamber so they could slumber undisturbed.

In the opposite tower of Dumfries, Robert Bruce slipped discreetly through a chamber door and shot the bolt securely. Jory awaited him, wearing only an inviting smile. "It took you a few minutes to recall the Roman phallic symbols on Hadrian's Wall."

Robert grinned. "I knew I'd seen the ribbon and bells decorating something or other." He began to laugh as he tossed the trinket from one hand to the other. "You don't seriously expect me to put this on, do you, wench?"

"Of course not, my lord earl, I intend to put it on for you. Get those clothes off!"

High in a tower of Dumfries, the merry jingle of Christmas bells could be heard, on and off, all through the night.

24

When the first day of the celebration dawned, Grace Murray took charge of Jane's son the moment he was fed.

"Dinna worry yer pretty head over the wee lordling, Lady Jane. I'll keep him under my wing like an' old broody hen, so ye can have a wee bit of fun."

"The Bruce brought over a beautiful cradle that we've put front and center in the hall. Since we're celebrating Christmas, New Year's, and Lincoln Robert's christening all at once, I want him to spend as much time with us as possible. Today is just for the castle people and the de Warenne men-at-arms, but tomorrow will include all the townspeople of Dumfries. Hundreds of people will want a good look at him in the next few days."

"Aye, and *look* is all they'll do, I shall see to that! There will be no pokin' at the wee lordling or pickin' him up and jigglin' him till he heaves up his milk!"

"Good heavens, I hadn't thought of that. Do you think they would do such a thing?"

"If I wasn't standin' guard, they'd have their dirty hands all over him, passin' him about like a secondhand haggis!"

Jane was suddenly glad that Grace Murray resembled a

dragon. "Bring him back upstairs before the noon meal is served and I'll feed him, then I'll feed him again before dinner tonight."

Marjory and Elizabeth arrived at Jane's chamber unable to hide the excitement that bubbled inside them. "Good God, aren't you bathed and dressed yet?" Jory demanded.

"I'm bathed, I just have to put on the beautiful dress you gave me last night."

"That wasn't from me, that was from St. Nicholas and I suspect he has more surprises in store for you, Lady Jane Tut!"

"Jory, you're so good!"

"Damn, I'm *very* good, but for the next few days I'm going to be bad, and if you have any sense, you will too. We have a castle full of men, so let's make them dance to our tune! For the first time in nine months you can think about yourself. You are slim and beautiful and I want you to enjoy enough fun and laughter to last you through the dark, cold winter."

Jory turned her attention to Elizabeth de Burgh. "We must both see to it that Elizabeth has a happy time. She's away from Ireland, away from her lovely home, and hardly ever gets to see her father. She hoped to see him at Christmastime, but the Earl of Ulster has pledged to help Edward Plantagenet win France."

"And with de Burgh on his side, the king cannot lose," Lynx de Warenne said as he came down the stairs from his own chamber. His glance fell on Jane in her fine lawn petticoat. "I came to help Jane dress if you'll be good enough to give us a little privacy."

"Dream on, Brother, there isn't time for Jane to indulge your dalliance this morning. Come back in a week if you want her to ride your cockhorse to Banbury Cross!''

Elizabeth's cheeks turned bright red and she began to giggle. She was just beginning to understand the naughty sexual innuendos that Jory came out with.

''For shame, corrupting the child,'' Lynx said sternly. ''I suspect you are a bad influence on Jane as well as Elizabeth.''

''You will be the beneficiary of my corrupting Jane, but I've barely touched the surface. You'll have to plumb the depths yourself to finish the corruption!''

Suddenly, the Lord of Misrule threw open the chamber door. ''Where are all the beautiful women hiding?'' Nigel Bruce demanded. ''You will each pay me a forfeit of one kiss for keeping us waiting!''

Elizabeth insisted on being first, then Jory paid her forfeit with a kiss that was both long and lusty. As Nigel captured Jane in her petticoat, Lynx said, ''I don't think Jane wants to play this game.''

Nigel gave him a pitying glance and Jane said saucily, ''Lynx is too old to remember what fun is all about!''

When the merry group arrived downstairs, the hall had never been so crowded in the castle's history. Tables piled high with food and sweet delicacies sat against the walls and its center was a vast open space from which the dining tables and benches had been removed and replaced with a throng of merrymakers.

The only chairs were up on the dais, alongside the magnificent Bruce cradle. Lynx de Warenne parted waves of celebrants so that he could reach the dais. He deposited

Lincoln Robert in the cradle and Grace Murray, accompanied by Lynx's two squires, sat down in the chairs to guard Dumfries' newest treasure. A line began to form immediately to climb to the dais to view the child.

The festive customs they celebrated were a mixture of English, Scottish, and Welsh. A pine yule log over fifty feet long and three feet in circumference was carried in by over a hundred of the brawniest males. Christmas cheer flowed freely from wassail bowls of hypocras, barrels of ale, jugs of whisky, and flagons of honeyed mead. Every windowsill was strung with holly and ivy, and from every door and archway in the castle hung a huge bunch of white-berried mistletoe.

Music of every description filled the air. Scots pipers roamed the castle, mingling with Welsh harpers and English drummers. Others had flutes and timbrels and handbells, but all the instruments combined could not drown out the laughter of the celebrants who were hell-bent on fun and games. The Lord of Misrule was everywhere, stirring up mischief, demanding forfeits, and leading the crowd in hilarious hijinks, while his brothers Alexander and Thomas aided and abetted his antics.

At eleven o'clock, the hall was cleared and all the children of Dumfries were ushered in. Their excitement was contagious. Jane, Marjory, and young Elizabeth led them in games, races, singing, and dancing. Then Jane stood beside her father while the prizes and presents were handed out. As well as a toy and an article of clothing for every child, they were encouraged to help themselves to sweets. Huge trays of butterscotch, treacle toffee, and quaint marzipan animals sat alongside a mountain of apples and nuts.

As Lynx watched Jane run about with the children, it was brought home to him how young she was. And yet, as she stood with her father, distributing the gifts, he could sense that she had organized most of it and he experienced a great pride in her. While he had been away in Edinburgh, Dumfries must have been a hive of activity, planning these festivities.

After the noon meal, the food was cleared from the tables and they were piled high with gifts for the castle people who served Dumfries. Again, Jane, with the help of Jock and her brother Andrew, the assistant steward, distributed the presents to each and every servant. She gave each of the Leslie women elegant warm cloaks and all her brothers received new doublets. For Megotta there was an intricately carved medicinal box.

Finally, Jane caught Lynx's eye and she beckoned him to join her. She held up her hands until the roar subsided to a low din, then with tears in her eyes she announced, "This largesse is possible only because of Lord de Warenne's unfailing generosity." She stood on tiptoe to kiss his cheek as the crowd went wild, cheering and shouting loud enough to raise the rafters.

As Lynx looked down at her, he knew the generosity was hers. Jane had spent all the monies he had left with the steward for her personal needs on her family.

Lynx spent most of the afternoon with his men-at-arms and Welsh bowmen. They were a long way from home and he greeted each and every man in his mesne and wished him good fortune in the coming year. Meanwhile in the hall his knights, the Bruces, and the ladies were playing games presided over by the Lord of Misrule, who made sure that the hijinks left their dignity in shreds.

When Lynx came into the hall he saw that Jane was blindfolded, with a circle of men about her, in the middle of a game of Blindman's Bluff. Thinking to join in the fun, he walked a direct path to her and lifted her high.

Jane immediately knew it was Lynx who held her feet off the floor, for he was the tallest man in Dumfries. Jane's wicked juices were bubbling and she couldn't resist the urge to tease him. "Robert," she squealed, "you've had enough kisses!"

She felt Lynx stiffen as he set her feet to the floor and lifted the silk mask from her eyes. "Robert has been kissing you?" he demanded in a hurt tone.

Jane took pity on him. "Lynx, I'm teasing . . . I knew it was you!" She dimpled. "But Robert is a devil with the ladies, he even dragged Megotta under the mistletoe!"

Lynx took her hand to lead her to a chair on the dais. "Come and have a rest, you are giddy and breathless."

"Just for a moment," she conceded sweetly. "But some of your Welshmen are putting on a magic show and they've promised to reveal some of their secrets to me." She was elusive as quicksilver and as he gazed at her, he pondered what it was that was making his desire for her mount higher by the minute.

In the brilliant fuchsia velvet, with her red-gold hair tumbling about her like a blaze of fire, she was vividly beautiful, but that wasn't the mysterious essence that captivated him and every other male who had crowded about her all day. An aura of joy and happiness surrounded her as she was caught up in the excitement of the celebration and she seemed determined to wring every ounce of pleasure from the festivities.

It wasn't until the evening meal was over and the dancing well under way that it began to dawn on Lynx what her fatal attraction was. For over an hour he hadn't been able to take his eyes from her, as one man after another competed to partner her, to tease and flirt with her, their only reward a brilliant smile, or a brief glimpse of her elusive dimples. Suddenly he understood what it was that had made his mounting desire for her turn to raging lust.

It was her innocence!

Here was a young girl who had never worn a jewel, nor painted her face in her life. Until recently she had never even owned a pretty gown. She was so innocent, that even though she was a mother, she was not yet a woman! Her female sexuality had not yet been awakened. He had mated with her for the sole purpose of procreating, but she had never been taught that sex could be for pleasure.

All that lay before her! And every man in the hall sensed it and longed to be the one who would introduce her to sensuality. And the thing that made her so tempting and enticing was the fact that she was ripe and ready without even knowing it! Jane was flirtatious and saucy, desirable and seductive, exotic and tantalizing. She was as alluring and provocative as Jory de Warenne, but with the added fillip of innocence, which made her both titillating and utterly irresistible.

Watching Jane had aroused him so much that he could not dance, he could not even walk. All Lynx could do was sit and observe her until the dancing was over and it was time to open the last gifts.

Lynx watched Jane's face suffuse with pleasure as she opened gift after gift for the baby. His knights had outdone themselves, gifting his son with silver rattles and inscribed silver mugs. There were gold medallions commemorating his birth and miniature swords and shields bearing the de Warenne coat of arms. The Welsh archers, who were extremely clever with their hands, had carved toys for the child, including a great wooden rocking horse and a whole army of soldiers guarding a wooden castle. They had also stuffed toy animals with wool and covered them with sleek otter skin.

Lynx kept his present until last. He wanted to see her face light up with joy when she saw the beautiful gown. He watched her fingers begin to tremble as she realized that the gift he had given her was not for the child, but for herself. The gown was made of rustling taffeta in shimmering viridescent green, shot with blue, constantly changing color with the light. It had a high collar at the back and a plunging neckline in front. To enhance the breasts, its bodice was encrusted with emerald and turquoise beads.

Lynx threw Jory a quick glance of gratitude, then his eyes were irresistibly drawn back to Jane's face, as he watched a look of pure rapture transform it.

Still clutching the gown, she went down on her knees before him. "My dearest lord, did you really choose this for me?"

Lynx saw the teardrops clinging to her lashes and suddenly wished with all his heart that he had chosen the gown. He took her hands and raised her for his kiss. "Jane, do not kneel to me, you have given me my heart's desire." In that moment he determined that tomorrow he would search all of Dumfries until he found a gift worthy of her.

A long procession climbed the stairs of the Master

Tower, led by Grace Murray carrying the baby and his squires and castle servants carrying up the gifts. Lynx followed Jane, barely able to bank the fires of his desire until they could be alone. He watched her hang her precious new gown in the wardrobe with loving hands, then he helped her remove the fuchsia velvet dress that had made her so vividly beautiful today. His hands cupped her soft shoulders possessively as he waited with barely concealed impatience for the last maidservant to leave.

Lynx had forgotten that Jane would have to feed his son. He sat down on the bed to watch her lavish her baby with love and attention. Finally, when she had fed him and tended to all his needs, she laid him down beside his father and climbed onto the wide bed.

"At long last I have you to myself," she murmured. She touched the tawny tufts on his head then traced her fingertips along his cheek. "Who is the most beautiful boy in all the world?" she whispered, totally engrossed.

As the baby gurgled and waved his tiny fists about, Lynx knew Jane had eyes only for her child; all his waiting had been in vain. With resignation he dropped a kiss on her head and then one on his son's. "Get some rest, Jane. Tomorrow the celebration begins all over again."

The rejoicing, mirth, and gaiety went on for three more days. The high spirits of the castle people and the townspeople of Dumfries never flagged. Finally it was time to christen the baby, and as the celebrants packed inside the tiny chapel, the atmosphere was jubilant. Lynx de Warenne, with his firstborn in his arms and Lady Jane standing beside him, looked and felt triumphant.

Robert Bruce stood as the child's godfather, and Jory

his godmother. The priest let each of them hold the infant for a special baptismal blessing, before formally christening him Lincoln Robert de Warenne. Then the godfather, carrying the child, led the procession through the castle and down to the hall.

Lynx saw his sister, Jory, wipe away a tear and he slipped a comforting arm about her. He looked down into her green eyes, so like his own, and murmured, "Thank you, I know how difficult that must have been for you."

Jory dashed away another tear. "Why difficult?" she demanded, ready with a denial.

"Because I know you would give anything to have his child."

Jory closed her eyes. "We've been so careful; how did you know?" she whispered.

"There is little about the Bruce that I don't know, Jory." He hugged her close, then tipped her face up so that their eyes could meet again. "He'll not wed you, Jory. His driving ambition to be King of Scotland stands in the way. The people would never accept an English queen."

"I know that, Lynx. I live for today; I'm not greedy enough to want tomorrow also."

That night in the hall a Welsh minstrel held them all in thrall with his epic tale of Beowulf. Lynx watched Jane's delight as she listened spellbound to the mythic tale, accompanied by the haunting notes of the minstrel's harp. Lynx became aware that he wasn't the only man who watched her. His squire Taffy imagined himself in love, and at least two of his younger knights paid constant homage to her. During the last few days of observing her, he had seen that the glances of many of his Welsh bowmen were openly covetous and smoldering whenever they fixed upon her.

Along with his desire, a feeling of possessiveness was growing within him. It was a new emotion for Lynx. Though he was not much given to introspection, Lynx admitted to himself that these feelings were prompted by jealousy as well as lust. He almost resented it when Jane bestowed her sweet smile upon another, or when she shared a moment of laughter that excluded him.

During the past week he had grown to begrudge the innocent kisses she received beneath the mistletoe and had begun to crave them for himself. Lynx knew that he could not go on in this aroused state any longer. He would erupt into violence if one more man so much as looked at her. Tonight he would put his mark upon her so that from this night forward she would be his alone.

His eyes licked over her as she came toward him. She was wearing a pink lamb's-wool gown that clung to every curve of her body. The silver chain that Jory had given her was fastened cunningly about her hips, so that its single ruby sat upon her high mons, tempting every male eye. Damn Jory, she had taught Jane too many tricks! It was time for him to take over as her tutor to teach her the things that would awaken her slumbering sensuality and fulfill her as a woman. It was time for him to take possession.

Jane held out a small package; a shy smile accompanied it. "I was very hesitant about giving you this because our beliefs are different. But it is a gift from the heart. You have given me so much, my lord; this is one of the few things I can give in return."

"Jane, you have given me a son . . . you have given me immortality. It is I who must gift you." He took a big box from beneath his carved chair and they exchanged presents. Lynx slipped the Celtic touchstone from its leather pouch and gazed with delight at the image of the proud lynx she had painted for him. It was in full flight, ready to pounce upon its prey, and it reminded him of himself.

"Thank you, Jane, I shall wear it with pride." He watched her face intently as she unwrapped the gift he had had made especially for her. Tonight he wanted to bring her more pleasure than she had ever known.

She gasped as she held up the emerald velvet cloak, lined with silver fox. "Oh, Lynx, it's magnificent!" She held it out to him. "Help me try it on."

"No!" He drew her close, then bent his head until his lips touched her ear. "When you try on your very first fur, I want you to be naked so that you will experience the luxurious, sensual softness against your skin."

Jane's lashes lifted in surprise. The corners of her mouth went up, revealing her dimples. "Do you often get what you want, my lord?"

"Always." His green eyes purposefully filled with wild surmise to set her all ashiver.

25

Lynx de Warenne signaled Grace Murray to carry his son upstairs, knowing full well that Jane would immediately retire. He bade the company good night, pitying the poor devils who would amuse themselves with their dice half the night and made his way to the Master Tower.

He stayed in Jane's chambers only long enough to retrieve his black velvet bedrobe, but she didn't even notice. As usual, Jane only had eyes for her son once she had him to herself. In his own chamber, Lynx stripped, bathed, and donned his favorite robe, allowing Jane ample time to feed his son. Then he opened the door at the top of the stairs that led to the chamber below and stood quietly observing the maternal scene.

Grace stood by with a fatuous look on her face as Jane cuddled, kissed, and cooed at the baby, far too absorbed in her motherly ministrations to be aware of the man who looked down at her with hungry eyes. When he spoke, his deep voice startled her.

"That young cub takes up every living, breathing moment of your time. You lavish all your attention upon him. His father would like some of that attention. Grace will stay with him tonight, while you come up here where you belong." Having delivered his ultimatum, Lynx withdrew inside his chamber.

Jane handed the baby over to Grace, then moved hesitantly to the foot of the stairs. She gazed up into the shadows, pondering what had just happened. Her pulse quickened with excitement. So, it hadn't been her imagination after all. During the past week, Lynx had hardly taken his eyes from her as she flirted outrageously with all the males who had conspired to lavish her with their attention. She had followed Jory's advice meticulously and at last it was going to pay off. For the first time Lynx de Warenne was seeing her not as the mother of his child, but as a female in her own right . . . a desirable female from the hunger she heard in his voice.

Jane glanced questioningly at Grace Murray. The nursemaid waved her hand, urging Jane to mount the staircase. "Go, go!"

With her heart hammering inside her chest, Jane took the first two steps slowly, tentatively. Suddenly she turned, ran back across the chamber, and picked up her fur cloak. Then with eager steps, she climbed the stairs to do her lord's bidding.

Jane secured the door, then turned to face him, breathless from her eager climb. Her breath deserted her entirely when she saw him clad in the robe. As his eyes fell on the fur she had brought up with her, he smiled in approval and held out a powerful hand. "Come to me. It is time we got to know each other . . . intimately."

His voice had the same black velvety texture as the robe she adored. Jane's heart turned over in her breast. How long had she waited for this moment? A lifetime?

An eternity? It seemed she had waited forever and a day, but at last the night had finally come.

"Have you enjoyed the weeklong celebration, Jane?"

"Oh yes, it has been the happiest time of my life."

He took the cloak from her and laid it aside. Then he took hold of her hands and raised them, one at a time, to his lips. "For me also, and you are the one who is responsible for bringing me the pleasure I've enjoyed. I want to repay that pleasure. Tonight is for you alone." His glance lingered on her lips, her breasts, then lowered to the ruby. "Have you the faintest notion how tempting you look?"

Jane thought she had a vague idea, until he drew her to the mirror and described what she looked like in his eyes. "Look at your face. Your eyes are like brown velvet pansies and your slanting cheekbones make you look like a witch at her enchanting. When you glance at me sideways or over your shoulder, I want to follow you to paradise.

"When you are happy or when you wish to tease me, the corners of your mouth lift and I find myself holding my breath, hoping that your elusive dimples make an appearance. The shape of your lips is utterly wanton." He ran his thumb along the fullness of her lower lip. "Your mouth makes a little moue when you concentrate upon my words, and I am left wondering if you want to spit on me or kiss me."

Jane's cheeks tinted pink with pleasure. She had known he was watching her, but hadn't the faintest idea that he saw her in such minute detail.

"A woman's hair is one of the things that attracts a man and holds him in thrall. Your long, silken mass floats about you, whispering in your ear, clinging to your shoulders, sometimes caressing your breasts or curling about your waist; always brushing and caressing your back. It makes me want to play with it. It makes my fingers ache to touch you as possessively as it touches you. It conjures visions of lying with you and becoming erotically entangled in it.'' Lynx threaded his fingers into her hair, lifted it high, then let it fall about her like a waterfall.

''This soft wool dress clings to your breasts so cunningly, it has been more arousing to me today than if you had walked about naked.'' He moved behind her so that he could cover the upthrusting globes with his palms. Jane watched in fascination as her nipples peaked and stood out jewel-hard. She gasped with delight as his thumbs brushed over the sensitive tips.

''And now we come to the heart of the matter. Your woman's center is decorated with a ruby! It has winked at me, teased me, taunted me, and tempted me to madness the entire day. Even in the chapel, or I should say *especially* in the chapel. I wanted to lay you on the altar and sacrifice myself upon you.''

His bold hands moved down the curves of her rib cage, down across her belly, and came to rest upon her hips. Then he pulled her back against his hard length to let her know the marked effect she had on his body. ''I have been waiting over twelve hours to get you out of this provocative dress. Who said I wasn't a patient man?''

As his fingers undid the tiny buttons down the back, his lips traced the satiny flesh that covered her spine. Jane shivered over and over as his mouth went lower. One moment her skin was on fire, the next, icy cold. The effect he had on her was intoxicating and she adored every moment of it. *Please God, don't let him stop!*

But Lynx had no intention of stopping; he had only just

begun. When he removed her gown, along with its silver chain, he laid them aside with reverence. "We must never let anything happen to this pink lamb's wool or the magic jewel."

Jane stood mesmerized by their reflection in the mirror. Her fine lawn shift was in startling contrast to his black-clad body towering behind her. She watched his hands pull up her shift inch by inch to reveal her creamy thighs. "The only time I've ever seen you completely naked, you were full term with my child. I found you absolutely beautiful that night, so can you imagine the effect your slim body is having on me tonight?"

She gave him a sideways glance up over her shoulder and Lynx groaned at the impact she had on his arousal. She could not have been more seductive if she had been an experienced courtesan. The shift followed the gown and Jane stood absolutely still while he looked his fill. She knew if he touched her bare flesh she would scream with excitement, but Lynx did not touch her. He simply stared at her reflection hungrily, devouring her with his eyes.

She held her breath as she saw him reach for the emerald cloak. When the fur touched her nude flesh, Jane gasped then moaned at the silken torment she experienced. The nerve endings over her entire body were heightened by her arousal. Beneath the silver fur her skin felt like hot silk and she began to quiver.

Lynx took her hand. "Come," he urged.

Incredibly, Jane realized he was taking her outside onto the parapets into the cold winter night. She followed him, knowing that whatever Lynx wanted, she would give him. Her body and her will were his for the taking.

He led her across the parapets to the high crenellated wall, then he lifted her so that she sat upon it. His hands slipped inside the fur to explore her body and he murmured, "Your stolen moments beneath the mistletoe have made you imagine you know something about kisses. You are mistaken. I intend to teach you everything there is to know on the subject of kissing."

Because she was elevated, their mouths were on the same level. When he pressed his lips against hers for their first full, frontal kiss, their mouths became ravenous. He deepened the kiss and at the same time explored the lush secrets of her body beneath the fox fur. What he was doing to her was shocking and primal and more intimate than anything she'd ever dreamed of. The hot sliding friction of his thrusting tongue and his insistent hands played in concert over her silken body, luring her to be splendidly uninhibited.

Jane slid her hands inside his robe and felt his heat leap into her fingers and spread up her arms. Without volition she opened her thighs to his questing hands and arched with pleasure at the sensations his knowing fingers aroused in her. She tore her mouth from his, opened his robe, and set her lips against his corded throat, then she slid her tongue down the muscles of his chest until her mouth fastened on a diamond-hard, male nipple.

They had an unquenchable thirst for each other that made them feel as if the night exploded about them. What began as tiny sensual tremors soon grew to full-blown shudders. Lynx traced the outline of her lips with the tip of his tongue. "I think that's enough cold air, are you ready to go back inside and let me warm you?"

"I'm hot," Jane panted, moving against him sensually.

"You are indeed, and I thank God for it." He lifted her from the wall, but did not set her feet to the cold stones. Instead, he lifted her high against his heart and carried her inside. He set her feet to the warm carpet only long enough to lift off her fur, then he removed his own robe and lifted her once more.

He carried her before the fire and after the coldness of the night, the heat of the flames felt delicious against her sensitized skin. "This chair served us well in the past and will again tonight," he murmured huskily. He sat down, holding her facing him on his lap. He did not have to tell her to put her legs around him.

Jane straddled him and looked down at his long, hard phallus that rose up between them. Her fingers could not resist exploring him and he covered her hand with his as he had done the night they first became intimate. Lynx was a big man and his size momentarily frightened her as she recalled the pain when he had first thrust through her hymen. But her mounting desire soon overcame her fear, so that even the memory of it was wiped away forever.

Lynx slipped his hands beneath her bottom and lifted her onto his engorged shaft. Then he pulled out until just the swollen head was inside her. "I don't want to give you another child just yet. It is too soon, I don't want to hurt you. I only want to give you pleasure."

Jane thought if he gave her any more pleasure, she would surely die of it.

Very gently his hands raised and lowered her on his shafthead until she caught the rhythm and began to move up and down herself, riding him as if he were a great stallion. When she took over, he removed his right hand from beneath her bottom and reached out with roughened fingertips to massage the tiny bud of her sex until he could feel it pulsing.

The sensations he aroused were so exquisite that she arched backward giving him a splendid view of her pink cleft as it became love-slick and her cries of pleasure began to mount with her passion. Suddenly, a throbbing began deep inside her and then she imploded, drawing him deeply inside her as if she would devour him. She moved rapidly up and down his long shaft until he was seated to the hilt.

Lynx held on to his seed with dogged determination as her hot and hungry body caressed him. He was anchored deep and it took an act of iron-hard willpower to withdraw without climaxing.

"Lynx, Lynx," she panted, overcome with the raw carnality of her first orgasmic experience. She unwound her legs from about his torso and slipped down on her knees between his hard thighs. Then she was kissing and tonguing the object of her adoration that had brought her such untold pleasure.

"Jane, sweet, you don't have to do that."

She stopped, mid-kiss, to murmer "Lynx, I must."

He groaned and gave in to her. She opened her mouth and took him inside the hot, wet cave.

After her wild exertions, he held her possessively cradled in his arms until their fever cooled. Strangely enough it did not cool and almost immediately Lynx wanted to pleasure her again. Because she had tasted him, he now craved the taste of her on his own tongue. But he wanted her to see him make love to her with his mouth. So once again he carried her to the mirror and set her down before it.

He took her fingers in his and lifted them to her cheek. He bent his head and bit down gently on her earlobe. Then he began to whisper. "I want to show you how to touch yourself. When I'm away from you and the night is long, I want you to know how to pleasure yourself."

He stroked her cheek with her own fingers, then slowly drew them across her lips. When he saw the corners lift with delight, he trailed her fingertips down her throat, over her delicate collarbone, and across the swell of her breast. He brushed her fingers around its lush, full roundness, then circled the nipple until she moaned with pleasure. As his tongue came out to trace the shape of her ear, he drew her hand across her belly and heard the swift intake of her breath. He felt her fingers stiffen as he approached her mons.

"Lynx, I can't," she whispered, shocked for the first time since she had come upstairs to him.

He nuzzled her neck. "Repeat after me, I will and I shall!"

Jane's objection dissolved in soft laughter. "I am so bad."

"What you are is innocent, and it is bringing me more pleasure than anything I've ever experienced with a woman."

With her fingers held firmly in his, he placed her fingertip at the top of her woman's cleft. "Just here is a tiny rosebud that blooms with the slightest stimulation. Let me prove it to you." He bent his head to cover her mouth with his.

She felt her rosebud begin to unfurl. Then his lips forced her mouth open and he thrust his tongue inside to taste her sweetness. Jane felt her rosebud throb and hot threads of desire shot up inside her. Lynx separated one of her fingers from the others and slipped it up inside her sheath.

"There now, does that feel bad?"

"No, it feels good, but Lynx, I need more, I need you!"

He withdrew her finger from her trembling body and kissed her eyelids. "Trust me to know just what you need." He went down on his knees before her and as she breathlessly watched in the mirror, she saw him separate her tiny folds and make delicious love to her with his mouth.

Jane threaded her fingers through his tawny mane of hair to hold his head at her woman's center. The act was so intimate, she knew that Lynx had breached all her defenses. She was a timid girl no longer, but a woman who was fast learning the power of her own sexuality.

This time her climax was quite different. A dozen small spasms strung together, yet were somehow separate in their intensity. The last one left her limp and languorous, and when Lynx picked her up and carried her to the bed, she marveled that he knew exactly the right thing to do.

Lynx reclined and drew her down to him. To Jane, he felt like a solid wall of muscle. He was the most powerful force she had ever known and she felt completely safe and secure for the first time in her life.

His fingers gently cupped beneath her lush breast, lifting it so that its pale curve swelled up from his calloused palm. His other hand stroked her back, going lower each time until his fingers splayed over her soft bottom, making her shiver, then burn. The last barriers that had stood between them had tumbled down tonight. She had never experienced such closeness with anyone, ever. She felt as if she were a part of him. She knew his scent had mingled with her own and would stay with her forever.

Jane loved him with all her heart and longed to tell him. Her lips opened to utter her fervent declaration, but Jory's words floated to her through the love-scented air. *Never tell a man that you love him until he has declared his undying love for you!* Jane caught back her words and instead yielded up her body to him, rubbing herself against his delicious hardness.

He crushed her against him and she felt his body's savage heat leap into her own, scalding her wherever they touched. Jane realized this was the way it was supposed to be between a man and a woman. When they shared their bodies, the male grew strong and powerful, while the female grew weak with love.

She felt his need become rough and elemental as he rolled with her to take the dominant position. Suddenly he had the ferocity of a lynx and she reveled in the fierce desire he unleashed as he lost control and lust consumed him.

As Jane floated in and out of slumber, she was vaguely aware that she lay sprawled across his magnificent body. Her cheek rested on the soft tawny pelt that covered his chest and the steady beat of his heart lulled her back to the edge of sleep whenever she stirred. She was completely happy. She dropped a kiss upon his heart and sighed with contentment.

Jane was confident that Lynx de Warenne had developed a burning desire for her and in her wisdom realized that this might be as close to love as a warrior like Lynx would ever come. Was she being foolish in holding back from marrying him when he had almost begged her? The thought of Lynx becoming her husband made her weak with love. No, she wasn't being foolish, she was being extremely clever, and enjoying every moment of his ardent wooing. Jane decided to let the passionate courtship continue for the present. A smile of pure bliss lingered on her face long after she drifted into a deep and dreamless sleep.

26

When the parapet door opened with a loud thud, Jane awoke with a start and bolted upright in the bed. A pair of powerful arms came about her and she realized she was sitting in Lynx's lap.

"Splendor of God, are you going to keep her abed all day?" Robert demanded with a straight face.

"You uncouth lout, the blush will never leave her face now," Lynx said, winking at his friend.

"Ha! 'Tis not I who put the blush there. I know what you're hiding under the covers!"

Jane gasped and her blush deepened as the evidence of what Lynx was hiding rose up beneath her. Then to her further dismay, the other door opened and Grace Murray marched in with their son. The nursemaid fixed de Warenne with a piercing glance and declared, "The young lordling will wait no longer. He's decided you've had her long enough and it's his turn now!"

"I know a Scots conspiracy when I see one," Lynx said with resignation, as he lifted Jane from his lap and set his feet to the floor.

Blushing down to the tips of her breasts, Jane lifted her arms and gathered her son to her heart. Grace Murray didn't bat an eye at Lynx's naked torso as he selected fresh clothes from his wardrobe and began to dress.

"I forgot you were leaving today," Lynx told Robert.

"Your lass is enough to make a man forget his own name," Robert said with unconcealed envy.

Before he left, Lynx rubbed the back of his fingers across his son's cheek and touched his mouth to Jane's. "Thank you, sweet lady." His green eyes held a promise that he would return and thank her more appropriately in private.

Lynx, with his sister, Jory, at his side, bade the Bruces farewell. He had received no firm commitment from Robert about quelling trouble in the Lowlands once it started again. Lynx could clearly see that the Bruce had divided loyalties. He took no pleasure in beating his own people into submission for the benefit of the English crown. Robert Bruce promised only to do what he had pledged and that was to keep open the western marches.

Within the hour Lynx was cursing the fact that for a week he had inadvertently kept the Bruces from their vigilance. Out of the six men he had sent to Carlisle for extra provisions, only four returned alive; two of the packhorses carried corpses instead of supplies.

When his knights reported that they had been set upon close-by at the foot of the Annandale Valley, Lynx knew immediately whoever had lain in wait had known that supplies were coming to Dumfries, and had also known that the Bruces were away from their castles of Lochmaben and Caerlaverock.

Lynx instantly made a mental connection between the missing supplies and the missing weapons, and his suspicions fell on the Leslie brothers. Without hesitation he summoned Jock and ordered him to have all seven of his sons attend him at once.

The small chamber off the hall where Lynx conducted castle business rang with denials as Jock's sons defended themselves. Lynx curbed his temper as he interrogated them over and over, asking questions about the missing weapons and the stolen supplies.

The only man in the room whom Lynx de Warenne trusted completely was Jock Leslie. The steward stood beside his sons, grim-faced, offering no excuses for them. After two interminable hours, Jock asked for permission to address his sons.

"Be my guest," Lynx invited in a deceptively quiet tone.

"If by word or deed ye have any involvement in this, get it off yer chests now. His lordship has two dead knights in the bailey and I know he will get to the bottom of this, no matter what it costs him or Dumfries."

Lynx de Warenne paced the chamber. Occasionally he stopped before one of the brothers and pierced him with an icy green stare, then moved to the next. He stopped abruptly before David Leslie, who was in charge of the stores. Lynx reasoned that David had the most to lose if aught happened to food supplies, since suspicion would fall on him immediately. "Do you have any coffins in your stores?"

David Leslie swallowed hard, wondering if he would soon be occupying one. "I do, my lord."

Lynx turned to Jock. "Would you and David see that my knights are prepared for decent burial?"

"Aye, my lord," Jock replied, heaving a great sigh of

relief that at least one of his sons had been exonerated in de Warenne's eyes.

After another hour of questioning, Lynx dismissed Andrew Leslie, the steward-in-training. Jock had brought him up in his own image and Lynx doubted Andrew would bring shame upon his father or Dumfries.

The hour of noon came and passed with no sign of food or drink being provided for the occupants inside the small chamber. After another round of questions and denials, Lord de Warenne addressed himself to the redheaded Keith. "I know you are not involved in this, but you have knowledge of it." He turned to the other four. "I could have him tortured, but the young fool would likely die before he would inform on any of you." Lynx jerked his head toward the door. "Go!" he bade Keith Leslie.

The four who remained exchanged quick glances. James and Alex, the two blacksmiths, wondered if de Warenne would punish the innocent with the guilty. Ben and Sim, the shepherds, hardened their resolve. They were Celts; there was no way they were going to knuckle under and confess their involvement with the rebels to this conquering Norman.

A knock on the chamber door interrupted the interrogation. When Lynx opened the door, he found Thomas, accompanied by a messenger from John de Warenne. Lynx stepped outside the room and closed the door, then he took the dispatch from the courier and broke the seal. The message was short; terse almost.

Return to Edinburgh immediately with full mesne.

Lynx frowned and swallowed a curse. John's timing was damned inconvenient. Besides this matter with the

Leslie brothers that required his attention, there was Jane and his son. Lynx wanted to be at Dumfries to enjoy his child, aye and to enjoy Jane too, now that they had become lovers. The last thing in the world he wanted was to run off to Edinburgh.

Frustrated, Lynx raked a hand through his hair. Trouble, it was rumored, came in threes or was it multitudes? He glanced down at the dispatch again and by its very tone he knew that he could not ignore it. He handed the paper to his squire and said with resignation, "Inform our knights that we are needed in Edinburgh and get the word to the Welsh lieutenants immediately so they can be ready to leave tomorrow. See that the messenger gets food and drink."

"*You* haven't eaten today, my lord," Thomas reminded him.

Lynx waved a dismissive hand. "My instincts are keener on an empty stomach. I should be finished in here shortly. Prepare one of the castle dungeons, I am about to place some of the Leslies under arrest."

Lynx returned to the chamber, paced its length once and began to think aloud. "The tension in this room is so thick I could cut it with my knife. That tells me only one pair is guilty or you would not be glowering at each other. The obvious pair is the blacksmiths, since weapons are missing, but I've taught myself to look beyond the obvious. So I ask myself, who had the opportunity to ally themselves with rebels? Only the shepherds, I'm afraid. Only the shepherds leave Dumfries every day to traverse the dales. The very same shepherds who were a month late returning from the Uplands."

Lynx's shrewd glance fell on James and Alex, and

when he jerked his head toward the door, they bolted through it. Lynx gave Sim and Ben his undivided attention. He scrutinized them for a full minute before he spoke. "I once told you I would hang any man who lifted Dumfries' sheep. Did you not believe me?" Lynx demanded. "Did you not understand that lifting weapons and supplies was also a hanging offense?" When their faces remained stony, Lynx threw open the door and shouted, "Guard!" Montgomery was there in less than a minute. "Arrest these men."

Blissfully unaware of the drama being played out elsewhere in the castle, Jane spent the morning in a state of euphoria. After she fed and bathed the baby, she carried him down to her chamber below and rocked him to sleep in the lovely carved cradle that Lynx had brought from Edinburgh.

As she looked at the presents her son had been given by almost everyone at Dumfries she was filled with joy. Jane handed Grace a silver rattle and told her she would be upstairs in Lynx's chambers if she was needed.

Jane leaned back against the heavy oak door as she surveyed Lynx's private lair. Last night she had climbed the stairs as a young girl filled with hopes and dreams, and he had fulfilled them beyond her wildest desires. Tonight she would climb those same stairs as a woman.

Jane put fresh sheets on the curtained bed in anticipation of the night to come. She lifted Lynx's pillow and hugged it to her tightly. Last night all the barriers between them had come tumbling down and she offered up a quick prayer of thanks to the Celtic goddess Brigantia.

As Jane began to tidy the chamber, her cheeks turned

dusky with delight as she picked up the fur-lined cloak he had had made especially for her. She rubbed her cheek into the soft fox fur and relived the delicious things that had happened to her out on the parapet walk.

When her eyes fell on his black bedrobe, she buried her face in the velvet, inhaling his male scent that lingered in every fold. With loving hands she carried the garments to his wardrobe and hung them side by side. She did the same with her pink lamb's-wool dress, marveling that a gown could have such an erotic effect on a man.

Jane longed to evoke the same effect tonight when he came to her and mentally went over all the clothing in her wardrobe. Suddenly, she had an idea. She would wear one of his silk jupons as she had on the night when he had first come to her. She opened his chest and gasped with delight as her hands lifted the black silk, emblazoned with the silver lynx. It was absolutely perfect!

The corners of her mouth lifted with happiness. *He* was absolutely perfect; she loved him with all her heart and soul. Tonight must be special. She would feed the baby, and take her bath early in the evening. She would have food brought up here to his chambers for them. She would not go down to the hall tonight, and imagined that Lynx would want to dine privately as much as she did.

Jane couldn't stop singing. She wished it was springtime so that she could fill the chamber with flowers. In the afternoon when she rested, she lay on the wide bed, savoring every word Lynx had said to her last night. She had been especially thrilled when he told her that he didn't want to give her another child just yet. That meant that he desired her for herself. He wanted them to be lovers. He wanted them to have time to enjoy their newfound intimacy.

Jane closed her eyes and imagined what he would say and what he would do when she told him she would marry him. She touched her lips, still feeling the wanton pleasure he aroused in her when his mouth took possession of hers. Never in a million years had she imagined there were so many different ways to kiss or how many other ways a man's mouth could bring such pure pleasure to a woman.

She shivered remembering the rough feel of his unshaven cheek against her breast and her belly. She shuddered at the thought of his calloused hands and how they felt on the sensitive curves and hollows of her body. She was becoming aroused just thinking about him, and she hoped and prayed that his thoughts lingered on her and caused him the same burning torment.

Some time later, Taffy came into his lord's chambers and was surprised to see Jane there. "I'm sorry, Lady Jane, I can come back later."

"No, no, come in if there is something you must do here."

Taffy hesitated. He had to pack his lord's clothes for Edinburgh and collect his war chest, but Jane did not yet know they were leaving on the morrow. She was glowing with happiness and Taffy did not want to snatch it away from her.

"It is time I fed Lincoln Robert. His nurse will think I have dropped off the edge of the earth. Excuse me, Taffy."

As he watched her leave, his heart was heavy. Lady

Jane hadn't the faintest idea how close her brothers were to being hanged for treachery. Taffy wished with all his heart that he could spare her the pain and anguish she would feel when she learned that Lynx had incarcerated them until he decided their fate.

Lynx had a hundred things to see to before departing for Edinburgh. He had the ability to separate one issue from another, so he set the problem of the Leslie brothers aside temporarily and concentrated on the tasks at hand. By nightfall the wagons were loaded with supplies and the baggage consisting of weapons, armor, and war chests was stacked ready to be put on the packhorses at the last minute. His knights and Welsh lieutenants were well-trained, capable veterans and Lynx knew he could depend upon each man to look after his own equipment, his personal needs and those of his warhorse.

In the stables, Lynx inspected his own destrier and found Keith Leslie assisting his knights as they fed and watered their mounts and checked their fetlocks and iron-shod hooves. Lynx knew it was love for the horses that prompted Keith. The lad reminded him of Jane. They shared a love of animals and the pair had a close bond. Suddenly, for Jane's sake, Lynx didn't want Keith to become involved in the treachery his brothers may have committed.

"You handle horses well; I'd like you to come with us to Edinburgh."

"To fight, my lord?"

"Nay, I'd not ask it of you. Overseeing the welfare of the horses is more than a full-time occupation. If you decide to come, just make sure you have sturdy boots and a warm cloak.'' Lynx made a mental note to ask Thomas to keep an eye on the lad.

When every last detail had been seen to, Lynx turned his thoughts to Jane. His body reacted immediately. He had intended to spend a rewarding hour or two alone with her during the day, but circumstances beyond his control had prevented it. Lynx fully expected that he would have to cope with her anger and her tears. It would be no easy task to persuade her that the business of Ben and Sim was separate and apart from their relationship and should in no way affect their feelings for each other.

Lynx was wise to the ways of women. Either they threw stormy tantrums or produced sulky silences to get their own way. When these tactics were met with indifference, they turned on the tears. He cursed himself for being such a cynical swine. Jane was different from other women. Jane didn't have a devious bone in her body.

Lynx climbed the steps of the Master Tower and entered Jane's chambers. She was conspicuous by her absence and Lynx experienced a pang of regret. He would have much preferred her to confront him honestly with her anger than deprive him of her company in an attempt to punish him.

The sight of his son diverted him. He bent over the cradle and reached out his arms.

''He's just been fed, my lord. Now would no' be a good time to jostle him aboot.''

Lynx cocked an amused brow. ''You make a formidable dragon, Grace Murray, but you don't intimidate me in the least.'' He swung his son up in his arms and bounced him gently.

Grace eyed the pair whose features were almost identical. "Then let me try more gentle persuasion. Lady Jane fed him early so the pair of ye could be alone up yonder."

Lynx felt his blood stir and his pulse begin to race. He handed his son to the nursemaid with a wicked grin. "I bow to your superior knowledge, Grace. Now would no' be a good time to jostle him aboot!"

Lynx strode up the stairs to his own chambers, considerably relieved that Jane was not purposely avoiding him. When he opened the door the tantalizing aroma of food set his mouth watering as he realized he was ravenous.

Jane's smile of welcome lit up the room. She was wearing a soft lamb's-wool bedrobe that made his loins quicken and he wanted to crush her against his hardness. Desire for her flared up in him as his legs carried him across the room and he watched her raise her lips for his kiss. *Is it possible she doesn't know?* Lynx asked himself doubtfully.

With her lips still against his, she asked softly, "Are you hungry?"

His mouth traced a hot path to her ear. "Starving," he teased, licking the delicate lobe. Either Jane was in ignorance or she was extremely wise, he told himself. It made a great deal of sense to enjoy their food before any unpleasantness began.

Jane set a small table before the fire, then with a sideways glance in his direction tossed cushions and bed pillows to the floor. Lust rose up in him, tempting him to slake his sexual hunger before his appetite for food, but Jane removed the covers from the dishes and offered to serve him. She savored her own food with zest, while at the same time she anticipated his every need, keeping his plate piled high until he devoured everything she set before him.

Lynx couldn't take his eyes from her as he watched her revel in her newfound power over him. He watched her set aside one of the new silver forks she had bought and pick up a pear tart with her fingers. She relished its sticky sweetness then very deliberately licked her fingers in a most provocative way.

Lynx stole her hand and lifted the tempting fingers to his own lips. He watched with delight as her mouth curved, revealing her dimples when he licked her fingers, then playfully bit down on them. As if to taunt him, he watched her withdraw her hand and in one fluid motion she gained her feet and moved away.

"I know what you would like," she murmured suggestively and walked across the room to the wine table.

"I'll just bet you do." His voice roughened with desire as thought of everything and everyone save this sensual woman melted from his mind. From across the chamber he watched her pour the wine, saw her turn to face him. His eyes followed her hands as they went to the neck of her bedrobe, unfastened it, and let it slide from her body.

His eyes widened as he saw the black silk emblazoned with the silver lynx. The jupon, slit up both sides, revealed her creamy flesh to his hungry gaze. She is seducing me, a voice inside his head warned. Like a flash of lightning, he experienced a revelation. *Splendor of God, she does know about her brothers!*

As she undulated toward him carrying the goblets of wine, his mind cried out, *Don't do this, Jane!* But of course, he knew she wouldn't stop. This was a seduction, quite blatant and quite effective by the reaction of his lusty body.

Lynx cursed himself for an unsuspecting fool. He thought Jane was different, but now he knew better. He watched her through cynical eyes as she drew close and sank to her knees before him, offering up the wine as well as herself.

Jane, please stop now. Only a whore barters her body. He felt his throat go dry as the perverse voice inside his head suggested, Let's see how far she will go!

Lynx took the wine cups and set them down on the carpet, then he pulled her into his arms. He would take what he could before she began negotiating. As he kissed her she became highly aroused and slid her hands beneath his doublet to caress the bare muscles of his chest. He wondered cynically if her arousal was part of the performance she had carefully planned.

"Help me, Lynx," she begged prettily, seemingly at a loss about how to undress him. He stripped off his clothes, wondering if she thought him more vulnerable when he was naked. He stretched his legs to the fire, leaned on one elbow, and waited for her next move. He didn't have to wait long. Jane pushed him back on the cushions and came over him in the dominant position.

In spite of the womanly wiles she was plying, Lynx thought her utterly lovely. She was small and delicate and more exquisite than any female he had ever known. How could he possibly have been attracted to bony blonds? He felt her soft thighs brush against his groin and his manroot rose up.

He saw her mouth curve with pleasure at the power she had over him. Lynx smiled too, deciding to enjoy the game she was playing. Slowly, delicately, Jane moved upon him until her hot cleft lay against his rigid shaft. Then, as if she were a queen, sitting on her throne, she picked up her wine and took a sip. She rolled it about her tongue with a feline sensuality, then growled deep in her throat.

His eyes fastened on her breasts beneath the black silk and the wildcat emblazoned across the jupon seemed to undulate. She shook her head until her flaming hair cascaded down over his naked chest, then she bared her teeth and lightly raked her nails across his hard belly.

"Have you ever experienced a she-lynx?"

At her erotic question, a throbbing began in his thick manroot. Slowly, slowly, she came down over him, inhaling the scent of his tawny mane of hair, then her pink tongue came out to delicately lick his cheek. When she heard him groan, her tongue moved down to lick his neck, then trace his collarbone. Her tongue, no longer quite so delicate, licked the muscles of his wide chest, then curled about a male nipple. Her teeth nipped him sharply and she was rewarded by his groan of pleasure.

Boldly, she moved lower, letting the rough texture of her tongue torment his belly. When she arrived at her goal, she lifted her head and murmured huskily, "A she-lynx toys with her prey before she devours him." Then she proceeded to make good on her promise.

Lynx's lust erupted. His thirst for her was so acute, he knew he must quench it. His powerful hands rent the black silk in half, baring her flesh to his savage mouth. The night exploded as he unleashed the fierce desire she had so wantonly aroused.

Jane met his body's every command, proud that her

sexuality matched his. As the last surging wave of need spent itself and their wild ferocity gentled slightly, Jane gazed down at him with slumberous eyes. He was still anchored deep inside her and she flexed her supple young muscles to hold him there.

"The time of our handfasting is almost run out. Soon it will be spring and I will have to decide whether I want to wed you," Jane teased. The corners of her mouth lifted. "Such a difficult decision. Do you suppose you can find a way to persuade me?" She lifted her cup of wine, dipped her finger in it, then slipped her finger into her mouth, relishing the taste of it and the taste of Lynx on her tongue.

27

Jane gasped as Lynx knocked the wine cup from her hand. She saw the desire in his eyes instantly change to anger.

"Damn you, Jane!"

She stared down at him in horror. "W-what?"

Lynx grabbed her wrists and rolled with her until he was in the dominant position and she was pinned beneath him. "What?" he snarled. "How many times have I asked you to marry? Your answer has always been, 'Oh, Lynx, I'm not ready,' " he mocked. "Now, you are suddenly ready! Just to save their miserable hides you are willing to discuss marriage. What a noble sacrifice!"

She looked up at him as if he had suddenly turned into a stranger. She could see that her words hadn't just angered him, somehow they had wounded him, and Jane was at a complete loss. "What have I done to anger you?"

"Stop pretending! You know damned well I had Ben and Sim arrested. All of Dumfries knows!"

Jane went cold all over and began to shiver. "Let me up," she said quietly. He reminded her of a beast, toying with its prey. He sat back on his haunches, allowing her an opportunity to escape him, yet knowing he was in full control. She got quickly to her feet and stood her ground. "You think I have been seducing you so that you would free them?"

"That's exactly what I think!"

"You are wrong. Tonight wasn't about seduction, it was about love!" Her eyes flooded with unshed tears.

"Save your tears, lady, they are wasted on me."

"You are so hard, and I understand that. You must rule over an army of men and fight wars, and you couldn't do it unless you were flint-hard and unemotional, but I thought you were beginning to feel a tenderness toward me." A single tear rolled down her cheek. "I didn't know about my brothers. However, you are right, I love them and I beg you to save their miserable hides, but I ask it openly without subterfuge."

Jane saw the doubt writ plainly on his grim face. "Not all women are deceitful, my lord." She watched from beneath downcast lashes as Lynx began to pull on his clothes. When he was dressed he searched her face. "When Taffy came for my war chest, are you telling me that he said nothing about your brothers?"

"Taffy would never say or do anything that would hurt me."

"You did not know that we leave for Edinburgh tomorrow?" he demanded, disbelief showing in every line of his hardened face.

Jane shook her head, unable to speak for the ache in her throat. She felt as if her heart were breaking. How could he leave her like this? Last night, when he had given her his body and showed how much he desired her, she had thought it was enough. Tonight, she realized that unless he gave her his trust, she had nothing.

He padded toward her wary as an untamed animal. He did not trust her because she was the female of the species. In that moment Jane made her decision. It was finished between them unless he gave her his trust.

"Don't touch me," she warned.

His green eyes narrowed. "Are you challenging me?"

"In your male arrogance you think me no match for you, but you are wrong, Lord de Warenne. I am more than a match for you." Jane drew herself up to her full height and walked regally to the door that led down to her own chambers.

As Lynx stared at the closed door, he wondered how in hell he had managed to turn his last night at home with Jane into a disaster. Christ, what if she had been telling the truth? What if she had remained in the Master Tower all day, absorbed with her baby, resting from the demands he had made on her throughout their night of passion? What if, in sweet submission, she had decided she wanted to be his wife?

Lynx grimaced as he realized how fierce he'd been with her. He had flung her offer in her face! In his male arrogance he had thought he knew all there was to know about women, but perhaps he did not. Lynx stepped out onto the parapet walk and filled his lungs with cold air, then he made his way down to the bailey where last-minute preparations were under way for tomorrow's departure.

With bleak thoughts for company, Lynx walked down to the stables and encountered his squires. "Taffy, did you tell Jane we were leaving for Edinburgh?"

"Nay, my lord. She was so happy this afternoon, I couldn't bear to take the smile from her face. I knew how grieved she'd be when she learned about her brothers."

Lynx looked at Thomas. "Show me where you put the Leslies."

They walked down an underground passage into the bowels of the castle. Lynx took the torch from Thomas and lit the one in the bracket outside the dungeon. Though the light was poor as Lynx peered through the iron bars, he could clearly see the look of defiance had fled from the faces of the shepherds.

"For Jane's sake, I am going to set you free. If you are determined to join William Wallace, I cannot stop you, but be warned that we go to hunt him down. I pledge to you that he shall be found and he shall be destroyed. If you are still here when I return, I will know you have pledged your loyalty to Dumfries. The choice is yours." Lynx turned the key in the lock and opened the prison door wide. His motivation was purely selfish. It was a gesture to Jane, asking her to forgive him.

"John, I have a son! You might well look amazed, but it is the truth. I can hardly believe it myself."

"That is the best news I've had in years. Congratulations, Lynx. I hope it is the first of many. I've never even met your wife yet. Is she well?"

"Yes, Jane is well." Lynx did not tell John that he was still unwed. "We named him after my father, Lincoln . . . Lincoln Robert de Warenne." When John frowned at the name, Lynx guessed that whatever the trouble was, it involved Robert Bruce. "Your message sounded ominous; I came as soon as I received it, though I wanted to linger at Dumfries.''

''The king has ordered me to reassemble the army. He wants us to sweep through the Lowlands from the border up to the Firth of Forth. He orders me to nip this rebellion in the bud, and he wants Wallace.'' John hesitated, seemingly reluctant to continue, and Lynx knew something unpleasant was sticking in his craw.

''Spit it out, John.''

''It's fortunate you didn't linger at Dumfries. The king has specifically named you and Robert Bruce to spearhead this operation as proof of your allegiance.''

''My loyalty to the crown is being questioned?'' Lynx asked softly.

''Robert Bruce's loyalty is being questioned, and because of your close association with him, you are being tarred with the same brush. The rumors and suspicions will be laid to rest now that you have answered the call to arms.''

''And if Robert refuses?''

''His English estates will be forfeit.''

''Splendor of God!'' Lynx's green eyes narrowed. ''Somebody has been carrying lies to Edward.'' A voice inside Lynx's head warned him that Robert could very well be involved with the rebels. ''Let me talk with the courier you sent to the king.''

John suddenly looked uncomfortable. ''It was Fitz-Waren.'' The name hung in the silence that blanketed the chamber. John's voice filled the void. ''Fitz arrived the day after you left for Dumfries. When my report was ready, he generously offered to act as courier. He caught up with Edward before he left York for the Cinque Ports.''

"I see," Lynx replied tersely, firmly clamping his jaw closed so that he would not begin hurling accusations.

"Treasurer Cressingham has a large force in Berwick. As well, I've called Percy and Clifford to arms and Fitz-Waren's light cavalry is already here. If the Bruce answers my call to arms, it will prove his loyalty, at least for the moment." John de Warenne rubbed weary eyes that were bloodshot from too much paperwork. "Lynx, I don't want trouble to erupt between you and Fitz."

"What prompts you to think there might be trouble?"

"He has Alicia with him."

Lynx began to laugh, but there was little mirth in it. *That son of a bitch has filled the king's ears with lies about my loyalty and you think the trouble between us is over a woman?* "Rest easy, John, I have no interest in Alice Bolton."

As Thomas lit the candles in the cramped chamber where Lynx and his squires were lodged in Edinburgh Castle, Montgomery memorized the message he was to take to Robert Bruce.

"Give the message to no other and make sure Robert knows it is from me. Tell him John's call to arms is a test of his loyalty. Tell him Edward Plantagenet is ready to confiscate the Bruce estates in Essex."

Lynx turned to his squire. "Thomas, my knights will know by now that Fitz-Waren's cavalry officers are in the barracks. Fights will be inevitable, but tell them I want no knifings, no matter how they are provoked. Oh, and keep an eye on Keith Leslie for me. Point out Fitz-Waren's men so he can avoid them."

"He has a wise head on his shoulders, my lord. He

may look like just a lad, but under that red thatch, he's a thousand years old!"

When Taffy went to get them food, Lynx was alone for the first time that day. He paced up and down the chamber like a caged beast. It galled him that Fitz-Waren had likely read all the reports he had prepared on William Ormsby, the justiciar, and Lynx's suspicions of the involvement of the Church of Scotland. Fitz-Waren could sell such information or use it for blackmail.

Why in God's name did the bastard volunteer to ride all the way to York in the dead of winter? Lynx asked himself. What can Fitz-Waren gain from discrediting me in the king's eyes? He must have another motive beside profit and power, Lynx decided. Fitz-Waren must be doing it for revenge!

Lynx heaved a sigh of relief when Robert Bruce answered the call to arms, bringing five hundred and pledging another thousand from Carrick. It was well past midnight when Lynx climbed to Robert's chamber high in Edinburgh Castle.

"I was determined to ignore the call to arms, and would have if you hadn't sent Montgomery."

Lynx nodded grimly. "My loyalty too is in question. I'm not surprised that someone is filling the king's ears with lies, but I'm bloody livid that Edward believes them!"

"It's my enemy, Comyn. The king was a fool to set him free on condition he put down Moray's rebellion. Comyn's dispatches to the king will say everything is quiet north of the Forth. But the truth is Comyn is in league with Moray and it won't be long before Comyn is in league with Wallace. They are all just biding their time until Edward Plantagenet sails for France, then all hell will break loose."

"What you say makes perfect sense. I thought it was my bastard cousin, Fitz-Waren, trying to discredit us with the king when he took John's reports to York."

"We could both be right; Comyn is my enemy, Fitz-Waren is yours. Sooner or later we will have to deal with them, my friend."

Lynx pushed the thought away. He did not want his cousin's blood on his hands.

During February and March an army of thirty thousand men, led by de Warenne, Bruce, Percy, Clifford, and Cressingham, began at Berwick and marched through the entire region known as the Borders: Lothian, Dumfries, Annandale, and Galloway. When they met no armed resistance, Treasurer Cressingham was adamant that the entire exercise was a ridiculous waste of the crown's money. He returned to Berwick and sent glowing reports to the king that the back of the Scots resistance had been broken and stating emphatically that there was no longer any insurrection in the Lowlands.

As a result of these reports, King Edward Plantagenet sailed for France in April, leaving the governing of Scotland in the hands of John de Warenne, Earl of Surrey.

In Scotland that year, winter changed into spring almost overnight. Lynx de Warenne and Robert Bruce sniffed the warm spring air and both smelled trouble. They knew it would come, but they did not know where it would strike. When it came, it was from an unexpected source.

William Douglas, who had garrisoned Berwick and gained his release by swearing an oath of obedience, had returned to his home in Lanark. Douglas immediately joined forces with William Wallace and they marched their army on Scone where Justiciar Ormsby had been reaping a fortune from levying crippling fines. Ormsby fled and the combined forces of Wallace and Douglas met no resistance. The common people of Scotland rejoiced that their sacred town of Scone, where all their kings had been crowned, was no longer in the hands of the hated English.

John de Warenne called an emergency meeting of his generals, cursing Cressingham for returning to Berwick and taking half of the army with him. "We have no choice but to march on Scone," John de Warenne declared.

"We should wait for Cressingham's forces to return," Percy insisted.

"We can't wait," Lynx pointed out. "Each day we delay, more Scots nobles will flock to join them."

"I should have heeded your advice, Lynx, and informed the king about Justiciar Ormsby's legalized stealing."

"Too late now, the justiciar will have destroyed any incriminating records."

"With all due respect, the justiciar is not the enemy," Percy pointed out. "Wallace and Douglas now occupy Scone."

"In the name of the king, I hereby confiscate all the English holdings of Sir William Douglas until he surrenders himself to us," the governor declared.

Robert Bruce made a rude noise of contempt. "That

won't bring him to heel. The lands belong to his English wife."

John de Warenne gave the Bruce a look of black hostility. "Then I charge *you* with the task of bringing Douglas to heel."

Bruce shrugged. "A simple enough task."

Lynx spoke up quickly before the sparks of enmity between his friend and his uncle burst into flame. "I propose we march on Scone immediately."

John de Warenne looked at the others for confirmation. One by one they all nodded their agreement.

The following morning as the armies made ready to leave Edinburgh, Lynx asked Robert how he would deal with Douglas.

"I shall simply ride to Lanark, take his wife and children prisoner, and send them to Lochmaben."

Lynx de Warenne was shocked. A picture of Jane and his own precious son rose up before him and he knew he would pay any price to keep them safe.

"Would you care to ride to Lanark with me, or will we meet in Scone?" the Bruce asked with a wolfish grin.

Lynx shook his head. "I've no stomach for making war on women and children. I'll meet you in Scone."

The English army came face-to-face with forces gathered by the Scots at Irvine, just outside Scone. Whenever a battle was imminent, the English forces joined together under one supreme commander.

John de Warenne did not believe the Scots army would be hard to defeat. He decided that heavy cavalry, followed by Welsh bowmen, would be enough to turn the tide. His light cavalry would be wasted in this operation, and war machines were completely unnecessary. He would attack at first light and inflict heavy damage. De Warenne estimated that one battle would be enough to make the Scots lay down their arms and capitulate.

The night before a battle was supposed to be for rest and prayer, but Lynx de Warenne had never been able to do either. He moved from tent to tent and spoke at length with each of his knights, then he walked among the campfires of his Welsh bowmen who slept in the open.

Lynx knew that men followed courage and if he displayed his confidence openly, boldly, his men could do no less. Following his example they would show contempt and defiance in the face of danger and fight with resolution and determination to emerge victorious.

When first light came a heavy mist still lay upon the ground. Lynx's knights were all mounted on destriers protected by armor. As well as lance and sword they carried battle-ax, billhook, and iron ball-and-chain at their belts. They peered through the mist, not daring to lose sight of their leader. Each man knew Lynx de Warenne would lead the charge as he always did, with Thomas on his right flank and Taffy on his left.

Lynx pushed his helmet down firmly and raised his clenched fist, giving his squires the victory sign, just as the order came to advance. Every man looked straight ahead, glancing neither right nor left as they spurred to meet the enemy.

The initial impact of lance and sword and ironclad hooves upon mortal flesh was horrendous. Men became unhorsed and were trampled to death. The screams of the horses over the clash of metal and the battle cries were deafening. In the melee, Thomas became separated from

Lynx. Suddenly, from behind, he was hit on the head with an iron ball-and-chain and he dropped like a stone. Another jumped into his empty saddle and fought his way to Lynx de Warenne's side.

Taffy glanced about wildly until he saw Thomas rejoin Lord de Warenne on his right flank, then with an overwhelming relief, he looked straight ahead and cut his way through the enemy.

Lynx focused on each opponent he faced. He unhorsed half a dozen with his lance before it broke off, embedded in the chest of an enemy. He threw away the broken shaft and reached for his battle-ax, guiding his destrier with iron-hard thighs. He was aware that Thomas no longer flanked him, but it was his squires' duty to protect his back, and Lynx assumed Thomas had moved behind him. Suddenly, Lynx felt a crushing blow to his head, then total blackness descended on him.

28

Keith Leslie had been up all night, making sure the warhorses were in fit condition to fight. He had examined the bits, bridles, and reins of every destrier that belonged to a de Warenne knight, and then two hours before dawn he had begun fitting the snorting, restive animals with the armor that protected their heavy chests, shoulders, and flanks. He kept Lord de Warenne's and his squires' destriers until last, making sure the saddles were well secured and the stirrups at the exact length required.

It was physically exhausting work and when his part was done, Keith lay down in the straw and closed his eyes. He drifted on the edge of slumber for almost two hours, but he was too keyed up to actually sleep and imaginary battle scenes filled his head.

Suddenly, he sat bolt upright, his eyes widening in dismay. Keith knew immediately that he was experiencing a vision, because what he saw had slowed down so that he could see everything in minute, horrific detail. He saw Thomas become the victim of treachery, as one of de Warenne's own men brought up his ball-and-chain and felled the squire with a single blow. Keith watched helplessly as the traitor vaulted onto Thomas's destrier and spurred it mercilessly until he came up behind Lord de Warenne. Once more in slow motion the iron ball-and-chain was raised.

"Noooo!" Keith screamed a warning that went unheeded. Lynx de Warenne's limp body rolled to the ground and lay supine. Keith watched helplessly as the traitorous soldier unsheathed his sword and impaled the unconscious man who lay defenseless upon the ground. Keith saw only the eyes, filled with hatred, bloodlust, and then triumph. Keith knew he would never forget those eyes; he would see them as long as he lived.

The red-haired youth struggled to his knees, then to his own disgust began to vomit in the straw. When he had voided the entire contents of his stomach, he gained his feet and began to run. The ground beneath his feet was soft and spongy from the spring thaw. He passed the wagons of the baggage train and stopped beside a group of men-at-arms who stood by with fresh horses and weapons.

Their mood was jubilant. Apparently, William Douglas had come over to the side of Robert Bruce, and the other Scots leaders, one after another, were withdrawing from the field. The Battle of Irvine looked as if it would be an undisputed victory for the English. Keith Leslie stood apart, mute, drowning in despair.

By midafternoon the battlefield held only the dead and the dying. The heavy mist rolled back in from the sea, as if to shroud the foul atrocities men had committed upon one another that day.

Taffy knew he was in danger of losing his sanity. He replayed the battle over and over in his mind, wondering what he had done wrong. He had sliced through the enemy as easily as a warm knife cuts through butter. But when he gained the other side of the battlefield and wheeled his destrier back into the fray, Lord de Warenne and Thomas were nowhere to be seen.

Taffy reined in his horse, glancing sharply about to locate them, but it was futile. His warhorse danced impatiently, seizing the bit between its teeth and plunging forward into the melee. Taffy had no time to panic. In battle it was easy enough to become separated, though it had never happened to him before. He had no idea how long the battle lasted, for time always seemed to pass with such lightning speed, all became a blur and what seemed only minutes was in actuality, hours.

Eventually the fighting ranks thinned until there were far more men and horses lying on the ground than were engaged in combat. Taffy recognized Montgomery and rode to his side. Both men realized the fighting was finished, the battle won.

''You got separated?'' Montgomery asked.

''Early on, Thomas fell behind, but he soon caught up again. Next thing I knew, they were both gone, so I fought on alone. I had no choice!''

''You came through unscathed, that's all that matters.''

But Taffy knew he should have stayed doggedly on his lord's left flank, no matter what. Gradually, more of the de Warenne knights gathered, but none had seen Lynx since he had led them into battle. Fear rose up in Taffy and sank its fangs into his throat. The thick white mist lay everywhere. ''Christ, we'll never find him in this.''

Montgomery cuffed him with a sticky gauntlet. ''Banish those morbid thoughts. He'll be celebrating the victory with the Bruce and the governor by now!"

But Taffy knew Lord de Warenne would celebrate nothing until his men were all accounted for. He spurred his horse from group to group, hope raging a battle with fear inside of him. He questioned Bruce men-at-arms and finally located Robert, who was busy looking for his brother. "We'll search him out, never fear."

They located Nigel Bruce on the infirmary field being treated for a flesh wound in his sword arm, but they could find neither Lynx de Warenne nor Thomas. Robert could see that Taffy was in a full-scale panic. "Lynx is no doubt searching for you and cannot find you in this fog. Go back to camp and let them know you are unscathed."

As evening descended, all the de Warenne knights were eventually accounted for. Many had flesh wounds or broken bones which were being treated by the Welsh healers, but none had seen Lord de Warenne since morning when he led the advance. Taffy's anxiety soon spread throughout the knights and Welsh bowmen who had returned to camp. They quickly organized search parties and set off on their grim task.

Keith Leslie knew he had to find Taffy. He did not know if Lord de Warenne and Thomas were dead or alive, but he knew they had gone down on the battlefield. Finding a specific soldier amid twenty thousand was no easy task, Keith soon learned, and at last he decided to return to camp. Young Harry Eltham, nursing a broken arm and collarbone, gritted his teeth and told Keith that every able-bodied man was out searching for Lord de Warenne.

It was two long hours before the men started to return

to camp. Keith busied himself tending the wounds of the horses, which almost broke his heart. Through the darkness, noisy celebrations could be heard from every direction, but in the de Warenne camp every face was grim.

When he saw Taffy slide wearily from his saddle, Keith ran up to him and clutched his blood-soaked gambeson. "I saw him go down . . . first Thomas, then Lord de Warenne . . . I saw it happen, I saw who did it . . . it was one of his own men!"

"You were at the battle?" Taffy asked skeptically.

"No, I had a vision!" Keith was shouting to make Taffy believe him. A group of Welsh bowmen gathered closer to listen to the lad's tale. They believed in visions and omens, and they knew from their own experiences that a few chosen Celts had the second sight. "I can lead you to him . . . we *will* find him!"

"We've searched for hours," Taffy said hopelessly. "This accursed fog blankets everything. We'll look again when it lifts."

Montgomery spoke up. "Lynx de Warenne would not give up on me if I were still out on that field."

Taffy knew Montgomery spoke the truth, but he was so afraid that all they would find would be a dead body. The lump of sorrow wedged in his throat almost choked him. If only Thomas were at his side to help in the search. "Do you really know where he lies?" Taffy asked Keith.

"No, but I have an unfailing instinct that I've learned to trust."

"Who goes with us?" Taffy shouted.

Every man within earshot set out once more for the battlefield. In less than an hour they found Lord de Warenne amidst a tangle of other bodies. The ground on which they lay was steeped in blood. Lynx's men gathered around him praying that he wasn't dead.

Taffy, the first to touch him, drew his hand back in horror when he felt that Lord de Warenne's body was as cold as a corpse. They looked closer and saw the sickening belly wound. Montgomery lifted the body slightly and felt the ground beneath the wounded man soggy with his lifeblood. "He lives—he's not yet stiff!"

Two dozen hands lifted with care and carried their lord as slowly and gently as they could back to camp. Taffy followed carrying Lord de Warenne's great battle sword. They laid him on the floor of his own campaign tent, then watched in silence as Taffy and Keith Leslie removed his helmet, gambeson, mail shirt, and leather chausses.

Then Taffy and Keith stepped aside so that the Welsh healers could examine the wound. Lynx's once tawny hair lay plastered to his skull, soaked with sweat and blood. They saw that he had a large lump on his head, but what they focused on was his belly. It was an undisputed fact that far more men died from putrefaction of their wounds than ever died on the field of battle.

One after another shook his head in sorrow. Any there who knew aught about battle injuries, knew that when the belly was sliced open, the stomach stabbed, and the bowel pierced, that it was a mortal wound. All knew that Lord de Warenne was a dead man. His life hung by a thread and not a few of his men hoped he would go peacefully without regaining his wits.

"Someone must tell John de Warenne," Montgomery informed the other knights. Then he realized he held the highest rank and it was up to him. When he arrived at the governor's campaign tent there were so many milling about, it looked like a circus. Dimly, Montgomery realized the governor was negotiating terms with the Scottish leaders who had capitulated after just one skirmish. Montgomery pushed his way through the throng and into the tent.

John de Warenne looked up and saw him. "Tell my nephew we are breaking camp and moving into Scone. We are finished here, the Lowlands are ours!"

"My lord earl," Montgomery rasped, "Lynx fell in battle."

"That is not possible—we won, they have capitulated!"

"My lord earl, his wounds are so grave, we fear for his life."

"Splendor of God!" John's voice cracked; he'd been shouting orders all day. "Percy! Take over here. I must get the physicians—"

Flanked by doctors, a haggard Earl of Surrey entered his nephew's campaign tent. Someone pulled aside the blanket so they could examine the man's wound. When they saw the damage, none of the battle doctors wanted to touch him. They feared making matters worse and they feared being blamed for killing him.

John de Warenne, the hardened supreme commander of all the English armies, broke down and wept. "Take him to his wife and child," John told Montgomery. "He might not survive the journey, but I know he would want to go home to them." John spoke with Taffy, who seemed to be paralyzed with grief. "Tell Lady Jane that I will come as soon as I may. I will confirm Lynx's son as my heir and appoint a legal guardian."

* * *

Roger Fitz-Waren and his light cavalry swept through Scone, ostensibly making it safe for Scotland's governor, John de Warenne, to take over the palace so he could finalize peace negotiations. In reality, Fitz-Waren knew of the priceless treasures that the fleeing Chief Justice William Ormsby had left behind in his haste to save his skin.

Fitz ordered his men to pack up the wealth of booty and transport it to Torthwald, promising to share the spoils if they kept their mouths shut. Then he himself took two wagonloads to Edinburgh and awaited his father's return. Fitz knew that Lynx de Warenne's death would devastate John, perhaps even speeding up his aging father's own demise. When John returned to Edinburgh, Fitz would be there to console him, ready, willing, and fully prepared to become the new heir.

The only medicinal herb the Welsh healers carried to staunch the blood of wounds was powdered yarrow. One of them held apart the torn edges of Lynx's flesh, while another sprinkled the yellow powder into the wound. The patient moaned, but did not awaken.

Taffy, spurred on by the actions of his countrymen, brought water and began to cleanse the blood and grime from Lord de Warenne's body.

Keith Leslie knelt beside Taffy, easily reading his thoughts because they mirrored his own. How were they to face Jane? "Thomas is still out there," Keith murmured.

"Thomas is dead," Taffy whispered numbly. "He's lucky."

"The Irish squire looked after me . . . I will find him," Keith said with solemn conviction.

"Take a horse . . . he'll be a dead weight," Taffy said choking off a sob.

At Dumfries, like everywhere else in the Scottish borders, spring had arrived early, and it seemed to Jane that nature had outdone herself this year. There was more sunshine, more flowers, more birds and butterflies than she ever remembered. Even the ewes were producing a bumper crop of lambs.

Jane helped Sim and Ben with the newborn animals that were troublesome, giving thanks that her brothers had decided to stay at Dumfries and do what they did best, which was tending their sheep flocks, rather than joining the rebels. The two shepherds worked night and day shearing the thick winter coats from the sheep, then with the help of their father, sold the wool at the best possible price to fill Dumfries' coffers. Jane had no doubt whatsoever that Lynx had freed her brothers for her sake and she would be forever grateful to him.

Lynx and his men-at-arms had been gone for three months and Jane missed him fiercely. Lincoln Robert was a big, healthy baby with fat, rosy cheeks. He was a happy child who laughed and kicked and seldom cried. On the rare occasion when something did displease him, however, he was capable of screaming down the castle. He now slept through the nights and recognized his beloved mother. When she carried him about, he always clutched two fistfuls of her long hair and crowed like a little cockerel. Jane couldn't wait for his father to return and see that his son was growing into such a beautiful boy.

Marjory de Warenne tutored Jane in her reading as well as her riding. Now that spring had turned into early summer, the three ladies, Jane, Jory, and Elizabeth, rode out every single day. Jane took them to her forest pool where they kilted up their skirts and played at the edge of the water, and she amazed her friends with her extraordinary rapport with the wild creatures who gathered to watch. She told them about her encounters with the lynx and lamented that she had never seen him again, once his wound had healed.

Life was quite serene without the men, but the three young women daydreamed constantly about their return. Jory and Elizabeth pined for Robert Bruce, while Jane longed for Lynx de Warenne, the lord and master of Dumfries; the lord and master of her heart. She missed her brother Keith, as well as Taffy and Thomas, but she didn't worry unnecessarily for their welfare. They were with Lynx and he would keep them safe.

One lovely warm day when the three ladies rode to Lochmaben, they learned the news that the two armies had confronted each other just outside Scone at a place called Irvine. A battle had been fought and the English once again had emerged victorious. Their hearts swelled with the knowledge that the conquering heroes would soon return. They carried the news home to Dumfries and all the people, both in the castle and the town, were relieved that the hostilities had been settled. There were many Scots who hated the English with a passion, but the people of Dumfries and most of Annandale knew they were far better served under the Bruce and Lynx de Warenne.

As Jane carried baby Lincoln into the bailey for his daily outing, showing him the hens and geese and pigeons that strutted about, a dark cloud swept across the sun.

Suddenly, the touchstone about her neck felt icy cold against her skin and her son stiffened and began to scream.

A feeling of dread swept over her, snatching away her serenity so swiftly, she had to fight for her breath. A picture of Keith flashed into her mind and apprehension for his safety almost overwhelmed her. According to the news she had been given at Lochmaben, the fighting had ended ten days ago and Jane realized some of the men should have returned to Dumfries by now. At the very least there had been time to send and receive a message.

She rushed back into the castle. *Something is wrong! Something is wrong!* When they encountered Jory, pulling on her riding gloves, the baby stopped screaming, and Jane could not bring herself to voice the dread that threatened to engulf her. She declined Jory's invitation to ride, handed her son over to Grace Murray, and made her way up to the parapet walk.

Jane gazed with unseeing eyes across the green dales. "Keith, tell me what it is!" The breeze carried her plea across the rolling hills, over the forest toward the mountains of the Southern Uplands. Jane listened intently, hoping to hear his voice. She heard nothing but her own heartbeat drumming in her ears, or was it galloping hooves and marching feet she heard?

Jane closed her eyes and emptied her mind of all thought. Once again the lynx touchstone turned icy cold against her skin. "Dear God, it is Lynx!" she cried aloud. Suddenly she was filled with an urgency that told her she must prepare. Time was of the essence.

Jane took up her big cloth bag and her herb knife and went to gather plants. The hawthorn was in bloom and she gathered the flowers to distil in water. She picked plantain, balm, and bistort. Then she pulled up madder root and gathered a large quantity of hemlock. When she returned from the forest, she went to visit Megotta and begged some white poppy heads from her grandmother's garden. Then she took all her precious plants to the stillroom and began distilling.

The fifty-mile distance from Scone to Dumfries would have taken Lynx de Warenne's mesne just a few days under normal conditions, but this journey had the feeling of a pilgrimage. His knights and men-at-arms opted to stay together; their common goal was to get their leader home alive, or even dead. Some days they managed to cover five miles, but others brought them only a mile or perhaps two closer to Dumfries.

Lynx de Warenne was still alive, but every man in his mesne knew he was dying. Whenever Lynx awakened they gave him water or a mouthful of broth or sip of wine, but he vomited everything back up. The flesh began to drop from his bones as if it were melting away. In just ten days he became emaciated, his large-boned frame showing prominently through the wasted flesh.

Taffy and Keith took turns nursing their lord. Keith had found Thomas stumbling about the battlefield with no memory of what had happened, but when Thomas saw Lynx de Warenne, he blamed himself completely and fell into black despair.

On the thirteenth day after the battle, Montgomery led the weary troops into Dumfries, escorting the critically wounded body of their lord. The castle people started to rejoice, but it was short-lived as they heard the devastating news. Taffy and Keith dreaded the moment when they would have to face Jane. Perhaps it would be best if they did not let her see Lynx. Both desperately wanted to spare her grief and pain, and they decided between themselves that they would nurse their lord until he drew his last tortured breath.

Marjory de Warenne rushed into the bailey before any could stop her. When she saw her brother on his litter she began to weep. Her weeping turned into uncontrolled sobbing, and a distraught Elizabeth de Burgh led her away from the appalling scene.

Jane watched from the parapets as the men rode slowly into the bailey. She had spent the best part of the last thirty-six hours up there, watching and waiting. At long last they had arrived and all her waiting was over. A strange calm enveloped her as she descended the castle steps and walked briskly into the bailey. She held up her hand in a regal gesture as Taffy and her brother tried to warn her away.

Jane looked down at Lynx without flinching, though what she saw was a thousandfold more horrendous than what she had expected, and Jane had thought she'd anticipated the worst. When Lynx opened his eyes, their green brilliance told her he was fevered. She gave him her loveliest smile, then calmly and firmly took over as Chatelaine of Dumfries.

"Please carry him to his own chambers in the Master Tower." Jane turned to her father, who stood by devastated by what he saw. "Fetch the priest, quickly."

It took a long, excrutiatingly slow time for his men to carry Lord de Warenne's litter up to his bedchamber. Then under Jane's instructions, they lifted their lord onto his own bed. The hastily summoned priest stood by with his prayer book and rosary, patiently awaiting his turn.

Jane slipped her hand into Lynx's and nodded for the priest to begin. "Hurry," she urged softly.

The priest made the sign of the cross and began giving Lynx de Warenne the last rites.

29

"What in the name of God are you doing?" Jane demanded.

"Administering the last rites, my lady."

"How dare you?" Jane was outraged. "I sent for you to marry us. Get on with it, can you not see he is in agony?"

The priest looked momentarily confused, but one glance at Jane's face told him exactly what he must do.

"We are gathered together here in the sight of God to join together this man and this woman in holy matrimony." He glanced worriedly at Lord de Warenne, then rushed on. "Wilt thou have this woman to thy wedded wife? Wilt thou love her, comfort her, honor and keep her, in sickness and in health; and forsaking all others, keep thee only unto her, so long as ye both shall live?"

Lynx's green eyes glittered and all watching thought they saw him nod.

"He answered in the affirmative," Jock Leslie said firmly.

The priest repeated the vow for Jane with the added question, "Wilt thou obey him and serve him?"

"I will," she vowed solemnly.

Jock spoke up quickly, "I give this woman to be married to this man."

Jory stepped into the chamber. The bittersweet moment was so poignant, the tears still streamed down her face. She placed her hand on top of Jane's, which in turn covered Lynx's. "I will plight my brother's troth," she murmured raggedly. "I, Lincoln, take thee, Jane, to my wedded wife, to have and to hold from this day forward, for better for worse, for richer for poorer, in sickness and in health, to love and to cherish, till death us do part—" Jory sobbed once, then continued, "and thereto I plight thee my troth."

Jane's clear voice rang out, rushing through the vow as quickly as she could. "I, Jane, take thee, Lincoln, to my wedded husband, to have and to hold from this day forward, for better for worse, for richer for poorer, in sickness and in health, to love, cherish, and to obey, till death us do part, and thereto I give thee my troth."

Jory slipped off her ruby ring and slid it onto the third finger of Jane's left hand. She took in a ragged breath and repeated after the priest, "With this ring I thee wed, with my body I thee honor, and with all my worldly goods I thee endow."

The priest omitted the psalm, the epistle, the gospel, and the blessing. "I pronounce that they be man and wife together. In the name of the Father, and of the Son, and of the Holy Ghost. Amen."

Jane turned immediately to the priest. "Thank you, Father. That will be all. If I need you, I will send for you." She turned back to Jory, who was valiantly trying to muffle her sobs. "I don't know if I can heal him, but I promise you I will love him." Jane looked at his knights who had gathered in the chamber. "Thank you for bringing him home to me. I will take over his care now. Thomas, Taffy, come with me to the stillroom, I need your assistance." Her eyes sought out Keith's. "Summon the Welsh healers to the adjoining chamber."

As the squires tried to keep up with her, they told her they would nurse Lord de Warenne; that his wounds were so horrendous, it was no job for a lady.

"Thank you both, I need your help, but I will tend his wounds and his body myself. Lord de Warenne has so much pride, it must humble him beyond belief to have his weakness exposed to his men."

It took all three of them to carry the decoctions, powdered herbs, distillations, and electuaries from the stillroom up to the Master Tower. "I will need a steady supply of clean linens." The squires hurried off to do her bidding, quite relieved to be told exactly what to do.

Alone with her husband, Jane lifted his hot hand to her lips, murmuring soft words to soothe him, then drew aside the covering that wrapped his body. The stench that arose almost staggered her. "I know how you suffer, Lynx," she murmured gently. "Give yourself to me . . . put yourself in my hands completely . . . turn your will over to me and I will try to take away your pain."

She watched him blink his eyes to show her that he heard, but Jane knew that even as ill and debilitated as he was, it would be almost impossible for Lynx de Warenne to give himself entirely to another's keeping. She smiled into his eyes and slid her hands into his hair so that her fingers touched the base of his skull. Jane focused on what she was attempting to accomplish and tried to ignore for the present the appalling filth of his once beautiful mane of tawny hair.

Along with the steady pressure of her fingertips, Jane crooned to him, telling him how to separate himself from the pain. "I love you so much, my darling, give me your pain . . . let it go, don't be afraid . . . I'll be here . . . let go a little at a time." Jane knew that the most important part of healing was touching. Her fingertips moved in ever widening circles at the back of his skull and her voice fell into the same mesmerizing rhythm as her fingers.

Inside her head was in stark contrast to her outward calm. Panic, fear, love, hope, and despair warred passionately within her. She wanted to treat everything at once, his fever, his filth, his wound, but her instincts told her that the first thing she must grapple with was his acute suffering. Jane knew she would do anything to take away even one small part of his pain, so she decided to bribe him. "If you will sleep, I will bring your son when you wake . . . sleep now, let the pain go, push it away."

Her heart ached for the plight of this once strong warrior, who had never given his trust to a woman in his life; now he had no choice. It took the best part of an hour before Lynx closed his eyes in sleep, but to Jane, there was no longer any such thing as time; no day and night; no past or future; only this present moment.

When she was absolutely certain he could not see her, she closed her eyes in dismay. His life hung by a thread as fine as a cobweb. It was a miracle that he had survived the journey home. Deep within the secret recesses of her mind Jane knew he was dying, but she vowed not to acknowledge it. Despite her tightly closed lids, the tears escaped and like scattered pearls dropped onto her tightly clasped hands.

In the adjoining chamber Keith awaited Jane with the Welsh healers. When she joined them, she cut straight to the heart of the matter. "I don't want to know how this happened, there will be time aplenty for the telling later. First, I want to know what you have done for him, then I want you to assess the extent of the damage for me, and finally I want your advice on the best way to heal him."

After consulting with the Welshmen, Jane turned to her brother. "Keith, go to the monastery for me. The Franciscans do scientific experiments with minerals. I want some permanganate salts and potash, and perhaps sulfur, if they would be so kind. Please hurry." When Keith tried to protest, she said, "Don't tell me again that my husband is dying. At this moment he lives, and this moment is all we have."

When Jane returned to the bedchamber, Lynx was no longer peacefully sleeping. His squires each carried in a stack of fresh linen sheets and towels, and Jane immediately set them new tasks. "Thomas, I want hot water right away and tell them in the kitchen to keep a good supply on the boil continually from now on. Taffy, ask one of the cooks to make Lynx some barley water."

When they left, Jane took up one of the decoctions she had prepared from the milky juice of the white poppy mixed with honey and water to help cover its bitter taste. She poured a small measure into a cup; it was not safe to give a man more than half an ounce.

Jane had no idea if Lynx heard or understood her, but she spoke to him as if he did. "I want you to try to drink this, my love. It could make you vomit, but enough will stay down to ease your pain and bring you sleep.'' She held the cup to his lips and tipped it. Lynx took the bitter white liquid into his mouth and swallowed. Almost immediately he began to retch and vomit. Jane was horrified by his agony, but knew she had to be cruel to be kind.

Thomas arrived with hot water and together they cleaned up and put fresh sheets on the bed. Then Jane kept her promise. She ran down to her own chamber and carried her son upstairs. ''See Daddy,'' she crooned, carrying him close. It almost broke her heart when she saw Lynx's mouth half curve into a smile. She prayed to every saint and every goddess she had ever heard of that the poppy would carry Lynx into the arms of Morpheus.

The moment his eyes began to close, she sat down beside the bed and fed her hungry baby. When she returned him to Grace Murray, she said, ''I'm not going to have much time for his lordling, Grace. I think we should get him a wet nurse, because there are going to be times when I can't even feed him. Ask Judith to come and see me, perhaps she will be generous enough to move into the adjoining chamber down here and bring her new baby with her.''

Jane hurried back upstairs. She lay down beside her husband and held his fevered hand. She whispered her magic words of love and hope, pouring them over him like gentle rain. Her eyes caressed his face, noting the sharp cheekbones and the slant of his jaw, now covered with a golden stubble of beard. Jane was too watchful to sleep, but she rested her body while the opportunity presented itself.

As she lay with him, she convinced herself that they were connected by an invisible thread that could never be broken. It had drawn them together in the beginning. It had been extremely tenuous until they had made a child together and now the magic thread connected all three of them. It was fragile at the moment, but it would grow stronger until it became a cord and eventually, with love and trust, it would become a cable.

Jane stubbornly refused to entertain negative thoughts, knowing they would sap her strength and debilitate her. This was a bad time, a wretched and devastating time that must somehow be gotten through, not necessarily with grace and dignity, but any way she could. They would have to live through the bad, so they could experience the good. Once she had heard someone say, "If I keep a green bough in my heart, the singing bird will come." And that is what Jane believed deep inside her soul. If Lynx meant enough to her, and he most assuredly did, somehow she would save him.

In her luxurious apartment at Edinburgh Castle, Alice Bolton could hardly believe that Fitz-Waren had accomplished what he set out to do. *My revenge is complete!* she told herself over and over. *Lynx de Warenne deserved to die for the things he did to me. I did what I vowed I would do: I destroyed him and used his own cousin to do it!*

Alicia had been terrified about her future, but now she realized that she had done the right thing. In all the time she had been with Lynx de Warenne, she had never been able to rule him, nor even influence him much. Fitz-Waren was entirely different. She could manipulate him as easily as a puppet. The trick was knowing which string to pull.

"Fitz, when your father arrives and tells you of Lynx's death, you must show surprise and shock. Both of us must mourn with him and shower him with sympathy and understanding for the loss of his beloved nephew."

"The old swine will have no one to turn to except me."

"I will go now and make sure his rooms are comfortable. There is nothing like a woman's touch to bring solace to a grieving heart."

Fitz stared at her with dispassion. The false bitch didn't even realize the irony of her words. She was the most cold-blooded female he had ever encountered. He thought longingly of Jory de Warenne and how he would like to comfort her in her hour of grief. Amazingly, Fitz saw no irony in his own thoughts.

When John de Warenne arrived at Edinburgh Castle from Scone he was exhausted physically and bereft emotionally. He was relieved that he would be able to send word of the English conquest at Irvine to the king in France, but personal satisfaction from the victory was impossible with Lynx's imminent death staring him in the face.

These days the governor traveled with his own personal guard of twelve, two of whom were his squires who acted as body servants and slept in an adjoining chamber. His squires immediately lit a fire, prepared his bath, and ordered him food, though lately his appetite was small.

John sat before the fire, gazing into the flames. He did not seem to notice that Fitz and Alicia had entered his chamber until Fitz-Waren spoke.

"Father, you look ill."

John lifted his chin from where it had sunk onto his chest and stared at the intruder. He seemed suddenly to become aware of where he was and what had gone before. "I am sick at heart. What good in gaining Scotland if I lose Lynx de Warenne? The price is too high."

"He died with glory, fighting the enemy, as any noble warrior would wish," Fitz said firmly.

John stared. Fitz spoke as if Lynx were already dead and most likely by now he was, God rest his soul. "God moves in mysterious ways . . . he gave him a son and a heir at the last minute."

"Lynx had a son!" Alicia murmured to herself before she moved forward with purpose. "My lord earl, the child is a bastard; Lynx de Warenne was not married to the servant girl who claimed to be carrying his child."

John stared at Alicia, seeming to notice her presence for the first time. "You are wrong," he said quietly. "Lynx left here after Christmas for the sole purpose of wedding Lady Jane, so that his child would be born in wedlock."

"How do we know it is his?" Fitz demanded.

John looked at him with sorrow. "Indeed, how does a man know if his son sprang from his own loins?"

Fitz's eyes narrowed with hatred. The urge to commit a murder gripped him by the throat and only the squires' presence stayed his hand.

"I intend to confirm Lynx's son as my heir to the earldom of Surrey as soon as I receive official word that my nephew has died."

"Lynx de Warenne lives?" Alicia demanded incredulously.

"When I last saw him, though I doubt he survived the

journey home to Dumfries; his wounds were horrendous.'' Tears streamed down John's face, oblivious of those who witnessed them.

The moment Fitz-Waren closed the door of their own chambers, Alicia turned upon him like a snarling she-wolf. ''You useless bastard, can you do nothing right? Lynx de Warenne lives!''

The back of Fitz-Waren's hand smashed across her mouth, sending her staggering across the chamber. ''That is the last time you will call me bastard,'' he hissed, stalking after her. ''All I ever get are crumbs from the de Warenne table. Even you are Lynx de Warenne's leavings!''

A terrified Alicia realized she had pulled the wrong string. She saw his intent and began to scream. His fist shot out to silence her. As Alicia went down, her head struck the solid brass fender of the fireplace, silencing her forever.

30

Lynx moaned softly. Lying beside him on the bed, Jane heard and her spirit flickered, then rekindled. She climbed from the bed and lit the candles to banish all the darklings, then she lit a small fire to help make the chamber even more cheerful.

Jane's breasts were full and aching, so she bathed and slipped Lynx's velvet bedrobe over her nakedness and was about to call down to Grace Murray and have the nursemaid bring up her son. Suddenly Jane paused on her way to the door and looked back at Lynx. *Breast milk! I'll try him with my breast milk.* Hope blossomed inside her. Slowly, she approached the bed and gently lay down beside him. She turned Lynx's head on the pillow and spoke to him softly. "Love, I want you to take my milk; I want to suckle you."

Lynx stared at her unblinking, while Jane wondered if he understood her meaning. Then he spoke the first words since he had returned. "For . . . baby."

"No, Lynx. He's fat as a little piglet. He doesn't need my milk. But you do! I want to nurse you . . . let me do this thing . . . don't resist me, Lynx, please let go of your will and give yourself to me."

Jane waited for him to give his consent. "If you won't do this for me, do it for your son . . . he needs you to live!" Jane waited no longer. She cupped his cheek and drew his head to her lush breast. With gentle fingers she slipped the nipple into his hot, dry mouth. Jane held her breath, silently willing him to take what she offered. It was the only thing she had left to give him. It seemed she had to wait an eternity before Jane let out her breath on a hope-filled sigh as she felt his tongue curl about her nipple.

Lynx was appalled at Jane's suggestion. He knew that he was dying and cursed heaven and hell that he had not died on the battlefield. Jane was so small and sweet; it was wrong that she had to face his horrendous wound with its disgusting stench. It was wrong that she exhaust herself over him when all she would have as reward was his death.

He could feel her nipple in his mouth. That she could even bear to touch him filled him with awe. She had ordered him, begged him, and now she was seducing him to give up his will to her. He knew if he did not take the last thing that she had to offer him, she would be deeply hurt by his rejection. Lynx was sure that the end was drawing close and his breathing would soon cease. At this moment Lynx acknowledged that Jane was stronger than he, and that he must bow to her will. He knew the moment had arrived when he must relinquish control. Almost, he did not have enough strength to suckle. He curled his tongue against her rouched nipple and began to draw.

Miraculously, Lynx's starving body did not reject the nourishment that he took from Jane's body. Later, though still fevered and in pain, Lynx felt comforted as he lay unmoving beside his sleeping wife. Her close presence brought him a peacefulness he had never before experienced. It was as if his thoughts hovered above his body. They were crystal clear and so unfettered they began to soar. Quite impassively Lynx wondered if this was what happened in the prelininary state of death.

He looked at Jane's sleeping face and knew she was exhausted. What an exceptional woman she was. The qualities she possessed were so rare, he had never encountered them in a female before. Jane was totally selfless. She gave without taking. She had given him his heart's desire, when he had always secretly feared a son was unattainable. But now he could die without regret, because Lincoln Robert had made him immortal. What more could a man ask for?

He knew Jane's devotion to him was absolute. She had generously shared her body with him from the beginning, putting her trust in him, even though she had been an extremely timid and frightened girl. And now she had shared her body with him in every way that it was possible. This time it was not to give him pleasure, but to give him life.

This is what love is all about! Jane loved him and Lynx realized suddenly that he loved her in return. It was a strange and wonderful emotion. Then panic rose up in him. He had never told Jane he loved her. What if he died tonight without letting her know that he loved her? His glittering green gaze traced her delicate features slowly, adoringly. She was exhausted; he could not waken her to tell her of his love, it would be a totally selfish act. And not the first one he had committed. Silently, Lynx began to pray that he be allowed to live until Jane awakened.

Thomas and Taffy both held their breath as they watched Jane bravely hold her hand over Lynx de Warenne's heart to see if it was still beating. She felt tears flood her eyes the moment her hand detected his heartbeat. To Jane, it felt amazingly strong. "He's very much alive," she said, smiling through her tears. "He's sleeping."

Lynx opened his eyes. "He *was* sleeping," she amended, as his squires looked on with extremely relieved faces. "My love," Jane murmured, bending over him tenderly, "I have to look at your wound . . . I'll try not to hurt you." As if touching a precious piece of porcelain, Jane opened the edges of the wound and looked into the abdominal cavity. She drew in a swift breath. "It's clean! Look . . . look, both of you!" She moved aside, allowing Thomas to examine Lynx with his eyes.

"The putrid smell has gone!" he said joyfully.

When Taffy bent over to have a look, Lynx murmured something to him.

Taffy's face lit up. "He must have retained some liquid . . . he has to pee! What was it he was able to keep down, my lady?"

For a moment Jane didn't know what to say. "I believe it was your barley water, Taffy," she lied sweetly, protecting the intimate secret she alone shared with her husband.

"I'll get some more!" Taffy said, rushing from the room.

Jane handed Thomas an empty jug so that he could help Lynx relieve the discomfort of his bladder. "I'm going to irrigate the wound again and leave it open to drain one more day. If it is still clean tomorrow, I intend to dust the cavity with sulfur and close it with sutures, then bind him up. What do you think, Thomas?''

''I think you have the true gift of healing, Lady de Warenne.''

Jane smiled down into Lynx's eyes and placed her hand upon his forehead. ''Your fever has lessened, darling.'' The look she saw on his face was neither relief nor gratitude. The look she saw was love. A tear ran down her cheek and she dashed it away with trembling fingers. ''If you die on me now, Lynx de Warenne, I swear I'll kill you!''

After Thomas helped her change the bed linen and Taffy brought another big jug filled with barley water, she thanked them sweetly, but made it plain she wanted to be alone with her husband. The moment they were private Jane undressed and lay down beside Lynx. ''Don't you dare to refuse me. I rule the roost at Dumfries. When you are strong enough you will soon overrule me, but until then, my lord husband, you will do my bidding.''

Lynx raised his hand and with his fingertips stroked the satiny flesh of her lush breast. When his lips were close enough, he kissed it. ''Love you, Jane,'' he murmured raggedly.

Jane's heart soared. Here indeed was a day filled with miracles! She stroked his temples as he took the nourishment from first one breast and then the other. ''I will drink Taffy's barley water. It will help make lots of milk for you, my love.''

* * *

Three days later, Lynx de Warenne had had his gaping wound sutured and he lay swathed in bandages from ribs to hips.

"Now, we are going to clean you up!" Jane informed him with hands on hips. Though her manner was confrontational, her hands were unbelievably gentle as she bathed him.

She had fully intended to wash his tangled mane of hair, but she could see Lynx was near exhaustion. "Help me change the bed," she told Taffy and Thomas, who were assisting her, "then we'll leave him in peace for a while."

After midnight came the first of many drenching night sweats. Jane knew that Lynx was still an extremely sick man. They had managed to keep him alive through a critical time, but he had no reserves of strength or any stamina to carry him through another crisis. Jane also knew his pain was constant by the way he drew up his knees and set his jaw. She told herself that it was good Lynx was fighting against it, instead of lying passively. She decided to cut the dose of poppy in half and try to ease most of his agony with her touch.

One afternoon, Taffy beckoned Jane into the adjoining chamber. "My lady, I didn't tell you before because I didn't want to upset you. Lord de Warenne's uncle John, the Earl of Surrey, said he would come to Dumfries as soon as he could. He asked me to tell you that when . . . er . . . I mean, *if* your husband died, he would confirm Lincoln Robert as his heir. He wanted you to know that he would appoint a legal guardian for your son until he comes of age."

Jane's hand went to her throat. She did not understand

the legal ramifications, but the word "guardian" to her implied that he meant to take her son away from her. "We must send a message to him immediately and inform him that Lord de Warenne is going to survive!"

"Too late, my lady, the governor just arrived in the bailey."

Jane's instructions tumbled over each other. "Run and tell Jory. I must change my dress. Ask my father to come up here to me . . . No, no, Dumfries' steward needs no instructions, even if our visitor is an exalted English earl and Governor of all Scotland! Ask my brother Andrew to come up instead." She snatched off her apron. "Where is Thomas? He can stay with Lynx while I greet John de Warenne and at least pretend to make him welcome."

"Thomas is making himself scarce, my lady. He is covered with guilt over what happened to my lord at Irvine, and there is no doubt the governor will be demanding answers to some hard questions."

"Dear God, why did the wretched man have to come now?"

"I'll stay by Lord de Warenne, my lady," Taffy offered, though Jane could see he also was very apprehensive about facing John de Warenne.

Jane raced down to the apartment below, and while she was selecting a suitable gown for herself, told Grace Murray to prepare his lordling for a visit with the exalted Earl of Surrey. Lincoln Robert began to chortle and screech the moment he saw his mother. He was five months old and as big as a child twice his age. Jane gave him a hug and a kiss as she was unplaiting her braided hair. The moment it flowed loose, her son grabbed two fistfuls with great delight.

When Andrew arrived, Jane said, "Fasten me up!" She presented her back to him so that he could button the pale green silk. "How many in the governor's retinue?"

"He has an escort of a dozen."

"Make sure the best chambers are plenished, make sure we have something special to eat. The forks! Don't forget the forks and rosewater bowls and towels after the meal . . . and a harpist too!" Jane raised her eyes heavenward. "Oh, St. Bride, send me strength . . . how do I entertain a bloody earl?"

It was the first time Andrew had heard his sister swear. "Calm down, Jane, we'll help you get through this. Father is serving them a stirrup cup."

"Damn the man! I should be with Lynx, I haven't time for dancing attendance on earls!" Jane gathered all her courage and drew herself up until her back was as straight as a ramrod. She was fully prepared to dislike the Earl of Surrey. When Jane arrived, she was thankful that Marjory was before her, gowned in exquisite peach, edged in deeper apricot. As Jory moved out of her uncle's arms, Jane got her first look at John de Warenne. The man was so haggard, Jane's heart immediately went out to him.

"This is Lynx's wife, Jane. She is a miracle worker and we love her with all our hearts," Jory said.

Jane swept down before him, but John would have none of it. He lifted her and enfolded her in his arms. "My dearest child, how can I ever thank you?" John's eyes were wet with tears.

"My lord earl, welcome to Dumfries."

"My name is *John,* whatever would you think if I continually addressed you as Lady de Warenne?"

Jane liked him immediately, but she exchanged an

alarmed glance with Jory over the earl's own state of health. Jane was no longer a shy maid and the chatelaine inside her, reinforced by her strong maternal instinct, took over. "John, you are gray with fatigue . . . you need some good food, some rest, and some pampering . . . thank heaven you have come to the right place!"

John searched Jane's face. "I don't know how he survived the journey home. Take me to him so that I may see with my own eyes that he is still hanging on." With Jane holding one arm and Jory the other, John de Warenne climbed to the Master Tower.

"Lynx, my boy, I deeply regret that this happened to you. I'll get to the bottom of it, never fear." John glanced at Jane. "They tell me your wife is a wonderful nurse, but I suspect she is an angel."

Jane slipped her hand into her husband's and squeezed. Miraculously, she felt him squeeze back. "He doesn't have enough strength yet to talk much, but you can see he is glad to see you, John."

Lynx managed to utter, "Our son."

Jane had Taffy move the big cushioned chair from before the hearth to the side of the bed. "Sit down, John, and I'll bring Lynx's son upstairs."

When Jane brought the chortling child, glowing with health, John turned from the silent, gaunt man lying in the bed, and held out his arms. "Splendor of God, he's the spitting image of his father!"

Jane knew he meant what his father used to look like. When John took the child from his mother's arms, Lincoln Robert's face screwed up as if he was going to scream down the rafters, then suddenly he seemed to change his mind. Opening his green eyes wide, he took hold of one of the earl's ears and crowed with curious exuberance.

John tore his eyes from the splendid child and gazed at the young woman who had produced him. She was small and delicately beautiful, but she had a luminescence of goodness about her that was so tangible you could almost reach out and touch it.

Jory smiled at her uncle. "She has the gift of healing on top of everything else. We are truly blessed in Jane."

"Nay, I am the one who is blessed," Jane insisted. "I am so very honored to be a de Warenne. All of you accept me for who I am."

John looked at Jory and shook his head, bemused. "She hasn't the faintest idea of her worth, Minx. Her price is above rubies!"

Jane blushed with pleasure and signaled for Grace Murray to take her son, whom she knew was a hard-to-control bundle of energy. "Dumfries has a steward worth his weight in gold. He also happens to be my dearest father, and he will see to your every comfort, my lord. My brother Andrew here is the vice-steward. He will prepare your chamber and your bath and tend to all your needs. I'll see you in the hall for dinner, my lord."

"John," he reminded her.

After a couple of days at Dumfries, John de Warenne began to look less tired and haggard. Relief that Lynx was still alive, combined with the respite from his heavy responsibilities in Edinburgh, did much to lighten his spirit. As well, Jane prescribed a tansy of balm mixed with eggs and honey, which acted as a tonic to the aging earl.

On the third day, however, the governor began an informal inquiry regarding what had taken place on the battlefield at Irvine. When Taffy told Jane that John de Warenne had requested a meeting with Thomas and himself, she and Jory approached the earl to ask if they could sit in on the questioning. Never able to refuse Jory anything she asked of him, John agreed.

They gathered in the small chamber off the great hall. John questioned Thomas first because he was Lynx de Warenne's premier squire.

"I remember nothing, my lord. I followed Lord de Warenne into battle, on his right flank, as always. Then nothing! The next thing I knew it was night and I was stumbling about the dead on the battlefield, feeling as if my head had bin caved in. I didn't know where I was or even who I was, till Lady Jane's young brother found me and took me back to camp."

Jane bit her lip. *How bravely Keith acted!*

John de Warenne turned his attention to Taffy. "I would like to hear your account of what happened."

"The three of us rode into battle—I flanked my lord on his left and Thomas was on his right. At some point I glanced around and saw that Thomas was missing. I feared he had gone down in battle. A short time later, I saw him return and felt much relieved. I cut through the enemy without too much difficulty but when I wheeled my destrier, I could see neither Thomas nor Lord de Warenne. I was forced to fight on alone. I didn't see either of them again during the battle."

John looked frustrated and called in Montgomery, who could add nothing. He told the governor that he had questioned all the de Warenne knights and none could shed any light on how their lord had received a wound that might still prove mortal.

Taffy hesitated, then spoke up. "My lord, young Keith Leslie said he experienced a vision. He said one of our own men attacked and wounded Lord de Warenne."

"I seek facts, truth, not visions!" the governor stated flatly.

"My lord," Jane spoke up quickly, "Keith Leslie is my brother. He is a seventh son and he has the second sight. Sometimes he can see things that happen without actually being there."

Montgomery too spoke up. "The lad led us to the exact place where Lord de Warenne lay. We had searched unsuccessfully for hours in the fog."

Taffy added, "He also knew where to find Thomas."

Marjory stood up. "I'll bring Keith so he can tell us in his own words. He has special powers, just as Jane does."

When Keith entered the chamber with Jory, Jane saw that he looked more a man than a boy these days. War did that, she realized. It stole men's youth away from them far too soon. The Earl of Surrey looked aged far beyond his years, and she could not bear to dwell on what war had done to Lynx. "Keith, you did not tell me about your vision. I suppose that's because I had time for no one save Lynx. But I want you to tell us all now, exactly what it was you envisioned."

Keith Leslie got a faraway look in his eyes. "It was a crystal clear vision, not indistinct like some of them. I had readied the horses for battle and I lay down to rest, but I was too keyed up to sleep. Time slowed and I saw a de Warenne knight fell Thomas from his horse with an iron ball-and-chain. The knight dismounted from his own horse and vaulted into Thomas's empty saddle. He spurred it like a madman until he caught up with Lord de Warenne. He came up behind him and raised the iron ball-and-chain again. When my lord's limp body rolled onto the ground, the knight dismounted, unsheathed his sword, and ran him through the belly."

"A de Warenne knight?" John demanded incredulously.

"My lord, I've searched every face of every knight since it happened, but I've not found him yet."

"You saw his face?" John de Warenne demanded.

"Only his eyes, my lord earl, but I'll never forget them as long as I live. They were filled with hatred and bloodlust, and after he plunged in his sword, they brimmed with triumph! His eyes were different from other men's—his left eyelid drooped markedly."

John de Warenne went ashen in the face. Jory also blanched. John and his niece exchanged a long, meaningful glance. Keith Leslie had just described someone they both knew only too well!

Thomas, Taffy, and Montgomery did not look at each other, not in the presence of the Governor of all Scotland. But any lingering doubts they had about the truth of Keith Leslie's tale were immediately wiped away. Each one of them now knew that Lady Jane's young brother had experienced a true vision of an attempted assassination.

31

Jane felt numb. She had assumed that Lynx had received his horrendous wound fighting the enemy. Now she learned that one of his own men had tried to murder him! *Who? Why?* her mind screamed. At all costs she must keep this alarming news from Lynx. He was not strong enough to handle the truth; it would devastate him, perhaps even kill him!

Jane knew that Lynx de Warenne was a hard man, often grim-faced and uncompromising, with a towering pride, but he was a natural-born leader of men who earned their respect. He was scrupulously fair and would never ask any man to do something he would not do himself. He set uncompromisingly high standards, but always set the example. *His men love him, yet there must be one who wants him dead!*

Jane suddenly realized she had left him alone in the Master Tower. "Please excuse me," she murmured, trembling at the thought of Lynx's vulnerability.

She crept into the bedchamber, trying not to disturb him, but as she approached the bed, Lynx opened his eyes as if he could sense her presence. Jane threaded her fingers through his and smiled down into his eyes. Her resolve hardened. She would protect him until he was strong! But what if he never regains his former strength? What if he is left permanently weak and crippled? she agonized. He will blame me for not allowing him to die! Stop it, stop it, she told herself fiercely, I have the power . . . I have all the power. He has done exactly as I asked: given himself completely into my hands! Now that he has given me his trust at long last, I cannot let him down, I must be strong enough for both of us!

"You are healing well, my darling, your body gains strength every day. But I know everything inside still gives you agonizing pain. Give it to me, let me take your pain, Lynx."

He never took his eyes from her face as she gently placed her hands upon his body. Beginning at his shoulders, she stroked soothingly, endlessly, down his ravaged arms, down his chest, over his protruding ribs. When she saw her touches begin to show their effect, Jane moved her hands lower, carefully avoiding his belly, beginning at the hips and stroking down his legs, once so heavily muscled, now only bone.

She eased his suffering so much that his mouth was able to curve into a smile for her. "I want to sleep beside you tonight," she whispered. "I want to touch you and hold you and love you all night. Do you think you could bear it, for my sake?"

Lynx lifted his hand to cradle her cheek and murmured, "Janie." The tender endearment almost undid her, but she willed back the tears that threatened to form. Tears were weakening to both of them. From now on, she would do only what was strengthening.

* * *

That night in the hall, Jane noticed that Marjory never left her uncle's side. She sensed that they were talking quietly about Lynx's attempted assassination. Perhaps there was someone they suspected, but Jane did not intrude upon their privacy. *Perhaps I don't want to hear the truth; perhaps I can't face it yet.*

When the meal was finished, John de Warenne approached her as she sat with Elizabeth de Burgh. "Jane, I shall be leaving in the morning. Unfortunately, my time is not my own and duty awaits me in Edinburgh. I have not yet appointed a guardian for your son, and will hold off for the present and fervently hope it will not be necessary."

Jane impulsively took his hands. "Thank you, my lord earl. I swear to you I will heal Lynx, if it is humanly possible."

"I know you will, my dearest child. Lynx is a lucky man to have found a wife devoted to him as you are, but I believe he knows that. God bless you, my dear. I pledge to get to the bottom of who did this grievous injury to him."

He knows who did it! Jane realized. But John de Warenne was a good man and she would put her trust in him. "Godspeed and thank you for accepting me."

Jane undressed in a glow of candlelight. She knew how much pleasure Lynx took from looking at her body, and her only desire was to please him. Gently, she turned back the snowy sheet and slipped naked into the bed. Lynx now had enough strength to turn his head toward her on the pillow, and she spoke to him in muted tones.

"The governor is leaving tomorrow. He wouldn't go back to Edinburgh if he thought you would not recover. I like John de Warenne." Her lips turned up into a smile, allowing her dimples to show. "Believe it or not, I think he approves of me."

Jane moved against Lynx, offering her engorged breast. As his hot mouth fastened upon her nipple, she heard him sigh with gratification. She wiped the dampness from his brow that formed in tiny beads from his exertion, then she threaded her fingers through his clean hair and held his head to her breast.

The bond between them strengthened with each passing day and night. She was everything to him: wife, lover, friend, nurse, and now mother. Joined like this, Jane felt she was a part of him, his breath, his blood, his bone, his pulse, his heartbeat, his pain, his very life. Jane smiled into the candlelight. She felt omnipotent. By giving her his complete trust, Lynx de Warenne had empowered her, and for the first time since he'd come home to Dumfries with his life hanging by a thread, she was absolutely certain her beloved Lynx would survive.

Jane fed him her breast milk for two more weeks, then she began to give him other food, and miraculously, his body did not reject it. Lynx gained strength rapidly after that and was able to turn on his side in the bed and eventually sit up. He was now able to speak without completely exhausting himself and Jane brought his son to him every day. At first she brought a sleeping Lincoln Robert and let him lie beside his father, but as Lynx gained strength, she let their son roll about on the bed, or on the floor, where Lynx could enjoy his antics.

When Jane joined Lynx in the curtained bed at night, a subtle change occurred. Where before she had enfolded him, now they held each other, never separating until the darkness melted into morning. It wasn't long before Lynx began to assert his authority again. "I want some fresh air," he declared one morning in June. Jane opened the door onto the parapet walk. "No, I want to go outside. Thomas!"

Jane instructed Taffy to take a chair onto the parapets in the sunshine. "Will you both carry Lynx outside?"

"Help me to walk," Lynx ordered his squires, overruling Jane's suggestion. She experienced one small moment of panic that Lynx didn't need her anymore, but then she began to laugh joyfully. She thanked the sun, the moon, and the stars in heaven that he had taken his first steps on his road to recovery. Jane knew that Lynx lived for the day when he would need no one. He hungered and thirsted for the world and everyone in it to need *him*!

As Thomas helped him into the chair, Lynx looked back at Jane outlined in the doorway that led out onto the roof. "Isn't she wonderful?"

"She is that, my lord . . . one helluva woman!"

Marjory and young Elizabeth joined them on the castle roof. "Oh, Lynx, you are doing so much better. You still look like hell, but I know your strength is coming back."

Lynx didn't seem to be listening. His eyes were glued to the doorway watching for Jane. When she finally emerged into the sunshine, he asked in reverent tones, "Isn't she beautiful?"

Jory's brows swept up as she experienced a revelation. "My God, you are in love!"

Lynx grinned wickedly. "Don't you dare tell her."

Jory rolled her eyes at Elizabeth. "Oh I vow, my lips are sealed!"

"They had better be, I am keeper of your secrets, don't forget," Lynx blackmailed. As Jane approached, he held out his hand to her. She drew near and placed hers in it. Immediately he pulled her close to steal a kiss. "Your fragrance is so heady, it steals my senses."

His sister laughed at Lynx and said dryly, "Don't worry, Brother, no one would guess your secret in a million years."

"Secret?" Jane asked innocently.

"Oh, didn't he tell you? Lynx has sworn a vow of chastity as penance for his sins."

Jane laughed and returned her husband's kiss. "I know better," she whispered to him.

"Speaking of sinners, here comes one now!" Jory cried, as she spotted Robert Bruce, riding in, hell-for-leather. Marjory picked up her skirts and headed for the outside steps and Elizabeth de Burgh followed.

"Please," Jane called out to them, "will you let me be the first to greet Robert?"

Jory's lovely green gaze searched Jane's face. "Of course," she conceded graciously. "We'll await you up here."

Jane met Robert Bruce as he strode into Dumfries' entrance hall. He opened his powerful arms and Jane felt herself enfolded. "I couldn't come sooner, lass. I was near torn in half for you; I thought Lynx had crossed too far over the line to survive. How did you save him?"

"I think he *did* cross over, but I have healing powers. Robert, he's nowhere near well. He is skeletal and soon exhausted. He won't allow you to see his pain, but sometimes in the night he suffers agony."

"I understand. How are you holding up, beauty?"

Jane's dimples appeared for a brief moment. "I am now Lady Jane de Warenne. My husband's plight has given me strengths I never knew I had."

"They were always within you, Jane."

"Robert, who is the knight with the drooping eyelid?"

The Bruce looked down at her warily. "He is Lynx's nemesis—his mortal enemy."

" 'Fore God, tell me something I don't know!"

"He is Fitz-Waren, John de Warenne's bastard."

Jane's hand went to her breast, "Oh, heaven help us!"

"Are you telling me Fitz-Waren is responsible?"

"Yes, but Lynx doesn't know. Jory knows, and John knows. They didn't discuss it with me, but the moment the eyelid was mentioned, I could tell by the looks they exchanged that they immediately knew his identity." Jane placed her hands on Robert's chest. "When Lynx finds out he will want to go after him and he isn't strong enough. In fact, I think that Lynx's fighting days are over."

The Bruce put his fingers beneath Jane's chin and raised her face so that their eyes met. "Is that wishful thinking?"

"Oh no, I want him to be restored to the same man of iron that he was. Anything less would be intolerable to him."

"Jane, listen to me. Lynx may be weak in the flesh at the moment, but there is nothing wrong with his brain. Believe me when I tell you he is strong enough to hear the truth."

* * *

When the two men embraced up on the parapets, all three ladies fought back tears.

"Damn it, I come to woo the widow and find you still kicking," Robert declared.

Lynx grinned. "I'll fight you for her."

"Horseshit! Your fighting days are over."

"Not by a long bloody chalk!"

Jane spoke up quickly. "Let's give these two some privacy. I know a cockfight when I see one."

Marjory went back inside with Jane and Elizabeth, but she protested, "Robert is acting as if there is nothing wrong with Lynx!"

"My first instinct was to protect Lynx from Robert's cutting tongue, but I think his words are strengthening. I know in my heart the Bruce would never do anything to harm Lynx; both of you know that too."

Lynx watched Robert hoist himself so that he was seated on the crenellated wall, between two merlons. "Your taking William Douglas's family prisoner won the Battle of Irvine for us. Did you know all along it would make Douglas come over to our side?"

"I had high hopes. I'm just back from Edinburgh. The governor has appointed me Sheriff of Lanark; he wants no more trouble from that quarter."

"How long will the victory at Irvine buy us?"

"A few months' peace, perhaps."

"Good. I need the summer to recuperate and regain my strength."

"John de Warenne has ordered Fitz-Waren and his cavalry north to aid Comyn. Rumor says they had a fearsome quarrel where the governor threatened to strip him of his rank. Good riddance, I thought, until I got home and read the message from my brother Edward in Carlisle. Ormsby, the justiciar, fled to Carlisle. Apparently Fitz-Waren dispatched one of his cavalry officers to warn him about Wallace's impending attack."

"Judas, the bastard is sharing Ormsby's ill-gotten gains and is obviously in league with Wallace at the same time, if he knew Scone was about to be attacked!"

"Exactly, and now the governor, thinking to rid himself of trouble, has sent the bastard north, straight into Wallace's camp."

"You still suspect Comyn and Wallace are in league?"

"Suspect, my arse! I know it for a fact."

Lynx narrowed his eyes. "You and Comyn and Edward Plantagenet are like three dogs fighting over the same bloody carcass."

"When Scotland bleeds, I bleed. That's the only reason I exercise patience." He gave Lynx a shrewd glance. "I've exhausted you; you look like a bloody cadaver. Come on!" Robert helped him inside to his bed. Jane was there, waiting to tend him. "What the hell do you see in this man? He's neither use nor ornament!" the Bruce growled to mask his grave concern.

Jane smiled and said lightly, "He may not be much to look at, but he makes beautiful children."

That night, after all at Dumfries retired, Jane removed the bandages that bound Lynx's belly. His flesh surrounding the wound was still quite tender. "I'm going to leave it open without binding. I know you aren't healing as quickly as you would like, but that's because your body was so physically depleted and run down. Now, turn over for me, but do it very carefully,'' she instructed.

Jane began to stroke his back, then she brushed the silky hair from the nape of his neck so that she could press her fingertips at the base of his skull. Then, with a featherlight touch, she began to stroke her fingers down the entire length of his back on either side of his spine.

''Lynx, I have struggled with my conscience all day about telling you something. You are nowhere near physically strong enough yet to deal with this matter, but Robert pointed out to me that there is nothing wrong with your brain. So in spite of my overwhelming urge to protect you, I am going to share my knowledge, because I fear you will never trust me again if I keep this from you.''

''Sweetheart, I have made you work so hard for my trust.'' He reached for her hand and stayed it, as she stroked away his pain. ''If this is about Fitz-Waren, I already know.''

Jane's mouth went dry with apprehension. ''How?'' she whispered.

''As soon as I could utter a coherent sentence, I questioned Thomas and Taffy.''

''Oh, Lynx, please promise me you won't—''

He touched his calloused fingers to her lips. ''Hush, love. The only thing I am going to focus on this summer is regaining my strength. I am going to start tonight. As much as I crave your touch, this is the last time you will take my pain away. I want to feel the pain; I need to fight the pain. It will make me stronger.''

''But, Lynx—''

''No, Jane.'' He drew her down to the bed. ''If you

want to stroke something, rub this,'' he said wickedly, moving her hand to his groin. Lynx closed his eyes. ''Lord God, how you make me quiver.''

''I don't want to weaken you,'' she whispered.

''It will make me feel stronger and more a man than anything else you can do for me,'' he confided.

Jane took off her night rail and slid her nakedness against his, ecstatic that Lynx was strong enough to achieve a throbbing erection.

''I'll be damned if I'll let the Bruce steal a march on me, for 'tis certain he'll be fucking right now.''

''Lynx!'' Jane reproved with a gasp. ''They will be making love.''

Lynx thought about it for a minute, then replied, ''Nay, they'll be fucking . . . then they'll make love.''

Jane traced his lips with the tip of her tongue before she kissed him. ''You are bad.''

''Mmm, in a couple of days when I'm stronger, I intend to show you the difference. It will be sooo bad, then sooo good!''

Lynx de Warenne became a man with a mission. Throughout the rest of June and all through the month of July he focused upon regaining his stamina and rebuilding lost muscle. Lynx began to participate in the tasks of manual labor that proliferated at Dumfries. He helped Keith Leslie in the stables, first by feeding and grooming the horses and, later on, mucking out the stables. He went into the meadows, scything and stacking the hay. Lynx spent an entire fortnight in the blacksmith's forge, repairing old weapons and fashioning new. He learned how to do everything from tempering a sword blade to shoeing a warhorse.

Lynx learned how to brew malt beer, then helped to fill and stack the barrels. At the mill he ground grain into flour, then filled up the sacks and stitched them closed. Gradually, steadily, his health improved, some of his strength returned, and slowly, he began to gain weight, which the manual labor converted into muscle.

Lynx never wanted Jane to be too far away. Midmorning and afternoon he stopped whatever task he was doing so that he could seek her out to spend an hour with her. With his encouragement, Jane sought him out when he worked in the fields, the forge, or the stables.

It was palpably obvious to one and all at Dumfries that Lynx and Jane were in love and seemed to fall deeper in love with each encounter. Gone was the grim-faced warrior who seemed mature beyond his years. On these bright summer days it seemed he never stopped laughing, and even his squires began to realize that he was a young man of barely thirty years.

Jane enthralled him. Her image was ever before him, day and night, and when they were separated by even a short distance, she haunted him. Lynx developed an unquenchable thirst for her. When he saw her across a chamber, he had to draw close to her. When he was close, he had an uncontrollable desire to touch her. Her voice enchanted him and her laugh stole his senses.

Lynx was filled with a compulsion to watch her, touch her, and taste her. He had tumbled head over heels in love for the first time in his life and he wanted the whole world to know it. Lynx stole kisses, teased her, tickled her, picked her up and carried her for the pure pleasure of holding her close. He couldn't resist caressing her bottom or pulling her into one of the stalls for a lingering kiss and an arousing embrace. His wooing was fierce and relentless and he enjoyed every moment of it.

Finally, at the end of July he began to hone his fighting skills with his knights and his Welsh bowmen. When he could once more draw a six-foot bow and let loose his arrows with deadly accuracy, Lynx felt a measure of satisfaction that he was making slow progress. He and Jane rode out together, sometimes along the pebbled seacoast where she gathered her touchstones, but more often over the dales with their breath-stopping vistas. She took him to her forest pool, where they swam together, then made love in the tall, fragrant grasses.

Each night they spent an hour or so with Lincoln Robert before they put him to bed. They bathed their son and fed him and played with him, immersing themselves in the joyous role of doting parents. Then later, in the wide, curtained bed, they explored to the full the mystical, compelling bond that lovers had forged since the beginning of time.

"I love you, Jane. It's important that I say it, and more important that you hear me say it, and know that I mean it with all my heart." The last thing he said to her each night became a ritual. "Jane, will you always love me as you do tonight?"

"I will and I shall!" she vowed fiercely.

32

One afternoon, late in July, at the forest pool, Lynx coaxed Jane from her garments. She clung to her shift, explaining sweetly that she had never swum without it. Jane was enjoying Lynx's delicious courtship so much that she gave him every opportunity to indulge his wooing. Pretending a reluctance she did not feel, she allowed him to render her as naked as he was himself. Jane dashed into the water and Lynx followed, swimming strongly until he captured her.

"Do you remember the lynx I befriended? I always dreamed that someday we would swim together in this pool."

"You have more courage than sense. Let me show you the danger of swimming with a lynx." To prove his point, he ducked her beneath the water.

When she came up, Jane did not sputter, rather she smiled her secret smile. "I know just how dangerous and wild a lynx can be," she teased, "but I hoped to tame him."

Lynx threw back his head and laughed. "What the hell would you want with a tamed lynx?"

"Absolutely nothing," she avowed. "I want you just the way you are, for always."

Lynx pulled her into his arms and kissed her wet eyelids. Then he lifted her high against his heart to carry her from the water.

"Don't lift me, I'm too heavy."

Lynx laughed again. "You don't weigh a hundred pounds soaking wet; besides, exercise is good for me."

"I know what exercise you have in mind," she teased, "and I don't believe it builds much muscle."

"Of course it does; feel this!"

When he set her feet on the grass, she molded her body to his. "Iron man," she whispered against his lips.

Lynx stretched out in the tall grass and pulled her down on top of him. "Let the sun play on your skin, it will make you hot for me."

Jane rubbed her face across the tawny pelt on his chest and inhaled deeply. "Mmm, I love the smell of sun-drenched skin."

"When I lay ill, your fragrance was so clean and fresh when you came close, I couldn't get enough of it. I love your scent, Jane." With the tip of his tongue he licked her throat up and down, then her breasts, her nipples swelling so temptingly for his enjoyment. "I love the taste of you too. Lady Jane, I believe you are addicting."

"Lady Jane Tut, if you please, my lord."

"How do you spell that? With an *i*?"

"You are a devil, Lynx de Warenne. I shudder to think what you'll be like when you regain your full strength."

"I'll make you shudder!" Lynx rolled her beneath him and did as he threatened. He was so hot for her after his forced abstinence, that his lovemaking was fierce and urgent. Lynx was completely aware of the violence of his feelings as he took her swiftly and brought them to a red-hot climax. He was amazed at her response to his blatant sexual hunger. She whispered his name and lifted her fingertips to his mouth, lazily tracing his lips as if she would never have enough of him.

Her touch aroused him again, instantly, and he turned her body beneath him so that she lay facedown in the fragrant grass. He curved his great body over hers and filled his hands with her beautiful breasts. Jane arched her back, raising her bottom, and he slid into her from behind. The sleek, wet thrusts of his marble-hard erection made her cry out over and over until his voice joined hers in a low, raw moan, and they both dissolved in hot shudders.

When they were replete, they slumbered in the warm sunshine with the lazy drone of bees humming on the breeze. When at last Lynx stirred, he whispered, "I wish our summer could go on forever. I had no idea being in love was so all-consuming."

Jane lifted her mouth to his and teased, "In love?"

"I fell in love, all right. I'm still falling . . . I hope I never hit bottom."

As the dining hall at Dumfries filled up for dinner, Montgomery approached Lynx with an apologetic glance at Lady Jane. "My lord, I saw a large mounted force approaching from the south and rode out to investigate. It is Justiciar Ormsby, he says he has been summoned by the governor."

"The fat swine! John must have ordered him to Edinburgh to answer the accusations leveled against him." Lynx left the dais to speak with Jock. "Prepare for company. Ormsby is such a coward he'll no doubt be traveling with a large guard. Accommodate them as best you can; our own men will have to double up."

Montgomery spoke up quickly, "He is accompanied by a large baggage train and a great body of foot soldiers."

"Splendor of God! John must have trouble again; trouble that he is deliberately keeping from me. Jock, when they arrive, line up the wagons in the bailey." Lynx turned back to Montgomery. "The foot soldiers will have to pitch their tents in the south meadows, but first, send a message to Robert Bruce." Lynx returned to Jane and Marjory on the dais. "You'll have to instruct the cooks to prepare a mountain of food; Ormsby thinks of his fat belly as often as he thinks of his fat purse."

Jane jumped to her feet. "I must prepare a bath for the justiciar."

Lynx took her arm and gently forced her to sit down again. "You are not bathing the fat swine."

Jory began to laugh. "Oh please, allow me to bathe him. I'm simply dying to see what he looks like unclothed."

"Jory, you have a damned perverted sense of humor," her brother declared bluntly.

When Ormsby was greeted by Lynx de Warenne he showed his surprise. "Rumor has it you fell on the battlefield at Irvine!"

"I did, but I am making a rapid recovery."

"I owe the de Warennes a debt of gratitude. If the governor had not sent Fitz-Waren to warn me of the impending attack on Scone, I would not have escaped with my life."

"Be sure to inform the governor of your gratitude, William. I am sure he will give all the credit to FitzWaren," Lynx said dryly. "My steward, Jock Leslie, has had chambers plenished for you, and when you have bathed, dinner awaits you in Dumfries' hall."

By the time Ormsby and his senior knights were seated in the hall, Robert Bruce had ridden the eight miles from Lochmaben. The justiciar bristled at the Bruce's arrival. "Have you not been summoned by the governor?"

"Not yet, I haven't, but he knows my men are spread out keeping the peace all the way up to the Forth."

"The governor appointed Bruce Sheriff of Lanark," Lynx explained.

"I've been expecting trouble north of the Forth," the Bruce declared.

"Why?" Ormsby demanded suspiciously.

"Use the brains God gave you, man. When Andrew de Moray started the rebellion in the Highlands, the king sent Comyn to hold him in check. Comyn, for Christ's sake, is a bigger threat than de Moray. The two of them are allies by now and it is inevitable they'll join Wallace."

"Wallace is a monster! He tried to seize me at Scone. He'd do anything to get his hands on me or the governor, so he could bargain with the king."

A sudden wave of fear for John de Warenne washed over Lynx. "All the Scots who lost their clan leaders at Irvine will flock to Wallace. I'm coming with you," he informed Ormsby.

"The governor will have enough without you. Cressingham has been summoned from Berwick and Percy from Roxburgh,'' Ormsby declared.

''You're not fighting fit yet,'' the Bruce said bluntly.

''It's true, I don't have my former strength back yet, but I'll manage and there's nothing wrong with my men.'' Lynx signaled Thomas, Taffy, and Montgomery and issued his orders.

Lynx waited until they were abed before he told Jane that he was taking his men to Edinburgh. Jane was appalled, but she loved him too much to point out his weakness. Lynx had worked so hard to regain his strength and rebuild his muscles, and he had accomplished much, but he was still lean as a hound, and not yet the invincible man of iron he had been before his close brush with death.

When Jane made no protest, Lynx knew she was keeping quiet to save his pride and he loved her all the more for it. ''I don't want you to worry about me, love. No power on earth will keep me from returning to you.'' She had a magic quality. ''You hold me in your spell.'' She was at once sensual and pure. It was as if the music of her siren song were inside his soul, telling him what to do, and he obeyed; he had no choice.

Lynx brushed back the red-gold tendrils from her temples, then traced her brow and slanting cheekbone with a finger. Everything about her fascinated and enthralled him. Lynx drew her into his arms and devoured her with kisses.

* * *

"I am taking the army all the way to Stirling and you are returning to Dumfries. That is an order," John de Warenne told Lynx flatly.

"Are you saying I'm unfit to lead my men?" Lynx challenged angrily.

"That's exactly what I'm saying. Swallow your towering pride and go home!"

"You think yourself more fit than I? You're in your sixties, for Christ's sake," Lynx shouted, revealing his fear for his uncle.

"I do not physically fight these days, I issue the orders, and I order you to Dumfries." John saw the stubborn set of Lynx's jaw. "My boy, there likely won't be any fighting. I'll offer them terms and persuade them to give up the struggle. I have a force of forty thousand. The best service you can render me is to regain your full fighting strength. It may well be needed in the not too distant future."

Reluctantly, Lynx capitulated. Becoming a liability to his men in battle would be more than he could live with. A picture of Jane rose up before him and he knew how relieved she would be when she saw his mesne ride into Dumfries' bailey. Before he left Edinburgh, Lynx went to a goldsmith's shop to buy her a wedding ring. He chose a wide band decorated with a Celtic knotwork pattern, representing a continuity of life and love with no beginning and no end.

That night, alone in his bed, he found it almost impossible to sleep without her. He tossed and turned for hours until an idea floated to him from some sacred, mystical place. When he returned he would take her to the chapel and marry her again. This time he would pledge his own vows. Once his decision was taken, Lynx fell into a deep and dream-filled sleep.

At Dumfries a nightmare awaited him. The moment Lynx entered the stable and saw Keith Leslie's face, he braced himself for bad news.

"St. Bride in her mercy must have returned you, my lord."

"What is it?" Lynx demanded.

"Come with me to my father. He has a message for you." Lynx followed him to the castle, impatient that the lad would not spit out what was amiss. When he entered the hall, the first person he saw was Jory.

"God be praised!" she cried. "I was on my way to Edinburgh to find you. The Bruce has gone back to Lanark and I didn't know what else to do."

"Will somebody tell me what's going on?" Lynx demanded. He raised his eyes to the stairs where Grace Murray stood holding his son while tears streamed down her face. "Splendor of God, it's Jane!" he growled. "Where is she?"

"We don't know!" Jory cried helplessly.

Jock appeared with a paper in his hand and automatically Lynx and his squires followed the steward into the small room off the hall, where Marjory and Keith Leslie joined them. Lynx reached out and took the parchment from a gray-faced Jock.

Turn John de Warenne over to William Wallace and your wife will be returned unharmed.

"Christ!" Lynx muttered, raking a frustrated hand through his hair as the blood drained from his face. "Put a guard on my son," he ordered Thomas. "Who delivered this message?"

Jock shook his head in dismay. "It could only have been the shepherds who knew Ben and Sim."

Lynx smashed his fist on the table. "I should have hanged them! Montgomery! Find Ben and Sim Leslie . . . I want them arrested immediately."

Jock said shortly, "I have them secure in the dungeon below, my lord."

"Fetch them up," Lynx said grimly. "Jory, you'd best leave us."

Marjory opened her mouth to protest, but thought better of it. Clearly, if Lynx did not get answers he was going to commit violence.

When the Leslie brothers came into the room, Lynx fixed them with an icy green glare, then he removed a mailed gauntlet from his weapons belt and laid it on the table before them. "You have something to tell me." It was not a question.

Both brothers spoke up at once, looked shamefaced, then Ben said, "We'd better start at the beginning."

"Yes, you had better," Lynx stressed.

"In the Uplands, in the autumn, we heard William Wallace speak. He spoke out for Scotland's freedom and made us ashamed we served an English master. He pointed out that we lived in slavery and though we were not harshly treated, others were. Most Englishmen are not known for their soft hearts."

Sim took up the tale. "Many joined Wallace in rebellion. We did not, but we were in sympathy and let them have a few sheep to keep them from starving. Later on, when the arms went missing from the forge, we knew who had taken them. A group of shepherds and homeless men who had been ill-treated banded together to aid Wallace any way they could. Under cover of dark they stole food, arms, anything that wasn't nailed down. We closed our eyes to the theft and didn't sound the alarm."

Lynx's face hardened. "The baggage train from Carlisle that was set upon?"

"I swear we had no knowledge of it," Ben vowed. "Only now do we realize we should not have talked openly about Dumfries with other shepherds in the dales."

"Get to Jane for Christ's sake!"

Sim's voice cracked with emotion as he tried to explain. "Two shepherds we knew sought refuge from their English lord. They swore they had barely escaped a hanging. We hid them in my house because Ben's wife was ailing and Jane was staying with her. The next morning, Jane was gone and that paper was nailed to the front door of the castle."

"That's all you know? Where did these shepherds come from?"

"Torthwald, my lord."

Lynx closed his eyes to blot out thought of Fitz-Waren, but it only brought his cousin's menacing image into sharp focus. "Lock them up," Lynx bid Montgomery. "If one hair on Jane's head has been harmed, you'll wish I had hanged you."

Lynx de Warenne with a company of thirty knights rode full speed to Torthwald. When they were not admitted immediately, they stormed the castle and hanged the guard on the gate.

There was only a token number of Fitz-Waren's men at the castle, left there to guard the treasures taken from the Palace of Scone. It did not take Lynx de Warenne long to make the men talk. They admitted that a red-haired young woman had been brought in by two shepherds, but Fitz-Waren had taken her away two days past. They swore they had had no hand in the kidnapping. They vowed they were cavalry officers loyal to John de Warenne and would never do aught to harm the governor. No amount of torture made them change their story that they had no idea where Fitz-Waren had gone.

The pain they suffered was naught compared with the agonizing torment Lynx de Warenne endured. Fitz-Waren was evil incarnate and Lynx dreaded what he might do to Jane. His sole hope lay in the fact that she was valuable as a hostage only if they kept her alive.

De Warenne would not remain under Fitz-Waren's roof, so they set up camp outside the castle, building fires to cook their food. The horses too needed a rest before the knights set out again on their quest to find William Wallace.

As Lynx sat staring into the campfire, his food almost untouched, he tried to fit the pieces of the puzzle together. He hadn't the faintest idea where William Wallace was hiding. His whereabouts was the closest guarded secret of the common people of Scotland. De Warenne knew he needed an intermediary, but no one came to mind.

Lynx's only option seemed to be to rejoin John de Warenne's army and learn if the governor's spies knew where Wallace was. Lynx stood up to order his men to break camp, when suddenly an idea came to him. He had always suspected that the Church of Scotland was behind William Wallace. Lynx was willing to bet his sword arm that Robert Wishart, Bishop of Glasgow, would have no trouble contacting Wallace.

At the bishop's palace in Glasgow, de Warenne left his men in the courtyard while he went inside with only his squires. After half an hour of cooling his heels, Lynx de Warenne grabbed a churchman by his cassock. "Tell Wishart that Lynx de Warenne seeks audience. If he doesn't show his face now, I'll torch the place."

In a few minutes Robert Wishart entered the room. De Warenne knew any man with enough guts to defy Edward Plantagenet and aid the king's enemy would not cave in to threats. Without saying a word, de Warenne handed the parchment to the bishop.

Wishart read what was writ there. "I take it you are the Earl of Surrey's heir?"

"I am, and the lady who Wallace holds hostage is my wife."

"You want the church to appeal for her return, my lord?"

De Warenne struck his mailed fist on the carved refectory table, marring it forever. "I want the church to cut out the bullshit!"

"I have sworn my Oath of Allegiance to King Edward's peace. I cannot contact William Wallace for you," Wishart said flatly.

"But you know someone who can," de Warenne said cynically.

The Bishop of Glasgow raised his hands in acquiescence. "Return tomorrow evening, after dark."

* * *

As Lynx de Warenne made his way to the Bishop of Glasgow's palace, he was amazed that he had gotten through the last twenty-four hours without spilling blood. His temper was in shreds, his gut knotted with sickening fear for Jane, and his patience had all run out.

With his hand on his dagger, de Warenne followed a black-robed priest through a maze of corridors and entered a chamber dimly lit by a few votive candles. The priest vanished and de Warenne stared unblinking into the shadows. A brawny figure stepped forward into the light and he found himself face-to-face with the Bruce.

33

A foul oath fell from de Warenne's lips. "Curse you, Robert, why am I not surprised that you are in league with both sides?"

"Only for Jane would I expose my position like this."

"Take me to Wallace tonight. If that scum has harmed her, he's a dead man!"

"I'll see Wallace; I'll get Jane back. Since you're not exchanging John de Warenne for her, I'll have to pay whatever price he asks."

"I'll pay his fucking price, it'll be more than he ever bargained for! Just take me to him."

"You are too incensed. Violence would be the only outcome if you dealt with him yourself."

"I'm coming," Lynx stated implacably.

"It would put Jane in jeopardy."

"She's already in jeopardy—it was Fitz-Waren who sold her to Wallace!"

"Then save your retaliation for him," the Bruce said bluntly. "Lynx, I know you are a facile negotiator, but you can't handle this one." The Bruce knew it would take more than money and he didn't want Lynx to be faced with the moral dilemma of betrayal.

''Then I'll just be one of your men. I'll stay back with the others; no one will recognize me.'' When Robert Bruce still looked unconvinced, Lynx added, ''I swear I won't interfere!''

A sharp bark of laughter fell from the Bruce's lips. ''Liar! At the least provocation you'd have a knife at his throat.''

''Then he'd better not provoke me.''

''All right then,'' Robert agreed against his better judgment. ''Just wear leathers, a hauberk, and a helmet. No colors or devices, we can't ride in flying a Bruce banner. Meet me in two hours at the Great Western Road.''

''I'm not that gullible; I'll stay with you now.''

The next two hours were taken up by secretly transferring a cartload of silver bars from a Bruce stronghold in Glasgow to the bishop's palace. Wishart obliged the Bruce with a signed receipt.

The Bruce party of ten rode six miles along the river to Clydebank where they were stopped and asked for a password. When Robert Bruce satisfied Wallace's men that he represented no threat, they were allowed to proceed toward Dumbarton. Lynx was amazed, since the castle of Dumbarton was governed by the Earl of Montieth, who had sworn his allegiance to King Edward.

Again they were stopped and made to wait in the predawn darkness. As the first hint of light touched the sky, a lone rider galloped toward the center of an open field, and the Bruce, unarmed, was allowed to ride out to meet him.

''I've been expecting ye,'' Wallace began.

''Is the lady unharmed?''

''Do we get John de Warenne?''

''That is impossible. Even if he were willing, Lynx de

Warenne could not hand you the Governor of Scotland. He is too well guarded.''

''If I hold his wife, he will find a way,'' Wallace stated flatly.

''If there was any way to seize the governor, don't you think Fitz-Waren would have found it, instead of stealing a helpless woman?''

''If ye won't give me the governor, why are ye here?''

''To negotiate a price . . . once I've seen that the lady is unharmed.'' The Bruce did not want Wallace to know Lady Jane held a special place in his heart.

''What price?''

''Five thousand pounds sterling.'' It was a great deal of money. Enough to buy weapons for a small army.

''Be serious, man,'' Wallace said with contempt.

''I have information as well as money, but first you must produce the lady so that I know she is unharmed.''

Pale eyes stared fiercely into dark ones and the Bruce knew he must not be the first to lower his gaze. He decided a threat would not be amiss. ''If aught has befallen Jane de Warenne, it is not Edward Plantagenet you must fear.''

William Wallace turned in the saddle and raised an arm toward the castle. ''I'll bring her out so ye can see for yerself, but then she goes back inside.''

The Bruce sat waiting in silence, far more worried about the actions of the man behind him than the one before him. Presently, a mounted guard led out a girl on a shaggy pony. Her blazing hair streamed behind her in the early morning breeze. Robert felt a deep pride when he saw the set of her Celtic head. She sat dry-eyed, her back as straight as a ramrod. Jane showed none of the surprise she must be feeling that he had come rather than her husband. Then he saw her gaze travel across the field to where his men sat waiting.

Jane saw him immediately. No other man sat a horse quite like Lynx de Warenne. Her inner turmoil, so at odds with her outward calm, swirled like a maelstrom. At one and the same time she wanted him close, yet wanted him far removed from this terrible ordeal. Jane felt the helpless impotence he was experiencing watching her, and knew he was only a heartbeat away from spurring his horse to her rescue. Jane knew if she did not look away from him, she would lose total control of her composure.

She swung her eyes back to Robert just as the morning sun appeared and reflected off his helmet. She felt suddenly strange and dizzy, and when she blinked her eyes she saw that Robert Bruce was wearing a golden crown. Almost immediately, Jane realized she was experiencing a vision. As she stared, she saw that he wore not only a crown, but splendid coronation robes. Robert Bruce was a king! And beside him Jane saw a crowned young woman who was obviously his queen. Jane's hand went to her head to dispel the queer dizziness and the next thing she knew, her mounted guard was leading her pony back toward Dumbarton Castle.

When Lynx de Warenne saw the small, proud figure of his wife astride the pony, he felt weak with relief. He wanted to make a sign to her, but managed to restrain the impulse. The sweat trickled down his spine from the effort it took. As Lynx watched her, he was consumed by a helpless impotence that almost unmanned him. When he saw her hand go to her head as if she were unwell, he rose up in his stirrups to gallop across the field. Then his heart plummeted as he watched her being returned to the castle and he knew that the deal was not yet done.

William Wallace waited until his hostage was secure, then he turned back to the Bruce. "What information do you have?"

"Information about John de Warenne. Information that will allow you to take him yourself if you are clever enough," Bruce challenged. "Is it a deal?"

"Perhaps," Wallace said, nodding.

Bruce knew it would be a stalemate unless he risked all. "The governor is on his way to Stirling. He commands a force of forty thousand." Bruce saw Wallace raise his shaggy head and his pale eyes went wide in surprise. "If you get there first you'll be able to choose the strategic ground. And once again, Percy's baggage train should be easy pickings—he joins Cressingham at Roxburgh. That's all I can give you besides the five thousand sterling."

"Make it ten thousand and ye've bought yerself a hostage . . . when the money's delivered."

"It's already delivered." Bruce showed him the receipt signed by Wishart, Bishop of Glasgow. It was for ten thousand pounds sterling.

"Ye anticipated me." Wallace grimaced and raised his signal arm once again.

This time Robert Bruce saw that Jane rode out alone. He handed William Wallace the receipt. "I'll throw in some free advice. Don't place too much trust in Comyn. You are an idealist who seeks to make vassals free men. Comyn has immense land holdings—an end to the feudal system would not be in his best interests." Robert Bruce took hold of Jane's bridle and the pair of riders trotted slowly across the open field to where his men waited.

"Thank you, my lord," Jane murmured.

"Do not thank me. It is your husband who will pay the ransom, but don't mark his presence until we are safely back in Glasgow; if they knew de Warenne was here, they'd have another hostage."

The de Warenne knights, cooling their heels at a Glasgow inn known as King's Crag, let out a great cheer as the dozen men in leathers accompanying Lady Jane rode into the inn yard. Taffy rushed forward to aid her from the saddle and was rewarded by a tremulous smile.

Lynx de Warenne was almost overcome with emotion as he strode toward his beloved wife. The tenderness he felt at the sight of her brought a lump to his throat that prevented him from speaking. He dropped a gentle kiss upon her brow and then wrapped her in his arms and held her against his heart. He knew he would protect her with his life from this day forward and cherish her with his heart and soul.

Lynx bade Taffy take her upstairs, then he embraced Robert Bruce and thanked him sincerely. "You'll have the money back immediately."

Robert grinned as he climbed back into the saddle. "I thought there was no point being tightfisted when you were paying. I'll bid you adieu." The Bruce men wheeled their horses and were gone.

Lynx de Warenne spoke low to Montgomery. "Come inside. I want you to carry a letter to the governor. He could be halfway to Stirling by now." Lynx set down on paper what had happened.

Fitz-Waren abducted my wife, Jane, and sold her to William Wallace, who offered to exchange her for you. I got her back safely by paying ransom, but urge you to beware of Fitz-Waren, who poses a constant threat to all the de Warennes, especially yourself. Wallace had a force of about ten thousand camped between Clydebank and Dumbarton, so he must be in league with Montieth as well as de Moray and Comyn.

Lynx chewed on the end of the quill as he pondered if Robert Bruce had divulged any information about the governor's plans. He decided a warning was in order:

Watch out for a trap at Stirling.

Snug under the rafters in a chamber at the King's Crag, Lynx and Jane shared a bath. The wooden tub was hardly large enough for Lynx's long shanks, but they couldn't bear to be separated any longer. He made a chair for her with his thighs and she lay back against his chest. "Doesn't your wound hurt anymore?"

"No, even my scars have started to fade." Lynx knew that now she felt safe, Jane would tell him everything that had happened to her.

"The shepherds from Torthwald didn't frighten me, even though they trussed me up and put a gag in my mouth. Fitz-Waren was another matter. I knew who he was the moment I saw him. I wanted to kill him for what he had done to you, but I was afraid of him. He never touched me," she said quickly, "but he told me he had killed Alicia, and would do the same to me, if I didn't cooperate. But once he turned me over to Wallace, I felt I would be safe."

The bastard killed Alicia? Fitz-Waren had much to answer for, but Lynx did not speak of retribution because he knew it would upset Jane. "Thank God John ordered me home, who knows what would have happened if I hadn't returned to Dumfries."

"You didn't hang Sim and Ben, did you?" Jane asked in a small voice.

"Do you have some inducement to make me spare them?" he teased gently.

Jane laughed with relief and slipped further down in the water.

Lynx dropped a kiss on her shoulder. "You are most alluring when you are reclining," he whispered, fascinated with her lush breasts bobbing up and down in the water.

She reached down innocently. "Where did the soap go?"

"That isn't it, you little cocktease."

They enjoyed a short erotic dalliance, but soon Lynx sobered as he realized how deep his feelings ran for this woman. It had been fully brought home to him just how much she meant to his very existence when he had almost lost her. He dried her carefully and carried her to the bed. "I have something for you, sweetheart."

"Oooh, I love surprises," she purred, but when Lynx held out the wedding ring on his palm, Jane began to cry.

He enfolded her in his arms. "Hush, love, this is a happy time." He cupped her face and kissed the teardrops from her lashes. "You are so beautiful, you take my breath away." He gazed intently at her face and began making love to her with his eyes. She had never felt more feminine and attractive in her life.

"I love you, Jane. Will you marry me again, so that I can give you my vows?"

"Lynx, that is so romantic."

"You make me feel romantic. I enjoy being your husband, but I want to be your lover too."

She lifted her mouth to his and whispered her joy against his lips.

He began kissing her and suddenly he couldn't stop. The loveplay of his mouth kindled a smoldering desire that ran through her veins like a firestorm. His hands cherished her body, stroking her hair, caressing her back, fondling her breasts, massaging her belly. His calloused hands cupped her buttocks. "Do you know that your beautiful bottom is heart-shaped?" he murmured huskily.

Thrilled to her core, Jane smiled her delight. "I had no idea you noticed such things."

"Good God, I notice everything about you!"

Her fingertips drifted down his chest. "Tell me."

"Your eyelashes are tipped with gold." He kissed her eyelids. "Sometimes, when you smile at me, your elusive dimples appear and make my heart turn over with love." He cupped one of her full breasts and ran his thumb over its tip. "When you know my eyes are on your breasts, your nipples peak and stand out like rubies."

Jane gasped with pleasure as she felt them swell at his touch.

"And your mons"—his hand slid down her belly—"is crowned with red-gold tendrils that would tempt the devil himself." He threaded his fingers into her curls and Jane went wild.

Jane responded so passionately to her husband's adoration that the loving went on and on. They did not separate even after they were weak with satisfaction. They lay entwined as Lynx held her close, cherishing her, still kissing her, enveloping her in his love. Their need to be one again overwhelmed them both, so Lynx made tender love to her, showing her how precious she was to him, honoring her with his body, until Jane felt worshiped down to her toes. It was the happiest moment of her life; she knew he would love her forever.

Later, as she lay in Lynx's arms, she told him what she had seen in her vision. "I've always had the feeling that Robert would be king someday, but now I'm certain of it."

"I won't oppose Robert's bid for the throne of Scotland when the time is right, but he will need more than my cooperation."

"The only part of my vision I don't understand is the lady I saw at his side. It wasn't Jory, it was young Elizabeth de Burgh!"

Lynx laughed and hugged Jane close. "By heaven, if Robert could get the power of the Earl of Ulster behind him, he'd soon be wearing the crown of Scotland."

Long after Lynx fell asleep, Jane lay in his arms, twirling her lovely new wedding ring around her finger and thinking about what he had said.

John de Warenne was advancing the army to Stirling by slow stages and Montgomery delivered Lynx's letter just before they crossed the Antonine Wall, which was the gateway to the Highlands. John reread the letter three times before he fully grasped the depths of depravation to which Fitz-Waren had sunk. He immediately wrote out a warrant for his arrest, cursing himself for sending his bastard into the arms of Wallace. He had always known what he was, but never had the balls to admit it.

The governor picked up Lynx's communication again advising him that Wallace had a force of ten thousand at Clydebank. "How many days ago did he encounter Wallace's army?" John asked Montgomery.

"Two days back, my lord."

John cursed. It would take days yet for his great force to reach Stirling. The river Forth snaked through the whole region making the ground wet and boggy with tidewater. He knew a smaller force not encumbered by heavy cavalry or baggage trains could easily reach Stirling before him. As well, Wallace could have gotten word to the rebels led by de Moray in the north. John de Warenne decided to press on at a faster pace.

The governor got his army across the river Forth at Abbey Ford and made camp on the lands of Cambuskenneth Abbey. This was by no means the last time they would have to cross the curling river that protected Stirling and its ancient castle, so John sent out his scouts to learn the enemy's whereabouts.

As he had feared, Wallace was there before him; his army encamped at the base of the Ochils, a steep ridge of hills north of the Forth. Nevertheless, John de Warenne, a veteran negotiator, believed that the Scots could be persuaded to give up their struggle in the face of the formidable and well-armed English. He knew the Scots were brave, but they were not well-trained soldiers and they had only crude weapons. De Warenne's army was the best fighting force in the world and behind it he had a constant supply of arms and food, something Wallace's army lacked.

When the governor sent his emissaries to negotiate with Wallace, he sent back a challenging reply: *We have not come for peace but to fight to liberate our country!* John was a patient man who decided to sit pat and try again. Cressingham, the treasurer, opposed this decision. He was all for prompt measures.

De Warenne pointed out that it was impossible to estimate the enemy's number, concealed in the thickets at the base of the Ochils. Moreover, to get to them would mean taking the army across the river via Stirling Bridge, which was so narrow it would take a full day to cross. John could not rid his mind of Lynx de Warenne's warning: *Watch out for a trap at Stirling!*

The governor asked himself why the bridge was still standing. Wallace had been first on the ground and should have destroyed it. Had the bridge been left intact as bait? When de Warenne suggested they send out scouts to see if a better way of fording the tide-fed river could be found, Cressingham accused him of cowardice. "There is no use, Sir Earl, in drawing out this business any longer and wasting the king's revenues for nothing. Let us advance and carry out our duty as we are bound to do."

His overbearing attitude divided the forces. Against John de Warenne's express orders, Cressingham commanded his men to cross Stirling Bridge. After his horsemen, came his foot soldiers and Welsh archers. There was no visible sign of the Scots and by midmorning almost half of the English army had crossed.

Suddenly the wild battle cry of the Wallace rebels and de Moray Highlanders rent the air. They poured forth with spears and hooked axes, seemingly without end, fighting barefoot so that the boggy ground did not impede them.

On the other bank de Warenne watched the carnage helplessly as Cressingham's forces were cut down. Cressingham himself was thrown from his horse in the first moments of the conflict and trampled to death. Within minutes the governor saw almost half his army slain by the fury of the wild keening enemy. When de Warenne realized that the battle was lost, he ordered Stirling Bridge burned and his army to retreat.

After this impossible victory, the common people of Scotland went wild. William Wallace was knighted and proclaimed guardian of the kingdom. His forces swooped down on the strongholds of Stirling and Dundee, capturing the castles and reducing the towns. The nobility of Scotland, however, held aloof from this commoner who was a threat to their hereditary power and privilege.

34

When Edward Plantagenet learned of the defeat at Stirling Bridge and the death of his treasurer, Hugh de Cressingham, he immediately returned from France and proceeded to organize his forces for the reconquest of Scotland.

Robert Bruce paid a visit to Dumfries to exchange information. He knew the de Warennes were privy to the king's plans and he wanted to pass on the dire news that Wallace's forces were systematically destroying crops and driving off livestock in as many counties as they could.

"Edward is on his way to join the governor in Edinburgh. He has the levies of many earls with him—Bigod, Bohun, and of course the Earl of Ulster's Irishmen," Lynx told Robert.

"When the vast army moves north of Edinburgh they will find nothing but blackened fields and burned farms. Wallace's forces are even moving the inhabitants north so that Edward's soldiers will be deprived of food or aid of any sort. They are moving into our territory; only nightly vigilance keeps them at bay."

Lynx looked shocked at such destruction. "We will ride out with you on night patrol, and I'll inform the governor immediately. Have any other nobles joined Wallace yet?''

The Bruce shook his head. ''Not openly at least, only de Moray, Montieth, and Comyn are allied with him.''

''They don't stand a chance this time.''

''My country is being torn assunder by both the English and the Scots,'' Robert Bruce said bitterly. ''Never has there been a time in history with more betrayals, treachery, and lies because of pride and greed! The result is mindless destruction. I wish it were otherwise. Our common goal should be unification.''

The ladies who had come to greet the Bruce overheard his words. Seldom before had they heard such bitterness in his voice. ''Poor Robert,'' Jory said with heartfelt sympathy. ''You wish the English out of your country completely, do you not?''

''In truth I do, present company excepted.''

''What about the Irish?'' Elizabeth de Burgh asked.

Robert ruffled her dark curls. ''The Scots hate only the English, not the Irish; probably because we share Celtic blood.''

''Elizabeth is excited because her father will be accompanying the king,'' Jory explained.

''I hope he won't be too busy to see me,'' Elizabeth said longingly.

''We'll invite him to stay at Dumfries,'' Jane suggested, looking to Lynx for approval. ''The king will have far too many for John to accommodate in Edinburgh.''

''I suppose I'll have to offer Edward the hospitality of Lochmaben and Caerlaverock, if I hope to keep them in my possession,'' Robert said dryly.

"John will be relieved to know he can count on your support."

"Did he arrest Fitz-Waren yet?" Robert inquired.

Lynx shook his head. "I have two of my knights watching Torthwald, but the bastard seems to have dropped off the face of the earth."

"Let's not speak of him," Jane begged. "Lynx is fully recovered and that's all that matters, at least to me."

"Now that you mention it, I think you've been feeding him too well, Jane. He's getting fat."

"That's solid muscle!" Lynx argued. "Try not to be envious, Robert."

Jane's dimples came out of hiding. "Will you stay the night, my lord?"

"All right, you've twisted my arm," the Bruce replied with a wink, all bitterness gone from his voice.

"Come to the armory, I want to show you a habergeon we've been working on. Instead of a shirt of heavy iron rings, we've invented a woven metal mesh that's almost impossible to penetrate."

The minute the men left, Elizabeth and Jory each sought their chambers to adorn themselves in prettier gowns. Jane followed Marjory up to her tower rooms and sat on the bed as Jory inspected her lavish wardrobe. "I cannot bear the thought of Lynx going into battle again . . . I'm so afraid for him!"

"Darling, don't ever let him know you are afraid for him. Let him think he is omnipotent."

"I love him so much! Why do they keep fighting wars?"

"Jane, wars are fought to be won and they cannot be won by anything but violent measures."

"Jory, do you love Robert?"

"Of course I love him, and someday he'll make a bid for the Scottish crown. That frightens me out of my wits, but I wouldn't dream of stopping him. Robert believes it's his destiny, so I must too!"

Thinking of her vision, Jane asked gently, "Do you want to be his queen?"

Jory laid the gown she had chosen across the foot of the bed and came to sit beside Jane. "I know that can never be. The Scots would never accept an English queen."

"Yet still you want him to become king?"

"Yes! I would do anything to help him achieve his goal."

"Do you love him enough to make a great sacrifice?" Jane asked softly.

"I love him enough for anything!" Jory declared passionately.

"I know Robert Bruce has the secret pledge of a few Scottish earls, but if he had the power of Edward de Burgh, Earl of Ulster, behind him, he could gain the throne."

"You are right, Jane. Oh, wouldn't that be wonderful? If only the Earl of Ulster could be induced to back Robert!"

Jane hesitated only a moment before she rushed on. "If Robert offered a betrothal, making de Burgh's daughter, Elizabeth, his queen, it would almost certainly induce Ulster to help Robert become king."

Jory's eyes widened with shock and the blood drained from her face so quickly, she looked as waxy as a corpse.

* * *

That evening in the hall, the talk was all about warfare. "Edward has told the governor his first priority is the immediate elimination of Wallace. He is offering rewards of money and land to any noble who aids in the fugitive's capture."

"The king is an evil genius at dividing and conquering. His favorite tool is bribery, either by gifts of land or remittance of debts," Robert declared. "I know . . . he's bribed me often enough."

To divert them, Jane brought Lincoln Robert to the hall. She fed him some custard while the onlookers marveled at the child's appetite.

"He needs something more substantial than custard," Lynx decided, handing him the crust from a loaf. When Lincoln Robert began to devour it with gusto, covering himself with sticky crumbs, the men couldn't help laughing.

Jane noticed that throughout the meal, Jory had been unusually pensive. In the candlelight her delicate face was shadowed with dark smudges beneath her beautiful eyes and Jane's heart ached for her dearest friend. Then Jane's glance was drawn to her husband, who was so like his sister in coloring. But there the similarity ended. Lynx's physique now exuded strength. He was more robust than he had ever been and Jane fervently thanked God for his recovery.

She watched with loving eyes as Lynx lifted his baby son onto his shoulders and galloped toward the stairs as Lincoln Robert clutched fistfuls of his father's hair and crowed his delight. Jory was right, as usual, Jane decided. She must keep her fears to herself and pretend Lynx was omnipotent.

* * *

Hours later, high in the Lady Tower of Dumfries, the Bruce lay spent, cradling Jory as she lay sprawled across his muscular body. "You are fierce as a tigress tonight, sweetheart. What prompts such ferocity?"

"Will you answer the call to battle?"

"The thought of losing me makes you insatiable?"

"Yes!" she told him, biting his shoulder.

"I'm needed to patrol Galloway, Annandale, and Lanark, or Wallace's raiding parties will have all the Lowlands blackened. Likely I won't be called to battle."

"I'm not talking about losing you in battle."

"How else could you lose me?" he asked, unwinding a pale strand of her hair from his forearm.

"You know as well as I, our parting is inevitable."

He placed strong fingers beneath her chin, forcing her to look into his eyes. "You've never had trouble before pushing away the future and embracing the present."

"Robert, there is a way to speed your bid for the crown," Jory said intensely. "If the Earl of Ulster backed you—"

"Sweetheart, de Burgh owns half of Ireland; for all intents and purposes he is a king himself. What could I possibly offer him that he doesn't have?"

"You could offer to make his daughter your queen," she whispered. "It's an offer few fathers would refuse."

"Elizabeth is a child!"

"If you'd stop looking at me, my love, you'd see that Elizabeth is on the brink of womanhood and already mad in love with you."

"Enough," he said, covering her mouth with his in a long, silencing kiss.

"Promise me you'll think about it."

"Jory, my heart, you know me well enough that I will think of little else."

In the opposite tower, Jane, who had downed two goblets of wine to bolster her bravado, was in a droll mood where the least word set her off laughing.

"You are very gay tonight and here I expected tears at the thought of my going to war again."

"Tush, I'm not the least bit afraid for you." She pushed him down on the bed and ran her hands up his bare legs. "You have muscles of iron, I warrant you could crack walnuts with your thighs. God, just the thought of that makes me weak with need!"

"You've been around Jory too long. You are turning into a shallow, selfish little minx who thinks only of pleasure," he teased.

Jane sat back on her heels, her eyes as round as an owl's. "You're wrong, Lynx . . . you'll see . . . Jory is capable of being completely selfless. She's always been generous to a fault with me and I *adore* her." An unbidden tear rolled down her cheek.

"And *I* adore *you,*" Lynx vowed, realizing immediately that Jane's tears were there, just beneath all her laughter. "I know what you need to banish those silly tears."

"What?"

"A damn good bedding."

The wine kicked in and Jane began to giggle.

"What's so amusing?"

"Our first bedding, after the handfasting. I was so pathetically green and ignorant. And you were so formal and stiff!''

''I bet I wasn't this stiff,'' he said, drawing her hand to his groin. Her fingers did wicked things to him and try as he might Lynx could not remember a time when he had not been rampant for her.

''Let's play stallion and mare,'' she invited, threading her fingers through his tawny mane and nipping his ear playfully with her sharp teeth. The bedding went on for hours during which Lynx de Warenne skillfully banished all his wife's tears.

At Edinburgh, Edward Plantagenet held a council of war with his generals to discuss strategy. Like John de Warenne, the king was in his sixties and the years had taken their toll.

''Numbers are not as important as weapons. How well equipped are they?''

''The last time I fought the Scots they were bare-arsed savages,'' Bigod declared.

''Since then they've managed to acquire better equipment, most of it ours,'' John de Warenne said dryly.

''How?'' Edward demanded.

''Sire, they pick over battlefields like crows, robbing the dead of armor and weapons, they mount raids on armories, and Wallace is famous for spiriting away baggage trains.''

''Whose?'' Edward demanded, his piercing blue eyes searching the room for culprits.

Percy looked sheepish; he had lost three. John de Warenne said quickly, ''Sire, their main weapon is the twelve-foot spear which is lethal to our cavalry.''

Lynx de Warenne held the opinion that the king relied on his cavalry too much when there were other viable alternatives. But since he was in charge of a large company of heavy cavalry, he risked sounding like a coward if he suggested these alternatives. Nevertheless he spoke up. "Sire, I have found my Welsh bowmen far more effective against the Scots. They sustain fewer casualties since they can fight from a distance. Their longbows discharge arrows three times the speed of crossbows; a most effective weapon against an enemy whose soldiers stuff tow in their tunics for protection."

Notoriously stubborn, the king argued, "I have always relied on my cavalry. It is a tried and true method of winning wars."

"In France, yes, but in Scotland, where moss and bog can stretch for miles, heavy cavalry can sink up to its hocks and flounder helplessly."

"We will put some of the Welsh in the front ranks before the cavalry," Edward declared.

"Nay, Sire," Lynx de Warenne objected, "the cavalry would trample them." De Warenne knew the English king was not above destroying his own troops if he destroyed the Scots as well. "The Welsh must have their own flanks."

Edward stared at him. "I heard rumors you were killed in battle."

"They were exaggerated, Sire."

"Have you read the Bruce's reports that the countryside has been laid waste to the north, Your Majesty?" John de Warenne inquired.

"Let us hope those too are exaggerated. I've ordered

supplies sent up from Carlisle in any case, so I see no reason why we cannot press forward."

When the king received a message from the Earl of Angus informing him that Wallace's army was encamped near Falkirk, Edward Plantagenet gave the order to march. Edward and his generals soon realized that the Bruce's reports were correct. The English saw nothing but blackened fields and burned towns.

By the time they reached Linlithgow, a few miles from Falkirk, the fodder for the horses was all gone. The English made camp in the darkness, rolling themselves in blankets and lying down wherever they could find a bit of dry ground.

Edward Plantagenet did likewise, too proud to order his campaign tent set up when his generals slept on the ground. In the middle of the night, Edward's restive warhorse stepped on him, breaking his ribs. Panic among his leaders ensued. Some even suggested they should abort the operation and return to Edinburgh.

The king stubbornly refused. His doctors bound him and he then donned his armor and mounted his horse, sitting stiffly in the saddle with John de Warenne at his side. He gave orders to strike camp well before daylight and the army moved forward at a snail's pace.

When dawn broke, Wallace's army was spotted ahead of them on a high ridge. The Scottish leader had drawn up his men in circular schiltrons, with spearmen on the outside and reserves in the center to take the place of those who fell. Between the schiltrons were Scottish archers who carried small, outdated bows and arrows. The cavalry, led by John Comyn, was being held in reserve.

The King of England sat his horse in agony, hating Wallace with a vengeance for occupying the high ground, knowing his own forces had an uphill battle ahead of them. To make matters worse, Lynx de Warenne's words had been prophetic—a wide, dank moss stretched before them. The English forces had to be diverted right and left to avoid it, but the Welsh archers proved their worth. The mighty longbows launched their arrows over the high ground, and they fell like hail on the schiltrons.

As the Scots began to die, Comyn's cavalry fled the battlefield. The King of England, now gray in the face from pain, ordered his own cavalry to swing far wide of the boggy moss and attack the foot soldiers from the rear.

The beaten Scots fled through the heavily wooded hillsides behind Falkirk, but not before ten thousand of them lay slaughtered on the battlefield. When it was reported to Edward that William Wallace was not among the dead, he swore his army would pursue him until the king's enemy was taken, but wherever the English army went, they found nothing but wasted lands.

Edward Plantagenet, now suffering ill health, and finding himself with a starving army on his hands, decided to withdraw to Carlisle on the English side of the border. Wallace was declared an outlaw and other warrants of arrest were soon issued from Carlisle, despite the king's deteriorating condition. Among those Edward wanted were Montieth and Comyn.

It wasn't long before Comyn sent conciliatory messages to Edward, pointing out the part he had played in the English defeat of Wallace. After due consideration, a shrewd Edward pardoned Comyn, knowing if he was arrested and beheaded, it would leave the way clear for Robert Bruce to claim the throne of Scotland.

The Earl of Montieth had not expected to come out on the losing side. He went into hiding, amazed at the number of Scots nobles, previously opposed to the English king, who now spoke out to blacken William Wallace's name and ability. Montieth watched Comyn's every move as he offered to accommodate Edward Plantagenet in return for a pardon.

The wily Earl of Montieth, following Comyn's example, entered into secret negotiations with Edward Plantagenet. In return for a pardon, reconfirmation of his governorship of Dumbarton, and the earldom of Lennox, the Earl of Montieth promised to deliver William Wallace into the king's hands.

35

"Is it true, is the king dying?" Lynx de Warenne asked Robert Bruce, who had just returned from Carlisle Castle.

"No such luck," Robert said irreverently.

"But didn't they send for Prince Edward?"

"Yes, the king had a seizure and his son came immediately. Never have I witnessed such a fucking poor excuse for a prince in my life!" Robert scorned.

"Young Edward was always spoiled and effeminate, but I haven't seen him for a couple of years. I hoped he would improve with age."

"He's totally unsuited to kingship. He's an immature fop who surrounds himself with male lovers. Edward must run mad every time he sets eyes on his heir."

"Such a feckless ruler would make things infinitely easier for you," Lynx said quietly.

"Aye, I would be more afraid of the *bones* of the father dead, than of the living son!"

"I have the governor upstairs in bed with an ague, coughing his lungs up. He rode in yesterday to tell me of a rumor Wallace had been taken."

The Bruce raised his eyebrows in consternation. "So

that's what brought about Plantagenet's rapid recovery! The king is suddenly well enough to return to London."

"If it is true, Wallace will be tried and condemned to death. There will be no pardon for the king's enemy," Lynx declared.

"Ironic, that such a valiant and brave warrior will be condemned, while false traitors like Comyn will thrive and prosper," Bruce said bitterly.

"Mayhap the time is ripe," Lynx said quietly.

Bruce's dark brows drew together, as he brooded over his friend's words.

"The Scots will never accept English rule, nor will the Church of Scotland ever submit. Someone will rise up to take Wallace's place and the battles will go on until Edward is dead. Then the son will lose all that the father has gained and the fighting and killing will all have been for naught. I am tired of war," Lynx said bluntly.

"If I took up arms against the king," Robert said low, "would you oppose me?"

Lynx shook his head. "I would return to my lands in England."

Bruce raised his eyes to the stairs. "And the governor?"

"His health is failing. I think I could persuade him to relinquish his office and retire to England."

Jory, who had been reading to her uncle, came downstairs to join them. She searched Robert's face, wondering if he had reached a decision about the private matter they had discussed. His face was dark and closed, telling her nothing.

Robert picked up his riding gloves. "I cannot stay. Will you ride out with me a short way, Jory?"

"With pleasure, my lord." Her face lit up with delight, pretending their time together would be infinite.

In the stables, the Bruce saddled Jory's palfrey and lifted her into the saddle. Then without a word they galloped swiftly to beyond the first dense copse of trees. They reined in, vaulted from their mounts, and fell into each other's arms. He kissed her until her lips felt beestung. Finally Jory pulled away from him.

"Did you speak with de Burgh?"

He searched her face with desolate eyes. "Beloved, why are you urging me to this action when you feel such passion for me?"

"Because I want you to fulfill your destiny! Let me make this noble sacrifice. Did you see de Burgh?"

"Yes. I did not broach this matter, but I invited him to Lochmaben."

Jory went on tiptoe to kiss him again. "I love you so much; you *are* doing the right thing, Robert."

He wrapped his arms about her and held her enfolded against him for long minutes. "You always smell of freesia," he murmured.

"Freesia is my favorite scent."

His face was bereft as he reached into his doublet. "Will you give this letter to Elizabeth? It is from her father, asking her to join him at Lochmaben."

Jory took the letter and in return gave him a radiant smile. It prevented the scream that was building in her throat from escaping.

Jane removed the cold brick from John de Warenne's feet and replaced it with a hot one. Then she measured out a generous dose of syrup made from speedwell and angelica to ease his coughing.

"You are an angel of mercy, my dear, I am so fortunate to be here at Dumfries with my family. I shudder to think what would have become of me if I'd stayed in Edinburgh."

Marjory came into the chamber and put into words what Jane had been thinking. "You shouldn't go back there. You've served the king your entire life, to the detriment of your own health. It's time your heavy responsibilities were shouldered by someone else."

"My dear Jory, I spoke at length with the king at Falkirk; both of us are feeling our advanced years. I believe he will soon appoint a board of commissioners to govern Scotland. One man cannot do it all."

"That is marvelous news, my lord, now try to get some rest," Jane pleaded.

Jory followed Jane from the chamber. "I have a letter for Elizabeth from her father. Will you come with me while I deliver it?"

Jane's eyes filled with speculation. Jory's tone made it clear she needed moral support. "Of course I will."

Elizabeth was overjoyed to receive the letter from her noble father, Edward de Burgh, Earl of Ulster. When she read its contents, she was ecstatic. "Oh, my father is visiting the Bruces at Lochmaben in a sennight and wants me to join him there!"

Jane saw Elizabeth's cheeks blush a pretty pink. "Oh, I will need a new dress," Elizabeth declared breathlessly.

As Jane looked at Jory, their eyes met in understanding.

"Not just one dress, Elizabeth, you must have a dozen new gowns," Jory insisted. "Don't forget that Robert Bruce is Scotland's most eligible bachelor."

Elizabeth de Burgh's face turned scarlet, but she fairly bubbled with excitement. "I must tell Maggie and Molly, they will be in a tizzy! Jory, will you come with me to Lochmaben?"

"What nonsense! I've taught you all I know. Didn't I teach Jane to be Lady Jane Tut? Now it is time for you to unfurl your petals and bloom, Elizabeth."

When the young girl ran off to find her women, Jane looked at Marjory with profound admiration shining in her eyes. "Oh, Jory, how selfless and generous you are. I don't think I'd have the courage to do what you are doing."

"Now *you* are spouting nonsense. Where do you think I learned such things, Jane, if not from your glorious example?"

In London, at the great hall of Westminster, William Wallace was charged with an endless litany of sedition and homicide, including putting to death old men and young, wives and widows, children and sucklings, and priests and nuns.

Since King Edward had declared him an outlaw, Wallace was not allowed to defend himself. He was immediately found guilty and sentenced to be hanged, drawn, and quartered.

When eyewitness accounts of William Wallace's execution reached Scotland, however, English as well as Scots were outraged at the unspeakable butchery. Wallace's body was bound on a hurdle and dragged at the tail of horses through the city of London from Westminster to the gallows at Smithfield. He was hoisted with a noose about his neck, but let down while he was half-living. Next his genitals were cut off. Then his bowels were torn out and burned in a fire while Wallace still lived. Only then was he beheaded and his trunk cut into four pieces.

His head was spiked on London Bridge; his right leg was sent to Berwick, his left to Perth, his right arm to Newcastle, and his left to Stirling.

Hatred toward Edward Plantagenet deepened over such barbaric butchery of the brave knight, especially since time and time again the king had forgiven the treachery of Scotland's nobles.

Word must have reached Edward's ears of the outrage of all in Scotland in general, and the Bruces and the de Warennes in particular, for suddenly they were out of favor. The king sent an official notice that John de Warenne had been removed from the governorship of Scotland and demanded an accounting of monies. In his place the king named four guardians, but Robert Bruce, Scotland's premier earl, was not one of them. To pile insult upon insult, King Edward appointed a new sheriff for Lanark and demanded the Bruce repay debts owed by his grandfather from two decades earlier.

Robert Bruce ground his teeth and wondered if documents taken when Wallace was arrested implicated him in any way. He knew such damning evidence would prevent any secret alliance with the Irish Earl of Ulster. But when Edward de Burgh arrived at Lochmaben for his promised visit, the Bruce heaved a sigh of relief.

He was gratified to learn that the Irish palatine found

Edward Plantagenet's treatment of Wallace beneath contempt. The Bruce lost no time proposing a betrothal between himself and Elizabeth de Burgh, in exchange for Ulster's backing when Bruce made a bid for the throne.

"Baliol is dead and we both know King Edward's days are numbered. His heir is no threat to any save himself," Robert pressed.

"You will have to fight Comyn. In the end it comes down to the two of you. Did you know he is claiming all Baliol's possessions because of their kinship?"

The Bruce laughed sardonically. "I cannot see Edward Plantagenet taking kindly to such a claim."

Ulster agreed. "No, at the moment Comyn too is out of royal favor."

As the two men talked long into the night, Edward de Burgh, with an eye to the future, saw that the advantages of Bruce's offer outweighed the risks. It did not take much persuading for the powerful Irish earl to agree to the secret betrothal.

The documents were drawn up and signed and Elizabeth de Burgh almost fainted at the midnight ceremony where Robert Bruce plighted his troth to her, under the watchful eye of her stern father.

At the end of the week when the visit was over, they escorted Elizabeth back to Dumfries before Ulster took her home for a quick trip to her beloved Ireland. Young Elizabeth was in a complete state of euphoria, even though Robert hadn't actually begun his wooing yet.

At Dumfries after all in the castle had retired, Lynx and Robert spoke quietly. "John looks much rested, but from what he said at dinner he is livid about his shabby treatment by Edward.''

''It's obvious one of our enemies has the king's ear,'' Lynx cursed. ''I suspect Fitz-Waren; he could very well be in England. If he is, I will find him and kill him. John and I have decided to return to our English estates. That way when Edward orders us to put down a Bruce rebellion, we will be far removed from Scotland and can turn a deaf ear to the call to arms.''

''I am convinced the time is right. If I don't act decisively now, it will be too late. I've never been so far out of Edward's favor, and for once, my enemy Comyn is in like case,'' Robert Bruce added with amused irony.

''How so?''

''Comyn is claiming all that was Baliol's.''

Lynx whistled. ''Christ, that's a deal of estates and possessions. Between the two of you, that's half of Scotland. Too bad you can't join forces against Edward.''

The Bruce smiled.

Lynx refilled his friend's goblet. ''You cunning swine, what plot are you hatching?''

''Comyn is close-by at his castle of Dalswinton. I'm going to send him a proposition. One of us will support the other for the crown. The loser receives the winner's lands and castles. What do you think?''

''It's brilliant! It's an offer he can't refuse—there is no real loser.''

''It's time I acted in my own interests.''

Lynx grinned, wondering when the hell he'd ever done otherwise.

''There is no trust between Comyn and me. I won't go

to Dalswinton and he won't come to Lochmaben. We need a neutral meeting place."

"You are welcome to use Dumfries," Lynx offered.

The Bruce shook his head. "I don't want you involved in this. I want you safely on your way to England before any bond is signed."

"How about the Franciscan monastery? Both of you would be safe in sanctified surroundings."

"Your suggestion is sound," Robert agreed. " 'Tis sad you must leave Dumfries, but when I am king and our countries live in peace, you must return."

"My wife and my son are Scots. We shall return to Dumfries someday, never fear."

"Is Jane unhappy?" Robert asked with concern.

"No, bless her heart, she is willing to do my bidding, even though the thought of England frightens her a bit."

"She has no idea of the luxury of the de Warenne estates in England?"

"Of course not, do you think she wed me for my wealth?"

"Why else would she wed an ugly brute like you?"

Robert Bruce quietly made his way to the Lady Tower and knocked low. When Jory opened the door, he slipped inside. "My own beloved heart, I have come to say good-bye."

Jory went into his arms, determined to shed no tears. She wanted him to remember her radiant smile. "Robert, my love, you'll be a part of me forever."

It was no small undertaking for the de Warenne mesne to vacate Dumfries and return to England. As well, John de Warenne had his own army who would accompany him back to Surrey. It was decided they would leave in stages, with John and his personal guard departing first, then in a few days the Welsh foot soldiers would follow, and the last to leave would be Lynx de Warenne accompanied by his knights, squires, and family.

Each army had its own baggage train of horses, armor, weapons, and supplies that would have to be transported in stages from Dumfries to their castle of Wigton near Carlisle, then to Lancaster and Chester on the border of Wales and so on to the vast de Warenne estates in the south of England.

Lynx found the services of Dumfries' steward so invaluable he offered to take Jock Leslie and his entire family to England with them. Jock shook his head. "We are castle keepers, my lord, and we will keep Dumfries running smoothly for you until you return."

"Jock, that may not be for years," Lynx urged, "and Jane will miss you sorely."

"We've had a family conference and we've all chosen to remain here at Dumfries, wi' the exception of Keith. He can no' bear to part wi' the horses!"

"Jane is thrilled that Keith is coming with us and she's already talking about sending for some of her older nephews and nieces so they can be educated in England."

Jock chuckled. "That would be over Megotta's dead body, nae doubt!"

Jory de Warenne's personal effects alone filled an entire wagon and Jane was busy from morning till night packing the household furnishings, their clothes, and Lincoln Robert's entire nursery. Jane persuadec' Grace Murray to come with them. The nursemaid was extremely wary of England and the English, but she had become firmly attached to the wee lordling.

Three days after John de Warenne departed, Lynx's Welsh bowmen set off on their long march, and three days hence his knights and his family would follow. It was not before time; the Bruce had informed Lynx that he had met with Comyn and documents were being drawn up on their secret agreement.

That night when Jane bathed the baby, Lynx helped her put him to bed. "We have to take both cradles and his baby bath, oh and remind me to ask Thomas to find room for our own bathtub."

Lynx groaned. "If you load any more unnecessary baggage we'll sink into the first bog we cross. Don't you think we have bathtubs in England?"

Jane went up on tiptoe and slipped her arms about his neck. "I don't care about bathtubs, but I will miss my enchanted forest pool. Will you take me there tomorrow one last time?"

Lynx loved her far too much to deny her anything.

36

After Falkirk, Fitz-Waren's options began to run out. Montieth shunned him, then went into hiding while he plotted to betray Wallace. The warrant for Fitz-Waren's arrest that his father had issued prevented him from returning to the army, and prompted even his own officers to turn against him. To save their own necks, they were ready to turn him over to the governor, and they knew far too much about his affairs.

As his funds dwindled away, hatred for the de Warennes seethed in his blood. He had treasures at Torthwald, but when he returned to that castle, he saw that Lynx de Warenne's knights guarded the gate. He returned to Edinburgh, hiding in the bowels of the city, changing lodgings constantly until his money was gone, then he furtively prowled about the castle under cover of night, reduced to stealing food from the kitchens and sleeping in the stables.

His father's guards made it impossible for Fitz-Waren to get anywhere near him and when he learned of John's ill health he fervently wished the old swine would die. Fitz-Waren also heard castle servants speaking of the king's deteriorating health and realized Edward Plantagenet's days were numbered. A spark of hope kindled in his depraved brain. Fitz-Waren decided to look to the future. It should not be difficult to cultivate the Prince of Wales. If he curried favor with young Edward, was it not conceivable the new king would bestow on him the earldom of Surrey? Provided of course that John and Lynx de Warenne were eliminated.

When John de Warenne journeyed to Dumfries, Fitz-Waren followed and found a safe haven close-by in Selkirk Forest. The summer nights were warm and the game so plentiful, all he needed was his knife and a hunting bow he fashioned from the long, sturdy branch of a larch tree. Fitz-Waren watched and waited, his mind obsessed with murder.

Lynx lifted Jane before him in the saddle as they rode out together to bid this beautiful place their last good-bye. As they meandered slowly down the bank of the river Nith, Jane pointed out a pair of sleek otters as they glided through the water and Lynx reined in so they could watch them climb from the water and chase each other through the tall reeds.

Jane leaned back against his chest, relishing the feel of his muscles restored to hardness. Lynx tightened his arm about her waist and turned their mount so that it headed toward the forest. A doe, suddenly startled, dashed away through the trees. "Your horse frightened her, we should have come on foot," she told him.

"Then I would have been deprived of the pleasure of riding with you between my thighs."

Jane glanced up at him over her shoulder. "It's usually the other way about."

Lynx, half aroused, suddenly hardened all the way.

Jane couldn't resist teasing him. "If you are hot and bothered, my lord, a swim will cool you down."

"Then we had better forgo the swim," he replied as they arrived at the forest pool.

"But, my dearest lord, if you don't want to swim, there is no reason to undress," she teased.

Lynx dismounted and lifted her down to him, letting her slide down the length of his hard body. "Is there not, my love?"

Her dimples appeared. "Trust you to find a reason."

Lynx undressed her slowly, savoring their building anticipation. He dropped a kiss on each portion of her lovely anatomy as it became exposed to the warm sunshine, then Jane did the same to Lynx as he threw off his clothes with more haste. Their passion kindled quickly, stimulated by the excitement of making love outdoors, in their own private Eden.

Lynx stretched out in the long grasses and delicate wildflowers, pulling her down to him so that they were half-hidden by the fragrant flora that grew so lushly beside the forest pool and wafted about them in the light summer breeze.

"I love you," he told her between kisses.

"When did you discover that you loved me?" Jane whispered, eager to be told over and over.

"I've always loved you," he vowed.

"Liar," she teased. "You never noticed me until Jory showed me how to make you jealous. Admit the truth, it was Lady Jane Tut you fell in love with."

Lynx kissed her deeply, then held her gaze with an intense look. "Do you want the truth? All the feminine tricks Jory taught you made me *desire* you, even *lust* for you, but it was your own sweet nature that made me love you. When I lay deathly ill and helpless, you gave me everything . . . held back nothing. That is the moment I tumbled hopelessly, deliriously in love with you.''

Jane's heart overflowed. ''Mmm, love and lust, what a glorious combination,'' she murmured, molding her body to his intimately and offering up her mouth so that words were no longer necessary, or even possible.

Hidden by a thick canopy of leaves, Fitz-Waren watched the lovers through malevolent eyes. The hatred he harbored for Lynx de Warenne pulsed through his veins like pure venom. Here was the author of all his misery, here was the reason for his father's rejection, here was the cause of his fall from grace and every misfortune he had ever suffered! Fitz-Waren cursed that his detested cousin had escaped his daring attack and survived. Not only was he still living, the son-of-a-whore was thriving, enjoying life to the full!

Fitz-Waren's view was obscured by the tall grasses, but he could hear every word, every rustle, every cry of passion. He curbed his impatience; this time he knew he must not fail. Fitz-Waren gripped the bow and arrow and sat back on his haunches to wait.

Lynx shook off the delicious lassitude that made him drowse in the warm afternoon. ''Are you awake, love?''

''Mmm, I'm watching something here in the grass I've never seen before.''

''What's that?'' he asked, unable to resist stroking his

hand down the length of her bare back, then resting his palm on her bottom.

"It's a pair of very beautiful snails that are mating, and it is absolutely fascinating."

As they watched, the snails touched and clung and caressed, moving slowly against one another in a sensual ballet of clasping, embracing, stroking, and fondling.

"That's how I want to make love to you," Lynx whispered.

"That's how you do make love to me," Jane whispered back.

"Am I that thorough?"

"You must be . . . you've made another baby in me."

Lynx looked stunned. "Janie . . . you shouldn't be running about the forest, naked."

She stood up and tossed her disheveled curls. "I will and I shall," she vowed, laughing, "and don't you dare tell me I can't ride or swim!" She glided gracefully to the water's edge, and looked back over her shoulder, knowing he would follow. She was breast-high in the pool when she heard his whoop of joy and turned, eager to watch him.

Suddenly, she saw a man emerge through the leaves and take careful aim at Lynx's back with a longbow. "Lynx!" The scream of warning was torn from her throat as her eyes widened in horror.

Lynx spun around, just as a deadly arrow sped past him, barely missing him. He knew it found another target, however, as he heard Jane scream with pain. He recognized the hated Fitz-Waren, who instantly took flight, but Jane's plight made immediate pursuit impossible. Lynx felt his gut knot with fear as he saw Jane disappear beneath the surface of the pool. He knew the arrow had pierced her body and desperately prayed that it had not taken her life.

Lynx plunged into the pond and dived down at the place he had seen her disappear, panic speeding his heartbeat and fueling his fear when he could not see her through the murky water. He came up for air, then dove again, desperately searching for his wounded wife. Finally, he saw her limp body floating near the bottom of the pool and knew at the very least she was unconscious.

His powerful arms closed about her and he thrust himself to the surface. As they broke the water, he could see the long arrow was embedded in her shoulder. Lynx knew such a wound should not be fatal, yet he could see that Jane was not breathing. He carried her from the water with all speed, snapped the shaft of the arrow off and laid her down gently. Then he bent and breathed his own life into her.

Jane began to cough and retch up water, then her eyes fluttered open. The minute she regained consciousness she was swept with a wave of pain that made her cry out in agony.

"Thank God, thank God," Lynx murmured. "Jane, you must be brave while I get you back to the castle. I know it hurts, but you are going to be fine, sweetheart." He pulled on his chausses and wrapped her in her discarded dress. His horse pawed the ground and snorted at the commotion, rolling its eyes, as Lynx firmly grasped its bridle and tried to calm it. The restive animal began to dance away from him, but he managed to gentle it while he mounted, clasping Jane in one powerful arm.

* * *

Fitz-Waren was not the only watcher at the forest pool this day. Green eyes gazed through the canopy of leaves, silently watching the man who crouched behind a tree. He was a master of stealth, motionless and infinitely patient. The lynx stared unblinking as if mesmerized. He licked his lips, his appetite whetted for the flesh that would slake his growing hunger. Never taking his eyes from his prey, he moved his weight so that it was more comfortably distributed as he crouched and waited for the man to flee so he could take hot pursuit.

When Fitz-Waren shot his arrow and hit the wrong target, he was momentarily rooted to the spot. He saw Lynx de Warenne recognize him and knew escape was impossible unless the fool chose to aid the woman rather than pursue him. Fitz-Waren fled in panic, but as he bolted along the forest path, he could hear someone following him through the trees. He ran faster, frantic, as he realized his pursuer was gaining on him.

Fitz-Waren felt as if his lungs were on fire and his heart felt as if it would burst. He knew he had no choice but to fight for his life. He unsheathed his knife and turned to face his nemesis. What he saw made his eyes bulge from their sockets. It was not the Lynx he was expecting, but a lynx nevertheless! The wild cat was in full flight, and as he turned he watched, almost hypnotized as it leaped upon its prey.

The impact knocked the knife from Fitz-Waren's hand and the last breath from his body as it took him to the forest floor. Fitz-Waren feared his sanity would leave him, as he felt the lynx's claws rip through his clothes and the large incisors slash into his throat. As he screamed, blood bubbled up through the holes its teeth had made and he watched in terrified agony as the lynx licked his blood with relish. The uncanny resemblance of green eyes and tawny pelt sent a deadly chill along Fitz-Waren's spine as he realized the wild cat was going to toy with him before it delivered its coup de grâce.

"Get Megotta," Lynx shouted to Keith Leslie as the boy took his horse. Taffy ran across the bailey and flung the castle doors wide. As Lynx carried Jane through them, he ordered, "Take some knights into the forest and hunt down Fitz-Waren!"

When Marjory saw the pair covered with blood, she cried out in alarm.

"She'll be all right, Jory. She's been hit with an arrow—get hot water and bandages." Lynx carried Jane upstairs and laid her down gently on the bed so he could examine the wound. The arrow had pierced her shoulder deeply, but he saw with great relief that there was no metal head embedded in her flesh.

Jane's face was blanched white and she was biting down on her lips in an effort to silence her moans of distress. "You will have to be brave, love, while I pull out the rest of this arrow."

She nodded, trusting this man above all others to help her.

Lynx unsheathed his knife and knelt beside her. If he could not pull it out, he would have to dig down with the blade. "It's all right to scream, Jane, you don't have to hold it inside." He knew he must be cruel to be kind. Her pain would be unbearable, but he was confident the wound was not fatal. Lynx was far more worried that the shock of it all could make her lose their baby.

With a sure hand and steady fingers he grasped the broken shaft and pulled. It was so slick with blood, Lynx felt his fingers slipping. He gripped it more firmly and pulled hard. It came out with a little whoosh; the hole quickly filled with blood. He saw the tears streaming down her face, but he had been concentrating on his task so intently, Lynx had not heard her scream.

Jory stood by with the hot water as Lynx bathed Jane's shoulder, sprinkled powdered yarrow into the wound, then bound her up. "I've sent for Megotta, she'll give you some poppy for the pain."

Jane looked alarmed. "No! It might harm the baby."

Lynx brushed the back of his fingers across her cheek in a tender gesture, not the least surprised at her selflessness. "I love you, Janie." He dropped a kiss on the top of her head and beckoned Jory to follow him from the chamber.

"Is Jane with child again?"

"Yes, keep a close watch on her for me. I have some unfinished business."

Thomas had a fresh mount waiting in the bailey. Lynx put on the doublet his squire handed him and led the way into the forest in the direction of the pool. It didn't take them long to make the grisly discovery. Fitz-Waren's throat had been torn open and a huge chunk of his flesh had been devoured. Lynx bent down to pick up the body.

"I'll do it, my lord," Thomas proffered.

"Nay, I'll do it," Lynx said grimly. "I don't want him buried anywhere near Jane's pool."

* * *

Lynx de Warenne and his knights had been all set to leave Dumfries the following day, but now their departure was delayed. Jane assured him she was fit to travel, but Lynx, ever protective, insisted she have a few days of bed rest, telling her there was no reason for any great haste. The following day, fateful events took place that proved Lynx de Warenne wrong.

Robert Bruce with two of his men at his heels rode hell-for-leather into Dumfries' bailey. Lynx, noting his gray pallor and his agitation, immediately knew there was trouble. The Bruce refused to come inside, refused even to leave his saddle. "There is no time! Why in Christ's name are you still here?" he demanded.

"Jane wasn't fit to travel," Lynx said shortly. "What has happened?"

"Comyn betrayed me! He dispatched our signed bond to Edward Plantagenet. We intercepted his messenger with the incriminating documents on him."

"Christ, he must have a death wish to betray you."

"Then he got his wish. I just stabbed him by the high altar at the monastery."

"Judas, what will you do?"

"I am riding to Scone immediately to be crowned. There is no alternative; they will arrest me for treason."

"You killed Comyn on holy ground—you will need absolution!" Lynx said wildly.

"I have the clergy on my side. Don't worry about me, my friend, look to your own safety. Get out of Scotland today!" He wheeled his destrier and spurred away. Lynx stood staring after him. Somehow their destinies were strangely linked. Both of their enemies had met death within hours of each other.

* * *

"There has been a slight change in plans," Lynx told Jane and his sister, Jory. "We are leaving today, but I think the ride too rigorous for you and Lincoln Robert. I'm sending you by ship from the Solway down the coast to Chester. I'll meet you there in a sennight."

Both his wife and his sister protested, but Lynx was adamant. He took Jory aside and gave her an explanation he hoped would satisfy her. "I know you are capable of riding and keeping up with my knights, but Jane isn't, and then there is the problem of Grace Murray and the baby. I want you to go with them and watch over Jane for me."

"You are right. It *will* be less rigorous for us to go by ship. Don't worry about Jane. I'm a wonderful sailor; I'll take good care of her."

When Lynx went back into the chamber, Jane put her hand on her husband's arm. "Lynx, something is wrong. Only yesterday you told me there was no great haste."

He searched her face and knew he must always share the truth with her. "It's the Bruce—he's riding to Scone to make a bid for the crown. If we remain in Scotland, we could be implicated in treason." He covered her hand. "Whatever you do, don't tell Jory. You know how impulsive she is—God knows what she would do—at the very least she would worry herself into a decline."

"Jory will be just fine; she's very strong."

"Headstrong," he said dryly.

She went up on tiptoe to kiss him. "It's a family trait."

He slipped a possessive arm about her, taking special care to be gentle with her shoulder. "As soon as I put you aboard, I want you in bed. I'm worried about the baby as well as your wound. Damn and blast everything, you shouldn't be traveling!"

"We'll both be fine, I promise you."

"I'd better sail with you," he said decisively.

"No, Lynx, you know your place is with your men. In only a week we'll be in Chester."

"Then I'll have Thomas and Taffy sail with you."

"Oh dear, they will love you for that!"

Less than two hours after they set sail, Jory was hanging over the ship's rail, retching up everything she had eaten that day. Jane led her down to her cabin and washed her hands and face with rosewater. "I want you to get into bed and I'll give you a little bistort; it's wonderful for nausea."

Jory groaned. "I'm supposed to be looking after you!"

"And so you shall. The bistort will settle your stomach immediately."

Within half an hour Jory was no longer green about the gills. Jane closed her medicinal box and sat down on the berth. "There, what did I tell you?"

"Jane, I'm amazed you have no nausea, are you sure you're having another baby?"

"Very sure . . . my monthly courses have stopped, my breasts are extremely tender, and I have to pee every five minutes."

"Ahh," Jory said thoughtfully, the corners of her mouth lifting with self-satisfaction.

Jane studied her rapt face for a moment. "Jory . . . you're not . . . ?"

"I have reason to hope," Jory whispered joyfully.

"Oh my dear, Lynx was right, you *are* headstrong."

"Don't you dare to tell him. I want to savor my secret as long as I possibly can before all the ranting and raving starts."

"Does Robert know?"

"Of course not! His destiny lies one way and mine another, but now he will always be a part of me."

A week later, when Lynx de Warenne and his mesne clattered into the courtyard of Chester Castle, Jane, who had been eagerly watching for his arrival, ran out to greet him.

His anxious eyes swept her small figure from head to foot and he could tell by her radiant face that all was well with her pregnancy. Lynx dismounted quickly and gently slipped his arm about her. "How is your shoulder, love?"

"It's healing well, though still tender, damn it! I wanted to fling myself into your arms to show you how much I've missed you!"

He covered her mouth with his, delighted with her sensual response. "Mmm, I'll have to leave you more often if this is the welcome I get."

"Just wait until you see how grand our chambers are. I had no idea castles could be this magnificent."

"Wait until you see Chester Cathedral. That's where I'm taking you today. I never did get to properly say my vows to you."

Jane, wearing Lynx's favorite pink lamb's-wool gown, stood before the high altar while she and her adoring husband confirmed their wedding vows. Before they left the cathedral Jane gazed about in wonder. "I've never seen anything so splendid!"

"Do you feel truly wed to me, now?"

She turned her face up to him. "Yes, I truly feel like Lady Jane de Warenne."

Lynx couldn't resist teasing her. "Now that you are in England, you will have to behave like a lady at all times. No more swimming naked, no more running about the woods unclothed. This is a civilized country."

Jane hid her smile. Two could play teasing games, she decided.

Lynx de Warenne's knights and those of the Earl of Chester enjoyed a wedding feast in Chester's vaulted dining hall. When it was time for the newlyweds to leave and seek their chamber, Jane seemed reluctant and lingered over the wine and the music. She hid her amusement as Lynx's hints to retire became more pointed by the minute. After listening to him for an hour, she decided to put him out of his misery.

"Shall we leave the men to their dicing?" she suggested intimately, and was rewarded by an overwhelming look of relief on Lynx's face. Jane smiled her secret smile; she wasn't done with him yet!

When the door to their chamber closed, Jane went into his arms. "Lynx darling, thank you for bringing Blanchette. I have a special fondness for my lovely white mare, but of course I know how strict your rules are when I'm with child." She left his arms and put a little distance between them. "And I promise to obey every last one: no riding, no lifting, no lovemaking, no overexertion of any kind."

No lovemaking? Lynx looked at her intently to see if she was serious. She certainly looked serious.

"Now that I am Lady de Warenne I want you to be proud of my accomplishments. I have learned how to play the lute and how to play chess so that I can entertain you on a long winter's night. Let me show you," she said eagerly.

"But it isn't winter," he said miserably.

"Please play with me?" she begged prettily.

Her titillating words aroused him instantly. Lynx sat down reluctantly and eased the tight material across his swollen groin. His eyes never left his beautiful wife; he hardly looked at the board as he moved the pieces absently.

"Lynx, am I boring you?" she asked innocently.

"No, sweetheart, but why don't we make it more interesting and play for forfeits?"

"Whatever you desire, darling."

Within seconds he took one of her pawns and with a sigh, Jane removed a satin slipper and offered it to him.

"Ah, no, my love; I get to choose the forfeit." His green eyes narrowed. "I'll have your dress, 'tis my favorite."

Most reluctantly and very slowly Jane unfastened the buttons and peeled off the pink lamb's-wool gown. Her movements were so provocative and tantalizing that Lynx became suspicious. The little minx was playing sex games, if he wasn't mistaken! He deliberately made a vulnerable move with one of his knights and watched her swoop down on it.

"I lose," he said with resignation. "Take your gown and put it back on."

Jane stared at him in dismay. "But I don't want to put it back on," she blurted out.

"English ladies don't play chess in the buff," he said reprovingly.

"I'm not in the buff, I'm in my shift."

"Not for bloody long, you're not!" He made a grab for her and she danced away across the room.

As he began to stalk her, he removed his doublet, then the rest of his garments, tossing them aside as he gained upon her. Just as she thought she had eluded him, he pounced and carried her down to the thick-piled rug. Then pinning her beneath him, he pulled off her shift and rubbed his swollen shaft across her breasts and down her belly.

"Lord de Warenne, have you no control?"

"Lady de Warenne, where you are concerned, I have not."

Jane arched her back, unable to wait a moment longer for his ravishing. Buried in her sleek heat, he tongued every naked inch of her skin until she was writhing with liquid tremors. Their bodies were so perfectly attuned, they erupted together and she cried out with passion as his white-hot seed spilled into her. She clung to him, loving his weight, his scent, his hardened warrior's body.

"What a pity to waste that beautiful curtained bed," she whispered languorously.

"I have no intention of wasting it, there are things I'm going to do to you that require the privacy of curtains," he teased.

Later in the big curtained bed, the lovers touched, kissed, and whispered the night away. Lynx lifted the touchstone from between Jane's breasts and gazed down at it. "Perhaps the magic symbol of the lynx does protect you."

"I ofttimes wonder if you and my lynx are one and the

same,'' Jane murmured softly. ''Are you a shape-changer, sometimes a man, sometimes a beast?''

"I am whatever you want me to be,'' he growled softly, licking her throat with his rough tongue.

Later, when all their love games were played out, Lynx looked deeply into her eyes. ''Jane, will you always love me as you do tonight?''

She touched her lips to his and vowed fiercely, ''I will and I shall!''

Author's Note

Bruce was crowned King Robert I at Scone by the Bishops of Glasgow, St. Andrews, and Moray, the most powerful churchmen in Scotland. In defiance of Edward Plantagenet, the north rose in his support. Sixteen earls from Perthshire, twelve each from Angus and Fife, eleven each from Aberdeen, Banff, and Moray, six from Lennox, four each from Stirling and Argyll, and one from Dunbarton declared for Bruce.

Robert wed Elizabeth de Burgh, daughter of the Earl of Ulster, and the union lasted twenty-five years.

It was not until the decisive Battle of Bannockburn in 1314 that King Robert won Scotland's independence.